"Can you look further?" Lannes asked. "Go further out to sea? It is only a few miles to England. Dover should be visible from Lion's topmast."

It was like uncoiling, like movement swift and sure, rising up from Captain Arnold, up the length of the ship's mast, sails taut in the wind. She was tacking out to sea, her wake a zigzag down the coast. And behind her and northward, lights on the horizon, lights along the shore spread like a crescent, brighter and then dimmer as they curved westward, the southern coast of England laid out before me like a map

I stood on the wind like a gull in the night, white wings spread over Lion below. Fifty feet above her decks I hovered, watching sailors running about, the complicated and graceful business of changing her course again.

There was England. A few beats of my wings and I soared toward it, low and fast as a gull, not even leaving a shadow on the water. There was Dover, port marked by so many masts, Dover Castle above all. There was the curve of coastline, chalk cliffs glimmering white in the darkness. They were almost beneath me.

And then something rose out of the darkness, vast and strange as a great wind. It hovered, impenetrable, a shape of cloud and trouble.

I veered off, and it tore at me, gull's wings wildly beating. Time to go, I thought. This is what Lannes means by superior force. I darted, diving low, and for a moment beneath its rolling clouds I saw something different, a garden enclosed by hedges, an old woman looking up, a swan's feather in her hand.

Then the winds hit me, tumbling and shaking, buffeting at me with unearthly force. The sea came up like a wall beneath me, flat and hard and cold.

Cover illustration by Cécile Jacques
Interior design by Aaron Rosenberg
ISBN 978-1-937530-47-1 — ISBN 978-1-937530-48-8 (pbk.)

For information address Crossroad Press at 141 Brayden Dr., Hertford, NC 27944
www.crossroadpress.com

First edition

The Emperor's Agent

Jo Graham

CROSSROAD PRESS

For Amy Griswold,
with love

Other works by Jo Graham:

Novels

Stargate: Atlantis

Death Game

Homecoming: Book I of the Legacy Series

The Lost: Book II of the Legacy Series

The Furies: Book IV of the Legacy Series

Secrets: Book V of the Legacy Series

The Inheritors: Book VI of the Legacy Series

The Order of the Air **(with Melissa Scott)**

Lost Things

Steel Blues

Silver Bullet (Coming Soon)

Collections

The Ravens of Falkenau

Unabridged Audiobooks

The Ravens of Falkenau / The Hand of Isis/Stealing Fire

Lost Things/Steel Blues (with Melissa Scott)

When you are old and grey and full of sleep
And nodding by the fire, take down this book,
And slowly read, and dream of the soft look
Your eyes had once, and of their shadows deep.
How many loved your moments of glad grace
And loved your beauty with love false and true,
But one man loved the pilgrim soul in you,
And loved the sorrows of your changing face.
—W.B. Yeats

Shadows on the Republic

The dark bulk of the Chateau de Vincennes reared up across the sky ahead of me, and I shivered for reasons that had nothing to do with cold. "Vincennes?" I said.

In the seat across from me, the big man said nothing, his arms crossed on his chest. He swayed a little with the movement of the carriage as it shifted, the sudden difference in the rhythm of its wheels evident as it turned off the cobbled streets of the town of Vincennes onto the differently shaped pavers of the Chateau's drive. I had not really expected an answer. He had shown no inclination to answer my questions since we'd left Paris an hour before.

I could no longer see the castle. We clattered across the bridge over the dry moat, the carriage slowing as we came up to the guard post at the curtain wall. I stilled my gloved hands in my lap.

I could hear the other man, the one who was sitting beside the driver on the box, exchanging words with the guards, joking about something. The light of the torches at the guard post did little to illuminate the interior of the carriage.

"...for Senator Fouché," I heard one of them say, and clamped my hands together more tightly. I was not surprised.

I had been leaving the theater after a performance when the two men had been waiting at the stage door. "You are coming with us, Madame," one of them said, flashing papers in front of me. "We have a special warrant." One on either side, they had escorted me to the carriage standing ready, and before five minutes were passed we had been blocks away.

"Will you not tell me where we are going?" had met with no answer, nor had any other question.

At one point, as the carriage stopped in heavy traffic on one of the bridges, he had reached forward, taking my hand from the door. "I wouldn't do that if I were you," he said, and any notion I'd had of leaping out screaming into traffic died. I could not escape them, and any attempt to do so would make it worse. He would break my arm before I had gotten ten steps.

Instead I leaned back against the seat and attempted to marshal my thoughts. Vincennes was not good. It had not even been two months since the Duc d'Enghien had been shot there, part of some complicated plot to kill the First Consul and reestablish the Bourbon monarchy, a plot that unfortunately a former lover of mine had been implicated in. I wished I could believe he'd had nothing to do with it, that he was innocent. However, I knew Victor Moreau too well to believe that.

The carriage rolled forward past the guard post, and I was surprised to see a working portcullis raised. We passed beneath, and I heard the groan of the ropes as it was lowered again. "Very dramatic," I said, hoping I sounded arch rather than panicked.

The big man said nothing.

There were not, after all, so many pleasant reasons for being hauled off to meet with Joseph Fouché in a fortress in the middle of the night. Though he was no longer Minister of Police, he was still perhaps the most dangerous man in France. And his use of the Chateau de Vincennes suggested that he had nothing to fear from the First Consul. Indeed, he had probably been instrumental in the shooting of Enghien.

The carriage stopped in an interior courtyard. After a moment, the door opened and the man who had ridden on the box held out a hand for me. "Madame?"

I took it and stepped down. Above, the pale walls of the keep blocked the stars. They escorted me, one before and one behind, though neither of them touched me again. My heart was pounding by the time we had gone up one flight of stairs.

The room on the second floor of what had been the medieval donjon was spacious. Candles gleamed in wall sconces and from a massive iron floor stand beside a carved desk. At the desk, in a green velvet chair, sat Senator Fouché.

Joseph Fouché steepled his long, bloodless hands and regarded me. He did not stand, and there was no other chair in the room.

"Madame," he said.

I made my best courtesy, hoping that he had indeed left his Jacobin past behind. The setting seemed to indicate so. "Monsieur."

"You may go," he said, and the two men nodded, closing the staircase door behind them.

I stood perfectly still, hoping he could not hear my heart.

He studied my face, and after a moment put his head to the side as though I were a curiosity. "You have no idea why I have sent for you, Madame?"

"I assume it has to do with General Moreau," I said, and was pleased that my voice did not shake. "But I have nothing that I may add to your case against him. My relations with Moreau ended six years ago, and since then I have not had his confidence."

His voice, a light tenor, was pleasant, as though we were merely discussing some matter of art at a party. "You were not surprised by his arrest for conspiring with the Royalists?"

"Not surprised, no," I said carefully. "I know he has never liked the First Consul. But six years ago things were very different. At the point where Moreau and I ended, the First Consul was in Egypt, and the Royalists in disarray. Any plot which Moreau joined necessarily began much later."

"You seem very certain of that," he said.

"It is only logical," I said. "And what plot should remain secret for six years?"

"What indeed. You have no loyalty to Moreau?"

I met his eyes quite squarely. They held no expression whatsoever. "If you have investigated General Moreau's past thoroughly enough to bring in his mistress of six years ago, you will also doubtless know the terms upon which we parted. Moreau treated me very badly. I have not spoken with him for six years. My loyalty is to the Republic, not Moreau. If I knew anything that would be helpful to you, you would only have to ask for my assistance."

"I am glad you are so helpful, Madame," he said, reaching for a paper on the desk before him and pretending to consult it. "Because you see, I know that Ida St. Elme does not exist. And unfortunately I have before me here a warrant for the arrest of one Elzelina Ringeling, and an order for her extradition to Holland." He looked up at me, his gray eyes milky under thin brows. "It seems the poor woman is mad, and that her family has been searching for her for many years. I have here the sworn statement of one Claas Ringeling, her father-in-law, who intends to remand her to the gentle concern of the experimental hospital of one Dr. Kuller, who has had great success in curing hysteria and other ills through the application of electrical currents to the brain." He laid the paper upon the desk. "You would know nothing about this poor woman, I assume?"

I said nothing. I could not speak.

"You are pale, Madame," he said. "Could it be that you do know something about this Madame Ringeling, who left her husband for Moreau all those years ago?"

"Moreau told you that?" I whispered.

Fouché's lips twitched in what might have been a smile. "Moreau had no reason not to. As you say, you have not been on the best of terms."

"That bastard...." I murmured.

"He did no more than give me your real name. The warrants have been outstanding for some time, unable to be served because the lady could not be found."

"Since the business over my husband's will, no doubt," I said.

He spread his hands. "No doubt. But your problem remains, Madame."

I lifted my chin, trying to keep my voice from shaking. "Are you going to send me back to Holland then?"

"That remains to be seen," he said. "You do see my difficulty. You are at present an illegal alien living under an assumed name. At best, you are a runaway wife. At worst, you may be criminally insane like the poor Marquis de Sade, who spent so many years locked up within these very walls." He looked up, as though de Sade still dwelled somewhere in the corners of the ceiling. "He's back in prison, you know. He really should have known better than to dedicate Juliette to the wife of the First Consul."

"How very indiscreet," I said.

Fouché smiled as though I had said something clever. "However, it is possible that I may be able to assist you in finding an alternative that will please everyone. You wish to stay in France?"

I bit my lip. "Yes," I said. If it was that he wanted me, I could think of worse. I could do it. I could do him if I had to. I made myself smile at him coquettishly. "If you think you could help me."

"Not in that manner, Madame," he said shortly. "I do not share General Moreau's well documented tastes in vice."

I felt the blood rise in my face, wondering exactly what he had heard, and from whom.

"I have need of an agent with certain talents," he said. "A former merveilleuse would be ideal. A courtesan, yes, but also a woman who can handle a pistol and who can travel discreetly." He looked at me over the documents. "Your exploits traveling with the army are not as secret as you might wish, Madame. Very little is secret from me. I am quite aware you have papers that the naïve General Ney procured for you, stating that you are a handsome Dutch youth named Charles van Aylde. But for now you will not need them. The plans I have for you do not involve leaving Paris."

"And what would those plans be?" I asked. My hands were sweating, and I could feel a trickle down my back as well.

"Then you are amenable to my offer?"

I unclasped my hands, letting them fall at my sides. "I have no reason not to be," I said. "I presume I will be paid?"

Fouché nodded as though satisfied. "Of course. All of my agents are reasonably compensated for their work. Am I to understand that you consider yourself for hire?"

I tossed my head. "If you know so much about me, then you know that I have no patron at present. Work is work, Monsieur. If I am, as you say, reasonably compensated, then you have no need for threats. I must pay the bills, Monsieur."

"Then I believe we understand one another, Madame," he said. "You will be paid upon completion of your first assignment. Which will begin now."

He searched among the many green paper folders on the desk, then laid one open before me. It was a drawing of an elderly man, well dressed, with the white wig of the last century. He had a square face and a nose that had probably been broken more than once, a clean face running to fat. "Do you know this man, Madame?"

I could answer entirely honestly. "I have never seen him before."

Fouché spread his hands as if to say, well it could not be that easy. "The gentleman is Dr. Alasdair Fraser, a Scotsman and a Jacobite who was resident in Paris for many years. I want you to find him for me."

I looked at him in confusion. "But surely you can find this man much better than I, Monsieur! I've never seen him before, and I am only one woman, while you must have dozens of agents who can…."

"Find him, yes, but not without arousing suspicion. You, however, can do so with utmost discretion."

"Why?'

"He's an abortionist."

I clamped my mouth shut. Surely Fouché….

"A woman of the world such as yourself might have good reason to seek him out without any suspicion at all, whereas my agents...." Fouché spread his hands. "Let us say we do not wish to alarm the good doctor. All

I require is that you find him and make an appointment, to which you may be escorted by a gentleman much concerned for your welfare."

"I see," I said. I looked down at the drawing again, and wondered what he had done to merit this attention from Fouché. "That seems simple enough."

"Then we have a bargain?"

"Yes," I said. He had a point. I could inquire after this doctor reasonably enough, among theater friends and various connections.

"Good," he said. "Maurice will contact you and make sure you are progressing in your work."

He snapped the folder closed and handed it to me. "Take this with you. And do try to remember his name." Fouché rang the small bell on the corner of the desk. The stair door opened immediately. "Maurice, please escort Madame St. Elme back to her lodgings. She will be playing with us now."

I fell into bed the moment I got home, and did not wake until mid-morning. Coffee, I thought. Nothing could be considered without coffee. Half an hour later, sitting with bread, butter and café au lait outside the café down the street, I tilted my head back so that my face caught the sun and thought.

Not for a moment did I believe that Fouché trusted me. Of course he could never trust his agents, not the ones recruited this way. And this matter must be very simple for him to give it to me. It would test me, and also be much more convenient than sending a thug after this man. If he hadn't already been found, it suggested that he did not want to be for some reason or another. While abortion before quickening was not specifically illegal, it existed in a legal gray area, and of course no legitimate medical practitioner would admit to providing it because of the damage it would do to his own reputation. If this Dr. Fraser were a real physician, he probably kept that part of his practice quiet.

However, if he could not be found openly practicing in Paris at all, that presented a more complicated problem. If he had changed his name, then I should have to make a great many enquiries, and finding him might just be a matter of luck. And if he had left Paris....

And what if I simply left Paris? No doubt Fouché had considered such an eventuality. I should be stopped and brought back, or more likely simply shipped off to my father-in-law as a matter no longer worth pursuing.

Who would then not have to deal with my hands still in the business that had been my inheritance, nor with the terms of the divorce that left income still coming to me. Given my mother's madness, which was a matter of common knowledge, and the way in which I had lived these last nine years, he would have no trouble at all locking me up. It would be for my own good, really.

So running was not an option.

Running as Charles? Fouché knew about Charles, my alter ego, and had doubtless considered that too. I should be stopped, et cetera.

I took a long drink of the coffee, thick with milk, and looked up at the poplar trees just beginning to burst with leaves above.

Moreau. He had gotten my original papers to stay in France. But that had been years ago, when he loved me. And when he had not just gotten himself arrested for treason. His public trial would begin in a few weeks, and if he were lucky he would escape the guillotine. If not....

Most of my friends had no power to help me. Actresses and courtesans, soldiers and artists and low ranking officers, there was certainly nothing they could do against Fouché, one time Minister of Police and enforcer for the dreaded Committee of Public Safety. It was said he had been eased out of his position because the First Consul did not trust him, something I heartily agreed with. And yet he still seemed to have his fingers in everything, acting as though his capacity were still official.

Which left Michel. He had lately returned to France from the Helvetian Republic, but I had not seen him. I had not tried to. I did not know whether he would see me. But if he did, he would be angry at Fouché, that I knew. And in his bullheaded way he would rush straight in, making enemies and demanding answers. No, I could not go to Michel, no matter how much I might wish to. Not if my life depended upon it.

Which really left me no choice at all.

The search for Dr. Fraser was no harder than I expected. Among friends at the theater, I made a point of mentioning his name in the chorus dressing room, and wondering aloud where I might find him. He had, I said, been recommended by a friend for feminine complaints, and I wondered....

Which resulted in nothing at all, except some blank looks and the names of two midwives.

I was still trying to decide how to proceed a week later when I came out of the stage door to find Maurice lounging against the wall. He ambled over to me and leaned in. “The gentleman would like to know what you’ve done.”

“I don’t know where Fraser is yet,” I said. “I’ve asked some people, but I don’t know anything.”

Maurice sneered. “You’d better work a little harder then. The gentleman doesn’t like for people not to work hard.”

“I see,” I said, trying not to shudder as he leaned into me with his rank breath. “I’ll have it for him. Soon.”

“You’d best,” he said.

“I will.”

And so I began my enquiries again.

I had lunch with Doreé the next day, sitting in the spring sunshine just off the Palais Royale, and casually professed that I had forgotten the address of a doctor that Lisette had recommended many years ago, did she happen to know of a Dr. Fraser who specialized in women’s complaints?

“Oh, you mean the old Scotsman?” Doreé shrugged. “I heard he was expensive. But he’s a good doctor, people say.”

“Do you know where he lives?” I asked. “I do want to find him.”

“If you need a midwife,” Doreé said, tossing her dark curls back, “I know a good one too.”

“I think I really want a doctor,” I said. “I’ve been irregular for years and I’d like to see what he thinks. Lisette recommended him and said he’d helped her.”

“I think he’s in Rue Hubert,” Doreé said. “I think he lodges there. In the third or fourth block.”

“I’ll look for him,” I said.

That afternoon I walked that way. Surely there could not be so many lodgings in a few blocks of Rue Hubert. It was a quiet, respectable neighborhood, not too far from where I had first lived when I came to Paris, in the small house belonging to Moreau, the one he had bought at bottom prices from people condemned by the Committee of Public Safety. Most of the houses were not for rent. There were only two that seemed to take in lodgers.

I was lucky the first time. The old lady seemed somewhat deaf, but she knew who I meant. “Dr. Fraser? Oh yes! He lived here!” She gave me a wide smile, her eyes almost milk white with cataracts over clear blue.

“Did he move, Madame?” I asked. “If so, I would appreciate it if you could tell me where he now lodges.”

"Where we must all lodge someday, even you pretty young things!" She grinned again, and I thought that she could not see me properly at all, if she was taking me for so young. I was twenty-seven, and scarcely a girl. "He died a year and a half ago."

"Oh no!" I said.

"Did you know him then? Or more like, that girl of his, Laura?"

"No, I didn't," I said. "Do you know what he died of?"

"A winter fever. It went in his chest, you know. I helped his daughter nurse him and we laid him out at the end. Poor man! It happens even to doctors! And my, he was a good one! He made my Simone's dropsy go straight away!" She sighed, and looked a little less ecstatic now. "But then his Laura picked up and moved out. Went to live with her aunt, she said."

"Do you know if she took all his papers with her?" I asked. "Or perhaps some things were left with you, Madame? And where did she go?"

"Aberdeen," the old woman said cheerily. "Oh gracious yes! Laura only came here because her father was so stubborn about the Pretender and all. Once he was gone she went straight home to Aberdeen to live with her aunt. Said she'd had enough of Jacobite nonsense. And no, she didn't take a thing with her. Burned the whole lot of his papers, except for his medical books that she sold to pay for her passage home. She said it was just a mess of receipts and bills he'd never be able to collect."

I took a deep breath.

The old woman squinted at me, as though trying to see me better. "This doesn't have anything to do with secret maps to the Bonnie Prince's lost gold, does it?"

"I truly don't think so," I said. Though who could tell what Fouché might be after.

"Burned the whole lot," she repeated with satisfaction. "Nothing but a mess, Laura said."

"Thank you for your help, Madame," I said, and gave her a small coin. Fouché might not like what I had found, but it was at least information. It did not seem there could be any mistake that Dr. Fraser was dead. I hardly thought the old woman would be lying, or mistaken that she'd helped lay out a corpse.

I wrote down all that I had found out, and gave it to Maurice as I left the theater that night. He took it without a word, and was back the next day with a purse full of small banknotes. It seemed that Fouché's agents certainly didn't get rich at their work. I should make as much in one evening with a big spender. Still, I hadn't done very much, and I failed to see how anyone else couldn't have done as much. What was the point, I wondered, of playing heavy handedly over so little?

It was several weeks before I discovered more. I almost thought Fouché had forgotten about me until I had a knock on my door early one morning. It was Maurice, and freshly shaven and dressed in clean clothes he looked almost respectable. He even took off his hat as I opened the door.

"The gentleman would like to see you. If you will accompany me?"

Of course I did, and not entirely without qualms. But it was daylight, and there was no one except Maurice in the hired carriage. I wondered if even he might be disposed to talk.

"What is it this time?" I asked him in a confidential manner, friend to friend, as though we were colleagues at the theater. "The last was tedious but not difficult."

Maurice leered. "I think this one probably involves fewer clothes."

"Oh," I said, and sat back in my seat and said nothing else.

Instead of the intimidating bulk of a prison, we came to a very reasonable second floor office in one of the buildings surrounding the Place Vendome, busy with tradesmen and clerks coming and going, their Morocco cases of papers under their arms. I waited in a green-papered antechamber with four or five people for the better part of an hour before a clerk called for me, and I went into what was obviously Senator Fouché's office.

"Madame St. Elme," he said, and this time gestured with one hand to a chair drawn up on the other side of his desk. "I see that you are fledged in my service."

"Yes, Monsieur," I said, and thought it best to say no more.

He looked me up and down, glancing over my plain day dress. "Have you nothing more feminine than that? Something pink, perhaps?"

"Yes," I said, though very little of my wardrobe ran to frills and ruffles. "I have a pink dress."

"Good, because you are wearing it tomorrow to plead your case to the Minister of Foreign Affairs, Monsieur Talleyrand."

"Oh good Lord!" I exclaimed. "Why in the world would I do that?" I had met him once or twice when I was with Moreau, but I hardly knew him.

"Because I am telling you to, Madame," Fouché said politely. "You will confide in him all the details of your sad case, and let him know that you will do anything, absolutely anything, to be allowed to stay in France. You will make yourself very amiable. Do you understand?"

"I do," I said evenly, though I felt the blood rush to my face.

"Good." Fouché steepled his hands, as though over a dossier. "He likes blondes, and he has a particular weakness for damsels in distress. Especially generously endowed damsels in distress. You will wear a dress lower than that, Madame. And make yourself most persuasive. Your goal is to insinuate yourself with him to such a degree that in time he will talk freely to you."

"I understand," I said.

"He is not an easy man to please," Fouché said. "But then I understand that you are quite adept at accommodating a variety of vices. See that you make yourself agreeable to whatever he might propose. I do not want to hear that you have disappointed him."

"Of course," I said, wondering what he knew. There had been that time with Moreau and Therese that half a dozen people had witnessed....

"Good. You may go." He half turned away, as though already moving on to the next case. Fouché gave me one last glance as I gathered my skirts. "And do try to cry. He likes tears so very much."

On that note, I was dismissed.

Three Rivals

I went to see Talleyrand the next morning, wearing my pink dress with a little lace shawl. It was very thin, and while one might call it intended for modesty, it revealed far more than it concealed beneath its tiny scrap of dainty lace. I waited nearly two hours in his antechamber, wondering if my curls would hold up in the warm room, until at last I was called.

The Minister of Foreign Affairs had a very grand office, with a great marble desk in the style of the ancien régime, while behind him the windows were bathed in enormous blue velvet curtains that might as well have been sprinkled with fleurs de lys. He looked up from his work as I was announced, and made no attempt to disguise the spark in his eye as he looked at me. His gaze was frankly admiring as I swept in and the clerk closed the door, so I wasted no time.

I threw myself on my knees beside his chair, begging and kissing his hand.

"You must help me," I pleaded, his ringed fingers against my lips. "Oh, you must, Monsieur! You are my last and only hope!"

"There now, Madame. What is this?" he asked, but he did not sound displeased. His hands tasted like powder and smelled faintly of lavender.

"Monsieur de Talleyrand, you may be my savior! You and you alone! I do not know what I can do, and I have only your mercy to throw myself upon. Oh please do not fail me!" I looked up at him, my eyes brimming with tears, affording him a view straight down the neck of my dress. I wore no stays, and my buskin stopped just below my breasts, thrusting them up and out. I had rouged my nipples slightly.

"Surely it is not so bad as that, Madame," he said gently, his eyes going exactly where I wanted them to go. "You may rely that I will hear you out, and that I will do what I may to alleviate your distress."

"Oh, Monsieur, you are too good!" I said, blinking into his face with an expression I hoped showed a lack of good sense. "I am so very frightened."

He took my hand in his. "Then tell me what is the matter, Madame." He wore fine clocked stockings with heeled slippers, an old fashioned mode of dress that reminded me suddenly and sharply of my childhood in Italy, of a friend of my father's that I had once seen making love to both my parents at once. One slipper was heeled differently, no doubt to compensate for the difference in the length of his legs that gave him a pronounced limp.

I leaned in, my breast brushing against the inside of his thigh. "I was a very dear friend of General Moreau once, as you may remember. It was only for love of him that I was persuaded to leave my husband and my family in Holland and to enter upon a most precarious and libertine existence. But beauty wanes, Monsieur." I blinked at him again, dropping one shoulder to once again provide a glimpse of nipple. "Moreau cast me off. But now! Oh now! I can scarce bear to think of it!" I buried my face against his knee, pleased to see that I was at least having some effect on the state of his trousers.

"There now," he said, and I felt his hand brush lightly over my blonde curls. "Moreau was a very great fool to do so."

"I am glad you think so, Monsieur," I said, looking pleadingly at him again. "But now he stands accused of treason, and I am so very afraid! Monsieur, Moreau did not talk about politics with me! I had no idea he was involved in any kind of plot! Please believe that he never brought politics into the bedroom. He said that our time was for pleasure, and I should not worry about such things!"

"And he was very right," Talleyrand said, playing idly with one long spiral curl. "You are much too beautiful to waste time talking about politics."

"But now I am afraid, Monsieur! I am so afraid I shall be sent back to Holland, now that Moreau is fallen!" I rested my hand on his knee. "Oh please, Monsieur! Please don't let them send me away! I know nothing about politics, and only long to remain in Paris, where I shall not be punished for the license I have enjoyed." I held his eyes and did not blink, trying to let nothing else show there.

He pursed his lips, and for a moment looked like nothing so much as a well-bred cat who has got a bowl of cream. "I am sure I can help you, Madame. It is such a little thing, really."

"A little thing to such as you, a very great man, but a great deal to a young woman like me."

For a second I thought I had overdone it, but he smiled complacently, almost kindly. "I will look into your case, Madame. Unfortunately, I have a luncheon appointment in a few minutes, but if you might return at two the day after tomorrow, I shall be pleased to review all the particulars of your case."

"Oh!" I clasped his hand to my bosom and rained kisses upon it. "You are too good!"

"Come then." He got to his feet with some difficulty, as I was between his knees, and helped me up. "Dry your tears. A woman as lovely as you should not cry. You may rely upon me."

"Day after tomorrow?" I looked at him hopefully, trying to look up, which was more of a trick standing, as he was not tall, and I am tall for a woman.

"At two," he promised, petting my arm. "I will see you then. Go home, Madame, and be of good cheer."

"I shall," I promised, and made my escape.

I reported all to Maurice when I left the theater that night, and the next evening he was there again, with the verbal message, "The gentleman is satisfied."

Well, I thought. That was something. It was enough that I had arranged another appointment.

The following day I dressed carefully. I didn't want to wear the same dress again, so instead I chose a pretty sprigged muslin and added a broad pink sash, powdering my breasts and rouging my nipples. I debated whether or not to shave my pubis, but opted in the end for a quantity of lavender water, and a careful trim with a pair of little scissors. After all, I was not entirely certain of his tastes. An enormous hat with pink ribbons added to the effect, and I went to meet Talleyrand looking something like Madame de Tourvel in Dangerous Liaisons, only with a good deal less brain. I hoped that was his fantasy. It was a bit late now to switch to ambergris and black dresses.

This time I did not have to wait in the antechamber long. It was only a few minutes before I was announced, and the clerk closed the door behind me with what might have been a smirk.

I gave the Minister my best smile. "Monsieur, I am so grateful that you have given me even a little of your time today."

"How could I not?" he asked. "You were such a charming suppliant."

"I am gratified that I charmed you, Monsieur," I said, "As I have often heard that you are the most charming man in France."

He nodded affably. "Then come and kneel by me again, as I confess this little matter of yours may be instantly resolved. You need have no fear because of your former association with Moreau. If every beauty were in the confidence of a man, there should be no secrets in France!"

I came and knelt by him again, pooling my skirts about me pleasingly, and leaning forward a little to promote the view.

"And we must take your hat off," he said. "Such lovely hair should not be covered indoors."

"Here," I said, reaching up, "I will...."

"Allow me." Carefully, Talleyrand untied the ribbon and drew out the hat pins, each curl I had spent ten minutes on that morning cascading from combs in charming disarray. "You do have lovely hair."

"Thank you," I said, leaning against his knee. "I have been so fearful, since Moreau. You do not know what it is to live without a man's protection, Monsieur!" I was laying it on thick, but he seemed to like it.

He ran his fingers through my hair, playing with each curl. "Not dyed. Your hair is as fine as a child's."

"Thank you, Monsieur," I said, one hand gently caressing the inside of his thigh. He gathered my hair up, kneading to the scalp, brushing it the wrong way so that a chill ran up my back. I pressed my face against his leg.

"I understand Moreau was very devoted to you," he said, and I heard the quickness of breath in his voice.

"He was my master and my teacher," I said. So close, I could smell him, almost feel the heat of his arousal.

Again the hands playing in my hair, drawing the spiral curls out. "And what did he teach you?"

"This," I said, and began to undo the buttons on his breeches. "This, Monsieur." He was fifty, but still he jumped at my touch, and I gathered the weight of him into one hand, licking delicately at his swollen cock, laving it with my tongue while he gathered up my hair again. I felt his carefully trimmed nails on my scalp, and a great breath escaped him.

I took him in my mouth, drawing with long, luxurious strokes, deep and slow as possible, while all the while he kept kneading at my hair, like a cat with a toy. A few dust mites danced in the light slipping between the velvet curtains, and the oriental carpet was soft beneath my knees. It seemed to take a very long time. He said nothing more, and my mouth was otherwise occupied. Just when I had begun to think this would surely go on all morning, he moaned, his hands clenching on my curls, and came almost silently.

I swallowed convulsively, as nothing else would do in the precious neatness of the office.

Wordlessly, he handed me his handkerchief, with which I wiped my mouth while he rebuttoned his breeches. "There, you are neat, Madame," he said.

I hardly knew what to say to that, so I blinked prettily instead.

He drew one long ribbon of hair across my shoulder. "I have left you in disarray," he said. "I have ruined your morning's work."

My hair felt like a ball of yarn that has been batted about the floor. "It is nothing," I said, feeling vaguely sick on my stomach and wishing I could be gone.

"Oh, but I cannot let you go out like that!" he said. "Here, let me take a hand."

"It is nothing," I said again, wondering if I should ask if we could meet again, or wait for him to bring it up. "I do not mind."

"I shall mind, if you leave here looking ruinous," Talleyrand said, brushing his fingers ineffectually over my draggled curls. "Come, let me restore you. Bend your head like a pretty thing."

I bent my head, and he pulled out some small paper, with which he proceeded to tie up an errant curl.

"You will be as fine as ever," he said, dexterously rolling another curl in paper, for all the world as though he were my ladies' maid. "You will put your hat on when you go out, and not take your hair down until you get home."

Where he could not see I rolled my eyes. It seemed my main attraction was my hair, and I was more than tired of this already. Two, three, four curls, each one fussily arranged and papered. I looked up, trying to see how many he planned to do. The slip of paper he was folding to put around my curl was a thousand franc note!

He glanced down, catching my eye, and his thin aristocratic lips bent in a smile. "You see, I am not insensible after all."

I pulled a bit of hair forward from the other side. "Here is another piece that needs doing!"

Talleyrand laughed. "For the sake of your curls, Madame!"

"Oh yes," I said.

There were eight in all before he put my hat back on, arranging the pins and ribbon just so. "Now you are decent, Madame," he said.

"I am," I said, getting to my feet. "And I hope you are left with an impression of my case that is favorable."

"Quite," he said.

I waited for him to suggest another rendezvous, but he was already looking at the papers on his desk. "I shall be going then," I said.

"Good afternoon, Madame," he said, rising to his feet to see me out. He stopped, one hand on the door handle, prepared to let me out. "And Madame," he said courteously, "You may tell my dear friend Fouché that this was an excellent try, but in the future I prefer to arrange my own assignations."

"Ah!" I gaped.

He glanced at my hat. "But I believe it's been worth your while. I know how little Fouché pays his agents. Good afternoon, Madame."

"Good afternoon," I managed, and somehow got myself downstairs and into the carriage before I burst into laughter. It was that or tears.

I told "the gentleman" in person. He made no comment, only waited for me to tell the entire story, as baldly as I might. I would not seem squeamish to him. Nor did I attempt to conceal the money, though I certainly had not brought it with me.

Fouché's only comment was a shrug, as if to say he had expected no more. "Well," he said, "Talleyrand is no fool." Which I thought should have been self-evident. They had been playing deadly games, sometimes at cross purposes and sometimes not, for the better part of ten years.

"Since you have already been amply paid," he said, "I see that you need no more. Until I next summon you, Madame."

And with that I had to be content. It was true that, though the currency was inflated and 8,000 francs was not worth what it had been a few years before, it was still more than I might have hoped for in the run of a play. The price for Talleyrand in scoring off Fouché, and probably a bargain at the price.

It was only a few days later that the verdict came down in Moreau's trial. While it had not been specifically proven that he had been part of the Royalist assassination plot, it was clear that he had known such a plot existed and had done nothing to avert it. For this he was convicted as a mere accessory, to two years in prison, rather than the death sentences that were pronounced on the others.

I thought he had done rather well for himself. But then, Moreau had always been cautious, and doubtless there were no incriminating papers, only word of mouth from unreliable witnesses and thugs hired to do the dirty work.

He served four days of his term. On the fifth day, Bonaparte commuted his sentence to exile, giving him ten days to quit the country. This was, I thought, quite a masterstroke. In prison, Moreau would seem a martyr. Living peacefully in retirement elsewhere, there was little to be said of him, and the First Consul should look magnanimous to someone who had plotted his own murder.

I was glad, for I should not have liked to hear that he was killed.

To my surprise, a letter came for me the next day.

My dear Madame St. Elme,

I do not know whether you will be glad to hear from me, or rather the opposite, but as I am preparing to leave I have come across some documents belonging to you, letters and legal papers relating to your marriage that I think you will want. Is there some time when we might conveniently meet that I may deliver them to your hand? Day after tomorrow at noon in the Boulevard Madeleine would suffice, if you can think of no better.

I am your obedient,

Victor Moreau

I stared at the paper, and for a moment I felt all of that old thrill, all of that frisson of desire I had once known, staring at his spidery writing. Perhaps I had not loved him, but I had desired him. I had hated him. For a moment I thought of nothing more than crushing the paper between my hands or burning it. If Victor had some papers of mine, he could have sent them as easily as the note. Why should he want to see me, so many years too late?

Curiosity won. Or perhaps I wanted some denouement, some ending. I could slap him. I could curse him. I did not know what I would do. But what I should not do was wait at home, wondering what would have happened if I had gone.

That day was a day of rain, with fitful summer squalls racing across the sky. I stood in the Blvd. Madeleine fully half an hour, waiting for him. I almost didn't recognize him. He was cloaked against the rain, his hat pulled low on his head, his steps quick and abstracted.

When he lifted his face, I drew in a breath of surprise. His hair which had been ebony only touched with gray was now almost white, startling with his dark, sharp eyes. He looked so much older. I had thought he would be as he had been, when we had begun almost eight years ago, but he was nearly fifty and looked it.

"Ida," he said, and once again I started. He had never called me that. It was not my real name, and he had never called me by it.

"Victor," I said.

His eyes looked me over, and I saw a hint of that old amusement there. "You haven't changed."

"You have," I said.

"Misfortunes," he said, and shrugged.

"You should have known better," I said.

He shrugged again and offered me his arm. "Probably."

I took it and we walked together, not going anywhere in particular. "You had papers for me?"

"Yes." He dug a packet from his pocket and gave them to me. "I thought you might need them."

"You might have thought that six years ago," I said. "Why did you keep them?"

"One of life's mysteries," he said, and I took his arm and we walked again.

I glanced sideways at him. "Where do you go?"

He laughed, a short laugh like a bark. "New Jersey."

"New Jersey?"

"New Jersey, in the United States," he said. "A pleasant enough place, I'm told. It lacks palaces, but I understand that it at least has restaurants."

"Why ever in the world?" I would have expected London, or Rome, or even Cairo.

"Why not?" I was getting tired of his diffident shrug. "Are you going to ask me now if I am guilty of all I was charged with? A present for a new master?"

"I know you're guilty," I said evenly, "and I expect I would have a harder time proving it than the prosecutor. You forget how well I knew you, Victor."

"I suppose you did." He stopped and we stood facing one another in the rainy street. His eyes roved over my face as his hands once had. "I should have expected you to be coarsened by now."

"From the life you left me to?" My voice was bitter, but not as much as I had expected. "You underestimate me. You always have."

"I never have," he said mildly. "Did I not say that when a man makes a pet of a tiger he should not be surprised when one day it bites his hand off?"

"It was you that bit my hand," I said.

"And it was you who loved Ney." He took my arm again and we walked, stepping carefully on the slick stones. "I saw you together in Munich, you know. I knew you were there."

"And said nothing?"

"I had other things on my mind," he said. His profile was gray and impassive. "You are a tiger, and you will outlive us all."

"I hope so," I said. "But if I do, it will be no thanks to you."

He smiled as though at some pleasant memory. "You can still thank me for delivering you from that odious marriage, and for seeing to your education. That, I think, I did well."

"Yes," I said. "You did. But I am not done with it yet. My husband's family is still trying to get me back to Holland and lock me away."

"My dear, if I could I should intervene," he said. "I did all those years, while I could."

"Did you?" This time it was I who stopped and faced him. "Until your arrest?"

He nodded, one eyebrow rising. "Who else did you think? But I have no more power to do anything of the kind."

I put my gloved hand on his arm. "Victor, why would you do that?"

"Tigers don't belong in cages," he said, and steered us around a boy taking dustbins out.

I said nothing. The rain dripped down from my bonnet.

"I do not think I will see you again," he said conversationally.

"I don't imagine so," I said, trying to make light of it. "I am seldom in New Jersey."

"I wouldn't think you're missing much." The corner of his mouth quirked. "How will you remember me, I wonder? An ogre? A failed conspirator? A general not quite as good as Bonaparte or a lover not quite as dear as Ney?"

I stopped and took both his hands in mine. "As my Valmont," I said. "My dark seducer, dangerous and fascinating, cruel and lost. That is what I will remember of you, Victor. That is the story I will tell about you in years to come."

For a moment he smiled. "Better to reign in hell, then?"

"Much better," I said, and kissed him goodbye in the rain for the last time.

Playing for Queens

My third assignment for Fouché was not until the eve of autumn. I had hoped, after the failure of throwing me at Talleyrand, that he would lose interest in me. Of course not. Of course Fouché didn't simply forget about me.

However, this time instead of sending Maurice or one of his other thugs, he simply sent a note for me with the instruction that I should present myself immediately. He had been reinstated as Minister of Police since the spring, and I supposed he thought there was no reason he could not simply summon me to his office now.

It was a beautiful day, though rather warm, and I was not surprised to see that his windows were open, letting in all the racket of the Place Vendome two stories below. I made my courtesy briefly. "Monsieur."

"Madame." He did not look up from the folder before him, only waved me to the chair opposite his desk.

A chair, I thought cynically. I am really moving up in the world. I settled myself, wondering who he wanted me to sleep with this time.

At last he looked up from the papers, as though suddenly noticing me. "Madame, do you recall Dr. Fraser, the gentleman I asked you to find last spring?"

"Yes, of course," I said. "But as you know, he died nearly two years ago. Or so I was told by reliable people. Is that not true?"

Fouché's mouth twitched in a thin line, what perhaps passed for a smile from him. "Dr. Fraser is indeed dead. A pity, but something that can be worked around. He can no longer provide the evidence I require, but fortunately it is likely that it can be obtained in other ways."

I waited, a cold pit of dread in my stomach at what those ways might be. I had heard stories of the Terror, of course, and of his means of obtaining information.

As though he read my face, his lips twisted in a real smile. "Nothing so draconian, Madame. Much can be accomplished with money. You are to act as my go between, to persuade a certain lady to sell me the documents I desire. I had reason to believe that she has them, and they are far too valuable for her to have disposed of. Your job is simply to persuade her that it would greatly be to her benefit to work with me, and to convey those documents to you for a reasonable sum."

"Who is the lady?" I asked.

"Therese Tallien. I understand she is well known to you."

I took a breath. "Yes," I said. I certainly knew Therese. Once I had thought we were dear friends. Until Victor disposed of me, and I was no longer of any importance at all.

"M. Tallien has divorced her," Fouché said. "Some small matter of her bearing three children who were not his. She is now living quite retired in the Loire, until her new lover, the Comte de Camaran, is free to marry her without losing any part of his inheritance. His uncle is acutely ill, I hear, and once he is gone his edict that his nephew will have nothing to do with her is meaningless. And alas, Madame Tallien is barred the capital. Some little fracas with the Emperor, I understand. He suggested that she would prefer to live away from court." Fouché looked at me and his gray eyes sparkled maliciously. "Is it not nice that we once again have a court?"

There was no possible answer to that which would not cause me great trouble, so I held my tongue.

"I see that you are prudent, Madame," Fouché said, with a quick nod. He reached into a desk drawer and brought forth a purse, which he gave to me. "There is a draft within for fifty thousand francs, as well as some travel money for you. If Madame Tallien is cooperative, the draft is hers in exchange for the documents I want."

I kept my voice steady. I did not want to see Therese, did not want to talk to her, not after all that had passed between us. But I knew better than to refuse Fouché. "What are these documents and how shall I know if they are the ones you want?" I asked. Fifty thousand francs was a lot of money. Therese had always had lavish tastes, and I supposed that since her divorce, and since her affair with the banker Ouvrard ended, she might be feeling the pinch.

"Letters or notes to Madame Tallien from Madame Bonaparte," Fouché said. "Requesting her assistance in a matter of delicacy. You will get these documents from Madame Tallien and bring them to me. That is your sole part in this affair. I send you because I expect that you can be exceptionally persuasive to Madame Tallien."

I felt the blood rise in my cheeks. Servants talk. He had heard, then, what had once passed between us.

"Is that clear, Madame?"

"Yes," I said.

I had a long time to think on the way to the Loire. The roads were good and the days warm and pleasant, and my funds more than adequate for inns as I traveled. I went dressed as Charles for more than one reason. The obvious one was that it was simply far easier to travel as a man than a woman, who would need to have a maid if she pretended to decency, and who would be held back by the slow pace of a carriage, which I should have to rent. As Charles, I could simply saddle Nestor and go.

The other reason was much more complicated. I had never had the upper hand with Therese, a hanger on in her stellar orbit, a rather ordinary blonde among the ladies of fashion who circled around her. I had thought, perhaps, that I was a friend. I had been wrong. When I had gone to her after Victor threw me out, she had refused to have anything further to do with me once it became clear that Victor was done. I was valuable only while I was with him. Without him, I returned to being nothing.

That still stung. I had not gotten over that yet.

I supposed most women would have seen through her. But strange as my early life had been, and as solitary as my adolescence, a wife before I was a woman, I had never had the crowd of girls around me that most women had. I had never been part of the circle of maidens whispering and gossiping, never learned how to tell what was true and what was false. I counted myself lucky in some ways to have missed it, but in missing it I had never learned to survive in the world of women. I did not know how. In retrospect, I thought Therese had played me for a fool more than once, only I had been too naïve to realize it.

Charles was another matter. Charles had always had the upper hand with her, sometimes quite literally. If I had to see Therese again, much less needed to try to get her to do something, it was better to be Charles than Elza.

And yet Fouché thought I might prove "exceptionally persuasive." Could it be that quiet, respectable and comfortable exile was wearing on her? Without the political circles that were her meat and drink, without lovers to seduce and games to play, what did she have, exiled to a beautiful house far from the capital?

It came to me that Napoleon understood all of us far too well. Victor might a thousand times rather languish in jail rather than in unremarkable exile in New Jersey, as though he were so little threat that he might be dismissed. Therese would, I was sure, rather be locked up dramatically in a convent or thrown into the Conciergerie, where her plight would attract a great deal of sympathy, than simply be barred the capital and the court. After all, who would pity her, with a lovely house and all the rest of the world at her disposal? She might go to Rome or London if she liked, or live in palatial comfort in the country. How should she parlay this into poor treatment? Meanwhile, his reputation for mercy could but grow, if enemies received clemency.

And so it was with some trepidation that Charles van Aylde presented himself at her chateau.

Therese took her time receiving me. At last I was ushered in to her morning room, a lovely small chamber on the ground floor with gold wallpaper with a pattern of twining roses. French doors opened onto a green lawn and the distant landscapes of a glowing English garden. She was reclining on a pale pink chaise, her fine lawn gown the palest shade of yellow. It set off her skin to perfection, which time had seemingly not touched at all.

Still, she was not entirely the same. Her breasts were fuller, her arms plumper, and her hands where they rested on her lap were not entirely still. She was not completely the master of the situation. She did not know why I was here.

"Good afternoon, Madame," I said with a dancing master perfect bow, Charles' hat in my hand and a fine leg before me. "It is a pleasure to see you as ravishing as ever."

She smiled, and there was something of the old predator in it. "Good afternoon, M. van Aylde. I confess I am surprised to see you in my humble country house." She had decided to play along. Perhaps entertaining her was my best course.

"I happened to be in the neighborhood," I said, straightening and toying negligently with the riding crop in my hand. I never used it on Nestor, of course, but it made an appropriate and provocative prop. "As a matter of chance. I thought that I would see how you are keeping, rusticating in the country as you are."

"Were you? By chance?" Her eyebrows rose, plucked and perfect as ever.

"I heard that you were in Bavaria some time ago, engaged in...." Therese paused delicately. "Martial endeavors."

"Alas, Madame, I fear the army grew too dull." I paused with my back to her, before one of her large gilt mirrors. I could see her reflected over my shoulder, a study in pink and gold.

Charles van Aylde was a very handsome young man. Fair hair cut in the latest Brutus cut just touched the top of his high collar, white linen setting off a dove gray riding coat to perfection. His features were even, almost pretty, though his mouth was too cynical for beauty, the first fine lines appearing at the edges of it, belying one's initial impression of youth. No, Charles was not as young as he looked, not anymore. His eyes were too cool, and his rakehell manners did not quite hide far too much steel. A man so inclined might wonder if he played the girl in the bedroom, but would be unlikely to find out.

"Did it?" Therese said in the mirror. "I am surprised."

"It lacked sufficient scope for certain amusements," I said, turning about, the riding crop still in my hands.

Therese smiled sweetly, but I saw the shiver that passed through her. "Did it now?"

"It did," I said, taking a step closer. "And certainly the salons of Paris are much duller without you to ornament them."

My eyes held hers, but it was she who looked away. "What is it you want?"

"Besides your charming company?" I asked innocently. "Surely you remember what good friends we have been in the past." I cocked my head, one foot forward in its tasseled leather boot.

"I do," she said. "But we did not part friends, did we?"

"That, I fear, was your doing, not mine," I said, arching my back just a little as Victor had when he played this game.

"It was," she said. Therese gathered her legs under her and sat up. "So now I'm wondering what you want. You look well turned out, and you have no reason to think I would give you money. You haven't any proof of the things you might say, and my dear Comte de Camaran has heard all the nasty, unsubstantiated rumors before. If such things mattered to him, we should not be where we are."

"Oh?" I asked, raising an eyebrow rakishly, "Does he like the crop too?"

At that she did color just a bit, and I felt with a rush the sudden jolt of desire unfeigned, as though suddenly the seams of these trousers rubbed in entirely the wrong places. I had gotten to her, which I never used to do, and there was a thrill in the power of that.

"Perhaps, Madame, I am here instead to do you a good turn." I looked about the room appraisingly. "You seem quite comfortable, however, and probably not in need of fifty thousand francs."

That got her attention. "Where in the world would you get fifty thousand francs?"

"From a certain gentleman," I said, pacing around behind a pink brocade slipper chair. "A friend who has my interests at heart." I stopped and looked at her, one gloved hand resting on the chair back. "Fifty thousand francs, Madame, for some trifles of yours. If you are interested."

"Ah." Therese lounged back on her chaise, smirking like a cat in cream. "Now we come down to it. What sort of trifles?"

"Letters," I said. "From Joséphine de Beauharnais. Written in the spring and summer of the Year IV."

"Say rather Madame Bonaparte, as she was at that moment," Therese said. "Of course I have some little notes, but why should they be worth that?"

I bent over, my elbows on the chair back. "You know what I want," I said. "I saw the flash of cupidity in your eyes. I am prepared to pay exceedingly well, if they contain enough interesting material."

"Joséphine is a dear friend of mine," she said. "I should not want to betray her confidence for so poor a sum."

"A dear friend who is only too happy to have you exiled from Paris," I observed. "Could it be that you stepped upon her one time too many? I remember how you used to enjoy cutting her, dear friend that she was. It's a pity she was the one who wound up married to the head of state!"

At that Therese's eyes snapped. "And that only because Barras made her! She never wanted to marry him! But Paul Barras demanded it, and she had to jump. And then she nearly ruined the whole thing. Empress of France! It's folly!"

I chose my words carefully. "Perhaps Empress. Perhaps not. That may rest on those little notes you have. But of course if they contain nothing of interest...."

"Who are you working for?" Therese stood up, kicking her skirts out before her.

"I am not at liberty to reveal that, Madame."

"You're working for one of the Bonapartes, aren't you?" she demanded.

"They don't want Joséphine crowned. They want him to divorce her. That's it, isn't it?"

"It could be." I shrugged negligently. "But if you do not have any papers of interest, then it is a moot point. I am not authorized to pay unless it is actually of worth."

"It's of worth," Therese said sharply. "It would be worth a good deal to them. I'll see your money."

"I'll see the paper first," I said, holding her eyes.

"Wait here," she said, crossing the room and closing the door behind her abruptly.

I waited. Outside the bees were in the flowerbed. I went to the mirror and straightened the folds of my cravat. Oh yes, Charles, I said to myself, you do this quite well. Aren't you the devil?

It was not long before she returned. "Here," she said, thrusting a letter at me, a packet of others tied with blue ribbons still in her hand. "This is the one you want."

12 Floreal, Year IV

Therese, you know I hate to beg favors of you, but I do need the name of the doctor you mentioned. It has been more than four décades now and I am quite certain. I fear that it is growing too late to end this safely, and I must very soon before people notice. If you would make an appointment with this man for me I would appreciate it, or if not at least give me his name. I do not dare use one of the midwives here, for fear they will talk too freely. My husband is writing me twice a day, begging me to come to Italy, and I am running out of excuses. Already his sister Caroline writes to him saying that she thinks I am with child, and I have told him that I am not. I've told him I'm just ill with a spring cold, but I cannot expect to be believed very long, not with that sister of his nosing about. I'm telling the footman to wait for your reply.

Joséphine

I read it over twice, as though to make certain of its worth, though my mind was spinning. I had been there, that spring. I had stood with Joséphine at one of Moreau's receptions, had hardly paid attention when she said her husband wrote her too often, though I remembered she had seemed distracted. Yes, I thought. I knew just when it was. Therese had arrived with M. Ouvrard, and Joséphine had pounced on her, pulling her away to talk. I remembered that.

If we had been better friends, perhaps it would have been I that she confided in rather than Therese. I was a better friend to have. I should not have saved her notes to sell.

I schooled my face to boredom, as though I were merely satisfied with merchandise offered. "Hippolyte Charles, I assume."

Therese shrugged. "She didn't tell me which lover. Hippolyte Charles or Paul Barras. I don't know precisely when she and Barras broke it off. But it won't be important to your buyer. It doesn't matter which lover." She smiled maliciously. "I wonder what Caroline will think of the nice things her new sister-in-law said about her?"

"I am sure she will be very interested," I said.

"The money?" Therese prompted.

I got out the draft and handed it to her. "Fifty thousand francs, drawn on the Bank of France. It is always a pleasure, Madame."

She took the draft eagerly, glancing over every detail, then looked up at me. "Is it?"

"It is," I said, and with a feral smile seized her chin in one gloved hand, tilting up her lips as mine descended, hard and very thorough. I felt her respond, moving closer, her full breasts pressed against me, her warm body and her seeking hands.

I stepped back, putting the letter in my pocket with a flourish and making a little bow. "Very nice," I smirked, "But not as good as I remembered."

And I took my leave.

It was a long way back to Paris. I slept with the letter beneath my pillow, of course, in every inn where I stayed.

I dreamed, and in my dream I stood in a garden, stark rectangular pool bordered by a weeping almond tree, walls about carved with ancient princes, and above the clear azure sky of distant lands. I dreamed, and in my dream I sat beside a young man with long black hair, his green eyes reflecting the waters, the light dancing on his face, beautiful and serene.

"I come here," he said, "To remember."

"As do I," I said.

He reached out and stirred the water with one hand idly, long and graceful fingers, a beauty just past his prime. "I did not want to be in this story," he said. "I didn't. But fate left me no choice. And now for better or worse I must play the queen. It is not what I intended."

I bent my head, flashes of fire on the water, fire and the memory of fire. "Would you truly be free of this if you could?"

"Not now," he said, looking out over the pool, a breeze stirring his hair. "Not now. But when I was younger I only wanted heart's ease. Can you not understand that?"

"Of course I can, my friend," I said. "I have known a little of sorrow too."

"And once again you will choose your own way, master all or be mastered." He smiled, and I thought it was a fond smile, though his face was drawn and tired. "You act as though we can choose who we will be. I told you that before, if you remember."

"I do," I said, "And I believe it still. I am a Companion because I choose to be, not because destiny binds me. I choose out of love."

"As do I," he said. "Choose well."

I woke. It was dawn, and I slept in the loft room of an inn, Charles's shirt about me and the letter in my hand. And I knew what I would do.

A Rose Without Thorns

"Her Imperial Majesty will not see you." The footman was officious, barely glancing at me. I did not look like much, come from the south in autumn rains wearing men's clothes as I had once, in wilder times. And even then I had not dared to show my face at Malmaison without invitation. How much worse to turn up now, six weeks before her coronation!

Perhaps it would be her coronation, perhaps not. Perhaps in six weeks Joséphine would be Empress of France. Or perhaps she would not be. It might depend on what I carried.

I fumbled in my waistcoat pocket and brought out the note I had prepared. "Will you at least take her my card? It is a matter of the greatest delicacy and importance."

At that he sniffed, but he deigned to take it while I stood beside my horse outside the gatehouse. Someone had planted very pretty red geraniums in the windowbox of the second story of the gatehouse, and they bloomed still. The autumn had not been harsh.

"There, Nestor," I said, smoothing his unruly mane. He was a little blown from the journey. I had not dared to stop once we were close to Paris. Even now, Fouché might be hearing of my return. He, at least, would know in a moment what it meant that I had gone instead to Joséphine. He, like I, knew I had probably signed my own death warrant.

The footman returned, picking his way over the puddles of the drive careful of his white silk stockings. His demeanor was entirely different. "Please come in, Madame. The stable boy will take your horse. Her Imperial Majesty is awaiting you in the garden." He gestured politely, and I handed over Nestor's reins.

With my head high, I walked over the cobbles and around the side of the lawn. A beautiful Lebanese cedar stood only as high as my waist, a specimen tree brought back by the expedition, no doubt. I wondered if it would thrive in France.

The roses did. Even though it was late in the year, the rose garden was a riot of color, blossoms from palest shell to the color of rich Burgundy intermingled. At Malmaison, transplanted roses bloomed even though the leaves were already falling from the trees. In an ash barrel along the far walk a fire was smoldering, casting a pall of smoke from the damp leaves that burned, the scent of autumn.

She was standing among the trees, where a path led among the trees to a little Greek pavilion, a statue of Aphrodite Cythera lifting an urn. Joséphine's dress was white, and the cashmere wrap around her shoulders was shades of rose and cream. I thought she looked pale.

"You said it was urgent."

"It is," I said, and stopped opposite her, my boots hard on the damp ground. I reached into my shirt and gave her the letter that rested against my heart. I said nothing more.

She opened it, and I saw her hands tremble as she saw what it was. A chill passed across her face, as though she were already dead.

"Therese," she said.

"Yes," I replied. "She gave it to me for what Fouché gave to me to offer her."

"You know what it says."

"Yes," I said.

She held it lightly, as though afraid it would bite. "If you know what it is, then you know what it is worth to him." Her eyes searched my face, dark and curious, even in this terror, and I knew what she saw—a merveilleuse as she had been, tattered now in my mud-spattered men's clothes, while she would be Empress of France. I had not particularly been her friend. "Why have you come here instead of to Fouché?"

I met her eyes evenly. "Because it is the right thing to do."

A tiny frown began between her brows. "And what will you do with this?"

I spread my hands. "Nothing. It is yours. You will do with it as you want."

"Your word, Therese's word, is nothing without this," she said. "Gossip."

I nodded. "The word of a courtesan with ample reason to be jealous. Nothing more."

"And what will happen to you?"

I took a long breath. I had thought it through over and over on the long ride from the Loire, and I knew. "I will be deported to Holland, to spend the rest of my days in a madhouse, however long they may be. If I do not do as Fouché says, he has been clear about what the consequences will be."

"And you are giving this to me?" The line between her brows grew tighter.

"Yes," I said.

Swift as a marten she flew across the grass and dropped it in the gardener's fire. I followed and saw it already half consumed. I watched while the flames reduced it to ashes.

Joséphine took a deep breath and lifted her eyes to mine. "Come in the house," she said, "And have some coffee. It's cold out here."

We went in and I stood while she told the footman what to bring, then followed her in to a sumptuous library, its dark green velvet drapes framing a view of the lawn. The fire was lit, and I stood close by, trying to shake the chill that had come over me. Above, the ceiling was half finished. I could not tell if the painting was to be the gods on Olympus, or their modern counterparts here.

The coffee came, and Joséphine fussed about with milk and sugar while I stood by the fire, the enormity of what I had done washing over me.

"Why?" she asked.

I shrugged. "I could not let that be used against you. I was there, remember? I was at those parties of Barras' when I was with Moreau. I was there. You told me your husband had gone to Italy, and that he wrote too often."

"Did I say that?" She looked at me over the rim of her cup. "I should not have said that."

"No," I said. "But you did not know then what he would become."

She shook her hair back, dark curls falling back over her shoulders from their pins. "I didn't," she said. "And I did not want to marry him. Did you know that?"

"Not in so many words," I said. Therese had said that, but like everything else Therese said, I took it with a grain of salt.

She gave me a rueful smile, her lips tight over her teeth. "I was in love with Lazare Hoche. We were in prison together during the Revolution. I can't explain to you what that was like, spending each day in those barns full of prisoners, waiting to be called to the tumbrels. Each day might be our last. He was kind and strong, calm and philosophical no matter what came. He was my rock. He made me strong. He made me kind." She put her cup down on a gilt table, poured more coffee in it. "And then Barras came with his infernal bargain."

That I knew. "Your life and the lives of your children and the lives of the little Auguié girls if you would be his mistress. The guillotine if you would not."

She nodded, glancing up, and I thought her eyes were beautiful, dark and timeless as the night sky. "If I had been more like you perhaps I would have said no. But I did not want to die. I did not want my children to die. I was not brave enough."

I shrugged. "I would not have been either. There are too many good things still in the world."

"That may be," she said, and lifted the cup to her lips, Sevres porcelain banded in gold. "I agreed. And Lazare and I made promises. If we could get through this, we said, if we could survive, we would be together. My husband was dead. When this was done, he would get a divorce from his wife. Barras would be through with me someday. And then we would marry. Then we would be happy forever."

I tasted the coffee, rich with cream. "I understand," I said.

"Do you?" she said, her eyebrows rising. "I did as Barras wanted. And of course before long his interest began to wane. That was when it happened. Bonaparte, he said, is in love with you. Bonaparte adores you. Bonaparte worships you from afar. And I need Bonaparte as a counterbalance to Moreau."

Joséphine looked at me and I nodded. "Oh yes," I said. "Moreau wanted the Republic."

"Bring me Bonaparte, he said. You can entrance him. You can play him. And I? I knew little enough of him, practically a schoolboy who didn't even own a dress sword, writing me the most absurd letters full of declared fire!"

"And so you did," I said.

She shrugged. "It was easy. A day, two days and he was eating out of my hand, calling me his destiny, the other half of his wandering soul."

I drew a breath.

"He wanted to marry me. I told Barras it was impossible. He said if I went through with it Bonaparte would be off to Italy before the wedding breakfast had been eaten, and that as soon as he was tired of me I should have my divorce and so should Lazare. We could finally be together. If I could just keep Bonaparte entranced a few more months...." She reached for the cream, stirring more of the heavy liquid into the coffee. Outside, there was the first spatter of rain. "You know what happened then."

I did. I had been there in those days, on Moreau's arm. "He went to Italy with his paladins. And you stayed in Paris. And then?" I cut my eyes toward the garden, to the undistinguished ashes in the gardener's can.

"And then. He was begging me to come to Italy, writing me every day. He was threatening to resign his command if I would not come. I needed Therese's help. Not a word could ever get back to him. Therese can get things done discreetly when money is no object."

My throat was dry. "Because it was not your husband's child."

"No." She lifted her eyes to mine. "Because it was."

A swirl of wind threw the rain against the window and I felt the world still.

"Do not you see? If I gave him a child he would never let me go! All I wanted was to be free to marry Lazare. If I had his child, son or daughter, he would never divorce me." She paced away, her cashmere wrap dragging against the floor where it had fallen from one arm. "And therein lies the irony, of course." She took a deep breath, and I saw her shoulders square. No doubt she had never told this whole story to anyone, but I of all people would understand. And if I repeated it, no one would ever believe it. "Lazare lost interest. It was one of those things, he said. People feel very passionately when they're in danger. Lazare fell out of love. And I fell into love. With my husband." She turned, her face in shadow. "Surely you can understand that."

"I do not see how anyone could fail to love your husband whom he wished to," I said, remembering Milan and the man I had known there.

"He did not trust me. He didn't know what had happened, but he knew something had. He thought it was about some flirtation with Hippolyte Charles, or something like that. Some minor indiscretion, some harmless game that meant nothing. He forgave me. He forgave me completely. But he has never entirely trusted me since. I lost that." Her voice was unflinching. "And I lost the thing that he needs most of all. A son. An heir. I have never been able to conceive since."

"And an emperor must have an heir," I said.

She stood against the window, the darkening garden behind her. "His family wants him to divorce me. And Fouché wants to own me. If he had that, he would. I should do whatever he wanted for the rest of my life."

"And through you rule France," I said, and cautiously wet my lips. It was worth it, I thought, this thing I did. It was worth it if it kept that evil man from ruling France, though no one would ever know what I did or what I died for. I had come so far from that heedless mistress of Moreau's to stand here, grim and cold and certain. Valor in the face of danger is easy, I thought. It is this that is hard. To know what will come—the prison, the extradition, the chains, the drugs for my own good....

Joséphine nodded. "And now...."

"Now it is gone," I said.

"I will be Empress," she said.

"Our Lady of Victories," I said. "France's sacred queen, crowning the victor with her love."

She looked up at me, startled.

I smiled. "I am glad to have been of service," I said, and made my bow like a man. "I bid you good evening, as I have far to go tonight."

"Where are you going?"

"Paris," I said. "To my own apartment. I cannot evade Fouché, and there is little point in having him hunt all over town for me. It will simply put him in a worse temper when he finds me."

I made my farewells and went out to find Nestor. I led him out in the evening drizzle, mounted as soon as we were past the gates. We were a kilometer down the road when I heard the escort approaching and pulled to the side to let the carriage pass. I caught a swift glimpse of him in profile in the carriage lights, lit like a cameo against the dark, Bonaparte going home in the gathering night.

I rode on to Paris.

I went home. I sent the letters to my friends, knowing that I would not be able to write later. I did not write to Michel. What could I possibly say?

I waited for the knock in on the door.

Night turned into morning. I drank coffee dressed in a sensible blue broadcloth dress that I thought would wear well in prison. It felt a bit surreal, like picking out one's own funeral clothes. No one came.

Morning turned into noon. The sun came in through the window, making patterns of light across the floor. There was no sound. It was so quiet that an enterprising mouse came out and wandered about, freezing when he saw me.

I could hang myself, I thought, and at least spare myself some of the pain of what was to come.

Yet my heart misgave me. I thought there were yet cards to play. I would not do that except at the last turn of the dice, as the final gambit.

Afternoon came. I was starting to get irritated. How entirely ridiculous, to leave me hanging about all day waiting to be arrested! If I had known it would take so long, I should have gone out to lunch and enjoyed one last day in the clean air.

There was a heavy knock on the door.

Prepared for it as I was, I nearly wet myself when it came. It was nothing but pride that enabled me to cross the room and calmly open it.

An officer of dragoons stood outside. "Madame St. Elme?"

"I am," I said. Why was Fouché using soldiers, rather than his usual thugs? I was hardly in a position to resist arrest.

He bowed over my hand politely. "If Madame will accompany me?"

"I would," I said, and picked up my bonnet and overstuffed reticule. I had no idea when it would be taken from me, but until then the bread and fruit packed within could save my life.

He was joined in the street by two privates standing beside a waiting carriage, a plain affair with matched horses. He opened the door for me, then sat opposite me while the two privates swung up behind.

His hat was on his knees, and I saw that one of his gloves had been ripped and neatly stitched. His moustache had a few threads of gray, though he didn't look more than thirty. Was his face the last I would see in freedom?

"It's a beautiful day, isn't it?" he said.

"Yes," I said.

He glanced out the window. "It's nice for this weather to hold. I'm not looking forward to the cold, let me tell you."

"No, not at all," I said, wondering why in the world he was trying to make conversation. If this was Fouché's newest brand of intimidation, it was baffling rather than threatening.

The carriage drew up. "Checkpoint," he said, and I glanced out the window in utter surprise.

We had only gone a few minutes from my apartment.

We stood at the main gate of the Palace of the Tuileries, and the driver was presenting his papers to the guard at the gate.

"Oh Jesus Christ," I said. I had gotten it all wrong.

I should have worn another dress. The blue broadcloth was dowdy as hell. The soldier stared at me as I madly hunted through my reticule for a comb.

We were led in through a side door under a portico, and along a lengthy mirrored gallery into a waiting room. Three or four men stood about, one in uniform. There were chairs, a small bookcase, and an abundance of gilt tables. On a plinth under a swag of crimson velvet was, life-size, a beautifully rendered copy of a classical bust of Alexander the Great.

All the men looked up when I entered, but none spoke.

The soldier vanished, no doubt to report that his errand was accomplished.

I paced about the room, wandering over to the bust, my exceedingly heavy reticule banging against my legs, clad beneath the dress in sturdy half boots of leather treated with garlic to make them unattractive to rats.

Alexander seemed to give me a curious half-smile.

"Madame St. Elme."

I spun about to see a tall man in splendid livery beside the doors. "This way, if you please, Madame?"

I nodded and followed him mutely into the room beyond.

Napoleon was seated at a huge desk with a green blotter, wearing the dark blue uniform coat of the chasseurs with a white waistcoat. His hair fell forward over his eyes as though he had been working and had not noticed. At the window, thin curtains of white silk embroidered with bees swayed in the wind.

"Come in, Madame," he said. "You may go, Duroc."

I took a deep breath.

Napoleon stood up, his face transformed by a brilliant smile. "Good afternoon, Madame. I understand that you have done my wife a very great service."

"It was nothing, sire," I said with a courtesy, trying to guess what in the world Joséphine had told him I had done, since she could not possibly have told him the truth.

"It does not seem nothing to me to save her from Fouché's blackmail when he has you by the throat," Napoleon observed, perching on the edge of his desk.

I must have gaped, for he waved a hand. "Yes, I know you are loyal to her and do not wish to say that you had some silly letters she had written to Hippolyte Charles years ago. That is all in the past. I have forgiven my Joséphine long since and there are no secrets between us."

"I am relieved to hear that, sire," I said. He did not know. She had told him it was about the Charles affair. And I would say nothing.

"It puts you in a very bad position to say the least."

"It does," I said evenly. "Fouché has me, as you said, by the throat. At best I expect to be deported to my former husband's family in Holland, where I will spend the rest of my life locked in an asylum."

"At best."

"As you say, sire."

He put his head to the side, considering. "Joséphine said you had never been a close friend. Why did you do this for her?"

"For her, or for you?"

At that he broke into a broad smile. "I see what you have made of yourself, then."

"You gave me money," I said, "And let me go, saying you were curious what I would become. Four years have passed, sire. This is what I have become."

He nodded. "You asked me what the price of a general was."

"And you said, the same as a companion."

His dark eyes were alight with amusement. "And so you are, Madame. Your wits are too sharp for me to allow you to remain Fouché's agent." He forestalled my reply with a gesture. "No, don't bother to say you aren't. I have already had my conversation with him this morning. A private conversation. I have in the past relieved him of being Minister of Police, but clearly that was insufficient, if he then turned to blackmailing the Empress upon his reinstatement."

"Sire...."

He rested his chin on his hand, his head to the side. "So here is my proposition for you, Madame. You do not wish to return to Holland. You wish to be a French citizen, safe forever behind our laws. You wish for the powerful friends to make it so, and you do not want to work for Fouché. And yet you make an ideal agent, clever, loyal, equally capable in the ballroom or the battlefield. A pretty woman who is not afraid to kill." One eyebrow rose. "Perhaps a clairvoyant, if the rumors are to be believed."

A blush rose on my face.

"You are rash, yes. Daring to a fault, which is not an uncommon flaw among my paladins. And you are a little too fond of sleeping with generals."

In my confusion I dropped my reticule. Three apples and a bun rolled out, stopping just short of his feet.

Napoleon bent down and picked up the bun. "And prepared," he said, his eyes lively.

"It was for...."

"I am not mocking you, Madame. Or if so only a little!"

"I see that, sire," I said, and smiled back. "Believe me, I am grateful if you are offering to intervene with Fouché for me, but I do not know what good there can be for you in it."

"I have already spoken with Fouché, as I said, Madame. You have nothing more to fear from him. I give you my word on that. I will not have it said that service to me or to Joséphine is rewarded so badly."

I had not thought it was possible to be more relieved. "Thank you, sire."

He got up from the desk and stood opposite me, exactly of a height. "I want you to be my agent."

"Your agent, sire?"

"I sometimes employ special agents of my own, outside of the parameters of the Minister of Police, agents who are loyal to me alone with no Fouché as intermediary. They report directly to me, or to whomever I deputize as necessary. I must be able to trust them absolutely." His eyes searched mine. "Your personal oath, Madame. Irrevocable. You may think on it."

"I do not need to think," I said, my eyes squarely on his. "I have known for a long time. I, Elzelina Johanna Van Aylde Versfelt Ringeling, do swear to you, Napoleon Bonaparte, Emperor of France, my undying loyalty and service, that I may in all things serve you and France, waking and sleeping, in danger and luxury, in omission and commission, as a true Companion in all things, until death or you release me." I knelt and took his hand in mine, my lips to his finger where a ring should go.

He gripped my hand and raised me up, and there was nothing but a knowing half smile in his eyes. "Welcome to my service, Elzelina. I shall act as your liege in all things, and shall in no way disappoint your expectations while life and breath last." His eyes fluttered shut for a moment.

Did he remember? I did not know. I remembered the humid garden, the sound of the water playing in the bathhouse in Babylon, the fever in his flesh when he had taken my hand. I barely remembered myself. And yet it was there, like celestial music barely heard.

"I am yours, sire," I said.

An Education for an Adventuress

I had expected the life of the Emperor's private agent to be much more exciting. For the first few weeks I waited with bated breath for the messenger that would come to give me my first assignment. As much as I had dreaded the idea of a summons from Fouché's minions, now I eagerly awaited one.

And yet no summons came.

Surely there must be a use for a private agent as the coronation approached! The eyes of Europe were on Paris, where in a short time Bonaparte would be crowned Emperor of the French in a grand ceremony lasting most of a day at Notre Dame Cathedral. Surely there would be assassins seeking his life, both Royalists as Cadoudal had been, and British and Austrian agents alike. Surely those assassins needed thwarting!

But apparently not by me. No summons came, no messengers left anything for me.

At last, the week before the coronation, I sent a short note to the Tuileries, reiterating in neutral terms my desire to be of service. I received no reply. Nor did I hear a word from Fouché. If at least Napoleon had freed me from Fouché's domination, that was something. There were no threats, no communications at all.

The coronation procession closed streets and businesses alike, a holiday of the sort few people in France could remember. After all, France had had no monarch for nearly thirteen years, and all in all it had been thirty years since the coronation of the unfortunate Louis XVI, two years before my birth. Napoleon was determined this should be an event to remember, and like a great many others I waited in the freezing December morning to watch the processions, cheering and shouting with the rest, watching the carriages pass and the guardsmen with their prancing parade mounts.

Michel, of course, had a part in the ceremony. His wife was one of the ladies in waiting who carried Joséphine's train. I wondered how she liked that, Joséphine who had not wished for this office at all and now took on the role that history gave her. I had some part in that, and I could warm myself with that knowledge despite the day's cold.

And yet no word came for me as the year turned.

But if there was no money in being a secret agent, I did have a job. The company patronized by Regnaud de Saint-Jean d'Angely was doing a production of Alexander the Great, and I had the role of Cleofile, an altogether imaginary Indian princess whose love for the king is thwarted by her brother. I had a great many high blown lines in the style of the 17th century, beautiful as one expects Racine to be, but not in any way close to my love for his later work, Phedre. Cleofile was a pale precursor of Phedre.

With the coronation, there were fetes and balls and plays almost every night, and we gave the play a dozen times to thunderous applause that I felt I had not quite earned. I could manage the mannered and exaggerated diction necessary to play Racine only because it was not supposed to be quite believable. I did a very good job of being a grand actress pretending to be an Indian princess. I should have made an abominable Indian princess.

Once, I saw Michel. I was arriving at Regnaud de Saint-Jean d'Angely's house, wrapped warmly in a cloak with a fur collar, waiting as a lady should for the line of carriages to move so that I might get out near the door where the ice along the curb had been melted. I was part of the evening's entertainment, but only in the most respectable way. Delacroix, who was playing my brother Taxilus, and I were to do a scene after dinner by way of a change from the usual harpists and girls on the pianoforte. We were doing Alexander the Great, and also a scene from Racine's Andromache as an encore.

It was late, and dinner had ended, though the windows of the house were blazing with the light of a hundred candles reflecting on the ice that had accumulated on the topiary trees outside. Delacroix was opposite me, running over his lines as Orestes. I glanced out the window and there was Michel.

He stood at the bottom of the steps wearing a dark coat with a fox fur collar, reaching up to help a lady down. She was petite and dark, with a white dress ornamented with crystals beneath a white cloak trimmed in fur, and her delicate white kid slippers gave her no purchase on the slippery steps. He took her arm and she clutched the rail with the other hand, stepping carefully on the ice. The candles illuminated his broad forehead, one strand of red hair escaping from his hat.

It went through me like a dart, seizing my chest so I could hardly breathe. This, then, must be Aglae Auguié. His wife. The Empress' goddaughter. She was twenty-two, tiny and fragile looking.

And there was Michel, so close I could see his breath steaming in the winter air.

In a moment he helped her up into the carriage, folding in the hem of her cloak as though he were the footman. He straightened, then, looking back at the door and about, as though he had heard someone call his name.

I looked away from the window, and when I looked back he was gone and the line of carriages was in motion again.

Was he happy? How could one know? They had two children, a boy nearly two and an infant three months old. There was no gossip of strife between them, no separate residences or at least no more of such than his duty required. It had been three and a half years. Did he think of me sometimes? I rather doubted it. Such things were not meant to last, not for a young man on his way up.

If I had no lover at the moment it was rather a relief. I had spent too many years at the beck and call of one man or another to want one just now. I did not need to have a patron at the moment, and I must face that I was not as young as I once was. Of course twenty-eight was not dead and buried, but there were younger, fresher faces in town. It was time to learn to declaim Racine rather than to rely on looks alone.

Of course, being the Emperor's agent ought to eventually pay something. He had been generous enough in the past that I had not liked to bring up money. But I would hardly expect a purse for doing nothing, which was precisely what I had been doing.

Best to prepare while one could, I thought. And so as that long winter turned into spring, I did my theatrical bits and spent an afternoon a week with Signore Vincenzio, the fencing master Michel had originally taken me to in Paris. I also added two mornings a week of shooting. While I had killed a man with a pistol on the road from Milan, it required no special marksmanship to hit a man at point blank range. Now, clad as Charles, I practiced target shooting industriously until the instructor asked me if I intended an affair of honor.

"It is always possible," I said mysteriously, and let that stand. For all that I enjoyed fencing more, I had no doubt that under many circumstances a pistol would serve me better. A bullet pays no attention to size or physique, and I was well aware that I did not have the strength or the reach of most men I would face. So my father had taught me when I was a child, and so I had learned well.

In my earliest memories he had been a fencing master—sometimes. Sometimes he had been a gambler and made our way at the gaming table, my father, my mother, my younger brother Charles, and I. It had always been only the four of us, the four of us against the world. But sometimes he had been a fencing master, giving lessons for pay to guardsmen and children alike. He had taught us together. Charles needed someone to practice with, and after Charles had died there had been only me.

My father had laid the saber in my hand, spreading my fingers a little and laying my thumb over the pommel. "Like this, princess. Don't clutch it. Hold it firmly and lightly. It's not heavy."

It wasn't, even for my childish hands. It was a practice saber, thinner and lighter than a real one, but it curved just as a saber should, with a basket hilt to protect my hand. Even with my left arm held straight out in front of my body and the foil extending outward, it was no strain to hold it. I straightened my body in my boy's clothes, eight years old and tall for my age.

My father smiled. He was a big man with brown hair pulled back in an untidy queue. He shaved in the evening for the gaming table, and so morning always found him with a prickle of beard along his chin and across his upper lip. He smelled of sweated velvet, brandy, and tobacco smoke. "Get the feel of it. You move from the wrist and shoulder, not from the elbow. The elbow just flows along." He took my right arm and moved it down and low. "Now when I was learning they were doing this silly thing of holding your off hand up in the air next to your shoulder. It ruins your balance when you're using a real sword. And now the fashion is to tuck your off hand behind your off hip. It minimizes your profile in a duel, but again, it throws you off with a real sword."

"Have you used a real sword?" I asked. I had seen him fence with students and with friends often enough over the years, but never with anything more than a dress epée.

A shadow crossed his face. "I was a hired sword for five years before I went to Amsterdam," he said. "Yes, I had a real sword." He took my right hand and positioned it low again. "Keep your off hand natural. It helps your balance."

We were in the garden of a house in Genoa. It belonged to some friend or other of theirs, smaller than the place we had had in Rome, but exquisite, all rosy stone and gardens with antique bronzes. We had left Rome as soon as we could travel.

My father and I had recovered well from the fever that had killed Charles, though my mother was sick for weeks, and when at last the fever broke she was left so thin and pale that her skin seemed little more than paper stretched over bones. Her glorious platinum hair had been cut, and it made her head look like a skull.

She would not believe that Charles was dead. She had not seen him die. She had not seen his body, and a gravestone could belong to anyone. My father explained over and over that Charles had died while she was so ill that she could not attend him, could not see to the funeral. She did not believe him, or for that matter anyone else. She was certain that Charles lived. Now she stayed mostly in her rooms, walking a bit about the house and gardens, eating little and regaining little of her strength.

My birthday had come in September, and I was as strong and active as before. And I had my father to myself.

There were no parties here, just card games for a few gentlemen that broke up well before dawn, sometimes leaving my father flush with coin and sometimes not. There were no masques or balls. My mother had no friends here. And there was nothing to remind her of Charles.

Nothing but me.

My father was correcting my stance, moving my breeched knees into the right pose, when she called out from the door of the house. "Charles! Dear sweetheart! Come here right now and give me a kiss!"

My father and I looked at each other. I dropped my point, and my father took the practice saber. We walked to her together.

"Adeline, this is Elzelina," my father said quietly. "You know that Charles is gone."

She seized me in a hug and kissed my brow and my cheeks. "Dear, darling boy! Oh my sweet boy!"

"Adeline, this is Elzelina," my father said again, one hand on my shoulder, his voice low and urgent.

She glared up at him. "Leo, it's unkind to play games with me. You know I hate to be reminded of our lost angel. Elzelina died in Rome."

A chill ran down my back and I stood stock still while she caressed me.

My father took her hands and drew her up, searching her face. "Adeline, dearest, this is Elzelina. Charles died in Rome. We lost Charles." His face was white beneath his tan.

"We didn't," she said, and her face was paler than his, a fine film of platinum down covering her head, a finger's length long. "We lost Elzelina, and it was better that way. I could not have stood losing Charles."

I don't know what my father said, because I broke from them and ran out into the gardens, running until I found the most remote corner. There was a place where the rosy bricks of the wall made a small walk beneath an arbor, a love nest with a fountain. There were roses in abundance climbing up the wall, their blossoms nearly spent. When my father found me later I was sitting on the rim of the pool watching the droplets fall from an urn held by a laughing cherub with an erect phallus. I was not crying.

He came through the arbor quietly and sat down beside me. He was only thirty-four, but for the first time I thought he looked old. His jaw was beginning to sag a little, his waist was broader than it had been, and his eyes were bloodshot. His lace cravat was mended, and as usual he hadn't shaved. "Elzelina," he said. "Your mother isn't well."

I shrugged, watching the fall of the water.

"She's not right in her mind. She can't help it."

"She loved Charles more," I said.

He trailed one hand in the water. "We can't help who we love. All parents try to love their children and love them equally, but we can't. Because we're not perfect, and there are things we like better than other things and people we like better than other people. We try to be fair and kind and do what's right. And when we're in our right minds, we never say things that hurt. But your mother isn't in her right mind. She's very sick. And she can't help the things she said."

I watched the water falling off his fingers, splashing back in the fountain. "Do you love me?"

He smiled and didn't raise his head. "I love you more than anyone in the world. You're fearless and clever and beautiful and warm. You love dogs and cats and horses, roses and sunshine and beat up old bronzes. You can make anyone smile. And you want to know everything there is to know in the world, questions I have no answers to. Why do clouds move? What is there above the stars in the firmament? Why do people have wars and fall in love? You'd stump a philosophe."

I looked at him sideways. "I want all the stories there have ever been," I said.

He lifted his eyes and met mine. "I love you more than you can possibly imagine, princess. You're the most wonderful daughter in the world, and I am proud of you every instant of every day."

I felt the prickle of tears in my eyes, and asked what I knew I shouldn't. "Do you love me more than Mother?"

"God help me, I do," he said, and looked away. The fountain ran on, water endlessly recirculating. "Differently, of course. But more. Adeline has never had your courage. The world is a dangerous place, Elzelina. If you're not quick and brave enough you get swallowed up by it. It has nothing to do with being good. Only with being strong."

I waited.

My father shook his head. "She's not weak, or she'd never have survived the childhood she had. But it's left her…damaged. I don't know if she can ever be whole. You know your grandparents died when she was a baby, and she lived with her uncle, yes?"

I nodded.

He ran one hand through the water. "He did things that were wrong, things that men shouldn't do with little girls, with his own niece and his own daughter both. Adeline was fifteen when I met her, and she was getting over a miscarriage. He had beaten her when he found out she was pregnant." He didn't look at me, but his mouth twisted wryly. "These things happen, even in the best families."

I said nothing. I wasn't entirely sure what he meant.

"I convinced her to run away with me. We're not all like that, I said. I promised her I would keep her safe."

"You loved her," I said. I understood that.

My father almost laughed, tilted his head back in the sunshine. "I did and I do. And I've done everything I could to keep her safe. We've built a life. Not much of one, sometimes, but we get along. And every time I start thinking about mercenary work in Bavaria or Hesse, or of going off to the Indies or something, I have you and her like a silver chain. And I will never leave." He looked at me. "I will never leave, do you understand, princess?"

"I do," I said, and put my arms around him, pressing against his worn frockcoat. "I love you too, Daddy."

It was in the autumn a year later that the letter came. My mother's uncle was dead, and there was some legal matter. I heard my parents arguing about it when I came in from the garden covered in mud from climbing vines and falling off the wall. I stopped outside the door and listened.

"You said we'd never go back," my mother said. "Leo, you promised! You promised I'd never have to go there again, never see that house again."

"Dearest, your uncle is dead," he said gently. "He can't harm you now."

"You don't understand," she said, and I knew from her voice that she was crying. I slipped closer, so I could see them through the crack with the hinges where the door stood half closed. She was sitting on the sofa and he was kneeling in front of her, holding her hands. "You don't understand. You promised me, Leo."

"Adeline, it's a great deal of money."

"I don't want any money from him."

He shook his head. "It's not from him. It's your parents' money that he had in trust for you. He should have given it to you when you came of age, if he'd been an honest guardian. Your parents would have wanted you to have it."

"I don't remember anything about them," she said. "You can't appeal to me that way. You know my father died before I knew him and then my mother committed suicide."

My father sat back on his heels, releasing her hands. "Adeline, we need the money. You know as well as I do that we can't go on like this." His voice was low and sad.

"I know," she said softly.

"And what kind of future can we give Elzelina this way? A dowry if I win at cards? Who's going to marry her? No respectable young man. Don't we want better for her than being the mistress of anyone who can afford to keep her, or worse?"

"And what kind of career for Charles?" she said. "He'll be old enough that he needs to go to school soon. We need to send him somewhere. I don't think we can afford a tutor who is any good."

My father dropped his head, but let it go. "Adeline, it's a fortune. And it's yours. All we have to do is go to Amsterdam and sign some papers. Then we can come back to Italy or go wherever you want. We never have to set foot in Amsterdam again."

She shivered and reached for his hands. "Leo, you don't understand. There's a curse on that house. Everyone who lives there is unhappy. It's haunted by old slaughters. By our tainted blood."

He stroked her fingers. "There are no ghosts, dearest, except in our minds. It's a place of horror for you. I see that. But your uncle is dead, and no harm will come to you now. You are beyond his power forever and ever. Is it worth it to throw away our entire future because you're afraid of his ghost?"

She searched his face, and seemed to draw some strength there. "You will be with me, Leo? You will protect me?"

He nodded. "I promise. I will be there. Nothing bad will happen in Amsterdam."

I don't remember much of our journey. It was in the early fall, and the weather came down to meet us in Grand Saint Bernard, lashing freezing rain at us in the pass. We pressed on, my mother and I huddled in furs and lap rugs. My father rode beside the carriage on his great gelding, quiet and concerned. My mother was prone to fits of shaking, when her body would convulse and her limbs tremble. It got worse the further we went from Italy, as though the pass itself were a barrier in her mind. She spoke seldom, and then did not know me at all. I was only Charles.

One morning I woke in some inn I did not remember arriving at, got up and went to the window. The mountains rose to one side, snowswept on the heights, the road already a handspan deep in snow where we had traveled yesterday. Below, the valley gave into a rich plain, trees bright with autumn, leaves of a million colors bright as paints, the wind coming to me cold and touched with the scent of apples from the orchard just below the wall. The sun had not yet risen, but the sky was primrose and birds were calling.

My mother was still sleeping but my father was not there. I got up and dressed quickly, went down to the inn yard and climbed onto the wall.

Somewhere below a dog barked. Morning came. The sun was rising behind the mountains, spreading their shadow onto the town and fields. Grapes were purple on the vines. I hugged my arms around me.

My father came and stood beside me.

"It's beautiful," I said.

"La Belle France," he said. "Frenchmen say there is no more beautiful country on Earth. And they may be right. I have seen some beautiful places, but this is beautiful indeed."

"I had to get up and see," I said. "I might miss something." I sniffed the air like a hunting dog. "Anything could happen. There could be anything just over the hill."

My father laughed. "Do you suffer from pothos then, like Alexander the Great?"

"What's that?" I asked.

He thought a moment. "Longing," he said. "But more than that. It's hard to translate, and I had only started Greek when my father died. The desire that has wings."

"Like an angel," I said.

He ruffled my hair. "There are no angels or demons either. No ghosts or evil spirits. Those are just things that people made up to help them explain the world. But now we can explain the world rationally, through logic and science. We don't need those things anymore."

"We don't?"

He smiled at me. "Because of pothos. Because people wanted to know. Because there have always been people like you and me who wanted to understand things and know how they work. And because of that we've sailed the seas and tamed the earth. Religion and superstition just give people an excuse to fight with their neighbors."

"What happens when we die?" I asked, and he knew I was thinking of Charles.

My father folded me in his arms. "We end," he said. "And nothing more."

Perhaps he meant it for comfort, but I had found none in it as the years passed and one after another went ahead of me into the dark.

The Emperor's Hand

The Emperor's coronation was past, and soon winter passed as well. Spring came, the glorious days when Paris was at her most beautiful. Roses bloomed in every garden, and the theaters made ready for their summer hiatus. I had nearly stopped waiting for the Emperor's summons. Perhaps he had forgotten me, or perhaps he had never intended for my fevered promises to come to anything.

It was a warm night on the cusp of summer. I was coming in from dinner with Delacroix and some friends a little short of midnight, and almost did not pay attention to the immaculately groomed lieutenant of the Imperial Guard waiting downstairs in my apartment building. He sprang to his feet when I came in. "Madame St. Elme?"

"I am," I said.

He bowed very politely. "If it would not inconvenience Madame to accompany me? There is a certain gentleman who would like to speak with you immediately. He sends his regards, and hopes that you are still amenable to your agreement."

"Yes," I said steadily, though my heart was suddenly beating fast. Anyone who had heard us would think we were speaking of an assignation. But I knew who it must be.

It was after midnight when I was ushered in to the Palace of the Tuileries, but Napoleon was still at his desk, wearing evening clothes as though he had come from some reception first.

"Sire," I said, sinking into a deep courtesy.

"Madame St. Elme," he said, looking up from his papers and putting them aside. "Do you take coffee?"

"Yes, sire," I said, somewhat bemused as a servant poured out a cup for me from a pot left standing on the sideboard, steaming hot and very black. He refilled the Emperor's cup as well, and then bowed himself out.

Napoleon gestured to the chair before the desk. "You may as well sit down. I do not expect this conversation will be brief."

"All the better to have in the middle of the night," I said, thinking of the long lines of people waiting in the antechamber during the day.

He laughed. "Not that sort of conversation, Madame, though I did find you delightful company! I had something different in mind. Are you engaged for the summer?"

"No, sire," I said. "I have not yet signed anywhere."

"Good, for I do not expect you will have time for it. Have you a lover?"

"Not at present, sire," I said, and was pleased that I did not color at all.

"Also to the good, as no one will be asking too many questions." He slid a brown Morocco folder in front of him and looked up at me keenly. "You know we plan to invade England."

"Everyone knows that," I said. Our armies had been poised by the channel for nearly a year, in camp from Boulogne to the Pas de Calais, waiting for the war that would inevitably come.

"Everyone does, but everyone does not know when it will happen, or how."

"And the British very much would like to," I said, trying to sound as though I discussed the highest matters of foreign policy with heads of state every day.

"Indeed. But of course they do not. Yet." He let the last word fall ominously in the air. "You can imagine, Madame, the difference in our casualties, and indeed in the success of our expedition, depending on whether or not they know the date and location of our landings in advance."

"Yes," I said. There was a tremendous difference between an unopposed landing on a deserted bit of beach, and a pitched battle to get ashore, with the British Navy picking off targets among our transports.

"They have spies, of course." He took a sip of his coffee and I followed suit. It was scalding hot. "And we have spies. The usual minuet. However, a situation has arisen that gives me particular pause." Napoleon looked at me over the rim of the cup. "There is a spy in the camp of the Grand Army, Madame. A spy who is either someone so highly placed that they are in the midst of the most delicate planning, or someone who is very close to someone who is. And not a wife or companion. A wife or companion would not have access to headquarters documents that do not leave the custody of the most senior officers. A very senior officer, Madame, or the aide to such."

It clicked into place for me. "You think it's one of the Marshals."

"Eighteen men," he said. "I have raised eighteen men to the highest military title France has ever had. Eighteen men who have fought for the Republic and shed their blood for ten years."

"And one of them is a traitor." I nodded slowly. "Like Moreau."

"Exactly like Moreau, Madame. The rewards are the same, after all."

"To be the new head of state, or to be the power behind the throne of a Bourbon restoration," I said. Oh yes, the rewards were easy to imagine.

"Four of the eighteen hold honorary titles with no real military responsibility," he said. "So I believe we can clear Kellermann, Lefebvre, Perignon and Serurier. And while there are others who are not part of the Army of the Coasts of Ocean, they must to some extent be part of any plans at the highest levels eventually. That is why those plans are being prepared in absolute secrecy, and only myself, Marshal Berthier, and two others are as yet aware of their contents. But before long we must open the secret to the men who must execute it."

"And so you must trap the spy before then," I said. I met his eyes across the desk. "Before the end of summer?"

The Emperor just smiled. "For a number of reasons which will be made clear, I am quite certain that the agent is working in the camps of the Grand Army at Boulogne or Montreuil-Sur-Mer. I need you to catch him for me."

"Why me?" I asked.

"Because I cannot be certain that Fouché himself is not in communication with the Royalists," he said. "And because I need someone who can move about freely, outside of the chain of command, and yet have plenty of good reasons to be in our camps."

Michel was stationed at Montreuil. I did know that, but it did not bear thinking about. I took a cautious sip of my coffee. "What about the aides?" I asked.

Napoleon shrugged. "There are dozens, of course. And while some of the Marshals are discreet, there are others who are careless. Too much said to the wrong person, codes too easily accessible, letters and correspondence too easily reached by a trusted aide. To make matters more complicated, Montreuil is also the site of the new School of War."

I must have looked blank, for he continued. "Marshal Ney and I have ventured to begin a new thing. In other trades and professions, a man must study a great deal to master his work. And indeed, military academies are not new. I attended one myself as a boy. But that was not the case with many of our officers. Most, like Marshal Ney, came up through the ranks learning as they went, putting together a bit of practical experience and a bit out of dog-eared copies of Caesar. Of course such training is incomplete. They have never had any comprehensive study of their work." He got up from the desk and paced to the curtained windows, his hands behind his back. "And how shall we get better, except by study and by fighting against our equals in the field? The School of War gives us the opportunity to not only fight one another on paper, but to take the field in miniature against the greatest masters of any age. I understand it was quite something to watch, last month, when Marshal Lannes and Marshal Ney refought the Battle of Gaugamela!" He sounded amused, but I could not see his face.

"And who was who, sire?" I asked.

"I understand that Darius won this time," he said. "But it is only fair, as Marshal Lannes knew what Darius did not and made far better use of his horse archers on the Macedonian right." He turned around in front of the windows. "And that is to whom I am sending you. Marshal Lannes will be your contact and your commander in this."

"Lannes?" I had never met the man, though of course I had heard of him. He had been with Bonaparte in Italy rather than on the Rhine with Moreau and Ney.

"Marshal Lannes is the only one I am certain of. Not only would he never treat with Fouché or the British, but he is also the only one discreet enough that I am certain of his staff. Davout, Ney…." He waved a hand and I knew what he meant. They might trust the wrong people. "I am sure you and Marshal Lannes can think of an adequate cover story for why you are there."

"I am sure we can," I said. The obvious sprang to mind. Right in front of Michel, who would think….

"I will not tell you to trust no one else. You must do as you see fit in the situation, and confide as you need to." He looked at me, and I thought he sounded amused. "I will not tell you not to tell Ney, to spare your conscience when you do!"

"Sire, Ney and I have been done these three years," I said a bit stiffly. "As you should well know, having had a hand in bringing it about."

His eyebrows rose. "I arranged his marriage. Why should I think he would throw you over for it? What reasonable man would, Madame?"

"None," I said dryly. "Except him. But that is all distant history, sire. I assure you I have no desire to confide anything in Ney."

"Marshal Lannes will give you a complete briefing when you arrive in Boulogne," he said. "And explain what we know of the matter. You may go to him for assistance at any point, and he will request periodic updates from you. You may also request from him any incidentals you may need, transportation, funds, a troop of grenadiers…." He grinned at me like a schoolboy who is enjoying a game of spies. "I trust you will not be too extravagant in your requests."

"I will not be, sire," I said. I hesitated, and then said what I meant. "I am sensible of the opportunity to serve. It is not something I expected."

"You will do well, Madame," the Emperor said. "I have faith in you."

And so I journeyed to the camp of the Army of the Coasts of Ocean, hugging that faith close in my heart. If he believed in me, surely I could not fail!

I had never met Marshal Lannes before, and as I approached the camp of the Grand Army at Boulogne the weather became decidedly uncooperative. Thus it was with a sodden bonnet and dripping plumes that I was escorted into his headquarters.

Despite the dismal weather, or perhaps because of it, it was extremely crowded. Young men in the uniforms of every branch of the service hurried to and fro, while four desks strained with the paperwork upon them, uniformed clerks struggling to keep up. The nearest appeared to be dealing with provisioning, which was hardly a surprise as there must be more than fifty thousand men encamped along this coast. The logistics of supply were daunting.

Of course it took forever to get the attention of someone who would give me the time of day.

"A letter!" I shouted over the din. "A letter from Marshal Berthier. For Marshal Lannes. I am to give it to him myself."

"Give it to me, Madame," the aide assured me, so young he still gangled. "I'll pass it on."

"I will not," I said. "I am to give it to him myself."

He looked doubtful. "Your name?"

"Madame St. Elme." I could barely hear myself over the din. A pair of messengers had come in muddy and were flinging droplets of water in the air as they took their cloaks off.

"You will wait a long time, Madame," he said. "The Marshal does not meet with ladies."

I sighed. Not that kind of meeting. "I have been sent by Marshal Berthier...." I began again.

"So you've said." He turned his back quite rudely and went to attend to the messengers.

I found it mildly humiliating to be taken for a woman on the make, an aging courtesan desperate for a pretext to talk to a famous man. But I could hardly shout to the room at large that I was on the Emperor's business. So I sat down to wait.

It was after five o'clock before a more senior officer deigned to notice me. He was a large man with perfectly massive brown sideburns and moustache, gorgeously attired in hussar's uniform with acres of gold lace across his chest. "Madame St. Elme? I understand you are carrying a message from Marshal Berthier?" He came and sat down in the wooden chair beside mine, and while I could see he did not believe me, his hazel eyes were at least frank and open. "I am Colonel Subervie, aide de camp to the Marshal."

"I am," I said, and produced the packet, showing it to him but not putting it in his hands. "May I have your word, sir, that you will put this into his hands immediately? I will wait here, if you like, but it is not to be put in a stack somewhere and forgotten about, or opened by a clerk."

"I'm not in the habit of losing the Marshal's correspondence," he said without heat, looking down at the packet. "I suppose it's too small to have a snake in it or something."

"A snake?" I almost laughed. "I would try to kill Marshal Lannes by handing him a letter with a snake in it? Why not a scorpion? Or a pit viper? Or a cobra? I might have a cobra in my reticule!"

Subervie looked abashed. "Stranger things have happened, Madame." He took the packet and stood up. "If you will wait a few moments, I will attend to this."

Having little other choice, I nodded and sat back to wait, hoping that he would indeed do this with dispatch. I should like to find the necessary, and I hated to leave while I was supposed to be waiting. Still, he seemed like a reliable man. I had long since learned to trust an impression that strong.

It could not have been five minutes before he returned, and Subervie's demeanor had changed entirely. "Come this way, Madame," he said, taking my elbow and hustling me quickly down the hall to the Marshal's office. "Marshal Lannes will see you right away."

The office was in the back, away from the din, with rain-slicked windows that looked out toward the sea, not that anything could be seen today. On an ordinary day, I supposed, one might even be able to see the topsails of the British ships patrolling just offshore, the Channel Fleet at their endless stations.

Lannes rose to his feet as I entered. Thirty-something, he was only of medium height, with a classically handsome face and light brown hair and the whippy body of a fencer, alert and keen. "Madame St. Elme," he said.

"Marshal Lannes."

Subervie shut the door behind me, staying inside.

Lannes' gaze ran up and down, from my sensible boots beneath my hem to the sodden plume on my bonnet. "So you are the Emperor's agent."

"I am," I said, coming in and taking the chair Subervie held for me, so that both of them might sit once more. "And you are the Emperor's friend."

He looked startled. "I like to think I am one of his friends."

"The one he trusts not to be spying for the Royalists," I said. "Wittingly or unwittingly. He has sent me to assist in your endeavors, and to find this man for you."

"So I see," he said, gesturing to the paper spread on his desk, the Emperor's own hand and his own seal. His eyes met mine squarely. Whatever doubts he might have, he did not give them harbor in the face of the Emperor's plan. "We have a leak. A substantial leak. And under the circumstances, a leak of our plans to the British could be the ruination of all. It would cost thousands of lives, to put it bluntly."

I nodded gravely. "So the Emperor said," I replied. "He said that the evidence pointed to a senior officer or one of their aides."

"Or one of the officers of the General Staff assigned to the School of War," Lannes said. "They also have access to some operational materials."

Subervie shifted in the other hard chair beside mine, and my eyes flew to him involuntarily.

"I've known Subervie since he was a boy," Lannes said, following my thought. "I'd stake my honor on him. But he's about the only one."

"There are too many people," Subervie said. "You saw the office out there. There are a hundred men in and out every day on business. We can't be certain that it's someone with legitimate access to the operational documents. There are just too many people."

"Don't you keep them locked up?"

"Of course." Lannes leaned back in his chair a little. "And many of them are in cipher. But it's not possible to keep everything locked up that could add up. Logistics and supply, for example. We have to order food, stockpile it, have powder and shot prepared and in the right locations. Every carter's order can't be in cipher or kept in a strongbox. Things add up. It's not the big plans I'm worried about. It's the hundreds of less secure things that add up."

"But surely everyone already knows we're going to invade England," I said. "Are the logistics that plain about date and time?"

Subervie and Lannes' eyes met over my head. The Marshal shrugged. "I think a smart man could put enough together," he said. "If he had the right pieces. Which is why we need to trap the spy, not just keep him away from the most classified materials. There are too many things that could give away something."

I had to accept that. "Do you have any suspicions, justified or unjustified? Any place I should start?"

"With the operational documents," Lannes said. "Subervie will give you a list of the men who have legitimate access, though I doubt that will tell you much. And then there are the aides. Dozens of them, and some of them aren't even French."

"No?"

"Jomini's all right," Subervie said. He looked at me. "He's Swiss, a volunteer who impressed Marshal Ney with his theories about classical warfare. Ney made him an aide and he teaches at the School of War."

I tried not to sigh. I had hoped to be here a few days before anything pointed straight there. But I knew Michel. If anyone was likely to hire a spy without realizing it, it was Michel, who always gave each man the best chance. "And what does this Jomini do?" I asked.

"He's been restaging classical battles for training purposes," Subervie said. "We fight each other in miniature, some of the great battles of history, learning what went right and seeing if we can change the outcome."

"The Emperor mentioned that," I said, looking at Lannes. "He said you recently won Gaugamela as the Persians."

Lannes laughed. "Oh that! Well, I had the advantage of knowing what mistakes Darius made. And besides, Hephaistion's no Alexander."

I must have started, because he looked at me a little sharply. "Marshal Ney was playing Hephaistion. In the game."

"Of course," I said.

A Passage of Blades

Colonel Subervie was charged with finding me lodgings in Boulogne, and I declined to accompany him, thinking that perhaps I had best be about my work as quickly as possible. After all, I had never done this before, and if I could not demonstrate expertise I could at least demonstrate energy. Subervie seemed to be under the impression that I was an agent of long standing, an experienced player in the espionage game, and I didn't want to disabuse either him or Lannes of the notion.

Of course it occurred to me to suspect Michel. How could it not? His wife's father had been an aristocrat, and her mother had killed herself when Marie Antoinette was guillotined. Aglae surely had no love for the Revolution, and I wondered, perhaps unfairly, if she had any for Michel. He was such a poor player at politics that I thought it would take very little for someone, either his wife or an aide recommended to him, to play him for a fool. He would trust the wrong person and betray his country unwittingly. I did not want the trail to lead to him, but I suspected that it might. I wondered if the Emperor thought the same, and if my employment in this matter had something to do with how close I might get to Michel.

Or could have once. I had not spoken with him in three years, since the summer of 1802. Passion does not well stand the test of time, especially apart. Especially with a wife in the middle. Especially with all that had passed between us.

I could not be fair about him, and wondered if I were rather too quick to indict where no crime had occurred. No, I must try other avenues first, and hope that the trail lead away from Michel, to someone else. I must try to investigate with as open a mind as possible.

So I wasn't looking for Michel, and my business in Boulogne was purely that—business. I was looking instead for Jean-Baptiste Corbineau. If anyone already knew everything that was happening in camp, it would be Corbineau. And I at least trusted that Corbineau would not turn spy for love or money. I could not tell him my charge, of course, but I could count on a certain amount of help and information from him for the sake of friendship, even if he did not know who I served.

He wasn't hard to find. Even in Boulogne, a quiet town swollen to four times its normal size by the Army of the Coasts of Ocean, people knew Corbineau when I asked for him by name. I was directed to the fencing salle of M. Clanet.

Even on an afternoon when a chill rain fell all up and down the Channel Coast, the salle was warm inside. It took up almost the entire ground floor of what appeared to be a former warehouse, with vast windows down one wall and mirrors down the other. The mirrors must have been a costly investment, I thought, but they doubled the size of the crowd. There were thirty or forty men there, and I eased the door open carefully. A couple of men looked back as I elbowed in. If they wondered why a woman was there, they didn't wonder long. Even dressed in female clothing I wasn't as interesting as the bout.

They stood around the room, a space cleared in the middle for what was clearly an exhibition of some interest. I heard the ring of steel almost immediately, but the spectators were dead quiet. A couple of hussars made room for me so I could see between them, even though my bonnet plume must have blocked the view of those behind.

I drew a breath. Michel was one of the fencers. He had taken coat and waistcoat off, fencing in just shirt and light buff trousers, and his cravat had come loose and fell over one shoulder. His shirt already showed patches of sweat, and his face was deadly intent. I had never seen him at practice with that expression of concentration, his eyes moving even though his foil was stationary.

The other fencer wore dark pants and a tightly buttoned waistcoat, his movements as controlled as his dress. He was Michel's height or a little taller, more lightly built, with short dark hair and olive skin, a nose a little too sharp for beauty. He was motionless as well. Even their points didn't move, waiting like dancers in a mirror, both in guard.

The other fencer moved first. The advance and the riposte were almost too fast for me to see, a disengage around another disengage as both of them tried it at the same time, following each other around like a minuet. Steel rang. Michel attacked with a triple beat, then a disengage and a thrust that I expected to connect. It didn't. The other man was just as fast, and the thrust met a parry to the outside, an abrupt disengage and thrust. Michel stepped back out of the way, and the full extension was just short.

And then they both recovered to guard, watching, the points of their foils both circling clockwise, round and round each other. Michel was grinning. The other man's face was solemn, all keen concentration.

Michel exploded forward, a combination ending in a deadly fleché I should have been reluctant to try, even with practice foils, when no one wore padding. It didn't connect. A backhanded beat and disengage opened a window, and I saw his foil come up, aimed at Michel's breastbone as he ran straight onto it. At the last second Michel swept the point away. It passed almost against his side, and they were shoulder to shoulder inside one another's guard, like lovers in a dance.

But both points were to the outside, and before the blindingly fast second when either could have scored, they both moved. They stopped seven feet apart, both in guard. I could see Michel's chest moving with his breath. His opponent must be half a decade younger, but he didn't seem in better state, and his off hand was dropping.

Corbineau put his hand on my shoulder. "Madame?" he whispered.

I glanced at him. "Hello, Jean-Baptiste. I was looking for you."

"And you've found me," he whispered. "My dear sister, all the way from Paris to bring me some comforts from home. Any chocolate?"

"You are incorrigible," I whispered.

Steel rang. I had missed the pass, but it was inconclusive again. Sweat dripped in Michel's eyes. His opponent's feet were slower. They circled in the round, abandoning the idea of a strip entirely. I wasn't sure whose idea that was, but their steps mirrored each other completely.

"Are you here for the Marshal?" Corbineau whispered.

I leaned in to whisper back. "We're not together anymore. You know that."

Corbineau raised an eyebrow. "Of course not," he said, in a tone that said he didn't believe me for a moment.

"We're through," I whispered. "We agreed to be friends. That's all."

Blades clashed again. This time a high thrust just missed Michel's throat. I wished he wouldn't play without a mask or padding, especially with someone who wasn't his inferior in either reach or speed.

Michel riposted, then went straight into a stop thrust that was short. There was a counter, and the blades kissed, beat and beat and beat. I almost missed the disengage and thrust, a quick tap to his opponent's sword hand.

It was the point.

The young man shook his hand out, grinning ruefully. Michel said something, coming over and slapping him on the shoulder as the entire room started talking.

"He's good," I said. I had never seen Michel's equal as a swordsman, but he wasn't far behind.

Corbineau nodded. He picked up a towel from a nearby bench and waved it. The young man elbowed his way through the crowd toward us, sweat dripping off his black hair onto his face. Corbineau tossed him the towel. His sword hand looked worse than mine, this latest welt on top of white scars that crisscrossed the back of his hand and wrist, over a bulge that spoke of a broken bone long healed. He ducked his head into the towel, scrubbing his dripping hair.

"I'd like to present my dear friend Madame St. Elme," Corbineau said. "Madame, this is Brigadier General Honoré-Charles Reille, a lethal man with a blade of any kind." He winked at me.

Reille had the dignity to look embarrassed. "Madame, the pleasure is mine," he said, a faint blush lending color to his dark skin. "I should bend over your hand, but I believe my state precludes it." He was a little rank, and seemed too aware of it. "With your permission, I will retire and make myself decent."

"It will take more than water and soap to make you decent," Corbineau said, as Reille bowed very properly.

He gave Corbineau a dirty look and went off with the towel, presumably in the direction of the dressing rooms.

I raised an eyebrow myself. "Is he your lover?"

"Honoré?" Corbineau laughed. "Good heavens no! He only likes girls. More the pity; I did try."

"And he didn't run you through with that lethal blade of his?" I asked with mock innocence. "Must be a patient man."

"Alas, no," Corbineau said, putting his hand to his heart. "Honoré saves both blades for other quarry."

I laughed. And looked up unerringly.

Michel's eyes met mine across the room. He had his coat over his arm, the sword belt in his other hand as though he had started putting the saber back on and stopped halfway through.

I looked away. When I looked back, he was looking down, fastening the buckles.

"Friends?" Corbineau said skeptically.

"Yes," I said.

We had dinner together in a crowded, noisy tavern at a table by the window as far from the bar as possible. Unfortunately, that wasn't very far. Our men gave good custom, but there certainly were a lot of them!

"You can tell me what you're doing," Corbineau said, "And not worry about being overheard. I can barely hear you myself!"

"What I'm doing?" I glanced around the tavern, hoping the barmaid would hurry. I was hungry.

He gave me a skeptical look. "Come on now, Elza. If you're not here for the Marshal, am I to believe you've come for the sea air?"

I took a deep breath. It was time for the cover story. "I'm here at the invitation of Marshal Lannes."

"Oh please!" Corbineau laughed. "Lannes is not your type at all! And the way you looked at the Marshal...." He waved exuberantly to attract the barmaid's attention. "I don't believe for a second you're here for Lannes."

At that moment Colonel Subervie pushed his way through the crowd, his scabbard banging into random diners. "Madame St. Elme, I wanted to tell you that your things are being put in Topaze House." He gave Jean-Baptiste a nod. "Good evening, Corbineau."

"Hello, Subervie," Corbineau said. "Care to join us for dinner?"

"Do you two know each other?" I asked. It was all beginning to seem a small and incestuous club.

"Of course we do," Subervie said.

"We're close as brothers," Corbineau expanded. He caught the look on Subervie's face and grinned. "All right, close as distant cousins. Exceptionally distant cousins who only see one another on holidays."

"We're both part of the School of War," Subervie supplied. "What was it we were teamed up for last?"

"Pharsalus," Corbineau said. "And a misery that was. I had Pompey's heavy cavalry. Might as well shoot myself right off. Gervais got to be with Caesar."

"I played the Eighth Augusta Legion," Subervie said. "It was a good game. Jomini ran Caesar himself and Ney took Pompey. But Pompey's in so deep he can't really win that one."

"The Marshal says it's important to learn how to lose," Corbineau said. "And admittedly it wasn't a total rout, like the real Pharsalus was."

Subervie winced. "I try to avoid losing, myself."

"Yes, well," Corbineau said. "Tomorrow it's Carrhae. There's no joy in that for anyone. Not either of us, anyway. Maybe for the Parthians. Who's playing Parthian anyhow?"

"Reille's the Parthian horse archers," Subervie replied. "Don't know who else has what. I suppose we'll see at nine. So don't stay out too late drinking with the lady!" He looked at me sideways, as if trying to decide if he was onto something or not.

"What do you learn by fighting these ancient battles?" I asked. "Surely this was a long time ago. They didn't have rifles or cannon, so how can this help?"

"The strategies of war stay the same," Corbineau said. "It's like a chess game. The capabilities of each piece may change over the centuries, but the game itself doesn't. The tactics don't. There's not a centimeter of distance between our flying wedge and Alexander the Great's."

"But the Persians didn't have riflemen in square," I pointed out.

"They had horse archers," Subervie rumbled, still standing in the aisle beside my chair. "Persian horse archers could fire at six times the rate of modern infantry, and at nearly twice the range. Also, because they were mounted they were more mobile. Modern infantry is more like hoplites in terms of their mobility and their ability to change facing." He shrugged, as though he had suddenly remembered who I was. "But that's a rather technical explanation for a lady. I apologize."

Corbineau snorted. "Don't apologize to her! My dear sister is a veritable Amazon! You should have seen her at Apfing. I turned about in the middle of it, and there she was with her saber sticking out of a man's breastbone, trying to get the point loose without breaking her wrist. I think Madame can comprehend our poor simulations."

Subervie blinked. "Is that so? Or is Jean-Baptiste having me on?"

"It's true," I said quietly. "A few engagements, and I do not claim to have played any part in the Battle of Hohenlinden, though I was there." I wasn't sure if I would have chosen to explain any of this, but there was little point in denying it now. I could see that there would be too many people here who had been with the Army of the Rhine on that campaign, and who would recognize me all too easily. I might as well own up to it.

Subervie blinked again. "I did not know there were any real Amazons, but trust Corbineau to find one."

"She's not bad," Corbineau said. "I'd have her for a troop leader. She'd be fine with light cavalry."

Subervie's brows rose toward his receding hairline. "Really? Knowing she's a woman?"

"I'd know, but you'd not guess seeing her kitted out as a trooper," Corbineau said. His eyes met Subervie's with a hint of a challenge. "Tactics isn't all about having a big prick, you know."

Subervie raised his hands. "Never said it was, Jean-Baptiste. Manhood's not the measure of a man. I know that."

I wondered what he knew of Corbineau's proclivities, and if words had passed between them. If they had, it had not gone too badly if Subervie was so quick to back down. He seemed genuinely determined not to insult a friend.

Corbineau shrugged, the tension in his shoulders fading a little. "Anyway, I'd have Madame for a troop leader. She's quick and she's got good common sense. She'd pick up the tactics in no time."

I had not seen the flying wedge, not in the snows of Hohenlinden, but I could imagine very clearly what it must look like, what horse and rider were supposed to do. I could do that, I thought. I truly could.

"It sounds fascinating, gentlemen," I said. "And is that what you are practicing?"

"To some extent," Subervie said. "At the lowest level we drill, practicing with the actual men and horses. But much of what we do in the School of War is learning how and when to use a tactic. We learn what it can do and what it can't, from the micro application to the macro, from the troop to the grand army."

"By refighting the battles of the past," I said. There was something fascinating in that, as though one could do it all again, do it right or better, or simply differently.

"With the best of us on both sides," Corbineau said. "We learn from our equals. And we learn each others' styles and weaknesses and strengths. That way when it's real we'll know who does what and how."

Subervie nodded. "In the heat of battle often you can't tell what someone else is doing. But at this point I know that Corbineau here is taking a middle course. He's not one of the aggressive ones who's charging everything that moves, but he's not hanging back in the rear either."

"Thank you for that," Corbineau said dryly. "I don't think you're milling around aimlessly either."

"You know what I mean."

"I do," Corbineau said. "And that's part of the point. We gain the measure of one another."

At this point the barmaid finally turned up.

"Staying for dinner, Subervie?" Corbineau asked, as he was still standing between tables.

The colonel shook his head. "I'm afraid not. I'm on duty still." I wondered what other tasks he had postponed, securing lodging for me, and how long it would take him tonight to finish.

"I do appreciate your looking to the matter of my lodging," I said with my most brilliant smile. "I will get Corbineau to show me where it is later. I am sure it is all very nice."

"It's where my wife stayed when she was here," Subervie said. "So it's respectable." He cleared his throat. "I mean, I think you'll like it."

"We know what you mean," Corbineau said with a wink at me.

"I do appreciate it," I said, and gave him my hand. He bent over it and swiftly disappeared among the diners, elbowing his way toward the door where another party of junior officers were coming in ten strong.

It was starting to get overly warm in the tavern. "Is it always this crowded?" I asked.

Corbineau shrugged. "Pretty much. This is what we do, Elza. We spend our days haring about on horseback and refighting the battles of the greatest commanders who ever lived, and our nights drinking large quantities of Calvados and wenching." He looked at me sideways. "It's an ideal life, actually."

"And how's the wenching?" I asked as the barmaid brought my wine. "Any particular wench?"

He looked off vaguely into the distance, and I thought he was avoiding looking at my face. We had not talked about this so baldly. "Not in particular. But you know, where there are enough men there are always wenches."

I picked my words carefully. "I hope you exercise good judgment."

"I always do." He toyed with his glass on the way to his lips. "I am too aware of the consequences not to. Some people take that sort of thing very seriously. It's not Paris, but there are...social events."

"Ah," I said. "That sounds interesting."

Corbineau raised an eyebrow at me. "A Chinese box, dear sister? A girl dressed as a boy dressed as a girl? No one would be quite certain what you were, without an intimate look."

"Which I don't intend to provide," I said. But it occurred to me, aside from the excitement of it, that one could find out all sorts of things on the shady side of the street, including which men had a lot to lose. Blackmail was a rationale for treason.

Corbineau leaned close. "Elza, what are you up to? Lannes doesn't have Subervie running errands for you because he thinks you're chic. Other people might believe that, but I know you."

I met his eyes levelly. "Jean-Baptiste, I can't tell you. You have to trust me on this."

I had expected that he would curse and push, but instead he leaned back, an inscrutable expression on his face. "It's about that, then."

"About what?" Surely Lannes wasn't on close enough terms with Corbineau to have told him. Surely half the camp wasn't in on this plan! What kind of way to catch a spy was this?

"That." Corbineau lifted his glass. "The Other Measures. I expect I'll be seeing you, then."

"What other measures?"

"I can't tell you."

I sighed. "Jean-Baptiste, now you are just being deliberately mysterious."

"You can't tell me, and I can't tell you. I know how this goes. But I'll see you there, and then it will all be clear." He touched his wine glass to mine. "I should have known when they said they needed a woman that it would be our Amazon."

"A woman for what?"

"Don't be coy," Corbineau said lightly. "You respect my oaths, and I'll respect yours."

"Shit, Corbineau," I said, leaning toward him. "Come on, now."

But he would not say another word about it.

It was nearly eleven when he walked me to Topaze House, a fairly large establishment on a noisy street. There was an attentive footman at the door, whose job was to make clear to all and sundry that this was a lodging house for ladies, not a bawdy house. Corbineau had to explain three times who he was before he could come in to the parlor, but even then he was not allowed upstairs. Gentlemen weren't, during the evening, unless they were the husbands of a boarder.

"Very respectable," Corbineau said with a quirk of the eyebrow at me.

"Would you care to come out and about tomorrow evening, or would Charles van Aylde prefer to come?"

I grinned. "I think it will be Charles. If that suits you?"

"But of course," he said with a bow low over my hand. "It can only do my reputation good to be seen with such a ravishing creature."

"Wicked boy," I said, teasing, and sent him on his way.

I went upstairs and stood by the window that looked out not over the street but toward the house behind, watching the shadows move on the curtains of the other window, hearing the sounds of the night. A small town grown brothels and lodgings, taverns and stables. What would happen when we were gone? Surely Boulogne would not go back to what it had been before.

We can never go back, I thought. We can never become what we were before. The best we can do is go on, hoping to be more complete.

Seeing Michel had been like a sword to the heart. It should not have hurt after so long. I should not have wanted him still, as much as ever despite all that had passed between us, despite the years. I had hoped that would change.

And how should it, I wondered. If I have loved him before unchangingly, as perhaps I have, how could that have gone away in three short years? It was there still, even if his primary response to seeing me had been irritation.

I squared my shoulders. I was here for the Emperor, not for Michel. I was here on a mission of vital importance. I must not get distracted. The only thing that mattered was the job, my chance to prove my worth. And that must happen, whether or not Michel turned out to have any connection to the spy I sought.

Theaters of War

The next day Subervie delivered to me the lists of the men who had access to headquarters, but he did not stay, both because the lady who owned the house and who had previously met Madame Subervie was eyeing him suspiciously as we spoke in the parlor, and also because he was in the midst of a wargame.

"And how is Carrhae?" I asked him.

Subervie grimaced. "Let's just say that the only one having fun is Reille."

"The fencer," I said, recalling the young man I had seen fencing with Michel the day before, though I supposed he was not so young as that. He must be about my age.

"The fencer," Subervie said. "But today he's running Parthian horse archers. I think I hate him!" He grinned to show that he didn't mean it, and hurried off to the campaign.

I retired upstairs ostensibly to write letters, under the glare of the landlady. I wasn't sure this respectable house idea was going to work.

Three hours later I put the papers down disconsolately. There were too many people. Dozens of men had access to the operational papers, and hundreds more to information about supply and logistics. How not? The officers of the Quartermaster Corps that supplied the camps of the Army of Coasts of Ocean numbered nearly a thousand, from noncommissioned officers on up. All of them had to know where fodder was going, where foodstuffs were being delivered, where powder and shot needed to go. The carters who carried and delivered it needed to know, though not far in advance.

It simply was not possible, I thought grimly, to supply an invasion force of 60,000 men without anyone noticing. There were so many details, so many things that could give away the invasion date. Every spy they could muster would be standing about on French country lanes, counting carts.

The location of the target beaches was a bit easier to keep under wraps. Whether we intended Dover or Portsmouth, our supply would look much the same. And surely this would be the most important priority of British intelligence. Every spy they could muster would be standing about on French country lanes, counting carts.

Well, then, I thought, scrubbing at my eyes, actual security is impossible. They will know more or less when we intend to go. The question is where. And that's a question that can only be answered by a highly placed man, not by agents bribing carters with drinks to find out where they're taking that load of hay. That's the man I need to catch.

The list at least was smaller. Roughly twenty-five men had access to some part of the planning and operational materials that were the most classified, the ones kept in cipher in strongboxes. Locks could be picked, of course, so strongboxes might not truly be secure, but presumably the cipher was good.

Unless the man in question had a key to the cipher. Or unless he could make a copy of someone else's legitimate key to the cipher.

My head spun. Did every man with a key to the cipher walk around with it on his person all the time? Of course not. They left them locked in desk drawers or under the blotter. They put them in the filing cabinet in some unlikely place. They stuck them in a book on their desk. Some of the twenty-five would be careful with them, but not all. Some would be careless. And any man with access to the headquarters offices could find them.

I got up and walked to the window. Yesterday's rain had cleared out, leaving a beautiful sunny day, a perfect sky marred only by a few puffy white clouds like whiffs of cannon smoke. I found my gloves and my summer straw bonnet. I could think outside in the wind, on the beach or the cliffs, and perhaps get a look at England across the channel. They said on fair days one could almost see Dover.

Boulogne itself was a good sized town, a sea port of long standing, and as a deep water port almost in sight of England, the logical place for the invasion fleet to prepare. Given the right wind, our men could be on English soil in half a day, if we chose to land at the closest point. However, sixty thousand men could not be billeted in Boulogne. The camps of the Army of the Coasts of Ocean stretched northward to Calais, southward and inland for many kilometers, various units headquartered in different villages, while the camps themselves were built on leased farmland, or on the windy meadows near the sea. V Corps, commanded by Marshal

Lannes, was headquartered in Boulogne itself, while Ney's VI Corps was headquartered in the pretty village of Montreuil, some 15 kilometers south along the road to Paris. Our men were thus spread over a wide expanse of countryside.

As I walked along the road in the bright summer air, I wondered how I should do this. Somehow I had to narrow the suspects down. I could not possibly investigate all the men who might have access in half a dozen different headquarters kilometers apart. Nor could I guess at motives. Any man might have the motive of money, while the Revolution had left many enemies. If it did not have to be a senior officer, but rather a man with access to a senior officer's cipher, there might be a hundred possibilities.

But were there? I had seen how busy Lannes' headquarters was. There were dozens of people in and out constantly. If a man were trying to get at papers not his own, he would not know who might walk in on him or when, given the constant bustle. Surely it was quieter at night, I thought. But of course at night there were guards. We did not leave our headquarters without even the preliminary protection of men at the guardposts. One could not just walk in with no justification besides idle curiosity.

Ahead, the road went round a curve, rising as it went up through scrubby underbrush instead of manicured fields. The air smelled of salt, though I could see nothing of the sea yet.

Could one just walk in if one had justification? I suspected one could. Surely people worked late and arrived early. Someone detailed to headquarters arriving early in the morning would not be questioned by the guards, and he might have the offices to himself for a while. That would be the time to search for a cipher and copy it, or to work with documents not one's own.

That was better, I thought. A man who either has access to the ciphers himself, or who arrives early or stays late. But that still left potentially dozens of suspects.

I sighed. I was chasing around in circles, coming no closer to what I sought.

I reached the top of the rise, and before me stretched serried ranks of sand dunes spotted with tall beach grasses, sloping down among stones to a sudden drop. Beyond, the sea glittered in the bright summer sun, still as glass from this vantage. In the distance I could see the white sails of a ship beating down the coast against the wind, a frigate from the look of her. Not ours. I thought I could see the yellow gunport stripe down her side. The Channel Fleet was keeping watch.

I climbed to the highest point, my bonnet shading my eyes, looking out at the panorama. To my right the road led back to Boulogne, but the curve of the coastline hid the town from me. I could just see the outer edges of the breakwater, but the lighthouse and the forts were hidden. To my left the track led off along the cliffs, a neat sign pointing the way to the village of Courcelles and to the observation pavilion that the Emperor had had built. Ahead stretched the sea. It was not clear enough to see across the Channel, or perhaps one couldn't from this particular place, but one could see clearly enough the faint haze on the horizon.

The frigate was taking in sail. I watched her mainsail come down neatly in reefs, passing by as tight in as she might, just a bit more than a cannon's shot offshore. She could not come closer, I thought, even with the tide at about half as it was, because of the rocks. It looked as though the water shoaled swiftly, and despite the seemingly soft looking sand, this was a rocky coast. No, even a frigate could not stand in more closely.

Which brought me to the next question. The Emperor had said that the British were getting the information very quickly. Our counterspies in Whitehall reported that information was coming in only five days old, and that consistently. It was relayed through Dover most generally by a Captain Arnold of the frigate Lion. I presumed the frigate in question was now before me, tacking slowly down the coast in the bright summer air.

How? Lion was very obvious in her movements. Surely everyone could see her from shore as plainly as I could, and should she attempt to launch a boat it would be met by our men. Of course we patrolled this coast constantly, and we had thousands of men to do it. It might be possible, once or twice, with luck and bad weather on his side, for this Captain Arnold to sneak a man ashore, but surely he couldn't do it consistently! Not on bright moonlit nights in high summer! A spy might come ashore, but how could he report back? And moreover, how could a British spy, no matter how well he spoke French, penetrate the most secure parts of the camp?

I raised my hand, shading my face as I watched Lion's leisurely progress. Two men, I thought. Two men if they do it that way. One man on the inside, and a spy coming ashore to meet him and pick up documents. In which case the weak point must be the rendezvous. The spy must come ashore from Lion and then go somewhere that this man can meet him. Perhaps it's out on the seashore. Perhaps it's in Boulogne, or one of the hamlets along the coast.

If the British were plagued by smugglers on their side, men willing to bring ashore goods or passengers from France for a price, so were we. Generations of seamen on both sides of the Channel had made a career of slipping things across clandestinely. Who and how? Emperor and Republic and Crown before had tried to catch smugglers with little success. If they met in some smugglers' den we should have to find it.

Three things, then, I thought, ticking them off in my head, three methods of approach: Identifying who could get to the documents and how, finding the spy coming ashore from Lion, and figuring out how the spy meets the man inside. For the middle one I would need help. I could not patrol the coastline myself, nor keep a watch on Lion. But surely we already had men doing that. I should speak to Marshal Lannes about that. If we could disrupt their rendezvous, we would cripple the spy at least. It would do the British little good for their man to have documents but be unable to get them to Captain Arnold. And sooner or later, in frustration, either Arnold or the inside man would make a mistake. That might, ultimately, be our best chance.

Having at least a preliminary plan made me feel better about this entire business. None of these options had the slightest thing to do with Michel, and with him in Montreuil and me in Boulogne, perhaps I would not even have to see him again. I could simply work on this plan with Lannes and Subervie, and ignore him completely.

So I turned, leaving Lion to her solitary patrol, and made my way back to Lannes' headquarters.

This time I did not have to wait so long, and the officer of the watch was polite. "If you will wait but a few minutes, Madame," he said, "The Marshal has a gentleman with him at present."

"I should be pleased to wait," I said, and sat down again in one of the chairs.

It had only been a moment when the officer glanced back down the hall to Lannes' office. "They are coming out now," he said. "The Marshal will see you next, Madame."

I stood up, smoothing out the front of my gown, as Lannes came down the hall, a civilian following him. Lannes was speaking to him over his shoulder.

I stepped around the chair, and in a second saw who he was.

"You!" the civilian said with a start.

"You!" I replied, like some ingénue in a bad comedy of manners.

"You know each other?" Lannes sounded baffled.

"We are acquainted," M. Noirtier said. His hair was more gray than it had been five years ago, liberally streaked where once it had only been touched, odd over such a young man's face.

I tried to make light of it. "Oh yes. Years and years ago. All those silly fake séances."

Lannes grabbed me by the arm and propelled me down the hall in front of him, Noirtier trailing behind. "Back in the office." He hurried me in and closed the door, releasing me and turning about. "What about séances?"

Noirtier still looked surprised. Perhaps he wasn't used to Lannes' precipitousness. "She's a Dove," he said. "The best Dove I've ever seen. She's the real thing."

"It was just some silly fake séances," I said to the marshal. "Years ago, when I was hard up for money, I worked with this man who staged fake séances. There wasn't anything to it. It was all mumbo jumbo. M. Noirtier was a customer a few times. But Monsieur, there wasn't anything illegal about it! It was just a stage act."

"She's the real thing," Noirtier said. "Absolutely the real thing. She said that the campaign in Egypt would be compromised because 'Orient's loss will blind the Eagle.' How was she to know that the expedition's flagship would be L'Orient, or that it would be destroyed by a shot to its powder magazine at Aboukir Bay by Admiral Nelson, and that without L'Orient and its fleet General Bonaparte would be stuck in Egypt?"

I opened my mouth and shut it again. Those had just been words when I uttered them, and I had not thought of them twice since.

Lannes' brow furrowed. "Is that true?" he asked me quietly.

I nodded. "Yes, but…."

"I saw her several times," Noirtier said. "She told a naval officer which ship he was about to be posted to. She channeled the Archangel Michael. She told me that you would rise, and likewise Augereau and Massena. I've never seen anyone handle angelic presence that well."

"It was just a game!" I said desperately.

Lannes' eyes met mine. "Really?"

I shut my eyes and opened them again. "Monsieur, please."

His voice was low, and he shifted so that he stood between me and Noirtier almost protectively. "Are you a Dove, Madame?"

"I don't know," I said. "I truly don't. It was a scam, but some of the things I said came true. And that night…." I cast my mind back to the

Walpurgis Night in question, when I thought perhaps an angel had spoken to me. "I don't really know what happened. I can't explain. But why in the world would you care, M. le Marechal? Why does it matter to you?"

Lannes sat down on the edge of his desk, pushing the hair back from his eyes in a surprisingly boyish gesture. "I am stepping off a precipice to tell you this, Madame, and if you repeat it I will swear I never said it. There is more than one war, here in Boulogne. There is more than one storm front. There is the one you and I have already discussed, and there is the one that we see before us, the sea and the Channel and the British Navy waiting. And there is a third. We are at war, Madame, on more planes than one. They sent forth a sortie, and we push it back. We sally forth, and they push us back. Control of the Channel is about more than a few kilometers of water. It is about controlling the powers of sky and sea, and at the moment we cannot do that."

"You're joking." I slid down into a chair. Lannes was a rational man in a rational age, the Emperor's friend, a Marshal of France. "That is something out of a fairy tale."

"You are the Dove, and you do not yourself believe?" Noirtier asked.

"It cannot be. This is the age of enlightenment," I said.

Lannes shot him a quick look, as if to say, let me attend to this. "Nevertheless, it is true. Should we dismiss forty centuries of humanity's accumulated knowledge, dismiss the experiences of thousands of men who have gone before us? That is much less rational. Our failure to understand something doesn't make it less real. Is it not far more rational to apply ourselves to understanding what we can?"

I took a deep breath. It did indeed make more sense. And had I ever truly disbelieved? I thought that I had not, for if I had, why should I fear something that was nothing but folly? What I feared was my mother's madness, and it seemed to me this path led all too clearly in that direction. She had said we were Doves, all the women of our family, but I had never asked her what that meant. I had not wanted to know. "What do you need a Dove for?"

Lannes leaned back on his hands, his trim form perched on the edge of his desk. His brown eyes were frank. "It's complicated." He seemed to search for the words for a moment. "In this war we fight, just as in the war we fight in our physical bodies, there are different kinds of troops, different men who are suited by nature and temperament and training to different endeavors. We have our roles, and we learn to use our talents most effectively, just as we do on the drill field. At the moment, however, we are lacking one particular talent we urgently need." He put his hands together, gold braid on his cuffs glittering. "Imagine that we faced a foe in the field, but we had no cavalry screen, no light cavalry made up of chasseurs or hussars who might scout for us. Our armies would be effectively blind. What would one do in such a pass?"

"Send out heavy cavalry, I suppose," I said. "To do the work of the other. But that would not work nearly so well."

"It would not," he said, and I thought there was something of the schoolmaster about him, teaching war and esoterica at once. It occurred to me that he must be a good teacher. "In this situation, a Dove is the equivalent of light cavalry, a seer who can scout ahead for us and who can slip through defenses and bring back a report. We have been trying to do this with the equivalent of heavy cavalry, with little success."

"With no success," Noirtier said. "The men who have attempted it are not suited by nature to the task. They are simply not natural oracles, and traveling bodiless is a talent that is more often associated with Doves. It's not working."

"And so you have been looking for a Dove," I said, and was surprised my voice was calm and steady. "But are Doves not usually women? Or at least virgin girls or boys?"

Noirtier shot Lannes a look, as if to say, she is not as ignorant as she acts.

"In some older practices this is so," Lannes acknowledged. "The Pléiade, for example, required virgin girls or boys, and in fact preferred fairly young children. More modern disciplines prefer adult women, and not necessarily virgins. But we are all men. And none of us are proving very adept at this."

"How unfortunate for you," I said. "But surely there are women aplenty, and if you do not want to hire an actress as M. Noirtier did before, don't some of you have wives?"

"We do," Lannes said, "But not just any woman will do. It must be someone with the right talent, and she must also be entirely trustworthy, someone who can be confided in upon the Emperor's business." His eyes met mine, and I knew what he was not telling Noirtier—I was the Emperor's agent, and so presumably already had his confidence. "If you are as talented as M. Noirtier says, you are a godsend, Madame St. Elme."

"I do not want to do this," I said, and my voice was steady.

Noirtier shook his head and began to say something, but Lannes spoke first. "M. Noirtier, why don't you go ahead to dinner? I will be along shortly."

He knew a dismissal when he heard one, and got to his feet. "If you think that is the best course, M. le Marechal."

"I do," Lannes said, and waited until the door had closed behind him. He sighed, and then came around and sat down in the other chair before the desk, turning it toward me.

"I am not what he says," I said. "I am not."

His eyes met mine frankly. "Can you honestly tell me you are not an oracle?"

I looked away. Outside the sun was setting behind the towers of the fortress, golden in an azure sky. He is one too, some part of me whispered. He is like you. He has sworn the same oaths, in one Babylon or another. "No," I said. "No, I can't say that."

He put his chin on one hand. "If you are the Emperor's agent you are as much a soldier as I. You too are responsible for your service to France, and to these other men we serve beside. Lives rest upon this, Madame. Hundreds of lives, possibly thousands. If it is in your power to serve, you must do so. We are soldiers. We do not choose how we serve and when, at our own pleasure. We must do things that frighten us, things we do not want to do. I ask no more of you than I ask of myself or of any man here. Are you made of steel, Madame?" He caught my rising glance. "Are you what I think you are?"

I nodded slowly, but did not name it, though the word hung in the air around us: Companion.

"I am, Marshal," I said. "I will do what you think needful. If you ask me on those oaths I have no choice."

"Nor I, Madame," he said. "I have no choice but to ask. Do you understand that?"

"I do," I said. He was in charge of the invasion plans. He must do whatever was necessary to bring it off, and in the end my fear was just a little thing. What was it, compared to what must be done? "I will help you if I can."

When Corbineau arrived just after nine to meet me I was waiting outside my lodging, coat and hat and boots all Charles.

"Good evening," Jean-Baptiste said jauntily. "All ready to go set Boulogne on its ear?"

"I need a drink," I said, standing up with sword cane in hand. "And you need to find me one. Now."

Strange Travelers

The house looked like any other, or rather like any other better brothel in an army town. The Army of the Coasts of Ocean had been in and around Boulogne for nearly three years now, and there had been plenty of time for the local economy to adapt. It was a three-story house of the sort one expected to belong to a family of comfortable means, and from the street one might have thought it still did. Windows were open in the warm summer air, and from the downstairs ones came the sounds of a piano and a young woman singing a popular air about lost love.

I raised an eyebrow at Jean-Baptiste. "Really?"

"Really," he said with a smirk, and knocked upon the door.

The butler looked more like a bouncer than a butler, or perhaps the bouncer had learned to answer the door like a butler, but either way his demeanor was deferential when he saw Corbineau. "Good evening, Major. Pray come in. Madame will be delighted to see you."

"Good evening, Renaud," Corbineau said, doffing his hat and handing it over. "This gentleman is with me."

The front hall was spacious, tastefully decorated, and once again gave no hint of anything besides bourgeois respectability. An enormous woman rushed in, her Chinese painted fan not quite matching an ensemble of turquoise silk, black curls bobbing from beneath a huge turban topped with cream-colored feathers and a great many rhinestones. "Major!"

She advanced to greet him, drapery fluttering, and he bent deeply over her hand. "Madame, it is once again my distinct pleasure. Allow me to present my friend, M. van Aylde. Monsieur, this is Madame Desbrieres, one of the lights of our little town."

"You flatter me," she preened, allowing me to make my leg before her.

"The pleasure is mine," I said. She absolutely towered over me. Madame Desbrieres must be six feet tall. Her hands in her evening gloves were wide and long as a man's. Ah, I thought.

She tossed her head at Corbineau. "The parlor? Or something more private?"

"Just the parlor to begin, I believe," Jean-Baptiste said, throwing me a wink. He did not precisely need a private room with me.

A number of banknotes discreetly changed hands as she led us to the right, to the room from which the sound of the piano came. The near end of the parlor held a variety of couches and chairs, all occupied by gentlemen in various uniforms or neat civilian clothes, as respectable a group of callers as one might want to admit, all listening intently to the music or speaking softly over glasses. Instead of the punch, some of them had brandy or whisky, but otherwise nothing separated the listeners from any musical evening in town, save that there were no women except the girl at the piano.

She was quite pretty, with golden curls caught up in a pink ribbon, wearing a fetching evening gown of rose silk that set off her complexion to perfection. Her playing was reasonably accomplished, but her voice left a bit to be desired, thready and too shrill. If I were her mother, I should tell her to stick to playing, or have some friend with a better voice accompany her. She finished her song, and the gentlemen applauded politely, including Corbineau, who blew a kiss.

I looked at him sideways. This sort of genteel playacting was not at all what I had expected.

The young lady stood up and curtsied deeply. "Thank you!" she squeaked in falsetto. "Thank you so much! It gives me so much delight to once again introduce to you my sister, Mademoiselle Camille!"

The lady in question came through the dining room doors like a Congreve rocket, white silk flying, plumes bobbing in her chestnut curls, a dress as diaphanous as any I had worn as a merveilleuse. It was wondrously low cut in the front, a swell of breasts half exposed and a pale cleavage adorned by false diamonds. The drape of the dress showed off slim limbs and the shape of her body. Or his body. He must have been taped within an inch of his life to look that good, as not a bulge showed beneath his tight stays.

The room came to their feet, applauding and whistling, while Mademoiselle Camille made a pretty courtesy and waved. She blew a kiss back to Corbineau, and various men stomped and cheered. It took quite a few minutes to get us all back in our seats.

As she launched into a sweet love song, I poked Jean-Baptiste. "I must say you did find some nightlife."

"My dear, I've been here more than a year," he whispered back. "It's less that I found nightlife than that I founded it!"

We remained two more songs, but I shifted in my seat.

"Not to your taste?" he asked.

I shrugged.

"You like it a bit sharper," Jean-Baptiste observed. "Come on, then." He edged out of the row, excusing us to others, and we made our way to the door.

"I was hoping for something a bit more…interactive," I said. I put my glass down on a butler's tray nearby. "And somewhere that served stronger drinks."

He looked at me keenly. "You don't usually drink a lot."

"I've had a day," I said.

We slipped out while the men were applauding and gained the street. It was a balmy summer night and the stars were bright, though there was no moon.

Corbineau dusted off his bicorn. "Not your taste?"

"Not really," I said. I didn't want to say I thought it was awfully dull.

"The real attraction's not the music," he said. "They serve a half decent if overpriced meal to eat with friends, and the rooms are clean, well-appointed and private. There's not really anywhere else to take someone, if you share a billet with three or four other men. If both of you do…." He shrugged. "It's much nicer than a sand dune or a back alley, and much more discreet. If one's tastes run more to assignations than orgies."

"As yours do," I said. I supposed I had thought that before, that he would prefer a lover to anonymous hands and mouths.

Corbineau shrugged again, still examining his hat for an imaginary speck of dust. "Generally speaking. I would rather a lover. But that gets complicated. It's been some time since I was comfortably settled."

I put my head to the side. He had never talked about this with me before. "What happened?" I asked.

"He died." Corbineau looked at me, his eyes bright in the dim light of the street. "Nothing baroque or tragic, I assure you. He was a naval officer. He went down with the Orpheé twenty months ago. These things happen. Fortunes of war, and it could as easily have been me as him."

"I'm so sorry," I said. I had not known about it. "You did not even write and tell me."

Corbineau put his hat on and tilted it to the correct angle. "It's not the sort of thing one puts in letters, is it? Besides, I have little to complain of. We had a good run, and that's all one really gets." He shrugged again, and if there was a catch in his voice it was only for a moment. "Now I will need that drink as much as you. Let's go find it."

"Indeed, my friend," I said, and we set off. "A drink is exactly what we need."

Nearer the port than the castle, it was a much rougher place. The music was raucous and came out into the street. A couple of working girls lounged outside, bodices artfully disarranged and reeking of cheap cologne. Only of course they weren't girls. Unlike their sisters in the first establishment, they had not waxed their arms.

One of them plucked at my sleeve. "Looking for a good time, handsome boy?"

The other rolled her eyes. "Wrong one, connard. That one's a pussy like you."

Corbineau put his arm around me. "Sorry, ladies."

It was a bit odd to walk in with his arm around me, and also to meet the kind of appraising looks Charles rarely got from men in public places. The tables were just board tables, the seats a motley collection of benches and mismatched chairs, and the room was filled with smoke from hanging lanterns which must burn the cheapest oil. In a near chair a man in a seaman's coat lounged, a boy with a painted face across his lap, a faint expression of boredom on his face beneath his rouged cheeks. I nearly gagged at the smell of opium, and dragged Jean-Baptiste to sit as far across the room as possible from the men with the pipe.

We settled down on a bench against the wall, his arm still around me behind the table. "Just staking my claim, my dear," he said, then raised his voice to the barmaid. "Brandy for me and my friend, and don't be all night about it."

She slunk back toward the bar with an unimpressed sneer. The seaman had his hand under the boy's untucked shirt, and as he moved I saw his hand on the boy, possessive and hard. At the bar, two ladies in dresses held court for five or six sailors, their hair piled up and their lips painted carmine. One of them seemed to be directing the sailor to kiss her shoe if he wanted further favors. He knelt and planted one on her ankle instead, one hand on the back of her calf. She wasn't taped in the least. I could see her erection through the thin dress.

"Oh, much better," I said, taking my cravat off and opening the buttons of my shirt, biting my lip all the while. I opened the shirt just enough to show the top of my stays, white lace and little pink ribbons beneath man's waistcoat and coat.

"You are going to get me into so much trouble," Jean-Baptiste observed, handing over a few coins as the barmaid dumped glasses in front of us. "You look like public indecency on two feet."

"Do I now?" I took a long drink of the brandy, feeling it burn its way down my throat. "I feel like trouble." My eyes met those of a heavyset man across the room with the five o'clock shadow of a man whose five o'clock was yesterday. I smiled.

"Oh God," Jean-Baptiste said.

He came right over. "I haven't seen you around here before," he said.

"I just arrived from Paris," I said. "My friend here was showing me the sights." I gave him a little smile. "Friend, not friend."

"Too bad," his eyes flicked to Corbineau, and then back to me. "I've got a few nice sights I could show you."

"Maybe later," I said.

He slid onto the bench on the other side of me from Corbineau, one hand on my thigh. "I bet you're a sight too."

"I try to be," I said, taking up the brandy glass again and flipping it back.

"I give as good as I get," he said, squeezing my knee. I scooted back before his hand reached for something that wasn't there. "Fair's fair."

I thought he had nice brown eyes, and there was something I liked about him, a starving kind of hunger but no malice. He probably had a wife who had no idea where he went drinking. "Out in the back, then, if there's a storeroom or such, but I'm back in ten minutes. Otherwise my friend here will come looking for me with his sharp, pointy sword."

Jean-Baptiste looked vaguely appalled. "Charles, what am I going to do with you?"

"I'll be back in ten minutes," I said.

"Jesus, Charles," Jean-Baptiste said. "I will come looking if you're not."

"See that you do," I said, and followed him behind the rough curtain that blocked off the storeroom from the tavern. "Popular place," I said. It reeked of men.

"Pretty much," he said, and pushed me up against the wall. I got my hand in the band of his breeches, undoing buttons one handed.

He tasted like brandy and salt, garlic from dinner and some kind of soup, exactly what I wanted, hard and raw and nothing except that. It took about three minutes to get him off in my hand, pumping and grinding against him, his face buried in my cleavage, in the top of Charles' stays. He swore and stepped back, stopping as I had him still, running my nail down the top of his drained member. "God Almighty!" Sweat was running down his face.

"More like Aphrodite," I said, and smiled a feral smile. The power of having him that way was intoxicating. I wanted to squeeze, to see how far I could push him, but he was only a stranger, not someone I could play those games with. I let go.

"Aye, Aphrodite," he said, beginning to do up his buttons. "I'll have you off. Turn about and all."

"No need," I said, leaning in and kissing him tenderly. "I've had my fun."

"If you say."

I nodded, the pressure unbearable. "I do. Go on now."

He took a breath, gave me one inscrutable look, pulled the curtain aside and went out. It had barely fallen back into place before I had my buttons open, stroking downward, one finger unerringly finding my wet quim, my pearl throbbing like a tiny knob. On the other side of the curtain fifty men were at their games. On the other side of the very thin curtain. That anyone might move any minute. I gasped and nearly screamed out my pleasure, shaking, my shoulders against the wall, my boot heels grinding on the boards. Light, dark, light and dark again.

I closed my eyes for a moment, catching my breath.

Then I wiped my hands on my shirttail, tucked it in neatly, did up my buttons and fastened my shirt almost to the collar. It was less than ten minutes before I came out.

Corbineau nearly jumped out of his seat. I slid in beside him, taking up the brandy and having a long drink. I really felt much, much better.

"I was about to come after you," he said in a low voice. "Damnation, Elza. You're crazy."

"Yes," I said levelly. "I know."

He snorted and refilled his glass from the bottle. "You think so, don't you?"

"I don't have any other word for it," I said. "But it works well enough for me. And that's all anyone gets, isn't it?"

"That it is," he said, and touched his glass to mine. "Strange travelers."

"Absent friends," I said, touching my glass to his.

We drank. He spread his hands around the glass as though examining each finger. "What happened?" he asked. "With you and the Marshal, I mean. You seemed so happy in Munich. And now he's…."

"Miserable?" I asked, cocking an eyebrow.

Corbineau shook his head. "Frustrated. Explosive. I don't mean that he does anything he shouldn't, but he feels like it's all coiled there, just beneath the surface, and if something touches the powder off it will all explode. Mind you, I love working with him. Always have. I think the world of him, don't mistake me. But he's tinder waiting for the flame, all the time now."

"I don't know," I said, and was surprised to hear the sadness in my voice. "I have no idea what he's thinking anymore. We haven't talked in nearly three years, Jean-Baptiste, not once."

"Why? What happened? Whose fault was it?"

I sighed. "I suppose in the beginning it was Moreau's."

"What did he do?" Jean-Baptiste asked, refilling my glass for me. "I know you were worried he'd find out and have his revenge on Michel."

"It wasn't that," I said. "It was that he gave him a lot of money."

Jean-Baptiste Corbineau refilled my glass again. "What did the Emperor do?"

I sighed and took another drink. The hanging lanterns swayed seductively in the breeze, and the crowd seemed quieter. "He didn't just double it. That would have been too easy."

"Too easy?"

I put my head on Corbineau's shoulder. "Too easy for Michel to refuse. No, he offered him everything he ever wanted, glory and beauty and the hand of a princess. And a place at his side. What have I ever had that could compare to that, Jean-Baptiste? What have I ever had that could compare to Alexander?"

"You are quite drunk," Corbineau said, his arm around me. "Alexander who?"

"Alexander the Great," I said, my mouth running on ahead of my mind. "Who else? I was fool enough compete this time. I should know better. I do know better. He is the perfect Companion. 'He too is Alexander.' I know better. And I held on, because I did not want to give him up. Because I did not want to lose him."

"You and Michel?" Corbineau seemed to be having some trouble following this, which was silly as I was making perfect sense.

"I tried to talk him out of it. I got him to ask to go on the Santo Domingo expedition instead when the Emperor offered him Inspector General of Cavalry. I got him to ask. But he wasn't assigned."

"And a good thing too," Corbineau said, taking a long drink of brandy. "Almost everybody on the Santo Domingo expedition died."

I held my glass out for more brandy, the room spinning in quite a comfortable way. "Do you remember Persia, Jean-Baptiste?"

"I've never been to Persia," Corbineau said. He sounded unaccountably baffled.

"The wedding." I waved my glass around. "The princesses. Stateira and Drypetis. Hephaistion married Drypetis, so that their children would be kin. His and Alexander's."

"That was a really long time ago," Corbineau said carefully. "And I'm not sure what it has to do with anything."

"I watched them get married," I said, my voice choking. "My wife was already dead, dead in Gedrosia. I watched Hephaistion marry her. And why not? Why shouldn't he? He was grave and beautiful and he would make her very happy."

"What in the world does this have to do with Michel and the Emperor?" Corbineau asked. "Elza, you have completely lost me."

"He offered him Drypetis, don't you see? The hand of Joséphine's goddaughter, Aglae Auguié. Inspector General of Cavalry, his son-in-law for all practical purposes—the money and the title and the honor and the princess—everything he could possibly want. Perhaps he knew the way to buy him. Or perhaps he caught that fire too. Michel came back from every meeting ablaze. The ideas, the conversation, the fire that leaps from mind to mind—they would build a new world together, a new world to be won! Do you see that, Jean-Baptiste?"

"Do we not all blaze from that fire?" Jean-Baptiste said quietly. "Do we not all see that new world to be won? Isn't that why we're here? That we may not return into the night of centuries past, but keep the best of the Revolution, tempering the white horse with the black? That we may move forward without the madness, without the blood of thousands running in the streets from the guillotine, the downtrodden paying back their oppressors a thousandfold? And yet that we may harness this lightning, schools and national law courts, freedom of religion and of conscience? Are we not all afire?"

I turned about and looked at him muzzily. "I've never heard you talk like that before," I said.

"I'm not really a lightweight, Elza."

"I never thought you were," I said drunkenly. "I knew you were a Companion too." I put my head on his shoulder, breathing in the smell of his sweat, the stale smoke of hours in a tavern. "My dear, true friend."

He patted my back. "Tell me about Mademoiselle Auguié, Elza. You can tell me it all."

Fortune's Favorites

All happiness, all idylls, have an end. The end of ours was due to Moreau, of course.

After the Battle of Hohenlinden, we stayed in a fine house in Munich all through the winter and into the spring, waiting for the final peace treaty to be signed, though Moreau had left for Paris as soon as the armistice was concluded. After four and a half months in his house, the doctor who owned it had more or less abandoned acting as a host, and treated us as the family we weren't. For our part, Michel behaved like some distant cousin imposing on a relative's hospitality, a little deferential and eternally polite, always at his host's disposal for a game of cards. It helped that Michel lost perpetually at cards. He was incapable of concealing the contents of his hand, and every thought was written on his face. Sometimes he lost rather more than I thought we could afford.

"Consider it the price of lodging," he said to me with a grin. "We're quartered on him, eating his food. If I lose half my pay at cards, surely that's no more than it's worth."

I rolled my eyes but agreed. I thought that I could win it back if I needed to. My father had taught me a number of ingenious ways of cheating at cards, but I forbore to use them. I wasn't sure it would help Michel with the Munichers to send to the table a female card sharp.

It was the middle of April, and Michel and I were eating breakfast companionably in the dining room, the windows open to the stable yard behind in hopes of catching the warm spring breeze. Michel had the newspaper and was frowning over it. I put more cream in my coffee and looked out the window at the branches of a blooming cherry tree over the wall. My German was considerably improved, but I spoke much better than I read, and the newspaper was beyond me.

The door opened and one of the footmen announced a dispatch rider, dusty and tired from the last leg of his journey. He came up and saluted Michel smartly.

"Citizen General Ney, I have dispatches for you from Paris, from Citizen General Moreau."

"Thank you." Michel took the packet and dismissed the rider. There were half a dozen small letters sealed with wax, addressed variously, and one large one for Michel. He broke the seal with his fingers and opened it.

"Oh my God." The paper dropped from his hand.

"What?" I got up and came around the table, alarmed.

He picked the letter up again, a piece of paper fluttering out of the fold.

I bent over his shoulder, reading.:

...in recognition of your services to the French Republic, it is my distinct honor and pleasure to convey to you this small token of the Republic's esteem, an honor well-earned by your martial prowess and your distinguished service at the Field of Hohenlinden. I have also enclosed some lesser awards for Captain Ruffin and those other officers that you recommended to me.

It is with the greatest pleasure that I convey these regards to you,

Your servant,

Citizen General Victor Moreau,
Commander in Chief, Army of the Rhine

I picked up the paper that had fallen. It was a draft on the Bank of France for 10,000 francs.

"Oh my God," I said. I had never seen so much money in one place before in my life.

"Surely..." Michel said. "Surely it's a mistake. Too many zeroes."

"No, Michel," I said. "It says ten thousand francs."

"I could pay off the farm," Michel said. "I could keep a carriage. I could buy you diamond something or others." His imagination failed him at that point and we stood there stupidly, holding the draft between us.

"I like diamond something or others," I said. "We could rent a bigger apartment. And hire a servant to clean it."

"I can't imagine what to do with ten thousand francs." Michel looked at me, his blue eyes honestly perplexed. His father had been the cooper at a vineyard in the Saar, making barrels for his betters all his life. Ten thousand francs would go a long way toward buying the vineyard and everything in it.

Something disturbed me about this windfall. "Michel," I said, slowly, my eyes on the draft, "Moreau doesn't even like you. I'm not saying you don't deserve this, but Moreau wouldn't just do this out of gratitude. He has a political reason. He always has a political reason."

Michel sighed. "I can't imagine what. I don't have any influence in Paris. I don't have any money, or didn't. I serve under him—he can take my troops away and assign them where he wants. What does he need me for?"

The pieces fell into place for me, the memory of the First Consul in Milan, talking about Moreau. "Bonaparte," I said.

"Bonaparte?" Michel raised an eyebrow. "I've never met the man. We've never been in the same command. I don't know what he has to do with me."

"Nothing," I said. "Or everything. Moreau thinks himself Bonaparte's one true rival for supremacy in France. Bonaparte has generals like Lannes and Massena in his train. Moreau wants to buy some generals of his own."

"Shit," Michel said. He sat down at the table again, his breakfast still getting cold on his plate.

I put my hand on his shoulder, brushing out the tangles in his long red hair with my fingers, a chill running down my back for reasons I couldn't put a name to.

"I'm not for sale," Michel said at last.

"Aren't you? Everyone is, for the right price." I sat down across from him, taking his hand in mine. "Money may not be your price. But what about glory? What would you do to have the supreme command on the Rhine? What would you do to command an army, not a division? What would you do to be a Marshal of France?"

Michel almost laughed. "Me? A cooper's son? Even if the Revolution hadn't abolished the title, Marshal is a title for heroes of the blood, for princes. I'm as likely to be a Marshal as I am a prince." He squeezed my hand as though I told him fairy tales. "Elza, you worry too much. Moreau wants to buy me with a big bonus. Fine. I'll take the money, but my loyalty isn't for sale. I'm not about to support him in some coup d'état. I'm not going to join some plot against the Consulate. As far as I can see, the government is working better than it has at any point in the last ten years, and the Austrians have finally sued for peace. I'm perfectly happy to thank God that Bonaparte was spared in the assassination attempt last winter."

On Christmas Eve, the same night that Michel and I had been rejoicing in Munich, Royalist agents loyal to the deposed Bourbons had set off a bomb in the streets of Paris, intending to kill the First Consul on his way to a performance at the Opera. Fortunately for him, the bomb had detonated seconds late, and the second carriage in the cavalcade had taken the brunt of it rather than the first. Among the wounded was Joséphine's sixteen-year-old daughter Hortense, who had been badly cut by flying glass. Fifty-two people had been killed or wounded, including a number of children in the crowds of late revelers on the crowded street.

There had been arrests, but no one knew for certain that the ringleaders were not still free, that there would not be more bombs.

"Moreau had nothing to do with that," I said, feeling certain. Moreau had been in Munich too, in the aftermath of Hohenlinden. There had been no time. And while I could imagine Moreau scheming with his former Jacobin associates, I couldn't imagine him joining a Royalist plot.

"I'm not having anything to do with any plot," Michel said, his stubborn chin rising. "I'm here to serve France, and her legitimate government, whoever that may be. I don't make policy. I'm a soldier."

"Michel, right now soldiers make policy," I said. "I don't think you can stay apolitical forever. Especially not if you rise any higher." I looked down at the draft, the zeroes stretching out to infinity. "That makes you a man of consequence. You are not going to be able to ignore politics. And Bonaparte is not going to be able to ignore you."

Michel picked up the draft, turning it over and over in his hands. "And if I burned it?"

"You'd be a stupid ass, " I said, taking it from him and putting it on the table. "Do you want to go back to the Saar and raise fruit trees? You could do that. Resign your commission and go home, marry some nice girl and wait for events to roll over you. Is that what you want?"

"No." Michel picked up his cold cup of coffee and took a sip, grimacing. "I decided long ago that I didn't want that. I wanted glory and war instead. I just never imagined rising so high." He looked at me and shrugged. "Perhaps that's being a stupid ass. I dreamed of being an officer, of earning some rare battlefield commission for gallantry. Because of the Revolution, I got that at twenty-two, an officer and a gentleman, something no one in Saar Louis could ever have imagined. And then I dreamed of being a general. I got that at twenty-seven. I'm thirty-two. What should I dream of next? A title? To be the founder of a noble house?" He put the cup down. "Or the guillotine. Fortune's favor is very, very fickle."

"I know," I said, having been up and down more times than I liked in twenty-four years. A chill ran through me, thinking of the engraving on the Tarot card, noble men rising and falling, lying at last beneath the turning wheel as a skeleton. "It's dangerous."

Michel reached for the coffeepot and refilled his cup. "What do you think Bonaparte will do when he hears what Moreau has given me?"

I looked down at the draft, lying between the solid silver plate, remembering gold coins spilling out onto the bed in Milan, a fortune for a bad actress. "Double it, possibly."

He didn't. Instead, Bonaparte sent a letter, very cordially inviting General Ney to visit him in Paris, saying that he had heard the most glowing reports of the General and was consumed with the desire to meet him in person.

I started packing.

Michel came into the celadon bedroom of the doctor's house while I had the cases open on the bed. I had also bought a trunk. We had both needed new clothes in Munich, and they wouldn't fit in the cases and saddlebags. In a way, I hated to leave. We had been five months in this room, and it was starting to feel like home.

Michel clearly felt the same way. He paced around, opening the curtains and looking out, poking behind the screen, wandering into the dressing room and back out.

"What's the matter?" I said, folding one of my men's shirts.

He shrugged and made another circuit.

I went up to him and wrapped my arms around him, my cheek against the gold oak leaves on his shoulders. He sighed and rested his chin on the top of my head.

"It will all be different," he said.

"I know," I said.

We arrived in Paris on a gorgeous day in May. I rode beside him on Nestor, cutting a fine figure in Charles' best clothes. The apartment was just as we'd left it, opened only for the maid to sweep occasionally. It seemed very small and cheerless after the fine house in Munich, and my gold curtains seemed gaudy and tawdry compared to the understatement of fine fabrics. Michel left the intricacies of moving to me.

The third day I went to look at apartments while Michel presented himself at the Tuileries. He wore his best dress uniform, dark blue coat crusted with gold, tricolor sash tied at his waist, his long hair tied back neatly and his hat ornamented with a black ostrich plume. And his tightest white pants. He looked like he could hardly breathe.

I giggled as I made a final inspection. "Planning to impress Madame Bonaparte again?" His first impression on the lady had been made in the nude, through a series of comic misadventures.

"She probably won't be there," he said, twitching under my ministrations. "My appointment is with the First Consul in his office."

"But just in case...." I laughed.

He shrugged a little sheepishly. "It never hurts to be well turned out."

"No," I said, "It never does." He had his vanity too, my beloved peasant general.

I saw him off with a kiss, and went to look at apartments.

I returned before he did, though not by much. He came up the street as I was going in, so I waited while he paid the hired carriage and climbed the steps. He still looked splendid, but his step was somewhat deflated. I waited until we were upstairs to ask.

"What happened? Didn't it go well with Bonaparte?"

Michel began undoing his cravat. "Not really," he said. "Nothing awful happened. But it wasn't good."

"Why?" Having met the First Consul in Milan, I had trouble imagining how Michel could have failed to be impressed. "What happened?"

Michel flung the offending cravat over a chair. "I don't know. It just seemed that everything was wrong-footed. I had to wait half an hour because someone was already with him, and the reception room was all done up like a palace."

"The Tuileries is a palace," I said reasonably. "It was the primary residence of the Bourbon kings in Paris. You know that."

"He had a bunch of busts," Michel said. "Mirabeau and Washington and the rest, which are fine. I have nothing against the Americans. Why should I? But right by the door he had a massive marble bust of Alexander, that one with the dreamy eyes."

"The one by Praxiteles," I said. "I've seen engravings. Go on."

"And another big one on the other side of the door of Julius Caesar. It was disturbing." Michel took off his had and threw it on a chair. The plume bent, so he picked it up and put it on the top of the cold stove. "So when he opened the door he was standing right between them, all three in a row, and all three heads on exactly the same level. Who does he think he is?"

"Lots of people have statues of Alexander and Caesar," I said. "They're famous works of art. And perfectly suitable to a public place. Martial success and all that."

"That's not it, " Michel said. "I can't explain it, Elza. It doesn't make any sense. But I was off on the wrong foot and I couldn't seem to say anything right. He congratulated me on Hohenlinden like he'd never heard of Moreau, so I said thank you very much but that the plan was Moreau's and not mine."

I rolled my eyes. "And sounded like a Moreau loyalist. Michel!"

"Maybe so." He shrugged. "I'm not good at politics like you are. But it's true. The plan was Moreau's."

"You didn't have to bring him up in the first two minutes," I said.

"So then he asked how I was liking Paris, and I said I just got here and I hadn't seen anything yet but it all seemed very noisy with the construction everywhere."

"He's building three hospitals and an aqueduct," I said. "And widening the streets around Les Halles. Michel, did you have to criticize everything you could think of?"

"I didn't criticize!" he said. "I just said it was noisy. Which it is. And how should I know it was his construction?"

"Whose construction did you think it was? George III? The Czar?" I put my head in my hands.

"I'm sorry I don't know everything like you do," Michel said hotly. "After all, I'm just some jumped-up bumpkin, not a lady in tatters like you!"

I stood up, face to face with him, my face as scarlet as his. "Did you have to be a complete idiot?"

"Do you have to be a complete shrew?"

"Shrew?"

"Shrew!"

I raised my hand to slap him, but he grabbed my wrist. I tried slapping at him with my right hand, but he caught that too. His grip was steel, and there was no way to break his grasp.

His hands were just a shade too tight around my wrists, and I felt a shiver that had nothing to do with anger.

He saw it in my face, and an expression that was almost a smirk settled over him.

I stomped on his foot.

He picked me up even though I was no lightweight and hauled me bodily into the bedroom.

Doing so involved letting go of one hand, however, and the buttons on his tight white pants suffered enormously from being ripped loose. And after that it was a different kind of passion.

Lying disheveled on top of my gold duvet in the afternoon, I got my breath back curled against his side, my skirts around my waist, one stocking on, one stocking off, wearing nothing else below the waist. His pants were a sad casualty on the floor, but he was still wearing his dress coat with shirt and waistcoat. The gold oak leaves on his collar had impressed themselves on the inside of my arm where it was pinned against him. I stretched lazily.

"I don't think you're an idiot, Michel," I said. The warmth of his skin felt good against the inside of my thigh.

"I don't think you're a shrew," he said. His voice sounded rough and half dozing, the tension drained away.

I rubbed my thigh back and forth against him, sticky with his seed.

"We forgot the letters," he said. "Does it matter? You just came off your courses."

"It should be safe," I said. "At least a day or two more. You forget all the time."

"So do you," he said, and nuzzled against my hair.

"We're both terrible about it," he said. "No common sense at all."

"I know," I said.

"Would it be so awful?"

"What? If I were to get pregnant?" I craned my neck to look at him. "You tell me."

He shrugged as though unconcerned. "I like children. And I like you. And I like the way we fight."

"So do I," I said. I put my head against his shoulder. I didn't want to think about it. If it happened, I would deal with it then. I didn't trust him quite that much. Or perhaps it was fortune I didn't trust.

"Am I an idiot?" he asked, and I knew he didn't mean with Bonaparte, but I pretended I thought that was what he meant.

"Yes, " I said. "No political sense at all. Was it a total disaster?"

He shifted his arm under my head. "I don't know. We talked about the Army of the Rhine and the last campaign. That seemed to go well enough. And then Madame Bonaparte arrived and walked me out. We ran into her daughter and a friend of hers in the garden. Did you know Madame Bonaparte grafts roses? She knows a lot about horticulture."

"I didn't know," I said. "And her daughter? Is she well? I heard she was injured in the bomb last winter."

"She seemed well enough to me," Michel said. "She and her friend Mademoiselle Auguié giggled at me behind their hands every time my back was turned."

"Well," I said, smiling, "Your pants were rather tight."

"I couldn't sit down," he said. "I had to tower over Bonaparte the entire time."

I rolled my eyes where he couldn't see. "And that was a wonderful idea."

"If you thought the pants were a bad idea you should have said so."

"I didn't know that you actually couldn't sit down," I said. "You should only wear them for dancing."

Michel glanced over to where they lay in a heap. "I'm not sure I'm going to wear them for anything," he said skeptically.

"I can sew the buttons back on," I said.

It seemed that Michel wasn't wrong about how badly it had gone with the First Consul. Spring turned into summer and he wasn't assigned. He continued on full pay, on indefinite leave in Paris. Of course, with the peace, it was possible there simply weren't many commands available, but I couldn't help seeing the shadow of Moreau's long disgrace, the year and a half when he had gone without a command, getting more and more bad tempered and unreasonable.

Not that Michel was either bad tempered or unreasonable. A summer in Paris with plenty of money and few cares seemed to agree with him after two years of more or less solid campaigning, ending in a difficult winter battle. We spent our mornings riding in the Bois de Boulogne, our evenings in taverns with my friends or his, or sometimes both together. His friends were mostly officers his age but junior to him in rank, the kind of young men who made high-spirited companions for actresses, free spending to a fault.

Michel was the soberest one. Perhaps it was because he was usually the ranking officer in any group, or perhaps he was simply more serious by nature, but he was the one who lost the least money at cards, the one who attempted to dissuade friends from betting on who could swim the Seine, made noxious by sewage in the summer. He was the first to want to leave the party at night, the least likely to be drunk. Perhaps it was because he had the most to look forward to at home afterwards.

I should not have been surprised that he took to Auguste Thibault, who was anything but a gallant. Isabella and her artillery colonel were still in Paris, and I asked them to dinner as soon as we had moved and had an actual dining room. Michel and Auguste sat at the table long after the last of the cheese was eaten, discussing increasingly technical details of gunnery over several glasses of my favorite Madeira, until Isabella and I wished we had another parlor to withdraw to. In the end, we went in the bedroom and sat on the bed while they went on and on.

Isabella kicked her shoes off and curled up on the foot of the bed, smiling. "I'm glad you see you found a man who suits you," she said. "You look very well, Ida. I was worried for a bit, last year."

I flopped back against the pillows, propping one under my head. "Oh, we suit. We suit very well." It was Michel's pillow, and it smelled like him. "I was worried myself, last year. But I came through, didn't I?"

"Even if he's not the First Consul?" Isabella grinned knowingly.

"Michel doesn't know about that," I said, glancing toward the door. He and Auguste were refighting something or other around the table, possibly an artillery duel at Lodi. "I don't see any point in bringing that up. He doesn't ask about my past and I don't ask about his."

"Does he have much of one?" Isabella asked.

I shrugged. "Men always have a past. I'm sure there are things I don't need to know. But I know what kind of man he is, and I trust that."

"I hope you're not given reason to be sorry," Isabella said. "Awful things happen all the time, and they're always done by someone else. Only not really. I don't want to know what makes Auguste go white around the mouth like he does. He keeps his secrets. And now he has these secret meetings on Tuesday night. I begged him to tell me if it was political, and he swore it wasn't, but he won't tell me where he goes or why."

"To protect you?" I sat up straighter. It had been only a few years since the Jacobin clubs met in the cellar of St. Sulpice, and revolutionary and counterrevolutionary societies continued to meet in secret, some to the left of the government and some to the right.

Isabella shook her head. "He says it's not political, but he's sworn to reveal nothing."

"That would make me nervous," I said.

It certainly made me nervous the next Tuesday night, when Michel went with him.

I paced around the apartment for hours, wondering what they were doing and what I should say, wondering how I could say it without seeming to attack Michel's complete lack of political sense. There was nothing of the conspirator in him, and if he played at that game I was sure he would be played for a fool.

Men had been denounced for nothing more than attending the wrong meeting, being in the wrong company at the wrong time. Men had gone to the guillotine for nothing more than that.

The hours went by. Eleven came and went, then midnight. It was nearly one when he came in.

I was still sitting at the table, the candle burned almost all the way down, a nearly empty glass of Madeira in front of me that I had been nursing for hours. I looked up, and all the things I had planned to say melted in sheer relief at seeing him.

"Elza?" He put his hat on the chair by the door and came over to me, his brow furrowed with concern. "Why aren't you in bed? You look awful. Did something happen?"

"No," I said. I stood up and took his hands, wanting to touch him.

"I was with Auguste," he said, "And the time slipped away. I didn't mean for you to sit up for me."

"I have to know," I said, and it came out all in a rush. "I'm not like Isabella. She doesn't want to know. But I have to. If you're part of something, if you're putting yourself in danger…."

He squeezed my fingers, his mystified expression changing to something more like discomfort. "Are you imagining me in some Jacobin conspiracy? I promise you, I'm not. I told you I had no interest in plotting with Moreau or anyone else."

"Then what are you doing?" I asked. "If it's whoring and gambling with Auguste and his friends, just tell me that so I'll know and not worry. I don't own you, and I wouldn't be hurt by that kind of thing."

"I would never do that." Michel looked honestly amazed. "Why in the world would I visit a whorehouse? I mean, all right, once or twice a few years ago, when I was on leave and didn't have any attachments, but why would I do that now?"

"I don't know." His hands were warm in mine. "Variety?"

Michel laughed, throwing his head back. "Variety? When we have an entire circus right here?" He slipped his arms around me, solid and comforting. "Believe me, Elza, there is absolutely no reason I would visit a whorehouse, with Auguste or anyone else."

"Then where were you?" I asked, looking up at him. "Michel, I need to know."

His eyes slid away from mine. "Need?"

"Yes," I said. I reached up, my hands against his lapels, the gold oak leaves scratchy under my hands. I found his eyes again and pulled them back to mine.

He searched my face and sighed. "It's a lodge meeting."

"A lodge meeting?" My voice sounded incredulous to my own ears. "You mean Masonry or something? My father was a Mason. Of course the ceremonies are secret, but he never hid that he was going to the lodge. There's no reason to."

Michel sighed again. "Something like that. I'm a Mason too and it's not particularly secret. This is…a more esoteric form of Masonry, I suppose. Not political. Just more esoteric."

"With Auguste."

"Auguste is a member, yes. He asked me to come with him." Michel met my eyes levelly. "I promise you it's nothing political. And I'm not supposed to talk about it."

"Esoteric." I suddenly wondered about Lebrun, about the legitimate lodges he had described in the days when I was acting as his medium. Auguste Thibault seemed an unlikely member for one of those groups, but I could certainly imagine Michel's interest.

"I'm not supposed to, Elza." " He put his head to the side, meeting my eyes fully now. "I have to ask you to respect my oaths."

I nodded. ""I understand. And I won't ask you any more." Isabella was right. There are things we don't want to know. And right now anything involving demons or angels was one of those things.

Michel pulled me close, his face against the top of my head. "Thank you. I promise you it's nothing to worry about. Now come to bed."

I did, and I asked him no more. And I told him nothing either.

Thermidor came, the hottest part of the summer when anyone who can leaves Paris for the country. It was too hot to wear nightclothes, even with all the windows open. We threw the duvet on the floor and slept naked on the bare sheets, waking skin on skin in the first morning light. There was something deliciously sensual about waking up beside him, one hand against the creamy, freckled skin of his back, about running my fingers over his thighs while he slept. Moreau had never liked being in a state of undress, and my husband, Jan, had never spent a full night with me that I could remember. To watch the first stripes of morning sun through the window slowly crawl up the bed across his scarred legs was almost more intimate than I could bear.

I had thought that I loved before. Now I knew I had been wrong. What I had felt for anyone else was nothing to this. With it came utter panicked vulnerability.

Sometimes I picked fights with him to prove I could. Angry words and slammed doors were proof against belonging to him utterly and completely, the last defense of a heart in surrender. I wanted to submit and to conquer all at once. Fortunately, it was possible to do both in the bedroom and still wake in the morning without recriminations, without apologies that stained the entire day with tears and promises of affection.

We had come in from riding in the Bois de Boulogne, a hot afternoon interrupted by a summer thunderstorm that left us both drenched and laughing, hurrying home while the lightning still cracked. I threw my sodden coat over the chair and took off my waistcoat in front of the empty fireplace while Michel unbound his queue and shook his head like a big dog, sending droplets of water everywhere. I laughed. "Stop that! You're getting me wetter!"

He only grinned and shook his head again, taking off his coat and draping it over the chair back. "It's just a little water."

"True enough," I said, throwing my soaked cravat at him so that it smacked him in the face.

"My amazon," he said, throwing it back. "Was there ever another like you?"

"If I were an amazon," I said, taking off my waistcoat, "I should not be yours. You should be mine."

"Should I now?" He sat down on the chair, incidentally crushing my coat, and started taking his muddy boots off. "Is that how it works?"

I nodded. His red hair was all over the place, falling in sodden threads about his face. "Oh yes. Some hapless soldier lost in the mountains and captured by fierce amazons. I think the captain would like you all to herself."

My eyes lingered on his face, watching the color rise in his cheeks. "And so pretty when you blush."

At that he truly did, turning red even as he dropped his second boot on the floor. "Would she?"

"She would," I said. I crossed the floor to him, standing very deliberately before him, hips tilted forward to show off female form in man's clothing, reached down and lifted his chin roughly. "Have you ever been tied up?"

Michel swallowed. He didn't look away, his eyes on mine. "No," he said.

"A big fellow like you would put up quite a fight, I imagine," I said. "But then you wouldn't be much use to me if you weren't a fighter."

"Use to you for what?" he said, his breath in his voice.

"Breeding stock," I said, tilting his chin up more tightly. "I expect my girls could get quite a lot of use out of you. After I'm done."

His eyes widened, anticipation warring with shame.

"Stand up," I said, "And take your shirt off."

He did it, unfastening the two buttons at the placket and pulling it over his head, shaking one of his hands loose where he hadn't gotten the cuff undone first.

"Very nice," I said, putting the flat of my hand against his chest, firm and implacable. "Now the pants. Or should I have my girls strip you?"

"I'd probably put up a fight about the pants," he said, even as his fingers tangled with mine getting the buttons loose.

"Then I'd have to teach you a lesson," I said. I gave him a little push. "Kneel over the ottoman."

It nearly broke the spell. "What, right here in the front room?"

"There's no one here but us," I said. The apartment only had two rooms. "Now do as I tell you."

"Amazons have ottomans?" He was nervous. I could see it in the way he moved, nervous but eager.

"I suppose I'd use a rough barrel, but I don't happen to have one in the parlor," I said. "So get down there and shut your mouth if you know what's good for you."

At that he did as I said, his knees on the floor, his chest stretched against the brocade fabric of the ottoman. His neck and forearms were sunburned, but his back and buttocks were all pale skin, redhead fair, a few freckles across the back of his shoulders.

"That's right," I said. "Reach over and hold the legs on the other side. Stretch as though you were tied to them." I wasn't sure he'd actually abide the ropes yet. "And get your knees apart." I kicked them apart with my booted feet, wider than comfort, wide enough to expose the cleft of his buttocks, the shadow of his scrotum beneath. "I believe you need to learn a lesson, troublemaker."

His breath was fast, but he bent his head like a boy in penance.

"There's only one thing to do with a defiant one like you," I said, and brought my riding crop down across his buttocks.

He actually cried out, more in astonishment than pain, as I'd stopped far short of giving him all I had, but he hadn't seen it coming. It had stung. And surprised. And somewhat more. His head rose, dripping red hair falling away from his face, from the line of his throat, passion writ in every line of his body.

"I have a lesson to teach you about amazons, soldier," I said, and laid it across the back of his thigh sharply. "You belong to me. You'd best not forget it." Another, this just at the join of leg and crack, hard enough to leave a red mark. "And get those knees apart!"

I shoved them apart again and he groaned. "Please."

"No pleading," I said. "It doesn't become you." Another one, sharp and quick with just the leather pad at the end. "You are here to service me."

"I won't," he breathed, his face against the brocade, his arms straining but still holding tight.

"You will," I said. Another stroke, this one on the inside of his right thigh, and he jumped under it, the muscles in his thighs working. "You will service me and anyone I tell you to. If I have to have you tied and mate you to my girls by hand, then I shall." The picture that made was enough to nearly make me lose my place, wanting to grind against something, imagining Michel tied in bonds, imagining my hands on him, my hands on a woman's slick cunny, mating her to him, feeling him slide into her against his will....

"No." He jerked as the crop came down again.

"You will. You won't be able to help it. You don't have self control enough." Unexpected movement, reaching for his right wrist at the same moment that I shoved his right thigh with my booted leg, pushing him off the ottoman and flipping him onto the hearthrug on his back. It was only a foot or so, as the ottoman wasn't tall, but intense, the more so for all exposed. Knees apart, his cock rose hard and full from a nest of red curls, straining and ready. I took it in one hand roughly, the crop still in the other. "Do you suppose that would hurt?"

"Oh my God," he said, and closed his eyes, arms splayed out to the sides as though held by invisible hands.

I caressed it instead, running my hands up to his belly, seizing him by the root. "I wouldn't want to damage your breeding potential. But I really don't think you have the self-discipline to resist."

His mouth opened but no sound came out, eyes closed, chin lifted like some ancient statue of a dying Gaul, noble and suffering and incandescent with desire.

I got my buttons open with the hand holding the crop, half tearing one loose in my haste. "I will have you if I want," I said. "Anytime I want. As often as I want. For whomever I want. Is that clear?" My privates were throbbing with the sudden rush of blood, my own pulse beating against the seam of my pants.

"Yes," he whispered, and his face tensed as the crop came down again across his lower belly, marking him with a red streak just above the thatch of hair.

"Mine," I said, tearing the placket loose and lowering myself onto him, the angle a bit awkward with the tangle of cloth. It took a moment to straighten that out. "Mine."

"No," he whispered.

"Mine," I said again, feeling him fill me, heavy and desperate, beginning to move on him. "You will do as I say. You are here for my pleasure. You are nothing but what I want you to be."

His breath caught, trying to thrust but instead ground down beneath me. I would set the pace and he must follow, his arms still stretched as if pinned, straining against the wool carpet.

I touched the leather tip of the crop to his lips. "Say it."

He shook his head, and I ground down again. So good, so tight, so utterly mine.... It was hard to remember what to say, not to become lost in it, not to lose control.

"No self-control," I said, "You have no self-control. You can't stop yourself no matter how hard you try. You will no matter how much you resist."

And he was resisting. He was trying to hold back, his whole face flushed, every muscle straining as though he were indeed that unlucky soldier taken by amazons.

"You can't help it," I said breathlessly. My climax was building, spurred by this power, this heady and unutterable wrongness, to own him, to take whatever I wanted like a man. Would he shake like this if it were my organ in him, if I could take him in truth? Red hair spread around him, white thighs straining....

The wave caught me early, lifting and spinning, quick contractions as I bit down on my lip to keep from screaming.

He did cry out, some wordless sound as I tightened around him, still holding on, still resisting while I rode out my pleasure on him.

And yet he was mine. "Say it," I whispered. "Surrender."

His mouth shaped the word no, but his hips snapped, surging against me as it took him at last, as though dragged out of him from the bottom of his being, a tear sliding beneath his closed eyelids. It seemed to go on and on, longer and deeper, and when I felt him soften I slid off and lay beside him on the hearthrug. I put my head against his shoulder and my arm about his chest, feeling his heart still pounding. Outside the rain was hammering against the window.

"Did I hurt you?" I said quietly. "Michel, not for anything would I." He would hold on out of pride, I thought belatedly. He would push beyond where he wanted, even unbound, even with nothing to constrain him but his pride.

"Yes," he said. He opened his eyes, naked to mine. "But I wanted you to."

I nodded. That I understood far too well.

He turned on his side stiffly, gathering me against him, and I came to him like a ship to port, linen shirt and breeches still tangled about my boot tops. "My dear," I whispered.

"We're mad," he said.

"I expect so." I put my hand to his face, tasted the one tear with my fingertips. "That was too much."

"No, it wasn't," he said. He ducked his head against my hair. "That's what I want. One thing I want. I need that. I need the pain."

"You need to surrender," I said. "As well as conquer." I ran my hand through his wet, tangled hair, suddenly filled with unaccountable tenderness. "I can do that. I can be that for you."

"Forever," he said, and closed his eyes against me like a tired child.

Afterward, we slept untroubled and woke stiff, side by side in the light from the window. Outside, the vegetable sellers were starting their day, hawking tomatoes and celery from their bins two floors down. I stretched against him and kissed him, mouthing his sleepy lips, the stubble on his chin, and felt him smile into me.

"Sunshine," he whispered. "Radiance and light. Fire made flesh."

"You're a poet," I said, my cheek against his shoulder. There was a spreading white scar there, like the impact of a stone on glass, where a musket ball had pierced it and been dug out. How long ago? Two years? Five? The ball had been nearly spent, he said, and hadn't broken the bone, just lodged deep in his flesh. I kissed it, and he tried not to flinch.

Ghosts of the Past

The next morning was the last day of our peace. A messenger came, the paid kind, not an Army courier. Paid messengers were expensive. Michel tore the letter open the moment the man was had his money, as though he already feared what it would say.

He looked at me and his voice was steady but his eyes were not. "It's from my sister Margarethe. She says our father is very ill. And that I should come quickly, if I want to see him." Michel looked away from me, out the window at the bright sun. "He's been sick a fortnight. It seemed like a summer cold at first, but it's gone into his lungs. She can hear him rasping with every breath, and all the plasters and camphor don't seem to do any good. This letter...." He broke off and took a breath before he went on. "This letter is four days old. I don't know...."

"You must go at once, of course, Michel," I said, going to him and putting my hand on his sleeve. "I'll put some clothes in your saddlebags, and some fruit and bread for the road. That will keep you to the first posting inn."

I had no warning when my father died. I couldn't actually remember it, oddly enough, though I remembered the funeral.

"Elza, I have to go." He was still looking at the letter, as though there were more of it to read. Or perhaps he didn't trust himself to look up.

"Of course you do," I said. "Let me run and tell the boy to go across to the livery stable and saddle Eleazar. It's not noon yet. You can get miles today."

Michel nodded. "I should take some nice clothes. In case."

"I'll pack your dress uniform," I said. "Though you'll have to do with one hat. There's not room for a hatcase on horseback." I packed his things swiftly. I had learned how to do that on campaign. By the time Eleazar was brought around, he was ready.

Michel stopped at the top of the stairs. The letter was still in his hand.

He looked at me, and for a moment he looked so young, younger than he had facing endless death in the field, younger than facing his own death, or mine. "Elza...."

"Go," I said, and kissed him. "Go. I'll write you."

He handed me the letter. "The address is there. So you know where to send it. La Petite Malgrange."

"I will," I said.

"I can't...." he began and stopped.

"I know," I said. "Whatever it is, I know."

He nodded and gave me a sideways, rueful smile. "Goodbye, then." He took his hat out of my hands and I heard him bounding down the stairs, his boot heels harsh on the polished wood.

I shut the door and bolted it. I walked around the apartment, picking up things and putting them away. I went in and lay down on our disordered bed. It smelled like last night's sex and suddenly I missed him with an intensity that brought tears to my eyes.

Of course he hadn't taken me with him. It would have taken time. Time, and explanations that had no place at a sickbed or a funeral. His father's house was no place for his mistress. His mistress should not meet his virginal younger sister. They didn't do things like that in Saar Louis. To my credit, I knew that. I knew which parts of his life I didn't belong in. To my credit, I knew how to say goodbye.

27 Thermidor of the Year IX
Dearest Elza,

I am in time. My father is very ill, and he hardly knows me, but he's alive. His breathing is very labored, and the doctor says that there is fluid in his lungs. There is nothing to be done for this, he says, except for warm plasters to the chest and a great deal of camphor that gives him some ease. He may yet recover, but the doctor is not reassuring.

It is strange to be here in the midst of crisis, needed and yet almost a stranger. At least, I feel strange. My sisters are very close to one another, both Margarethe my younger, and Sophie my older sister who has come to help with neither her husband nor children. Sophie is nearing forty, and she looks as I remember my mother, not as I remember her. And Margarethe is grown up. More than grown up. It seems to me that she should be a girl on the verge of womanhood as she was when I ran away to the army. Of course I have seen her many times since then, but that is the way she sticks in my mind. She's 27. And unmarried. Life is passing her by while she lives in Saar Louis with my father. I hardly know what to say to either of them.

I don't think they know what to say to me either. I'm a man. And I live in a different world.

It's so hot here, unusually hot. We sit beside the front window, watching the thunderclouds coming over the river and the branches beginning to move in a wind we don't feel yet, and the distant thunder seems to me the opening guns of some vast battle I can't see. We all hold our breath.

I miss you more than I can possibly say.

With all my love,

Michel

* * *

7 Fructidor of the Year IX

Dearest Elza,

You have no idea how glad I was to get your letter today! It was like a breath of home, and that's saying something I suppose.

My father seems a little improved. He can sit up in bed. He knows me now. I can still hear the rattle when he breathes, and he is terribly weak, but it is some improvement. He is surprised that I know anything about nursing him, which he should not be. We do not have our sisters in the field, and I do no more for him than I've done for friends in the past. He should know this. He was a soldier in the Seven Years War, for a while. But he hated it and the sins weigh heavily on his soul still.

Perhaps I am very wicked that every sin is not so heavy. But there are thousands of lives on my conscience, not a few, and if I thought about that every moment I should not be able to move, only press my chest to the floor and beg for mercy.

I am talking like this I suppose because I see things he has *done that he will not name weighing so much on his mind. There is no priest to be had in Saar Louis since the monastery was ransacked in the Terror, though there are in the German states. Sophie thinks she can get one to come over the border. Maybe that will help if he can talk to one and be shriven.*

Since my father has been ill, no one has done the haying, so I am doing it now. It's been a long time since I did it as a boy, but I still have the knack of it, though I made the mistake of working without my shirt yesterday because it was so hot and now I am sunburned and unhappy. I was going to put lard on it but Margarethe says that's an old wives tale and that lard makes it worse. She says the only thing that really helps is cool water from a well, though the cold makes you peel more.

I ache for you, my heart.

Michel

His letter was six days old when I got it. He did not have military couriers at his disposal in Saar Louis.

It came the same day as a letter from my cousin Louisa. I realized with a shock that I hadn't heard from her in more than a year, since last spring when I set out for Italy with Isabella. I had been on two campaigns since then, and had moved three times. If she had written to me, it was no surprise that I hadn't received it.

I held the letter in my hands, hardly daring to open it. When I did the first sentence made me catch my breath:

... I hate to put death in a letter, but I can hardly find you and I've written to everyone, including General Moreau, trying to guess where you might be now. I hope that this will get to you somehow.

M. Ringeling, Jan's father, was growing concerned about the rumors of unrest in Curaçao among the slaves at the estates that were your dowry there. You know that since the unrest in Haiti and Santo Domingo with Toussaint L'Ouverture and all this there have been rumors of slave uprisings everywhere. In any event, the properties are very lucrative and produce a large part of the income that goes to Jan and your mother, so Jan resolved to go and see what was happening.

Well, he had hardly been in port in Paramaribo for a day when he was felled with malaria. He lingered only a few days and died on the 2nd of December last....

I put the letter down on the windowsill and looked out. Below, the vegetable sellers were still bargaining for tomatoes.

Jan was dead. He had died of malaria in a tropical port on the other side of the world while we were engaged at Hohenlinden, while I fought with sword in the snow.

Jan was dead.

I was a widow in fact.

I picked up the letter again:

...needless to say, there are legal things to do. I don't know if you knew that Jan got a judgment against you in 1796—a divorce for adultery based on your desertion of him and the children. However, you were in France at the time, and never signed anything nor appeared in court. So the question is, are you a widow inheriting property? Or is the divorce previous to that valid, in which case everything should be immediately settled jointly on Claas and Francis, who are to be the wards of their paternal grandparents given their maternal grandmother's incapacity? That is the thing that no one knows. As for the property that remains your mother's but which Jan had been administering because of her incapacity, they are willing to make a cash settlement on you if you will agree to relinquish all claims to the house in Amsterdam and the sugar plantations in Curaçao in favor of your children when your mother dies.

Your mother seems amenable to this when she is lucid, and says that she never wants to see you again. She has become wondrously pious lately and faints of shame when your name is mentioned. But she is no longer convinced that Charles is alive, which is something.

In any event, whether you want to agree or contest this, you must sign things. If you get this please write to me immediately! I do not have any right to act in your behalf and I don't know what you want to do....

I had no idea what I wanted. The idea of my freedom from Jan was overwhelming enough.

Wild ideas ran through my head. I could go and get my children, sneak them over the border to France, live here in Paris with Michel in absolute bliss, or take the children and go live in the Saar, married and respectable, talking about apple harvests and haying.

For ten wild minutes I thought this.

Rationality intervened. Francis had no memory of me, and he was seven years old. For him, it would amount to being abducted by a stranger. Claas might have some vague recollections of a mother he had believed dead, but he was eleven now, not a cuddly child, a boy on the edge of youth who presumably had friends, went to school, had opinions of his own. He would not want to give up all that for an apartment in Paris, for a farm in the Saar where he didn't even speak the language and knew no one, a strange stepfather and a mother who dressed up like a man.

There would be no more campaigns for me. There would be no more of this life I was building. Who was to say Michel would want anything of the kind? I would be hopeless on a farm in the Saar, hopeless at any kind of life except that of adventuress. I did not want to live respectably in the country. The greatest happiness I had known was in the life of the road, in Italy and Bavaria, following the army. I wanted to stay with Michel in Paris, to go with him on his next posting wherever that might be, to know the world and everything in it with Michel, whose longings burned as hot as mine.

If I were pregnant, if there were a child that was ours from the beginning it would be different, but Claas would consider it a cruelty for me to rip him away from his life, and Francis—I could well imagine a child of seven taken in the darkness out of the country, away from anyone he loved. Francis would hate me.

I took a deep breath.

The children should stay with their grandparents then. I would not abduct them, would not try to fight in court the judgment of insanity that would surely be proffered against me, the taint of immoral living. No court outside of France would give them to me.

And the courts inside France wouldn't necessarily rule in my favor either, I thought with a shiver. Moreau had a great deal of influence, and Michel very little. An immoral woman who wanted to take two respectably-raised boys and bring them into a house where she lived as a kept mistress.... No, Republican virtue would not grant me my sons.

As for my mother, I hardly knew what to think. If she would not see me, then I would not try to see her. Whatever love there was had been broken so long that I didn't know what to do with the shards.

I put the letter down again. I wanted Michel. I wanted to put my head on his shoulder and feel worthy again. But he was far away with his father, tending a dying man. I could not ask him for anything, certainly not to hurry back to Paris so that he might take me to Amsterdam.

I shivered despite the heat. I did not want that house. There was nothing in it that I needed, and the thought of owning it disturbed me. As for plantations in Curaçao, I had never really considered them, had never thought about them at all. Hundreds of slaves might toil in the heat, lashed by overseers for the profit of owners on the other side of the world who did not even have to look at their handiwork. I did not want slave plantations. If they would settle cash on me to make it simpler, I would take the cash and leave the rest. I could use cash. Cash is always insurance against the future.

The future without Michel, some part of me whispered, and I tried to stifle it, but the part would not be still. Passion wanes, love dies. Do you think he will love you still when you are thirty? When you are forty? Do you think he will live twenty years, storming into the face of the guns? Your father did not see his fortieth birthday, and is not Michel the picture of the same careless gallantry, the same reckless will? If you do not want to die an old, mad whore you had best have money of your own put by in good Swiss banks, insurance against waning desire and bullets alike.

19 Fructidor of the Year IX
Dearest Michel,

I am glad to hear that your father is better. I hope that his recovery will be swift and complete.

I have had a letter from my cousin telling me that my husband is dead. As you guess, I do not mourn. But there is a great deal of legal paperwork that requires my signature. I wish I could talk with you about it, but I know that isn't possible.

I am leaving Paris for a brief time. I have agreed to meet the attorneys in Lille, so that I do not have to physically place myself in their power as I would if I went to Amsterdam. My cousin Louisa will be there, and you need not worry that something will happen to me. I will be very, very careful indeed. To that end, I have asked Auguste and Isabella to both go with me to Lille, and you know Auguste can be as dogged a protector as one could wish.

Perhaps I should be sad or sorry that Jan is dead. But I cannot be. No matter what comes, I can imagine no worse fate than to be a wife, tied forever to someone who owns you and can do as they wish with your body, your property, even your children. I will never be able to get my children back. If I had not been a wife, they would be mine. I wish they were bastards. Surely in all the world there is nothing that should be pitied so much as a wife!

I miss you terribly, and I hope that you are not too badly sunburned.

Love from your,

Elza

* * *

28 Fructidor of the Year IX
Dearest Elza,

I wish I could say that I'm sorry your husband is dead, but I'm not. What does this mean about your children? Why can't you take them? If they are coming to Paris with you we will work that out. It would be easier if I were there, but I'm not.

Dearest, I hardly know what to say. I am not good with words. If I could simply put my arms around you and tell you that we will do the best we can, you would know what I mean, what I want to say.

Do not you think there are some people who marry for love and who may be happy?

My father is doing better, and I begin to think that he will live. His breathing is better, and when the doctor puts the paper tube to his chest and listens he says his lungs are clearer than they were.

The barley harvest is upon us. Last spring my father put some in the field behind the apple orchard. It's not a big field, so I have been getting the barley in by myself, which is good hard work, which I need. Yes, I am very sunburned, but I have been before you know.

I miss you so much. I will be back to Paris soon, I hope. After there is the barley there are the apples, and my father can't do it this year, but as soon as the apples are in I will leave for Paris and for you.

With all my love,

Michel

* * *

9 Vendemiaire of the Year X
Beloved Michel,

I am still in Lille. No, nothing is wrong, other than the need of lawyers to run back and forth. The terms they proposed to me were not acceptable. Which sent them back to Amsterdam to talk to Jan's father, and then back here with different terms. They want to give me nothing, of course. And I do not think we will come to an agreement.

I'm so glad that Isabella and Auguste came with me! We sometimes make a gloomy and quiet little party, but I do not feel entirely alone under their eyes, under the way they say "Madame Ringeling ci-devant" as though I did not have a right to the name. I do not claim your protection, and Auguste bristles at any slight to my reputation, as soiled as it may be. I begin to feel that these good friends are more my family than those related by blood or law who are picking me apart.

You ask if I do not think that some people who marry for love may be happy. Some are happier than others. I do not see how one can call it love, wanting to own another person. Oh yes, some husbands are indulgent! You see I permit my wife to read, and to manage her own pocket change? She may even go out in the carriage for half an afternoon without telling me where she is going.

But I do not think that ownership and happiness can readily exist together, whenever one human being owns another. And in all countries in the world, ours less than most, marriage is nothing *else. It is as well to ask a slave if they are not happy! If I were a slave, I should prefer a soft master to a hard one, but better yet my freedom!*

Of course you are harvesting apples! And I miss you too.

Your adoring,

Elza

* * *

30 Vendemiaire of the Year X

Dearest Elza,

I am back in Paris, and you are still in Lille, I suppose. I trust it's all going well, and that you are probably on your way back. If not, I will come to Lille on the moment.

Is marriage such slavery for women? Could not one marry an equal and love them as such? Or do our laws, our society, render even that good intention impossible?

What do you think of Santo Domingo, just as a question? I mean, about going there?

Love,

Michel

I arrived home in Paris from Lille on a beautiful autumn day. When I took Nestor to the stable I saw that Eleazar wasn't there, so I wasn't surprised that the apartment was empty. And why shouldn't Michel be away? It was the middle of the afternoon and Michel had not known that I was arriving. There were dozens of places he might be and things he might be doing.

By nine 'o clock I was starting to get a bit irritated. I had arranged for a light dinner that I hoped he would be home to eat, but by ten I was getting hungry and considered just going ahead without him. I had not seen him in more than three months, between his journey and mine. I poured myself a glass of wine and nibbled on some olives and bread, telling myself to be fair. He had not known I was arriving. He had probably decided to have dinner in a tavern with one of his friends rather than a cheerless dinner at home alone.

It was after eleven when I heard his step on the stair, quick and heavy. He opened the door and the expression on his face was as joyful as I could have wished. I ran into his arms and there was a great deal of kissing and cooing before any coherent conversation.

"I saw Nestor," he said, "When I was bringing Eleazar in, and I knew you must be back. Elza." He ran his hands over my hair, as though reminding himself what it felt like. My hair had grown in three months, long enough to pin up again and to train in curls over my ears. His touch was light, and his eyes were warm.

Something else registered.

"What happened to your hair?" I asked suddenly. His hair was cut short in the popular Brutus cut, layered to a finger's length all over, just brushing the top of his collar in the back. It looked very fashionable and neat. But I missed that flow of long copper hair, long as the middle of his back.

Michel looked sheepish. "I got it cut."

"I see that," I said. It did look nice. Shorter, it had some fullness and body. And really the long tails had gone out of fashion entirely.

"Do you like it?" Michel looked unwarrantedly shy. "Nobody really wears it that long anymore. Not in Paris. I mean, they do in Saar Louis, but when I came back to town it seemed like it was time for a change."

"I think you look uncommonly handsome," I said, smiling.

"That's what Madame Bonaparte said," he said.

My eyebrows rose straight up. "Joséphine?"

"I just came back from Malmaison," he said. "You know. The country house she bought just outside Paris. I was at a picnic."

"With Joséphine?" I would not have thought he was Joséphine's taste, tight white pants or not. I would not have thought that she would have been indiscreet after all the talk about a man named Hippolyte Charles a few years ago, who had been rumored to be her lover to her detriment and the fury of the First Consul. Only Michel would be foolish enough to step into that fire.

He shifted from foot to foot. "She was there. So was Bonaparte and a whole lot of other people."

"Oh." Relief must have showed in my face. "That kind of picnic." I smiled at him. "Politics. You know, I can't really see you and Joséphine."

Michel didn't laugh. "No?"

"No," I said, wondering if it were all one sided. Joséphine inspired admirers, and I understood that, could even see how her kindness and quiet might attract. Michel was acting like a man with a guilty secret, or perhaps I was just being suspicious. And jealous.

Joséphine was beautiful.

"Is it because of my birth?" he asked, quite seriously.

"No, it's because she's married to the First Consul," I said. "Michel, he is not a man to cross."

"I wouldn't," he said. "I mean, I don't think of her that way. I can't imagine...." He seemed suddenly all confusion, and I wondered if I had misread something. "The First Consul is all amiability."

"He is?"

"Yes." Michel seemed now on firmer ground. "I've been out to Malmaison about a dozen times. We've spent hours in his study, talking about tactics and our different experiences in Italy and Germany. We've never been in the same command, so it's all different. I was in Army of the Rhine all along. We spent two hours talking about Hohenlinden. Very different conditions than Marengo. Marengo was close, let me tell you. Privately he knows how tight it was. Elza, he's the best I've ever seen!"

I felt my shoulders relaxing from a tension I didn't know they held. "Is he?"

Michel nodded, and went to take his coat off. He poured himself a glass of the wine. "Amazing. I've worked with men who were good, but I've never seen anything like him."

"Is he better than you?" I asked, watching his intent face. The haircut really did make him look different.

Michel grinned. "Ten times better. I would feel like a boy learning my trade again if it weren't that he makes it clear that he is as filled with admiration as I am. It's not hollow praise. I mean, I know what it is to be flattered. I'm not an idiot. He's not flattering when he wants to know what I would do with this situation or that, when he asks how I would take on a certain problem. He wants to know how best to use me. Because he knows I'm good."

"You are," I said. "And if you are not Moreau's creature, then he will use you. He has the power to give you a command. Michel, you are getting so much better at politics."

Michel shrugged. "It has nothing to do with politics. Bonaparte knows how to get things done. I understand it now. He's the kind of general anyone would give anything to serve under. He's that good. The kind of genius that comes along once in a century or two." His eyes met mine, clear and filled with light. "Grant me that I know what I'm looking at when I see it."

"I do," I said. I wet my lips, seeing not Michel but the First Consul as he had been in Milan, unanticipatedly kind. I had wanted to make foolish promises, to swear things that have no place in a courtesan's life. But Michel had a sword to give.

I went and put my arms around him.

"Do you see it?" he asked.

I nodded. "Yes. And I'm glad that you do."

Michel shook his head a little ruefully. "Sometimes you suddenly meet the person you were born to serve. That may sound poetic and silly, but I think you understand."

"He's our hope of keeping the things we've won. My liberty." I said the sensible things, and they were true, but they did not even begin to explain the complexity of it, of what I knew of Michel's yielding nature.

"Not to go all the way back to 1648," he said. "Not to lose everything we fought for in the Revolution, to have a Bourbon prince on the throne and the end of everything. Elza, I like Saar Louis, and I like being home, but that world is too small for me. If I had to stay there I would go mad. If I had to spend my life with nothing bigger." His arms tightened around me. "This is big. So very big."

I put my head against his shoulder. "I know." He smelled the same. That had not changed. "Like touching fire."

I felt him nod against the top of my head. "We were talking about a hypothetical campaign on Vienna, and he has never campaigned in Bavaria and Franconia, so I was telling him about the roads, and what I would do. He laughed and said I should be his Hephaistion."

I smiled against him, pressed my lips to the hollow of his throat above his collar. "You too are Alexander?"

"Hum?" Michel bent his mouth to my hair, nuzzling at me.

"Alexander in Asia," I said. "I've done that play two hundred times. I was Sisygambis, the queen mother of Persia. She's been captured after the Battle of Issos, and Alexander comes to see her, bringing Hephaistion with him. They come in together and Hephaistion is taller and more handsome so...."

Michel kissed me and the rest of the history lesson was lost.

In the morning we lay together in drowsy silence, lapped together in the warmth of the duvet.

"I'm sorry," he whispered.

"For what?" I was only half awake, and could not think how he had given offense.

"For not being in Lille with you."

I sighed, rolling into his arms. "Jan is dead, and I am glad of that. But he had filed divorce papers before that, charging me with adultery. So his father's lawyers are saying that I forfeited all my property to him before his death, and that rather than his widow, who would still have the rights to my dower property, I am only his former wife, disgraced. And that therefore I have no rights to anything, not my children, and not my own family's money."

Michel stroked my hair.

I bent my face against his shoulder. "I should never have married him. If I had not been stupid when I was young! But I thought he loved me, you see."

"I do see," Michel said. His hands did not stop, gentle and quiet.

"You asked me if I thought equals could marry." I put my cheek against his chest. "Not in this world, Michel. Not when a woman belongs to her husband, body and soul. Not when she cannot vote and cannot go to war, when she cannot divorce him on equal terms. Not when her children belong to him. If a man wants an equal, he must take Plato's advice and seek an eromenos, because only with another man can he find someone to stand with on even terms."

"I'm not sure Plato is saying we should all sleep with men," he said. He kissed my brow gently.

"You want an equal, Michel. And you can have one in Charles, the way you cannot in Ida. That's how it works. We can't escape the world we live in."

"I don't see why we can't change the world we live in, instead," he said, and I heard that stubborn note creeping into his voice. "Do as we please, and damnation to the rest."

"I wish we could," I said, and leaned up and kissed him softly. "Oh, my darling, I wish we could!"

Loves Lost and Found

Corbineau refilled my glass. "And yet," he said. "Somehow you managed to foul it up, the both of you."

"It wasn't Mademoiselle Auguié's fault, Jean-Baptiste," I said. "Truly it wasn't. She of all people was not to blame." I took a deep breath, half leaning against him. "She was eight when Marie Antoinette went to the guillotine, when her father was arrested for being an aristocrat. Her mother killed herself in front of Aglae. She was eight years old, Jean-Baptiste, when she and her sisters were thrown into prison, in to one of the cattle houses full of every kind of prisoner awaiting the guillotine. Her sisters were four and six." I took a drink of my brandy. "It amused the guards to throw in a basket of boiled potatoes and let the inmates fight for them. And yet she survived, she and her sisters, and in a few weeks one of their mother's friends was arrested and thrown into the same prison with them."

"Joséphine de Beauharnais," Corbineau said.

I nodded. "Her husband had been executed and she was scheduled to die. Separated from her own son and daughter, she took her friend's children under her wing, braiding their hair and picking the lice, caring for them as if they were her own daughters. And then Paul Barras came to her with his devil's bargain. He had wanted her, you see, when she was Vicomtesse de Beauharnais, but she had refused him. Now he had a bargain for her—to live with him as his mistress, obeying him in all things, and thus escape the blade."

Corbineau refilled his own glass. "A pretty offer," he said sharply.

"But Joséphine drove a bargain with him. Her release, and that of the Auguié girls. The Auguié girls remanded to her custody, and her own children likewise. Barras agreed, and so Joséphine and the five children lived together. When she married General Bonaparte, he took on all five of them, paid the Auguié girls' school tuitions as he did Joséphine's own daughter's, acted as stepfather to them all. Even when times changed, when M. Auguié was released from prison, Aglae stayed with Joséphine as a lady in waiting and companion to her daughter, Hortense, as much Joséphine's daughter as any other. This was the girl the Emperor offered Michel."

I took a long drink, letting the brandy burn down my throat. "I understand why. Joséphine wanted a man who would be kind to Aglae, who would cherish her and who would never frighten her or mistreat her. Someone who would be mindful of her scars and do his best to make her happy. That's Michel, of course. And she liked him, Aglae I mean. I don't think she fell madly in love with him, but that's not how aristocratic marriages are made. She liked him. She thought well of him. And the Emperor…" I took another sip and shrugged. "Well, what better Drypetis? Who dearer than a girl who was practically his daughter?"

"I see how that happened," Corbineau said.

"And Michel had to marry someone, didn't he? It wasn't going to be me." I was quite drunk, in that place of utter clarity between careless and asleep.

"Your past?"

I shrugged again. "My husband was dead by then, and while my past is bad enough there are more than a few merveilluses who have made good and become respectable. But can you see me a good wife, Jean-Baptiste?"

He shook his head, smiling.

"My husband is dead. And I will never put myself in that trap again, my friend. Not even for a man I love. And any man who loves me should know better than to ask. I will not be owned, and trying to own me that way again does not speak of love to me." My voice broke, and I was surprised to hear it so.

"Did he ask?"

"He asked if I thought it was impossible to have a happy marriage, a marriage of equals. And I said that it was not, for how can it ever be a marriage of equals when one holds all the cards? How can it be like this, like you and I, Jean-Baptiste, when one of us is a woman?"

"One of us is a woman," he said.

"You know what I mean," I replied. "Even Plato says it cannot be. True love, true friendship, can only flourish when no one owns the other. A slave may be grateful to have a kind master rather than a cruel one, but she would rather have no master at all. He should own me, body and soul. And that I will not bear, Jean-Baptiste! I will not."

Corbineau gave me a rueful smile. "He owns too much of your soul already."

I blinked, surprised to find tears in my eyes. "He does. I shall love him with all my heart, all of my life. I have always loved him, as much when it brought grief as joy. But I will not give him power over me, to have all my happiness in his hands. Do you see why, my friend?"

"I do," he said, his arm about me like a brother. "Too many wounds, dear one. And we do not live in Plato's world. We cannot have erastes and eromenos in this time."

"We are all the prisoners of our birthdays," I said, "Though we try to transcend them. We are creatures of our times, and sometimes our souls peek through the cracks and yearn for the sky. And then we are magnificent creatures."

"You are magnificent," he said, "For all your scars."

I blinked at him through tears. "I think you're pretty good too."

Corbineau laughed and handed me my cravat for a handkerchief. "Dear one, we should clear out of here. It's after three, and I unfortunately have to report in the morning. Some little matter of getting whalloped by Subervie at Cunaxa. But at least I will whallop back next week at Marathon!" He grinned at me. "I'm looking forward to dusting Reille, since he's got the dratted Persians again and I am all Athens!"

I laughed and let him help me up. The bar was almost empty, and the barmaid with dark circles under her eyes had begun wiping down tables. "Why does Reille keep getting the Persians?"

"The Marshal keeps giving them to him. Says he does the best job with them. And so he's Mardonias and the overall Persian command next week. The Marshal swears Reille's going to win Platea, though I don't see how."

"He could keep Mardonias from getting killed," I said. The night air hit me like a cool blanket as we came outside. "That would probably do it."

"Maybe." Corbineau shrugged. "I haven't done my reading for that one yet. I stake my life that we've got a hundred pages a day assigned, and Xenophon's not exactly light."

"Surely you're reading in translation?" I asked.

"Of course. Think we sans-culottes know Greek?" Corbineau steered around a dubious looking puddle. "I'm the son of a horse trader, Elza. I stopped school when I was fourteen. But I know horses."

"Which is pretty important in a cavalry officer," I observed.

"Well, yes. But we're new men, and we're hearing about all these historical things for the first time. Half of us thought Alexander the Great was some guy in an opera until we got to the School of War!"

"Michel was a cooper's son," I said. "He left school at eleven for an apprenticeship, when he'd learned to read and write and figure enough."

"Subervie's father is a tavern keeper," Corbineau said. "In Lannes' hometown. If Lannes can do it, why not the busboy?"

"Why not indeed?" I said. "And your friend Reille?"

"Oh, he's the best of us," Corbineau said, stepping around a puddle in the street. "His father's a merchant with business in the West Indies. His older sister was married to an impoverished Chevalier before the Revolution, his title and her Creole money, so Honoré went to proper school in Paris and learned to be a gentleman. He'd even got a little Latin, enough for an epigram or two, before the Terror blew through like a wind and consigned all to the rubbish heap. He was seventeen and ran off and joined the army. His sister's husband went to the guillotine, helped along by dear old Fouché. There's a man he's got no love for."

"Interesting," I said. That was one officer at least with reason for a grudge, and ready access to the School of War and headquarters.

Corbineau shot me a look. "I thought you'd find it so. You and Honoré wouldn't be a bad combination."

I laughed. Of course I could not tell him I was seeking a spy, so he had assumed my interest was purely prurient. But I could certainly ask more without suspicion. "Really, Jean-Baptiste?"

Corbineau nodded. "He's a year older than you, not quite thirty, a bachelor, handsome in a very tall and looming sort of way, and clever as a hare. He's a bit too self-conscious about his accent, he studies all the time, and he's lethal quick with a blade. You'd get along like a house on fire."

"You think I should be seeing a bookworm?"

"He's quiet, but when he says something it's worth listening to. Even the Marshal listens. He's that steady. You might do very well together." Jean-Baptiste looked at me sideways. "You don't have to always be looking for trouble. You could see someone who would be no trouble at all to you. It might be a nice change of pace."

"And you will be my fairy godmother?"

"None other," Corbineau said.

We stood in front of my lodging. "And you think he'd like Charles?" I found it hard to believe that very many men besides Michel would.

"He'd find Charles a little strange," Corbineau acknowledged. "But I expect Honoré would get used to him. Good night, dear sister."

"Good night," I said, and started up the steps, wondering if the door was unlocked. I should have to ring if it weren't.

It was. I was about to ring when a man's voice called out, "You do not belong on the porch, gentlemen!"

I looked about, at Corbineau standing in the street.

"I need to come in," I said.

"You have mistaken the house," the voice said loudly. "Now be off with you!"

"I have not," I said. "I need to see Madame St. Elme."

"Not at half past three in the morning, you don't," he said, stepping into the light, a heavy man with a cudgel in one hand, whom I'd seen yesterday afternoon splitting wood out back. "This is a respectable house, not a brothel. Now clear off!"

"I..."

He took a step closer, the cudgel raised. "Off with ye! Or I'll not wait for the gendarmes!"

Corbineau dragged at my arm. "Come on, Charles," he said. "My friend here is inebriated. Your pardon." He half pulled me down the street.

"What are you doing?" I demanded. "Jean-Baptiste, that is the right house!"

"Do you want the entire town to know that Charles van Aylde is Madame St. Elme?" he asked. "Because that's what it's going to take to get in there. If you want to be able to be Charles, you've got to drop it."

I sighed and sat down on the rim of the public pump down the street. "No, I don't want everyone to know about Charles. But I do want my bed."

"Well, you can't have it," Corbineau said. "You can't get in there in the middle of the night smelling like drink and dressed like Charles."

"Wonderful," I said. "I suppose I'll just have to walk around until morning."

"You could come to my billet," Corbineau said. "No one will care there. Everybody's in and out drunk when they've had leave anyhow. And then we could both get some sleep."

"You could just go sleep," I said.

He laughed. "And leave you on the town? No, thank you! I'd like for Boulogne to still be here in the morning! Come on, Charles. Come back to my billet and sleep."

"All right." I got up from the pump. It was still hours till dawn, the sky not even beginning to pale. It must be still short of four.

"The only catch is that I'm billeted in Montreuil," he said. "It's about 15 km."

"Lovely," I said. "A nice walk to clear our heads."

We veered off the main road as soon as it left the walls, following a track that led upward along the cliffs and south. Neatly lettered signs pointed to Montreuil and the little hamlets further along the coast, and to the observation pavilion the Emperor had built.

"It's a good way," Corbineau said. "Usually I'm on horseback, but I didn't want to have to find a place to put her in town while I saw you. She's a menace, and if you leave her with someone she doesn't know, she bites."

I scratched my head. "That dapple mare you used to have?"

He nodded. "Pomona. Pomme for short. I hate her."

"Then why do you keep her?" I asked.

"She's a good warhorse," he said. "A devil in a fight. She's fast and light, and she's the smartest horse I've ever seen. We just don't get along is all. I'd sell her in a heartbeat if I thought I'd get what she's worth. But everybody I know knows about her and wouldn't buy her on a bet."

"If you hadn't told me, you might have sold her to me," I said. "I need a new horse before long. I love Nestor, and he's all heart, but he's twenty-three. I rode him down the Loire not too long ago, in nice weather on good roads, and he was feeling it. He needs an easier life at his age."

"He's gentle as a lamb, isn't he?" Corbineau said. "You might talk to Subervie. He's looking for a horse for his son to learn on. The boy's four, and Gervais wants a well trained horse that will last him a few years, just going around the paddock and park teaching the boy. He doesn't want a hack, because he wants the boy to learn on a good horse with good habits."

"I might talk to him at that," I said, though my chest ached at the idea of selling Nestor. I couldn't afford to keep two horses, and I had no place to put an old horse out to pasture. Subervie had seemed like a kind man and a responsible one, not the sort to sell an old horse for meat when he got a little stiff, who would appreciate Nestor's steady temperament teaching a little boy to ride.

"You can buy Pomme anytime you want," Corbineau said darkly. "Special bargain price if you don't look at her first."

"That bad?"

"She hates me."

I burst out laughing. "Hates you? And you the son of a horse trader?"

"My father's to thank for her," he said. "Palmed her off on me. Swore up and down she was fantastic."

"What's her bloodline?" I asked.

"Half Lusitano, half heaven knows," Corbineau said. "My father had a cart horse accidentally serviced by one of his blood stallions. She's eight years old, with a mouth like steel and the temperament of my maiden aunt."

"I'll have to see this peerless gem," I said.

We crested a rise, and before us was the ocean. The tide was high, crashing on the rocks below, white spray flying and glittering in the starlight. Overhead, the stars of summer were sinking into the sea, Sirius the dog star rising in the east, herald of the sun. My heart lifted with it, as though its winking faint light held some gift for me, some dream or omen.

My head was clearing from the drink, leaving me with a small, nagging headache. Corbineau stopped. "Pretty, isn't it?"

"Beautiful," I said.

Out to sea I could see lights, a ship cruising northward along the coast, her white sails spread to catch a following wind, Lion about her solitary patrol. Captain Arnold must never get out of sight of France. Lion was the tip of the spear, their first warning of invasion.

"There goes Lion," I said.

Corbineau looked at me sharply. "How do you know her name?"

"Someone must have mentioned it," I said. How could he be slipping someone ashore? The currents must be treacherous around the rocks, and I didn't see how, with a sea like this one, it would be possible to bring a small boat in without capsizing. How was Captain Arnold doing it? And yet he must be, at least twice a week.

And, like clockwork, we heard approaching hooves. Two chasseurs came trotting along the path toward us, checked when they saw us. "Name and business?"

"Major Corbineau, VI Corps, attached to the School of War," Corbineau answered, stepping out. "My friend, M. van Aylde. On our way to Montreuil to the School of War."

"Very well. Pass, major." We went on, walking silently, sometimes in sight of the sea, sometimes not.

How was Captain Arnold doing it? How was the inside man doing it? Twice more along the heights patrols passed us, once requiring our papers. The coastal route was very heavily patrolled, and a boat coming ashore would be visible for a long time before it reached the beach. The thing this made clear to me was that the inside man must be in uniform, someone who seemed to have a likely reason to go back and forth along the cliffs at night. He must be able to answer the guards' challenges legitimately.

I was musing, the sea air clearing my head, and it startled me when Corbineau spoke. "The thing I don't understand is this. Why did the Marshal throw you over? All right, he was going to marry Mademoiselle Auguié. What's that to do with you?"

I sighed. It was on the tip of my lips to say, that's exactly what the Emperor said, but then I should have to explain why I had been gossiping about Ney with the Emperor. "It was complicated," I said. I tilted my head back, looking up at the stars now beginning to pale in the east, the sky dove gray on the horizon.

Respect for the Flag

We had gone back to Malmaison a few days later. There was lawn bowling to take advantage of the last of the good weather, though the leaves were off the trees and it was already late in the year. He excused himself early and I was surprised to see him in time for dinner.

We went out somewhere nice, a restaurant I had been wanting to visit, and said that I hoped he hadn't given offense by excusing himself.

Michel shrugged. "Napoleon wasn't there. He had business in town, so it was just Joséphine and the girls."

"The girls?" I nodded absently to the waiter as he put my fish in front of me.

"Her daughter Hortense and her friend, Aglae Auguié."

I put down my fish knife. "Joséphine had you all the way out to Malmaison to go lawn bowling with her, Hortense, and her friend?"

"Her goddaughter, really," Michel said, taking a mouthful of his fish. "Joséphine practically raised her and her sisters after their mother died in the Terror. They came to get her the day Marie Antoinette was arrested, and she committed suicide by jumping out of a window right in front of Aglae."

"Those little girls." I remembered breakfasting with Therese, the little girls she had mentioned whose freedom had been part of Joséphine's bargain with Barras. "But surely they're young," I said. Too young for matchmaking. Surely.

Michel didn't look up from his fish. "Aglae will be eighteen in the spring. It's been eight years, Elza."

"I suppose it has," I said. It had been five and a half years since I had left Jan, since 1796, the early days of the Directory. While I was in Lille I had passed my twenty-fifth birthday. And Aglae Auguié was seventeen. Which would explain why Joséphine hadn't invited me to Malmaison. A reason other than that while I had been Moreau's mistress at the same time she was Barras', she was now a wife and I was still a whore.

"Is she pretty?" I asked casually. "Mademoiselle Auguié, I mean."

Michel's eyes stayed on his plate. "Yes, she's pretty. Dark hair, dark eyes. She's very shy, graceful and quiet."

I felt the ice settle in my stomach. "I see," I said. Sensible. I would be sensible. I took a long sip of wine, proud that my hands didn't shake at all. "I suppose she would make a fine wife."

Michel looked up, and it was all written in his eyes, wretchedness and pride, desire and guilt.

I raised an eyebrow coolly. "I suppose you must marry, and it may as well be Mademoiselle Auguié as anyone. I'm sure she's a very accomplished young lady."

He opened his mouth and closed it again. "I'm not. I haven't...."

"Haven't what, Michel?" There was no tremor in my voice. I was very proud of that.

"Haven't made love to her. Haven't promised anything or said anything. Haven't done anything except lawn bowling and looking at plants in the greenhouse." He reached for his glass and knocked it over, sending wine spilling over the tablecloth. Fortunately, it was nearly empty, and he mopped at it with the napkin, hoping the waiter wouldn't notice. I sat perfectly still and didn't help.

"But you mean to," I said.

He looked up, the stained napkin, spotted as though with blood, held to his chest. "No. I don't mean to at all. It's flattering that she's interested. After all, she's the closest thing to a princess. Her ancestors fought for St. Louis in the crusades. They had a chateau before the Revolution that D'Artagnan visited. All that's gone now, but she is who she is."

"A princess," I said, "the goal of every heroic woodcutter's son." My voice was not acid. Instead it broke. "There's a fantasy you can attain. The hand of the virtuous young princess, a maiden descended from knights and kings. Of course. That's how all the fairy tales go."

"Elza." He reached for my hand on the table but it was too far.

"Do you expect me to stop you?" I asked. I wasn't crying. I wasn't. But I felt the tears choking in my throat. "Do you expect me to beg you and plead with you? If so, you don't know me well enough, Michel. I know the extent of your ambition. Hephaistion must have Drypetis."

He looked confused. "Who's Drypetis?"

I shook my head. "Michel, for Heaven's sake. Haven't you read Arrian?

The Campaigns of Alexander?"

"No," Michel said shortly. "As you've just pointed out, I'm a peasant. I have no fucking idea who Drypetis is."

It wasn't like him to use language like that off the field. He was usually very careful. "Hephaistion's wife," I said precisely. "The sister of Alexander's wife. So they would be related, you see."

"I don't," he said.

I looked away. "Michel, are you being stupid on purpose? Don't you see the political implications of marrying Bonaparte's goddaughter? Don't you see the pattern?"

He put his knife and fork down with a clatter. "Of course I see the political implications! Aren't you the one telling me to pay attention to Bonaparte? Aren't you the one who was saying that I needed to make a better impression? Now I'm trying to make a better impression, and you're complaining."

"I'm not complaining," I said. "I have absolutely no complaints that you're courting Bonaparte's goddaughter. As far as your career goes, it's a terribly smart move. Nothing could help you succeed in your ambitions more." My voice choked a moment before I went on. "I see you found your next goal, the one you were looking for. Hephaistion to Bonaparte's Alexander is a fine ambition. I don't imagine you could look much higher."

I couldn't speak without crying, so I got up and rushed from the table, out to the women's dressing room.

It was hung in pink silk, and there were Chinese screens around three or four necessary pots and basins. There was no one else in there, so I went in and stood behind a screen, trying to master myself. I don't know how long I stood there, my forehead against the lacquer.

When I came out, Michel was standing beside the door with his hat in his hand, shifting uncertainly from foot to foot as though he were considering barging in. "I've paid the check," he said. "Elza, let me take you home." He put my shawl around me, the nice new dark blue one that he had gotten me when we had come to Paris in the spring. I had hardly worn it.

"Yes," I said.

We walked. It wasn't really cold yet, and while we could have hired a carriage it just didn't seem worthwhile. We walked side by side, not touching. Overhead, there were stars. Orion was rising.

"Elza, I'm not going to do it," he said. "I'm not. It was just a thought. It was flattering."

"I know," I said, and took his arm. He tucked my hand against his side. "You are worthy of a princess."

He ducked his head.

"You are," I said, looking at his profile silhouetted against the distant lights nearer the river. He looked so different with his hair short. His strong jawline was clearer, jutting a bit too much for beauty, a good face but not a beautiful one, except to the eyes of love. "And I am no princess."

He sighed. "What do I really need a princess for? It's a fantasy, as you said. The kind of girl who would never have looked at me in Saar Louis, the kind of girl who rides past in a fine carriage and guardsmen salute her. They protect her or die for her but never even have names."

"And now she needs you," I said. "An impoverished princess, rescued by a kindly godmother."

"Hardly impoverished," Michel said. "Napoleon said he would dower her with 100,000 francs."

I looked at him sharply. "I see. Well, then. Not double Moreau's bid. Ten times Moreau's bid. And the girl too, of course."

He stopped, turned half away from me. I heard his breath quicken. "I already told you, I'm not going to do it. Even though he offered me Inspector General of Cavalry, command of all the cavalry in France."

"Oh my God." I put my hands to my face. "Oh Michel."

"I don't know if that's contingent on marrying Aglae. It may not be," he said.

"He wants you that much?"

"Does that surprise you?" His voice was a little hard, but I couldn't see his face.

"No," I said. "It doesn't surprise me at all." It didn't. It clicked into place like something that had always fit there. "I asked him in Milan what the price of a general was. He said it was about the same as a companion."

"In Milan? I thought you met him at some Directory party in Paris." Michel sounded confused, not accusatory.

"No," I said. "It was in Milan after Marengo. I spent the night with him." I didn't know if lies or truth would hurt worse, or whether I wanted to hurt or not.

"You didn't tell me that," he said.

"You didn't ask," I replied.

His fingers tightened on my hand, almost bruising me through the gloves. "Was he good?" he asked harshly.

"He was very good," I said. I bit down on my lip until I tasted blood, his hand crushing mine. "He was amazingly good."

"Better than me?"

Only the most absolute naïf would ask a question like that. The streets were silent around us, Orion's belt lifting over the city. "No, Michel. Not even close to better."

His hand loosened, then his arm went around my waist. I heard him exhale. "Well, that's something."

I let myself lean into his arm a little. "I'm sure you would enjoy buggering him, if that's what you mean."

"Elza! For God's sake!" He dropped his arm and stepped back, almost losing his hat. "Where do you get these things?"

"I'm going to buy you a copy of Arrian and make you eat it," I said. "And I can guess from Charles that you might like it a great deal."

"Charles. Now that's my twist, not yours?" His voice was dry. I wished I could see his face, but it was too dark.

"It's mine too," I said. "But I'm not the one who's troubled by you liking to pretend I'm a man."

He took three steps toward me, his hand coming up. It closed on air. His teeth were set, eyes blazing. "Elza, that is not fair. It's not fair to use that...."

"It's not fair to use that to hurt you because you're going to marry someone else? If I'm going to be out on the street again, at least I want to get a few licks of my own in first," I snapped. "I promise you, I will hurt you every bit as much as you hurt me."

"You're a bitch." He stood looking at me as if he'd never seen me before. I was sure his dewy eyed princess never acted like this.

"That's right. I am." I met his eyes. "I'm every bit as cruel as you are."

"I know," he said. "That's the thing I love."

I closed my eyes. "Michel, no." I took a step back, the cobblestones uneven under my feet. "Don't say you love me."

"But I do," he said, and his voice was choked too. "We're both cruel and proud and selfish, and we deserve each other."

I stepped forward into his arms. I knew they would be there, and they were. "We probably do deserve each other. You like to be kicked, and I like to kick you. And I don't have enough pride to walk away from you. You're going to marry some sweet weeping virgin, and I'm going to wish you well." I put my forehead against his shoulder, turned my head and brushed my closed eyes against his chin, letting him feel the prickle of tears on my lashes.

"I'm not going to," he said. "I'll do something else. I could join the expedition to Santo Domingo instead. I wrote you about that, remember?"

"Instead of being Inspector General of Cavalry? Michel, that's madness."

"Well, yes," he said. "Now let's go home."

"Yes," I said.

It would not resolve anything, the ballet of our bodies, the graceful, violent dance of joining. But there was nothing really to resolve.

Michel wrote to the First Consul requesting his official permission to join the expedition to Santo Domingo. There was no immediate reply.

The invitations to Malmaison ceased. Perhaps it was because the weather turned bad, cold and rainy, sometimes icing the trees in the morning, and the lawn parties ended. Perhaps it was because the First Consul took it as spurning friendship and patronage both. If it were so, he did nothing in retaliation. The invitations ceased, and the letter was unanswered.

Michel continued in Paris, on full pay, with no appointment whatsoever and time on his hands.

"I'll get Santo Domingo," he said over breakfast on the sixth day. "I'm sure I will. There may be a lot of generals clamoring to go deal with slave revolts and malaria, but it would be out of the way. Very, very far out of the way."

Leave on full pay is nice. After a little more than six months of it he was starting to get testy.

Michel poured himself another cup of coffee with three spoons of sugar. "The problem is that everyone wants it. Because there's peace. Nobody is going to see any action here anytime soon. It will all be better as soon as we're back in the field."

"We?" I raised an eyebrow.

Michel grinned and leaned back in his chair. "We. You're coming to Santo Domingo with me. So you'd better go order some tropical clothes for you and Charles. If I'm going to go off into a snaky jungle chasing Spaniards, pirates and runaway slaves, you're going to come get malaria with me. It might be fun."

"Palm trees," I said. "Warm white sand." I leaned forward on my elbows. "Tropical breezes whispering through the veranda."

"Alligators as big as a man. Yellow fever. Snipers. Oh, and the British navy to get past on the way." He didn't stop smiling.

"We're at peace with the British," I said. "So there's one off your list. And I see why everyone wants to go."

"I'll get Santo Domingo," he said confidently. "You'll see."

I was less certain, but I went and ordered some summer weight clothes for Charles just in case. The expedition was due to sail in a few weeks, and if Michel was appointed at the last moment there would be no time for shopping. I got him things too. He would never remember to have thin cotton shirts made up.

To my surprise, Christmas decorations began to appear in the capital. Bakeries began to stock Christmas cakes, and there were plans for a Christmas Eve ball at the Tuileries. Very secular, of course, with more gold and silver ribbon than Virgin and Child, but it was something I had never seen in Paris before.

The First Consul had let it be known that Christmas was back.

There was some grumbling to the left, but for the most part everyone embraced gaiety. There was peace and plenty, the end of a good year, and the economy was rebounding from the disasters of the last days of the Directory. Decked with a thousand candles, Paris seemed indeed the City of Light.

The week before Christmas Michel was invited to escort Madame Bonaparte to the Opera. He opened the note from Joséphine soundlessly and handed it to me.

I read it and put it down on the table, lifted my hands to my mouth and breathed into them.

"Elza?"

"Of course you have to accept," I said. "If you don't, it will be a deadly insult. It will demonstrate that you are not of Bonaparte's party. And I don't think that's what you want to do."

"I'm happy to be of his party," Michel said. "I'm just trying not to marry his goddaughter."

"Mademoiselle Auguié will be there," I said. "There will be the three of you or maybe Hortense, and then at the first interval Joséphine and

Hortense will run into an old dear friend like Fortuneé Hamelin, and go join her, leaving you and Mademoiselle Auguié in the Consular box."

"Why do you think that?" Michel sounded vaguely defensive.

I put my hands over my eyes. "Because it's exactly what I would do."

Michel sat down heavily. "I can't do this. He should know that I'm happy to be in his party, that I would consider myself a true friend. He doesn't need to buy my loyalty. All he had to do was earn it. With or without Aglae or her dowry, if I give him my sword I will mean it. He should know that, Elza. I'd rather talk to him than Aglae."

I paced across the room, kicking my skirts out of the way. Outside the window it was raining again, a slow gray drizzle that resisted turning into snow. I pulled the curtain back and stood inside it, dark blue velvet sheltering me. I refrained from saying anything about the rival attractions of Mademoiselle Auguié and Napoleon. I knew which one I could fight and which one I couldn't.

Michel came up behind me and ducked under the curtain too, putting his arms around me from behind. I laced my fingers through his and leaned my head back against his shoulder.

"You have to go, Michel," I said.

"I know," he said.

If only it would snow, I thought. The rain was depressing. Through the rain-streaked glass I could see the roofs of Paris. "You're going to marry someone," I said. "It should be someone who will do you good. I have to get used to that. I don't really want you to throw your career away for me. And you're not going to do it."

"No," he said, bending his face against my hair. "I'm not."

"We're not going to Santo Domingo," I said.

"The expedition has sailed from Brest," he said. "With Leclerc in command."

I nodded. "Go to the Opera, Michel. Do what you're going to do."

His face was against my hair. "I could confide in Joséphine that an old wound has left me impotent."

I started laughing, as he knew I would. I turned in his arms. "And what am I then?"

"A trophy?" He smiled back at me, but the wistful look never left his eyes. "Elza, I want to do the right thing."

"And you want to be a hero of France, to go as far as your abilities will let you. I can't resolve this for you, Michel. Your conscience and your ambition are going to have to fight it out." I put my hand along the side of his face, warm and freshly shaven. The one thing he had resolved was that he was not marrying me. And I could live with that. I had not expected any different. "I will love you even if I hate you," I said.

He closed his eyes and nodded. "I will love you. Even if you hate me."

"Then go court your virgin bride," I said, pushing away from him gently. "Go do the thing you're going to do. Just don't talk to me about it. I don't want to know her virtues."

"You won't hurt her, will you?" he asked. "No matter how much reason I give you to hate her?"

I blinked back tears. "Michel, why would I hate a young girl sold into marriage with a man she hardly knows and can't possibly understand? I was that girl once. It's your fault, or mine, or Napoleon's or Joséphine's, but it's not Mademoiselle Auguié's. Out of all the twisted lot of us, it's not hers."

"I know," he said, and I pretended not to see the expression in his eyes.

He went to the Opera, and I stayed home. I wished I had more self-respect than to lie crying on our bed, his pillow stuffed under me, having a good wail. I beat the pillow a bit for good measure too.

This took only three quarters of an hour, leaving me the entire rest of the evening to fill. We didn't even have separate rooms. When he came in I would wake up and have to hear all about his evening. Even if I pretended to be asleep I would really be awake and that would be almost as bad.

In the end, I decided not to pretend I wasn't sitting up. Yes, it would be more awkward for him, coming in from courting one woman to go to bed with the other, and I would look like more of a desperate fool, but sitting up I could read, rather than lie in the dark listening for his steps.

He came in at a quarter till one. I put the novel I was reading down on the side table beside my brandy glass and went to take his coat. He didn't say anything.

I hung his coat and put his hat on the peg. He laid his gloves on the table by the door. His face was flushed from the cold. He didn't meet my eyes.

"I haven't decided," he said.

I found my glass and took a long drink of brandy. He went and poured some for himself, came and sat beside the fireplace.

"It's snowing," Michel said.

"Is it?" I went to the window and looked out. A few thick white flakes were falling.

"Do you remember last year?" he said.

"How could I forget?" I said. Tears prickled at my eyes again. I kept them on the window.

"Do you want me to tell you or do you want to imagine?" he asked.

I looked down at the glass in my hand. The fumes rose from the bowl where my hands warmed it. "I want you to tell me," I said. I had laid out the cards. You can never read for yourself accurately, but I thought he was going to marry her. It really didn't take cards to tell me that.

"You were right that Aglae was there," he said. "And Joséphine left us at the first interval. No Hortense. We talked about the opera. And horses."

"You talked about horses and she listened," I said, smiling even though I was crying.

"Something like that," he admitted. "She rides a little. At least she's not afraid of horses."

"That's good," I said.

"She seems so young. So vulnerable." There was a note in his voice that I knew. I closed my eyes. "She's fragile. When I think about the things that happened to her when she was a child, the Terror, her mother's suicide…."

"It excites you," I said quietly. "I understand that. Like the girls in Franconia. Fragile, crumpled flowers. You wonder how she'll bleed."

I heard him take a ragged breath and waited for a retort. When he said nothing, I turned around.

Michel was leaning forward, the almost empty glass between his hands, staring into the fire. The expression on his face was desolation itself.

I came around the chair and knelt down on the hearthrug beside him.

"I would never hurt her," he said. "I wouldn't."

"No," I said. "You wouldn't. But you would think about it."

He took my glass out of my hand and drained it. He already smelled like brandy, but his hands were steady. I passed him the decanter. He filled the glass again.

"You will think about it," I said. "And you'll never do it. You'll imagine hurting her, all the while touching her as gently as a lover can. You will treat her like something precious, imagining how you would hold her wrists, how you would bruise her if you could. And she will never know."

He dropped his head into his hands, his shoulders moving with his sobs.

I put my arms around him, gathering him against me like a child. "My darling. My Michel. I know you won't hurt her. I know you well enough to know that."

"And you know me well enough to know I want to," he said.

"I do," I said. "And when it's more than you can take, you'll bring it to me. I can hold it. I can bear anything you need. I need you like fire needs fire."

"She's a sweet, shy girl of seventeen," he said. "She's pretty and she's nice and she flirts like she's not sure what she's doing. When I kissed her hand, she trembled as if she stood in a high wind. She has big brown eyes and she cries at sad parts in operas. In a white dress you can see that she has slim little hips and her skin is so white you can see the veins. And I can't help imagining...." His voice broke and he leaned against me.

"I know," I said. I knew what he imagined, her stretched beneath him, ravaged innocence beneath his assault, white gown in tatters, white skin marked where his fingers pressed. Something of that must show in his eyes, no matter how courteous and appropriate his behavior. No wonder she trembled.

"She's nothing like you," he said. "And I love you."

"My dear," I said, "You don't know her. You may want her, but you can't love her."

"I want her," he said, pulling back, his mouth set grimly. "And she can have no idea what kind of man I am. She can have no idea what I'm capable of."

"I know exactly what you're capable of," I said, stroking his hair. "Remember, I've seen you in battle. I know what you're like."

"It was better in the field," he said, turning his head and pressing his lips to my palm. "It was easier."

"It was easier when I was Charles," I said. "Eromenos in all but name."

"It was," he said. His lips brushed at my hand, warm and sensual. When he kissed her hand it was not like this, I was certain. This was as innocent as pillage. "Whatever name you give it."

I caught my breath. I shifted on the hearthrug, bending my face to his thigh, corded muscle beneath white evening pants, kneeling like a penitent while he held my hand in his, fingers opened wide.

"We are twisted people," he said. "Fallen and twisted."

"Yes," I said. He could feel my hardening nipple against his leg. "Debauched and depraved, the villains of the world. Libertine revolutionaries."

"I thought I was a jumped up brute whose pretensions of gentility were only a thin foil covering my inner savage," he said, lifting my chin with one hand.

"You've been reading Gilray again," I said, a little breathlessly. "You should avoid the British press whenever possible."

"They're off France for the moment and onto Nelson's mistress," Michel said. "I could find it in my heart to feel sorry for the poor fellow and Lady Hamilton."

"Do you?" I said. My other hand stole up his leg, following the shape of the muscle.

"He has a bacchante, but I have a goddess."

"And you will make me want you," I said, meeting his eyes with a feral smile. "Whether I want to or not."

He let go of my wrist and took the neckline of my dress in each hand, ripping the fragile muslin in half, baring me to the waist.

I yelped. "Michel! I like this dress!" My nipples stood out dark and hard in the chill of the room, puckered and erect.

"Then take the rest of it off," he said, pulling it down so that I crouched naked in the firelight. "And open your legs."

"No," I said, standing. I reached for the side buttons of his trousers, unfastening the left side while he fumbled with the right. I sunk onto him in the chair, wrapping my legs around his waist and drawing him into me, long and tight and more than ready.

"My dress uniform…." he gasped. He was still wearing every bit of gold he owned.

I purred. "It is, isn't it? I think I have a fetish for gold oak leaves. All that braid. And that lovely sash." I untied it and pulled it from behind him, the silk tricolor weighted with gold fringe. I trailed the bullion over his belly, just above where his phallus was sunk into me.

He flinched. I trailed it back again, blue and red and white silk whispering against his skin. My eyes never left his as I tied it around my naked waist, the fringe dripping down over our joined bodies. "Now you can move," I said.

"No," he whispered, "Now you can," and thrust into me hard and savage. There was no word for it but fucking, moving together, pounding and grasping at each other's bodies, the sash slick against my waist, the heavy gold fringe slapping against my pubis with every thrust.

Coming was agony. It seemed to go on and on, half anger and half desire, too much and not quite enough. It took my hand in the end, rubbing just above our joined bodies, feeling him filling me. I screamed. And when I had nearly finished, when I was half fainting, he pushed me further still, hard until it was enough for him, as though it were agony for him too. I leaned forward, feeling the blood rushing from my head, a little dizzy as I was sometimes. I put my head against his shoulder.

"Here, Elza." He handed me the brandy glass. It was still full. He must have put it on the table.

I took a long drink. My head cleared.

Michel gave me a sideways smile. He looked like a picture of dissipation, his cravat askew, his uniform coat and waistcoat open, his trousers down and his shirt raised. I rode him still, feeling him slack inside me, the glorious tricolor sash around my waist. I took another sip of brandy, then held the glass to his lips.

"Oh God," I said, shaking my hair down. It fell to my shoulders now.

He lifted the fringe. It was very pretty against my belly, against his copper curls. "Do you think this counts as disrespect of the flag?"

I laughed. "Possibly. If you need another vice. You can add disrespect of the flag to your list of sins."

"Why is it that sometimes we're so good and sometimes we're so awful?"

I took another drink of the brandy. "Possibly because sometimes we're good and sometimes we're awful. We never stop playing some fantasy or another."

"My whole life is a fantasy," he said. "I'm afraid if I stop playing I'll wake up back in Saar Louis. None of it will have been real."

"It's real," I said, and kissed him tenderly. "And if I stop playing I'll wake up and see that I'm nothing."

He put his arms around me and held me close. "Ah, Elza. You're not nothing."

"I've made a mess of my life," I said, "And I have no one to blame but myself. If I had stayed with Jan I would be a respectable widow now, a widow with a lot of money and my children."

"How would you know he would die young?" he asked reasonably. "Jan might have lived thirty years more. You couldn't count on being a young widow."

It was on the tip of my tongue. If I were, would you marry me? There was no point in asking about a what if. I was not a respectable widow with a lot of money. I was Moreau's cast off, and that was as it was. Better to make the best of it.

I leaned down and kissed him again. "Come to bed," I whispered, "and hold me all night long." I could guarantee that he would not think of Mademoiselle Auguié that night. If she dreamed of him, if she lay in her virgin's bed imagining him, it would not be like this.

"If you don't take the sash off," he said.

Hephaistion and Drypetis

Dawn was growing over plowed fields green with grain, an apple orchard beside a farmhouse. We walked down the hill to a little bridge where the road crossed a stream, then led up to the citadel of Montreuil. It was not much of a citadel, some crumbling medieval walls repaired by one of the Louis, looking over this lush valley.

"I'll show you where my room is. I don't have to share, but it's kind of noisy because it's right next to the exercise yard for the stables. You can get some sleep, and I'll find some coffee and report."

"I hate to send you to work like this," I said, thinking that I had not done him such a good turn, keeping him out all night.

"I've done it before," Corbineau said jauntily as we passed through the guardpost for the School of War with a salute. "Some coffee and I'll be fine. As long as I don't run into a senior officer first."

"Major Corbineau, I would like a word!"

"Shit," Corbineau hissed, turning about sharply, drawing himself up to attention, unshaven and smelling of drink and smoke and sweat.

I spun about too. Michel was standing in the nearest doorway looking thunderous. And how not? It was nearly six in the morning, Corbineau creeping in the worse for wear, a pretty civilian with him.

And then his face went entirely blank. I have seen the mortally wounded stand thus, as though only half aware what has happened to them.

"Good morning, sir," Corbineau began, his eyes front. "I was assisting M. van Aylde here, as he is locked out of his lodging and I thought…."

"Elza."

"Michel." His hat was off, but otherwise he was in full field uniform, white breeches and blue coat, gold oak leaves scrolling over cuffs and collar. His eyes were as blue as the lightening sky.

"How have you been?" he asked, his voice sounding almost normal.

"Just fine," I said. "And you?"

His eyes were devouring my face, as though he were memorizing every line, as though he were afraid he had forgotten something. "I've been fine," he said.

"With your permission, I'll be getting ready for the exercise, sir," Corbineau said, looking as though he wished he were anywhere else rather than in a courtyard in Montreuil-sur-Mer with the two of us.

Michel blinked. "Exercise? Oh, Cunaxa. You said M. van Aylde was locked out of his room?"

"Just a misunderstanding with my landlady," I said quickly. "Major Corbineau was kind enough to suggest that I might rest a while in his lodging, and perhaps clean up a bit."

"I see," he said. All the while he did not stop looking at me, as though Corbineau were suddenly invisible. "You are old friends."

"Yes," I said. And of course only friends, as Michel well knew, knowing Corbineau as he did. Of course they never spoke of it, but the anger in his voice in the beginning had been for Corbineau putting him in a position where he could not fail to see that which he did not wish to see.

He glanced at Corbineau then, quickly, as though afraid I would vanish. "Major, you go on and get ready for the exercise. I'll let M. van Aylde use my room."

"There is no need for that," I protested, but Corbineau knew the time to stand and the time to flee. He had saluted and left before the words had left my mouth.

And once he had, Michel seemed not to know what to do. He stood in the doorway still, a window box above his head alive with red geraniums, the first rays of the sun washing the stone golden. "It's just this way."

"I do not want to inconvenience you," I said, my heart thudding in my chest.

"It's no inconvenience. I will be at the exercise. War games. We're doing the Battle of Cunaxa today."

"Xenophon's loss," I said, as I followed him in and up an abrupt flight of stairs into a short hall washed in blue paint.

"Xenophon's disaster," he said. The hall was too narrow for us to walk abreast.

"Do you like to play disasters?" I asked.

"You learn as much from disasters as victories," he said, opening the door at the end of the hall.

The house's main bedchamber was not large, and I should have thought a marshal could do better, though there was a comfortable four-poster by the open windows, an unlit fire, wardrobe and such. We had been better lodged in Munich, or at least more elegantly.

On the other hand, the view from the window was amazing, out over the street and the houses down hill, over the old medieval ramparts and green fields beneath, all the way to the scrub and marshes that hugged the coast this far south of Boulogne. Summer blew in on a quiet breeze, tugging at white curtains.

"There's water and things behind the screen," Michel said, stepping aside to let me pass him. "No one will disturb you if you want to sleep."

I turned and looked at him. I wanted to take that step forward, but I would not. I would not throw myself at him, not after so long.

"Elza...." He too did not seem to know what to say.

"It is very nice," I said. "The room."

"I'm glad you think so," he said. "I'm officially in the Chateau d'Hardelot, but it's much more convenient for me to stay here than be off as far as that."

"I can see that," I said.

"What are you doing here?"

The cover story, not the spy. "I'm here with Marshal Lannes," I said. There was a certain perverted pleasure in seeing the flash of pain in his eyes, but only for an instant.

"Lannes is a good man," he said, though he sounded a little strangled. "A good soldier. I hope you're happy."

"Yes," I said. No, I wanted to say. No, I am not happy, and no, I am not with Marshal Lannes. I was being blackmailed by Fouché and now I'm the Emperor's agent trying to catch a spy and I have no idea how to do it and I am in over my head and I do not know how to do this thing, with so many lives resting on me including yours. "Yes," I said. "He's a good soldier."

Michel nodded gravely and took a deep breath, meeting my eyes. "Well, then. I hope that you and I can be friends. There's no reason for us to avoid one another, is there? I mean, if you're happy and I'm happy...."

"It's all for the best, isn't it?" I said with a brave smile. "Of course we can be friends. There isn't any reason not to be, is there?" Other than that my heart breaks at the sight of you, I thought.

"No, not at all," he said.

"And is your wife in town?" I did not stop myself quickly enough from asking, though it made me sound as if I cared. Obviously she wasn't.

He looked about as though he suddenly and incongruously expected to see her popping out of the woodwork. "Oh. No. Not right now. She was here a while in the spring, but she and the children have gone to the country for the summer."

The children. Of course. He had wasted no time, my Michel. Married not quite three years, with a son two and a son ten months old.

"I'm glad that you are so happy," I said.

"Yes, very." His brow furrowed, as though he were not sure if I meant it or not, and I knew in that moment he was not. He was no happier than I, and this no easier.

I could not bear to hurt him further, and I turned away, walking around to the window, my back to him. "You have a beautiful view."

"Yes," he said. "I do."

I waited, willing him to close the door, to come closer. Surely....

"Good night, Elza," he said, and I heard him go out and close the door behind him, his bootsteps retreating down the stairs.

I closed my eyes.

It was better, I said to myself. Better if we did not have to see each other. How could we bear this, so close and so far? It was over, and I must accept that, accept that all the decisions had been made. If we could deal with one another courteously in public, well and good. It would be cruel, surely, to throw mutual friends like Corbineau into the midst of it. And I was not here to do this. I was here to catch a spy. The best thing to do would be to snatch a few hours sleep, and then go about the business I was here for. Go back to Boulogne, talk to Subervie about the coastal patrols and their timing, and to enlist him to try to find out how Captain Arnold was getting a man ashore. That was what I needed to do. Michel was a beautiful distraction, but one I did not need.

I went behind the screen and washed with tepid water from the jug, running my fingers through my hair and taking off my coat and waistcoat. I sat down on the edge of the bed, looking out the window. Below, in the School of War, they must be beginning the Battle of Cunaxa. I could see nothing, of course. This window faced the town and the walls, not the courtyard.

I took off my boots and lay down, closing my eyes and curling into the down pillows. They smelled of olive oil soap and the scent of his hair. I bit down on my lip and cried, clutching his pillows to me, until in the warm breeze from the window I went to sleep as I had so many times before, when we had still been together.

Once, curled in bed on a spring night of rain, I mentioned that I was thinking of auditioning, wondering if Michel would object or think it beneath my dignity as Moreau had.

Instead Michel curled tighter around me, spooning against my back, squeezing a little too tight. "If you want," he said. "I wouldn't want you to think you had to. I would never leave you as Moreau did. I have enough to make a good provision for you." His voice sounded a little hoarse.

I turned over suddenly. "What?"

"If she accepts, I mean," he said. "I don't know that she will."

"You intend to leave me?" I sat bolt upright in bed, clutching the sheet up over my breasts. "What?"

He sat up too, tailor style, the sheet covering nothing. He looked confused. "We have to break it off if I marry. What else could we do?"

"Why?" I was more incredulous than shocked. "I accept that you need to marry. Why should we need to break it off?"

"Because I'm married," he said, and there was that dogged sound his voice that told me I had hit one of his bottom-solid Saar Louis facts.

I pushed my damp hair back out of my face. "But we're happy. Lots of men keep mistresses. Yes, it's more inconvenient to work around a wife, but that's all logistics. Why shouldn't we stay together?"

"And be unfaithful to my wife?" Now it was Michel who sounded incredulous.

"Everyone is," I said. "You make enough money now for two households, especially since I'm frugal. Everyone is unfaithful."

"Not me," Michel said. He lifted his head, and his mouth was set. "Elza, I have never been unfaithful to you, not since our first day together. Fidelity isn't a convenience, some outmoded convention like wigs."

"That is the most bourgeois patter," I said. I hardly knew what to say. It was as though he had suggested that he make a pilgrimage to Jerusalem.

"It's not," he said quietly. "Fidelity and honor are important. I've never hidden from you my intentions to marry Aglae, and I've never slept with another woman, or even kissed her while I have been with you. Not even Aglae, not even one kiss. I wouldn't break faith with you, and I can't break faith with her." He reached for my hand but stopped when I pulled it back. His voice was very low. "Do you really think that I can marry a girl of eighteen for her money, and then use her dowry to support a mistress behind her back? That I can stand in front of God and her family and promise to honor and cherish her while I keep you on the side? That I can go into this marriage and have it be a sham from the beginning? Is that fair to her? Is it right?"

"No, Michel." The tears choked me and I could say no more.

"Would I be the man you think I am if I used her the way your husband used you?"

"No, Michel." I couldn't see. I reached for him, and his naked arms went around me, pulling me against his shoulder.

He was crying too. "I almost hope she refuses. But if she doesn't, I can't do this, don't you see, Elza? I have to honestly try to make her happy. I have to try to keep my promises."

"You don't love her," I sobbed. "You don't love her the same way."

"No. And I never will. But perhaps in time I can come to care about her. I can respect her and be her husband, even if I'm never going to love her this way." He bent his face against mine, and I felt his tears on my forehead.

"I hate you," I said. "God, Michel, how I hate you!"

"You should," he said, holding me tighter.

"All your pious cant about honor and fidelity. How can that be more important than me?"

He touched my face with his fingertips. "Elza, aren't some things more important? Shouldn't we at least try to do what's right?"

"You fucking bourgeois from fucking Saar Louis." I buried my face in his shoulder. "I will hate you every day of my life. With your stupid Paladin of Charlemagne…." I couldn't talk any more. I just held onto him and cried.

"Elza, I can't do it," he whispered. "I can't take vows and make a mockery of them. I just can't do it."

"I know you can't," I said. "I know." He would not do to someone else what Jan had done to me. He would not marry her and be nothing but a stern taskmaster, an absentee owner she would try to please in vain. He knew the damage it did. He knew my scars.

"I'm not asking you to forgive me," he said.

"I won't forgive you. I never will," I said. "Never, as long as I live."

"I'll miss you every day of my life," he said, and he was crying as hard as I was.

"You have no right," I said. "You have no right to miss me when it's your fault. You have no right to say you love me or ever do anything for me again. I hate you. I hate you more than I hated Moreau. Can't you see that this is worse?"

"Worse than throwing you out in the street? Elza, I would never do that. I would never hit you or...."

I clenched my fist against his chest. "You have no idea what hurt really is. You have no idea. I would rather you beat me till I shitted than this. If you beat me I would forgive you."

"I wouldn't beat you," he said. "Elza. God. I don't know."

"I wish you would," I said. "I wish you would do something so awful you would feel damned for the rest of your life and then you would give up on doing the right thing and just be as evil as you can be, just rip and tear and take what you want out of life and not care about anything else."

"If you wanted a man like that there are plenty of them," he said, his voice low and shaking. "Elza, I thought you wanted more. Something finer. I thought you believed."

"You made me believe," I whispered. "All the grace I have ever known is you."

He raised my chin, desperately, urgently, looking into my eyes. "Elza, I don't deserve that kind of love. I'm just a man. I'm not redemption. I don't make you worthy. Your worth is in you. You are fine and brave and honorable and good. You're as strong as a man and twice as brave as most young soldiers, clever and sharp and quick on your feet, doing whatever needs to be done. You're a survivor and a scrounger and the best I've ever known."

"And a woman," I snarled. "If I were your eromenos, if I were your lover, I would have a future when you're done with me. But I'm stuck in this female body and there is nothing I can do. I can't swear my sword to Bonaparte and win some oak leaves of my own. If I could, don't you think I would? I would be better than Corbineau, better than Auguste Thibault. I would be damn good."

"And God help me, I would love you anyway," he said, ducking his head.

"You would. And it would be your problem, not mine," I said. I put my face against his shoulder. "I would do it anyway, and you would go on about God and law."

"Probably," he said with a wry smile. "I would fuck it up like I've fucked up this."

I ran my hand up his stubbled face. "Michel, you are the biggest ass in the world."

"I know," he said, lifting his head and blinking. "I don't know what else to do. Jilt Aglae?"

"And end your career?" I said. "Michel, this has gone too far. If you had ignored her in the first place, you might have gotten by with that. But now you're in too deep and if you do that you'll go back to Saar Louis on half pay. It will be the end of all your ambitions. And what would you do then? Take me with you so I could be a farm wife in the Saar for the rest of my life? I would hate that as much as you would. And we would hate each other and blame each other for the ruin of our ambitions."

"It would be honest and right."

"Michel, we would hate each other!" I pushed him back on the bed, put my head down on his shoulder. I felt shaken and tired.

"What do you want?" he asked, his arm stealing around me.

"To go with you wherever you go," I said. "To be your squire as I was in Bavaria. To fight for my friends and my lord and my liberty." I closed my eyes, but the tears still squeezed out. "To be as much as I can, as long as I can, and die well at the end."

I knew it would make him cry, and it did. "Elza," he said, and pulled me close. "You don't belong in this age of the world."

I took a deep breath. "I will say goodbye," I said. "I will say goodbye to you. And I will miss you, and I will go on living and I will think of you sometimes, and eventually I will love someone else." My heart felt curiously empty, as though all the fear had run out of me. I would lose him, and I would go on. I had done it before, and I would do it again.

He pressed his lips to my collarbone. "Goodbye," he whispered. "Oh my love, goodbye."

"But not tonight," I said. "Michel, it's not time yet." I drew him tighter against me. "Not yet."

"Not yet," he said.

After that, we were very gentle with one another. Our days had a sweetness as they had in the beginning, the fragile, tentative peace that comes from knowing that something is ending. With Moreau, I had not seen the season turning, had not savored the days. This time I knew. I knew exactly how many days we had left.

Mademoiselle Auguié said yes. The wedding was planned for 17

Thermidor, the height of the summer, with the signing of the marriage contract seven days earlier. The wedding would be at the Chateau of Grignon, where her father lived retired. Michel would leave Paris to go out to Grignon the day before the contract was signed.

I saw the contract. He did not hide any of his business from me. He left it on the table so I could read it if I wished, the contract and another document. The contract stipulated Aglae's dowry, and said that Michel brought to the marriage the estate of La Petite Malgrange, where his father and sister lived, and 12,000 francs in cash. I raised my eyebrows. Even given that we had spent part of the 10,000 francs from Moreau, he had been on full pay this year. There ought to be more in the bank than that. In fact, I was sure there was more. 12,000 francs was a pitiful amount for the bridegroom to bring to this marriage, given the income he should have.

I opened the other document. It was a draft for 12,000 francs made to me.

I put it down on the table and closed my eyes. Half of what he had. More than a fair settlement on a mistress. More than the dowry of a girl of good family. More than Moreau thought his price. Enough to live on for five years if I were careful.

I had never taken money from him like that.

I heard his step before I decided what to say. He knew that I had seen.

"Elza?"

I turned around. "I'll take it of course," I said, and my voice was brisker than I felt. "I'd be a fool not to. It's more than Moreau thought you were worth."

"I don't want you to need anything," he said. He did not look at me. "I don't want you to have to do anything you don't want to. I can give you your independence, at least."

"Yes," I said. I would not start crying again. I would not.

"We always shared everything," he said. "Everything we had." He walked over to the window, pulling back the heavy blue velvet drapes. I hoped he wouldn't start crying again.

"Even when it was just a couple of blankets," I said, thinking back to the nights before Hohenlinden.

"Even when it was a bowl of soup." He bent his head. I couldn't see his face. "It's not your price, Elza. It's half of what I have."

"I know," I said.

He had packed his things. The apartment was mine. I would not need to move. Nothing would be thrown in the street. After the wedding he would stay with the bride's family until they could buy a suitable house in Paris. I had no doubt that the dowry would buy an excellent house.

His wedding gift to her was a parure of cameos, very fine, the necklace strung on a thin chain in the newest and most fashionable style. The note was gallant enough.

> *These tokens from me to you are not worth very much. I cannot offer you pearls and diamonds because according to my beliefs the sword should be used to win glory, not wealth. May these adorn your beauty and may you take joy in them.*

"Very pretty," I said. They were nice but not lavish. And how should they be, with an outlay of 12,000 francs to his mistress, some wicked part of my mind whispered. Perhaps she would like them all the better for their classical simplicity and style. Perhaps she would prefer them to diamonds. I had no idea what her tastes were. Nor, I suspected, did he.

Our last night together we dined at home, for fear that we would both start weeping in a restaurant. We had the best of everything, our favorite foods, our favorite wines.

I lifted my glass to him. "As though you were being shot in the morning," I said, trying to find my wit.

"If I were being shot in the morning I should want nothing more than you with me the night before," Michel said. He touched his glass to mine. "Farewell, my dear one whom I have met too late."

"Don't," I said. "Let's not start crying again." I could tell that I would if he said one more word. "Not until after we've made love. I want it to be perfect. I want it to be something we'll remember."

"Of course," he said.

In the end, this too was sweet, as though we were drowning in the melancholy, warm and enveloping without an edge to it. It suited our mood. Afterwards, we lay together in the darkness, whispering and caressing, saying farewell a thousand times. If there were recriminations, they were for later. I could hate him another day. I told myself that I would. I would hate him when it didn't matter.

In the morning I dressed early. I would not say goodbye in a dressing gown, like some tragic heroine in a novel. He sent his bags down to the carriage, a bridegroom with dark circles under his eyes on his way to his father in law's house. It would take some little time to get out to Versailles. Perhaps he would be himself by then.

When the last bag had gone down he came back.

I stood facing him, trying to memorize everything so that I would remember. His hair was already damp with sweat, even this early in the day. He had a way of standing just so, legs slightly apart, as though he feared the floor would move.

He handed me his watch, the one his mother had given him when he was made an officer. "We may never see each other again. I don't know. But I will never cease to think of you as my dearest friend, whatever may come." He looked away, and then we both started crying again.

"I keep trying not to do this," I said, taking the watch and chain and holding them against me. "You've worn it, and it has your name engraved on it. I wish it weren't pointing to an hour of eternal farewell. I'm sorry, Michel. I can't stop."

"I can't either," he said. His mouth twitched. "You'd think we would have played the whole scene by now."

I started laughing through my tears. "We're doing it again, aren't we?"

"Doing what?"

"Being awful."

He put his arms around me and I leaned up into his embrace. "We could be awful one more time."

"We could," I said, and kissed him.

We did not say goodbye. He raised his hand to me, and took his hat under his arm and went off down the stairs. Michel did not look back, and I did not call after him. I went inside and closed the door. I did not go to the window to watch the carriage leave. I was worn out with tears.

I went and sat in the chair beside the fireplace. The apartment was quiet.

"Well," I said aloud. "What's next?"

The Lodge

I woke at noon, thirsty, hung over, and embarrassed to death. I shook the cobwebs from my brain, drank some water from the pitcher, and resolved to get back to Boulogne before anything else happened. I looked about for something with which to write a note.

Michel's desk was in the room next door, his old leather map case spread on a table. And right beside it, in plain sight beside the inkwell, a cipher key.

I took a deep breath. Anyone who walked in would not even have to look for it.

I thought about taking it, but instead tore off a piece of paper and wrote a note to leave on his bed: Thank you. E.

It was brief and to the point, but I could not think what else to say. I dressed and slipped out without anyone noticing at all.

As I hurried back along the cliffs it was beginning to get really warm. I loosened my cravat, and turned my face up to the sun. A glorious day, really, the tenth of Messidor in the Year 13. Or June 29, 1805, if one preferred. I did not see Lion offshore. Presumably even she must back off sometime, if for no other reason than to take on water from a tender. Or perhaps a ship had been sighted that I could not see from the cliffs. Our fleet was out, free on the high seas, trying to clear the channel of the likes of Lion while their Admiral Nelson tried to come to grips with us first. I should know nothing of that, except when at last weeks belated a bulletin came. The semaphores that brought the news so quickly on land, flashing signals over hundreds of kilometers in a few hours, did not exist on the sea. We should have to wait for a ship to bring the news, whether of victory or defeat.

By the time I reached Boulogne I was quite thirsty and decidedly hungry, so I found lunch in a café not far from the fortress before braving my landlady. I could see the main gates from where I was, the constant stream of couriers and soldiers coming in and out, mixed with townspeople, farmers coming to and from the markets, fishermen, and the unmistakable soldiers' families, women in cotton and straw bonnets, children running back and forth shouting. It was high summer, and I assumed a school holiday. Since we now had the ecoles populaires, most young children would be in school unless they were the children of farmers, who of course would be working at this time of year.

It startled me to hear the church bells ring. I had not realized it was Sunday. It had been a few years since the Concordat between Emperor and Pope had allowed the Church back into France, but I was still unused to it. A horde of little girls in white dresses, driven by their mothers like so many goslings, ran giggling and laughing up the street toward the church.

I had never had a daughter. I wondered what it would be, to have a child who loved me, a little girl who would put her arms around my neck and her face against my cheek. My sons had not, but then they were boys, and had been left to their nurses too often. Francis would be nearly eleven now, I thought, and his brother fourteen. They would not be running in a gaggle, but turning into young men, those years behind them forever. If there was sweetness in that life, it was lost to me.

From the looks of some of the officers arriving now, I thought that perhaps the Battle of Cunaxa had been brief. Some of them looked still caught in intense technical discussion. Perhaps it hadn't taken latter day Xenophon too long to be overwhelmed.

I got up and paid my tab, then walked the few short blocks to my lodging.

I had barely opened the front door when the landlady descended in a whirl. "You! What are you doing here?"

"I'm here to see Madame St. Elme," I said, altogether too conscious of my stale clothes. "I'm her brother, Charles van Aylde."

"I don't care if you're King Solomon!" the landlady shrieked. "You're that drunkard pounding on the door last night. And you are not going up unless your purported sister comes down to meet you."

"She can't do that," I began.

"Then you are not going anywhere. Out of this house!" She hustled me toward the door. "I do not want to call for Jerome to put you out, but I shall if you set foot in here again!"

Out in the street I paused, for once completely flummoxed. Madame St. Elme could hardly come out if I couldn't go in! It was beyond irritating.

Surely male spies didn't have this sort of trouble.

Well, I supposed they did. Were I really a gentleman I would not be getting in either.

Cautiously, I went around the side of the house. There was my bedroom window on the second floor, the window open in the warm summer air. If I could get up there, I could get in the window, change clothes, and reappear as Madame St. Elme. But I would need a tall person to help me....

Providence provides, I thought. Coming along the street from the gate, a book open in one hand, was the young brigadier Corbineau had introduced me to, Reille, the one who hated Fouché. And he was quite tall. Also, this would give me an excuse to make his acquaintance.

I rushed out and accosted him. "General Reille, have you a moment?"

He did not recognize me, it was clear, as he had met me in women's clothes. "I'm sorry, sir. You have the advantage of me," he said, stuffing the book into an inner pocket.

"I am Madame St. Elme," I said, "A friend of Major Corbineau's, who introduced us just the other day. I have a terrible problem, and I am hoping that you might be able to help me."

"I shall do my humble best, Madame," he said, blinking. Men did, when they first put me and Charles together.

"I need you to lift me up to that window right there. I'm locked out of my lodging, you see. If you might be so kind?"

Reille blinked again. "If it is necessary, Madame. But could you not use the door?"

"Not dressed like this," I said. "Not without a scandal. Could you please help me, General?"

"I suppose," he said, and followed me around the flowerbed to the side of the house.

"If you can just boost me up," I said.

"I think it will be better if you remove your boots and climb on my back," he said. "And then I will stand and you can reach the windowsill."

"Probably so." I shucked my boots and stockings and climbed up.

Which was where I was when the landlady and Jerome came around the house.

Of course there was great hue and cry, shouting and explanations, complaints that the gendarmes should be called and remonstrances of all sorts, culminating in my eviction with all my goods from the lodging and dire words about women like me who gave the entire fair sex a bad name, along with insults heaped on Reille's head, not to mention most of my baggage.

And thus we stood in the street again.

"Where would you like me to put these?" He gestured with my saddlebags, now draped over his arms.

"In Colonel Subervie's office," I said, now both hot and irritated. "I'm going to have to talk to him about finding different lodgings anyhow."

"Oh you're with Subervie!" He looked as though something had suddenly clicked for him, warm brown eyes looking me over more closely. "Now I see. You must be the lady he mentioned."

"I must be," I said coquettishly. I had no idea what lady or ladies Subervie might have, but I needed somewhere to stay that was neither in Michel's lap or chaperoning me as though I were a schoolgirl. This was getting ridiculous.

"Perhaps we should go find him then," Reille said, and we set off through the town.

Subervie was in his office, which I found a bit surprising. "Did you not have an exercise this morning?" I asked as I entered.

Subervie looked up from the papers on his desk. "It was the shortest battle I've ever seen. We were dead practically the moment we engaged, and Honoré just wiped us up." He glanced at Reille, who was holding my saddlebags. "Good fight, but Jesus, we were terrible today!"

"I've never heard of 'just charge everything with no regard for losses' as a strategy before," Reille said. "Marshal Ney was not playing a winning game this morning."

"Yes, well," Subervie grumbled. "We know Xenophon lost. But not in two hours. I was back here by lunchtime." He glanced up at my red face. "So what's the difficulty with your lodging, Madame?'

"I've been thrown out of it," I said, thinking that I must have rattled Michel seriously for him to blow the battle so spectacularly. "Colonel, I need somewhere that I can come and go at night."

Reille looked from one of us to the other. We were not talking like lovers. "I thought you said you were with Subervie?"

"No, I said I needed to find Colonel Subervie," I said.

Subervie was the one to blush now, his fair skin turning pink. "No, Madame is here with Marshal Lannes. I was merely assisting her in the matter of her lodgings!'

"Oh!" Reille said, seeming to relax. Presumably he knew Subervie's wife and small son, and was relieved to find out that I was not Subervie's mistress. Lannes' mistress was a different story. Subordinates might be run about tending to a marshal's mistress anytime. "Then I'll just leave your things here?'

"That's fine," I said. "Thank you."

Reille left, and Subervie shut the door behind him.

"I have to be able to go in and out at all times of the day, dressed in any way," I said by way of explanation. "Not being able to leave the house at night is very respectable, but I'm not here to be respectable! I'm here to catch a spy. And I'd like to get some information from you about Lion, if I may."

Subervie sighed and sat back down at his desk, gesturing for me to join him. I sat and accepted some coffee, though I did not take a pipe. "Lion," he said, "is a thorn in our side. Marshal Lannes and I are certain that it is through Lion that our plans are leaking to London, but we have never been able to figure out how. The patrols along the beach road are spaced fifteen minutes apart. It would take nearly twice that time for a boat to get ashore under the best conditions, if the tide were in and the sea calm at once. The coast is very rocky there, and Lion can't stand in very far. It's not like it is further south along the coast, where there are broader sandy beaches and it's mostly a sandy bottom."

"Could they be coming in further south?" I asked.

Subervie nodded. "It's certainly possible. The problem becomes the distance from Boulogne and the difficulty of getting to the beach. That area is marshland, and there are no roads, only tracks through the marsh that are submerged at high tide. Someone who knew the area could do it, but it would take them more than half the day or night to get from Boulogne out to the beach, and so much back. Which seems to me to preclude the frequency of correspondence that we know about."

"I see," I said. One of the officers at headquarters could hardly vanish for a full day several times a week without anyone noticing. "And do the patrols continue in bad weather as well as fair?"

Subervie nodded. "In all weather, and all through the winter. We think that perhaps the correspondence is more frequent in good weather, but that's easy to explain. I've been here through the gales of winter, and there are weeks when I should not like to try to get a small boat ashore, except within the shelter of the harbor of Boulogne."

"And what about the harbor?" I said. "Any chance of that?"

Subervie shook his head. "Nothing goes out now, not even fishing boats leaving sight of shore. We're blockaded by the Channel Fleet, essentially. Unless our fleet can draw them off, we can't launch the invasion. That's why it didn't happen last fall. We couldn't get control of the sea for 48 hours."

I nodded solemnly, thinking about what Lannes had said about not only mastery of the sea, but of the elements. Perhaps what we needed was not even so much to breach those wooden walls as to breach more ethereal ones that surrounded Britain. "And when we do?" I asked.

"We go," Subervie said.

Instead of a respectable boarding house in town, Subervie found lodging for me in a cottage a short distance outside the walls, an older house that was not nearly so convenient for the wives of officers, and I expected priced above the pockets of the families of the enlisted men. Here, as everywhere there was a camp, prices rose as the local people took advantage of the unexpected bounty, and charged what the market would bear. I disapproved of this, of everything from lodging to food going for four times what it was worth, because the burden sat most heavily on the families of the ordinary soldiers who had the least to spend. I thought that it would be fair to sell things for only twice the going price, and not try to gouge every sou.

There was a woman who came in and cleaned, and who for an additional fee would provide one meal a day, which suited me well. Subervie implied heavily that I was a famous actress, the lover of a very distinguished man, who wanted to keep me in a private love-nest. I thought he stretched the point a bit, but it did at least give me a certain amount of privacy, as well as assuring that comings and goings at strange hours would be excused as assignations.

He helped me move my things in, for which I was grateful, but as he left he turned. "Oh, I nearly forgot! Madame, Marshal Lannes requests that you be available night after next, for the ritual."

"You are part of this too?" I asked, taking a deep breath. I should not be surprised, as Lannes seemed to trust Subervie in everything. "I see. It is to be day after tomorrow, then."

"We usually meet on Tuesday night. Sometimes more often when it's needed, but it's hard for so many of us to coordinate schedules," Subervie replied.

"How many of them are you?"

"Ten or so," he said. "More like sixteen, but some of us aren't assigned to the Army of Coasts of Ocean, and so only come when they can. We'll expect ten or eleven on Tuesday."

"I see," I said again.

Subervie's eyes were kind. "Madame, please do not let it distress you so. We are not ogres, and I do not think what we will ask of you is very hard."

"I hope not," I said. "I am not very practiced, and I tell you frankly that it terrifies me."

Subervie put his hand on my arm. "It's really mostly dull. We try to get something, and sometimes we think we might and most of the time we don't. It's a lot like riding patrol, really. Most of the time you just go back and forth bored to death."

I smiled at him. "If that is how it is, it doesn't sound so bad."

"It isn't, Madame," he said. "Thus far none of us has sustained any injury worse than a stiff neck from sitting so long."

"I will bear that in mind," I said, and saw him off. I thought, after he was gone, that it had been very kind of him to try to allay my fears.

Tuesday was a beautiful day, hot and clear, with the sky a lambent shade of blue. To my surprise, however, the sea remained high. It crashed against the rocks with formidable waves, and though the wind was fair Lion labored down the coast, rising and falling on the heavy seas. I walked along the cliffs by day, hoping to find something of note, some clue that would help, but of course I did not. Only in novels does the heroine go for a walk along the cliffs and effortlessly stumble into the very clue which has eluded our heroes for most of the book! I found nothing and learned nothing except what I knew before: that our patrols were thorough and punctual. Certainly in fair weather it would be impossible to get a boat ashore by day. It could be seen for many miles.

Thus it was with certain frustration that I reported as ordered at seven in the evening at the old castle in Boulogne. Unlike many other castles, the ancient citadel of Boulogne had been modernized in the last century, and its courtyard showed it. It might have a moat and drawbridge, but the windows could not have been thirty years old, clear paned and tight against the winds that must challenge them in winter, while the fireplaces and other appointments were modern and tasteful.

As Lannes had directed, I had not eaten, and Subervie was waiting for me when I arrived. "Come up," he said quietly, "and meet the other gentlemen. We will be using a parlor upstairs, and no doubt you will want to talk to Marshal Lannes and get situated."

I glanced back at the silent grenadiers who had stopped me at the gatehouse. "What do they think is happening?"

"Senior staff meeting. Not to be disturbed except in direst emergency." Subervie winked at me. "There are some perks to being a Marshal of France, after all!"

The room above must at most times be used as a conference room, for two men were moving a huge carved table from the center of the room off to the side. The draperies over the windows along the courtyard side had already been drawn and the room was stuffy. Four tall brass candlestands had been brought in, the sort that grace churches, and were off to the side, unlit white candles as thick as my forearm on each.

One of the men moving the table looked up and gave me a smile. "Good evening, Madame." It was Reille, the young brigadier who had proved so helpful in the matter of my landlady. I supposed I should not have been surprised to see him. Still, his presence was not necessarily reassuring. He was the only officer so far for whom I had found any motive to treason—a brother-in-law sent to the guillotine, a matter of family honor against the Minister of Police. It was a thin lead, but so far the only one I had.

I nodded pleasantly to him as Marshal Lannes came over. "Good evening," he said. "Are you ready?"

"I will be," I said. "Can you tell me what we are doing?" I refrained from saying that I had never worked with a legitimate lodge before, only Lebrun's fake one, and my knowledge of procedure was likely to be spotty.

Lannes took me aside, steering me out of the way of a man I did not know carrying one of the candlestands. "We'll open the lodge as we usually do. You have no part in that, so just stand still and quiet. We'll ward for protection very strongly. Again, you do not have to do anything. And then we'll get to you."

"A blackened mirror?" I asked, recalling Lebrun's operations, and hoping I sounded professional and unflustered.

"Yes," Lannes said. "Unless there is some technique you prefer."

I shook my head. "That is what I have used before."

Good." He nodded approvingly. "Then we'll try to get a look at what aling with, what our opposition is doing."

"Opposition?"

Lannes gave me a rueful smile. "Did you think that we are the only ones who use such techniques, Madame? Standing against us are the witches of England, and they have no small power. They laid low the Spanish Armada in days past. It is no little feat to call a hurricane into the Channel, to drive the pride of Spain into wrecks on the rocks, or into Drake's fireships. Their witches are as good as their navy, Madame."

I blinked. "Surely the witches of England are not sanctioned by Mr. Pitt's government!" The idea of that Tory Prime Minister consorting with witches was ludicrous.

"Of course not," Lannes said. "But do you think that means they do not fight? The witches of England fight for a government that outlaws their existence, but fight they do. We cannot launch the invasion when wind and waves themselves conspire against us. We have been here almost two years, waiting for the confluence of tide and weather, for their navy to be distracted or called away, for the favorable moment for a crossing. We can embark 64,000 men in an hour and a half and we can be over in seven hours. But we must have those seven hours, and the guardians they have called do not sleep."

"The guardians they have called?"

Lannes sighed, though his face was patient, the look of a man who wishes he didn't have to explain things that doubtless everyone more qualified would know. "When you have worked before, have you called elemental guardians?"

"You mean to the circle?" I nodded. "We called maidens of the elements, Spirit of Air, Spirit of Fire, et cetera, with each one voiced by a girl."

"That's the mildest form of what I mean," Lannes said. "The Spirits of the Elements are very minor visualizations of elemental power, candy-bright, suitable for pretty engravings. But the true elementals are much different. Imagine if you can the power of elemental fire."

I bent my head. I had felt something like it once, I thought, when we had done the angelic possession. "I see," I said.

"But you're not going to be tangling with any elementals they've called," Lannes said. "You're just going to scout. Like a good cavalry screen, your job is to see what you can see and get back with word, not engage any superior forces."

"I understand," I said. I did. It meant there was a good chance there would be superior forces, and I should have to employ that time-tested technique of light cavalry, running away. Best not to ask what failing to get back with the word entailed.

I looked past Lannes' shoulder just in time to see Corbineau coming in, his hat in his hand, a broad smile on his face as he saw me. Perhaps he would have rushed up, if I hadn't been talking to a marshal.

"We're going to go change in a bit," Lannes said. "You can have the room to yourself after we're done." M. Noirtier was trying to get his attention and he hurried off before I could ask him what I was to change into. I had not brought a special chemise with me, like the ones I had worn for Lebrun long ago, but I supposed I could wear my regular one if they did not have a robe or such I could borrow. I would ask him about it later, when he was not so busy.

I went and embraced Corbineau instead, tremendously relieved to see him. "Jean-Baptiste, I should have known this was the mysterious thing you were talking about!"

"Wasn't it the one you were talking about?" he asked.

"I'm terribly sorry," I said. "I didn't mean to put you in such a mess the other morning. It was very inconsiderate of me. I promise you that I don't usually do such things. I hope you haven't gotten in too much trouble."

Corbineau shrugged. "Not so much. In fact, none. You would think that it never happened at all! Did you and the Marshal have a good talk?" He looked at me speculatively.

"No," I said. "Jean-Baptiste, you know it's over between us. Over. It's awkward and painful, and I hope that we do not run into one another again."

He opened his mouth, but I had already seen past him, appearing like a bad stage ghost right on cue. Michel came in, stopping to talk to someone just inside the door.

"Oh shit," I said. I grabbed Corbineau by the arm. "Why didn't you tell me Michel was involved with this?"

"I didn't tell you I was involved with this," Corbineau protested. "I couldn't. It's secret. That means we don't run around telling all our friends."

"Not even when…."

"Not even when what?"

"When Michel is going to kill you," I finished. Michel looked up from his conversation and saw me standing with Corbineau, and I saw the thought as clearly as if he'd spoken. He was going to kill Corbineau.

Corbineau spun around as his fate approached. "Sir! Good evening!"

Michel did not even look at him. "Lannes' Dove," he said.

"Hello, Michel," I said.

Michel frowned. "I wish you'd told me that you'd be here."

"How could I do that?" I asked. "I didn't know you'd be here."

"I'm the Ground. I have to be here."

As though whatever that was made sense to me. "Well, I'm the Dove, and I have to be here too." If he wanted to leave he certainly could, but Lannes had made it clear that I couldn't.

Corbineau was backing away silently, hoping nobody would notice him.

"I had no idea…" Michel began.

On the other side of the room, Lannes raised his hands. "Gentlemen, can we get started please? If you have not yet changed, please go and do it so our Dove can have the room by herself."

Michel looked as though he wanted to swear.

I touched his arm, just the lightest touch on his sleeve. "Michel, we both have a job to do. We don't need to like it. But surely we can manage to be brothers in arms."

He nodded and his face cleared. "We can," he said. "I'll go change, then." He followed Reille into the room beyond as Subervie came out.

Subervie was one of the few who had already discarded his uniform for something more atmospheric, an ankle length robe of heavy white silk of the sort worn by choirboys in churches, the high neck fastened with a white silk frog. It should have looked ridiculous, but instead it looked formal and seemly, like a priest clad in white instead of black. His waist was cinched by a white silk sash, into which he had incongruously tucked his dress sword.

"All right, Madame?" he asked.

"Yes," I said. "But I haven't a robe of my own. Do you perhaps have one I could borrow?"

"I don't," Subervie said, "But let us ask M. Noirtier."

We found Noirtier by the big table, his white robe tied with a black sash weighted with gold bullion fringe, fussing with the charcoal in a censer.

"Do we have a spare robe for Madame St. Elme?" Subervie asked. "She hasn't got her own."

"She won't need one," Noirtier said without looking up. "Doves work nude."

"Oh for Heaven's sake!" I said. It was worse than Lebrun's amateur theatricals, with the pretty elemental maidens.

Subervie looked shocked. “What?”

Noirtier straightened. “Doves work nude. Wearing clothing, particularly heavy silks, interferes with the ability to leave one’s body astrally.”

“I’ve never heard of any such thing,” I said.

“It is the tradition of the Pléiade,” he replied stiffly. “It is not for prurient purposes. It is merely because it makes the work easier.”

“For me to sit about naked among the crowd of you? All dressed up in your robes like anti-priests? It is like something designed by the Committee of Public Safety for a ridiculous spectacle!”

“Those spectacles were not ridiculous, Madame,” Noirtier said. “I had the honor to work on several of them with Jacques-Louis David.”

“That may be as it may,” I said, “But I have never before needed to be nude to see things.”

“What are you talking about?” I had not seen Michel come up behind me, now dressed in his robe with a sash of crimson silk.

Noirtier, of course, had heard none of our previous conversation, and had no idea we were not mere acquaintances. “Madame is protesting the necessity of proper dress. The Dove must be nude.”

Michel’s face turned as red as his sash. “I should think she would! How can you even suggest that?”

“It is the tradition of the Pléiade,” Noirtier said stubbornly. “We are trying to do this right, for maximum effectiveness. I would do it myself, if it were necessary.”

“But who cares about seeing you nude, Noirtier?” Michel demanded. “It’s not the same thing at all. That you should ask a lady to disrobe completely in a room full of men is incomprehensible. Apologize to her immediately.”

“I will not,” Noirtier said. “This discussion is between me and Madame, about the role she is taking tonight. You are not her husband, and you do not dictate her dress.”

I had to admire his tenacity, and he had a point. It was a bit rich, seeing Michel acting proprietary when he had no cause to be. “Michel, M. Noirtier has made a request which I am considering. Pray stay out of it,” I said.

“Elza, I will not allow this!” His face was scarlet.

“You will not allow it?” I felt the blood rush to mine as well. “You will not allow me to take my clothes off if I so choose?”

"No, I won't! Not in front of all these men!"

"You don't get to tell me who I can undress in front of," I snapped. "You have no right." I cast my shawl on the floor and put my hands to the buttons on my back just above the waist.

"Lannes!" Michel bellowed.

The entire room stopped and looked at him, Subervie with a jug of water in his hands.

"What?" Lannes asked. He had been across the room, and heard none of it.

"Will you permit your woman to strip like a harlot in front of your friends? As though she were nothing to you but a ten sou whore?" Michel stormed around me, his hands clenched.

"My what?" Lannes glanced from him to me. "Madame St. Elme? She's not my companion, and it is entirely up to her to dress as she likes."

I reached for Michel's arm. "Michel, don't carry on this way."

"The Dove is supposed to be nude," Noirtier said. I was beginning to think him quite a terrier, with an idea in his teeth that he would not let go of no matter how unwise.

Michel spun round. "And do you want to be?" he demanded. "That's not what it sounded like. It sounded like Noirtier bullying you in to stripping in a room full of men."

"I should rather wear a robe like yours," I said. "I do not wish to disrupt the atmosphere, but I am quite capable of doing what I do while wearing some clothing. Or if you do not have a spare, I am content to work in my chemise as I have done in the past."

"I don't think we've got a spare," Subervie muttered. "I can go look though." He hurried out through the door to the dressing room.

"Then I will wear my chemise," I said. "It's fine."

"You're going to stand in front of all these men in your underwear?" Michel still looked murderous. "So that they can look at you lasciviously, imagining what they'd like to do with you?"

"Is anyone having that problem but you?" I demanded.

"How about a sheet?" It was Reille who spoke. "If you put a sheet about you like a toga, nobody will be able to see anything. And linen is not a conductive material. In terms of not interfering with the ability to project her soul, a linen sheet should be materially neutral."

Noirtier threw up his hands. "If we are abandoning the principle of nudity, I suppose so."

"A sheet would be fine," I said. "I would be happy to wear a sheet."

"A sheet," Michel said.

Reille met his eyes, entirely unintimidated. "A sheet. She'll be covered from neck to ankles. She'll be more covered than we are."

"I suppose," Michel said. It was clear that Reille had more chance of calming him down than anyone else. He must respect the young general as much as Corbineau had said.

"Gervais! Grab a sheet!" Reille yelled through the door.

"Can we get started?" Lannes asked. "If we are through arguing about Madame St. Elme's clothes?"

"Let me go change," I said, and hurried through the door, taking the sheet from the bewildered Subervie as I went in and closed it behind me.

I took a deep breath. Calm. I knew I must be calm. It was a bad idea to go into something like this already agitated and upset. I need to calm down and try to mentally prepare for the task ahead. One thing Michel had done, I thought, was to completely distract me from my fears about the ritual.

He'd probably distracted everyone else too.

I took off my dress, stockings and shoes, and my soft bustier. There were no candles lit in the dressing room, and through the curtains of the one small window I could see that the sun was westering behind the walls. A stableboy went by, bucket in hand. It was evening.

Very well, then. It was time to get on with it.

I draped the sheet about me, wrapping it like Roman palla, hoping that it looked more Classical than silly. I glanced in the mirror and thought it did. I stopped then and unpinned my hair. It was not so long, but it did fall below my shoulders. I never wore it that way, unbound, and so I thought it suited this new persona, the one I would be when I did this, the one who knew how to do it. I looked at myself in the mirror, blond hair unbound, enormous blue eyes, the unrelieved white of the sheet falling in graceful folds. "Who are you?" I whispered. "Who are you, the one who can see?"

She did not answer, only regarded me solemnly.

I opened the door. The witches of England were waiting.

The Witches of England

"Asclepius, Healer of Bodies and of Hearts, Wisdom old as time and ever-revealed, harken to our call and grant us the benison of your grace this night."

I sat in the middle of the circle, a little table with a blackened mirror in front of me and Noirtier beyond that. There were no lights besides a taper on the table, and one fat white candle in the stand beyond Noirtier that a young man was lighting, his invocation hanging in the air.

He turned, the censer in his hand, and slowly began to walk around the outside of the circle. The heady scents of frankincense and myrrh filled the room. He passed each of the other seven men in turn, their heads bowed, hands clasped before them. Noirtier sat opposite me, likewise still, his eyes closed. The man with the censer passed behind me and around, returning it to its place hanging from a tripod beside the candle.

"Athena, Quickener of Minds and of Spirits, Guardian of the worthy, harken to our call and grant us the benison of your grace this night." Reille, off to my right, took his cue and lit another white candle from the passed taper. It flared into life as though it were a lamp, not a candle. I saw his face for a moment in profile, solemn and reverent, as a man who hears music only he can hear.

He was always the pious one, I thought, though I did not know where the thought came from. Doors opening, opened by the words, by the scent of the smoke.

From the scabbard tucked into his sash he drew forth his sword, gleaming and bright. It was pretty, but it was not a dress sword, not a toy. It was a saber with a curved blade, hilt with only a bar guard. He lifted it before him like a crusader, point uppermost, light reflecting off the steel, and in its gleam I almost saw the talons of an owl, the bright flash of its stoop. Then, sword before him, he passed behind me, going around the circle.

I closed my eyes. Now it was Lannes behind me, the sound of water pouring from a pitcher into a basin. "Aphrodite, Measurer of All Who Love, Lady of the oceans of the world, harken to our call and grant us the benison of your grace this night."

Pelagia, something whispered within me. Lady of the Sea who belongs to no man.... I felt it like a breath, like a whisper over my bowed head, as though someone had opened a window and let in the salt air.

But of course it was only the rustle of Lannes' robe as he passed about, a sprig of rosemary in his hands with which he sprinkled sea water. I wondered irrelevantly whose job it was to procure rosemary and sea water. Probably Subervie's.

"Serapis, Harvester of Lands and of Souls, vine and vinestock, harken to our call and grant us the benison of your grace this night." Michel was off to my left, lighting the last of the four candles. I opened my eyes to see him straighten, a bowl of salt in his hands which he sprinkled before him, passing in front of me and around.

A frisson ran down my spine. They are real, I thought. All the old gods and spirits, all the ancient names read in dusty books. They are real. They awaken.

Noirtier stood, his hands before him. "Selah. So may it be. We stand here, my friends, one in purpose and one in heart, that the fortunes of our nation may prosper, and so the cause of liberty on Earth. To that end, we have with us a Dove, who will, with our aid and protection, attempt to penetrate the defenses of the enemy." He glanced around the circle. "Your job is to protect her, and to grant these mighty patrons whose aid we have requested whatever they may need. Pray be seated, gentlemen."

With a sigh, they all sat down on the ground, a ring about us, the four white candles on their stands gleaming like pillars of light behind them. I would have looked at Lannes for a cue, but now he was directly behind me. It was Michel who put the taper back on the table beside the blackened mirror, carefully not looking at me as he placed it.

A moment of terror gripped me. I did not know what to do. Beside Michel, Subervie gave me an encouraging smile, and I remembered what he had said about nothing happening. If I produced nothing, it was no different than what they had already done. I would be no worse at least.

"Look into the mirror," Noirtier said. "Don't try to focus your eyes on it. Just let them play over the surface. Look, and dream."

I tried. We sat in silence what seemed a long time. My hands sweated, and I saw nothing but a mirror before me, Noirtier's lap and the eastward candle beyond him, the young man with glasses who had lit the flame for Asclepius. I am doing nothing, I thought.

The flames were better. I started to raise my head to tell Noirtier nothing was happening, but the reflection of the fire off the brass candlestick stopped me. It played on the brass, flickering and dancing.

You do not need this mirror, something whispered inside me. You only need the fire.

Fire, and the memory of fire. I let it grow in my mind, my eyes watering and closing when it grew too bright. Fire, and the memory of fire. Sparks of light flickering off water, coals coiled in matching darkness in a brazier. The memory of fire. Light on a pool, sun streaming through a window of stained glass, fire leaping on an altar. Fire.

Light played on the back of my closed eyelids.

"A hanging lantern," I whispered. I could see it in the darkness, swaying with each movement of the ship. "A lantern, the kind with shutters." It swung back and forth gently over the head of the man at the desk, his dark blue coat off, white shirt and waistcoat pale in the dark. Beyond him the stern windows of the ship showed nothing but darkness, sea and night beyond. There were papers beneath his fingers, pages in neat writing, one with a row of words and numbers. I saw his face a moment as he glanced up, fair haired, young, with the broad homely face that should belong to a farmer, nothing keen and bright about him but his eyes.

"Captain Arnold," I whispered. "Captain Edmund Arnold, of the HMS Lion." Captain Arnold sat at his desk a few miles away, a cipher key in his hands. "He has a message from his spy," I said. "A new one. He just got it a few minutes ago and has gone below to decipher it."

Somewhere, far away from this cabin on Lion, I heard a rustle and a stir, some low muttered words, but they were much less real than Captain Arnold, turning numbers into words. "No…something …." I could not read much, though I could see the words plainly, as I did not read English.

A different voice, this one at my elbow. "Can you tell where Lion is?" Lannes, I thought.

"South," I whispered. "She's tacking against the wind, going down the coast, close hauled to the port bow." I did not even know the meaning of what I said, but it was there in Arnold's mind, on the very surface, where his ship was, what it was doing. A moderate wind and high seas, tacking and tacking across her course southward. Even now, above, they were passing the word to come about, Mr. Walker's voice clear and strong.

"Can you look further?" Lannes asked. "Go further out to sea? It is only a few miles to England. Dover should be visible from Lion's topmast."

It was like uncoiling, like movement swift and sure, rising up from Captain Arnold, up the length of the ship's mast, sails taut in the wind. She was tacking out to sea, her wake a zigzag down the coast. And behind her and northward, lights on the horizon, lights along the shore spread like a crescent, brighter and then dimmer as they curved westward, the southern coast of England laid out before me like a map

I stood on the wind like a gull in the night, white wings spread over Lion below. Fifty feet above her decks I hovered, watching sailors running about, the complicated and graceful business of changing her course again.

There was England. A few beats of my wings and I soared toward it, low and fast as a gull, not even leaving a shadow on the water. There was Dover, port marked by so many masts, Dover Castle above all. There was the curve of coastline, chalk cliffs glimmering white in the darkness. They were almost beneath me.

And then something rose out of the darkness, vast and strange as a great wind. It hovered, impenetrable, a shape of cloud and trouble.

I veered off, and it tore at me, gull's wings wildly beating. Time to go, I thought. This is what Lannes means by superior force. I darted, diving low, and for a moment beneath its rolling clouds I saw something different, a garden enclosed by hedges, an old woman looking up, a swan's feather in her hand.

Then the winds hit me, tumbling and shaking, buffeting at me with unearthly force. The sea came up like a wall beneath me, flat and hard and cold. I righted myself at the last second, almost beneath Lion's prow, streaking like a shadow over the waves. The winds tore at me one last time, and then it was beach and marshland beneath me, the coast south of Boulogne sleeping under a quiet moon.

I turned and looked back.

There was nothing to see, except perhaps far out to sea a shape of cloud that momentarily obscured the waxing moon.

"Elza? Elza?" There was a voice, a touch on my shoulders, and reeling I spun away, drawn suddenly northward at a terrible pace.

"Don't do that." It was Noirtier's voice. "Let her find her way back in her own time."

"Elza, can you hear me? Can't you see she's in trouble, man?"

I opened my eyes, though the room still spun. "Michel?"

He was kneeling beside me, a worried look on his face. "Are you all right?"

My hands were clenched, and I opened them gingerly. "I think so?"

"What happened?" Lannes asked. "You stopped talking." He too had come around to my other side.

"I think I ran into that superior force you were talking about," I said, and related to him what I had seen.

Lannes looked grave. His eyes met Michel's across me. "We feared something like that," he said.

Michel nodded. "An air elemental?"

"It looked like a storm," I said. "A very small, concentrated storm, like one of those deadly thunderstorms, the ones that spawn cyclones."

Lannes looked thoughtful. "It is summer. And it has been hot."

"This wasn't natural," I said. I was quite sure of that.

"The woman with the swan's feathers...." Michel mused.

"Swans have a lot of correspondences," Reille said. He had not left his place at south. "I wouldn't know what else was done right off, but there are a lot of stories with swans in them, some of them Northern European."

"And some unique to the British Isles, no doubt," Lannes said. He stood up. "Corbineau, can you ask that Free Irish friend of yours about stories with swans?"

"Of course," Corbineau said.

"Subtly," Michel said.

"Of course!" Corbineau looked mildly offended. Michel was not the most subtle man in the world himself.

"I'm fine," I said to him quietly.

Michel got up and went back to his position. Glancing around the circle now, I saw that Subervie was no longer there. "Where is Subervie?" I asked.

Reille answered. "We cut a gate for him to get out. Marshal Lannes sent him to do something."

I glanced at Lannes, who shook his head almost imperceptibly. Interesting, I thought. He does not entirely trust everyone in the circle, though he sent Subervie out immediately when I said that Captain Arnold had just gotten a message. No doubt Subervie was out on the cliffs now with a patrol, hunting the spy. I did not think he would catch anyone, not because I doubted what I had seen, but it would take Subervie twenty minutes or more to get there, and if the man had been left on shore when

Arnold returned to Lion, he would have at least twenty or thirty minutes while Arnold rowed back out. All in all, nearly an hour would have elapsed before Subervie got there, and I didn't think our man would sit about.

Still, I told myself that I would go out in the morning and see if there was any sign, even a boot print that might tell me something about the man I sought. There might be something in the strip of sand along the base of the cliffs that Subervie would miss by night. Though more likely I would only discover what sort of shoes Captain Arnold wore.

"A promising start," Noirtier pronounced.

"Better than anything we've had so far," Corbineau said. "At least Madame is finding some action." He winked at me.

I winked back. Truly, it had been frightening, but also exhilarating. I could still feel the rush in my veins, as though I had actually battled the sky borne by swift white wings.

"Shall we try this again on Thursday?" Lannes asked.

The young man with glasses at east shook his head. "I'm on duty that night, sir. General Larrey will be in town."

Lannes made an annoyed sound. "That means we aren't free either, Michel. We've got to give him dinner."

Michel nodded. "We do have to. After all, he is the Surgeon General."

The chief medical officer in the entire French army, I thought. Dr. Larrey was also Napoleon's personal physician. Like the rest, he too was an innovator, his newest change being the use of modified artillery caissons drawn staffed with trained corpsmen whose job was to fetch the wounded from the field with all speed, and treat them while transporting them to field hospitals. These new Flying Ambulances were like nothing seen in modern warfare, where generally the wounded were tended by one's friends or not at all. The idea of having servicemen whose jobs were to fetch the wounded, provide first aid, and carry them in haste to surgeons was entirely new.

"I have a practicum with him in the afternoon," the young man said, "And I expect I shall see you at dinner."

"Of course, Max," Michel said. I was gathering that Max was one of the surgeons assigned to VI Corps.

"Can we take down before we get into Thursday's social arrangements?" Noirtier asked.

Everyone stood up. "Let's figure out when we can do this," Michel said to Lannes, who nodded.

"Send me a message tomorrow when you've looked at your schedule. I'd like to get another session in before next Tuesday."

"I am at your disposal," I said to Lannes.

I stood, head cast down, in the center of the room while Noirtier stepped back into the position that Subervie had held. Around me the lodge passed in reverse order, beginning with Michel, thanking each of the invoked deities for their regard.

When the last was done, and the final candle extinguished, there was a collective sigh. Max lit the tapers on the mantelpiece and on the side table, bringing light back to the room, and they waited while I went to dress first.

When I came out, having resumed my ordinary clothes, I saw that servants had begun bringing in a repast and laying it out as a buffet. Corbineau had a plate of chicken with mayonnaise, which he was engaging with great gusto. I suddenly realized I was ravenous.

I fetched a plate and stood with him while various gentlemen took turns changing. Reille came and joined us.

"That was very interesting," he said. "Have you done this much before?"

"Not precisely this," I said. "And it was interesting."

"You're very good," he said. "I've been trying to do it the last three times, and I couldn't get anywhere."

"Not your forté," Corbineau said. "Honoré is our technician, if you like. He has the mind for the operational end. He understands how the energy works, and he remembers every correspondence."

"How the energy works?"

Reille shrugged, a difficult gesture for a man with a fork and a plate. "We are a Hermetic lodge, Madame."

"Elza, please."

He smiled, and I thought it was a very nice smile. "Elza. We are a Hermetic lodge, which means we follow in the philosophical footsteps of that ancient sage of Alexandria, Hermes Trismegistus, who taught that everything in the world follows natural law, even those things that seem supernatural. And if it is so, then even things which seem supernatural may be codified and utilized. Just as it is not necessary to understand how to make gunpowder in order to fire a gun, we may find a practical basis for action even if the natural laws which govern the esoteric so far elude us. It remains for future generations to carry on our studies, just as we have carried on the studies of the ancients in every field."

"Have we?" I looked at him over the rim of my glass as I took a sip.

"We have," Honoré said. "The ancients knew five planets, and now we know seven. Copernicus and Kepler have given us ways of understanding them that Aristotle or Ptolemy could not have imagined. And yet we stand on their shoulders. We have sought, these last centuries, to recover lost knowledge, to find our way back to where we got lost. And now we have begun to move on—to see further than the ancients, to seek more just societies than they built, to build the temple they begun."

"To seek more just societies?"

Honoré looked at Corbineau, as if to ask if he were boring, but Corbineau nudged him with a friendly smile. "Slavery, for example. None of the sages of old could compass a world in which slavery was entirely abolished, in which the majority of mankind rejected the idea that one human being should own another."

"The majority of mankind does not reject that idea today," I observed.

"But many do," Honoré said. "We have reached a point where it is a matter of public debate, where our assemblies argue over slavery and whether or not it should be legal, whether or not it should be abolished. That would be simply unthinkable to Aristotle or Seneca. Throughout most of human history, slavery has been a given. Now it is challenged constantly. Is that not seeking a more just society?"

"It is indeed," I said. I could not help but see what Corbineau saw in him, the fire in this man. "Are you a Jacobin, then?"

Honoré laughed. "Heavens, no. I'm a moderate. The Left unbridled is no better than the Right. I have seen the guillotine, and I have seen the misery that revolution can bring when the downtrodden extract payback from anyone they deem their oppressor." He laughed, but a shadow crossed his face. "I cannot stand with them. It is not progress, to substitute one tyranny for another. For example, I agree completely with the principles of freedom of religion and freedom of conscience. I do not think the Church should rule France. Nor do I think that one can wean a people from Catholicism by killing priests, by drowning old nuns who have done no one harm! Freedom of religion means that people must be able to follow their beliefs without danger of censure or harm, whether or not those beliefs are ones I personally agree with." He looked about, drawing Max into our conversation where he had hovered outside, plate in hand. "Max here is a Protestant. He'd have no place in our army in other times. Nor could he serve in England's fleet, unless he were Church of England, not Lutheran."

Max bent over my hand, the one with the glass in it. "I don't believe I've had the honor."

"Madame St. Elme," I said. "Elza to my friends."

"Dr. Maximilien Duplessis, Surgeon attached to VI Corps," he said. "Enchanted, Madame."

"It's my pleasure," I said.

"Also Max to his friends," Corbineau said.

"How is it you come to be here?" Reille asked. "I wondered, when I met you the other day with Corbineau at the fencing salle."

"I am formerly acquainted with M. Noirtier," I said. "And when I heard that Marshal Lannes was in need of a Dove, I was happy to put myself at his disposal." The answer seemed to satisfy all, and in truth it gave a much better excuse for my presence than an imaginary affair with Lannes. That might do for landladies or servants, but it seemed not to work well with anyone who actually knew the man. Only Corbineau looked at me sideways, but he said nothing.

"Well, you did a nice job," Max said. "I tried it myself, and nothing."

"Have all of you tried it?" I asked.

"Pretty much," Corbineau said. "I was the worst."

"No, you weren't. Subervie was the worst," Honoré said.

"It's hard to say who the worst was when none of us got anything," Max said equitably, heading off the race to the bottom. "Let us agree that Elza did better."

"She's a woman," Honoré said meaningfully.

"And that's important?"

"It seems to be," he said. "I don't know why. But the ancients generally employed women as oracles, and most modern cultures that have a living oracular tradition prefer women. It seems logical that whatever natural ability or constellation of abilities make an oracle, it occurs more often in women." He spread his hands. "A fascinating subject of study for someone more inclined to the academic understanding of the esoteric than I am."

"That would be nobody," Corbineau said. "He's our brainy hare."

"Only in comparison to the likes of you," Honoré said good-naturedly. "Next to midgets I am a veritable giant."

Corbineau drew himself up, looking meaningfully at Honore still towering over him by a good six inches. "You are indeed a veritable giant. Outsized, even." It was true that Reille was very tall, the tallest man in the room by a good few inches, overtopping even Michel. "But is your...."

"The lady," Max interrupted meaningfully. "Let's keep it clean."

"Oh yes," Corbineau said, turning and bending over my hand gracefully, his eyes twinkling. "I apologize deeply, Madame. I did not mean to almost make an off color joke in your presence."

"Your apology is accepted," I said, for of course how could I reply suitably as he deserved?

Michel, who had been talking with Lannes, came over and stood at my elbow. "Elza? Would you let me walk you back to your cottage? It's sometimes a little rowdy in Boulogne late at night."

Corbineau looked as though he were going to pop with laughter. And it must be all of ten o'clock.

"Yes," I said. "In a few minutes, if you don't mind." I supposed I could not avoid it. We must try to deal with one another civilly for the good of all, and perhaps we could agree on how. "I will be there in a moment."

Companion

I waited in the courtyard while Michel reclaimed Eleazar from a groom. He had ridden over from Montreuil, of course, as why would he walk? I had not brought Nestor, so Michel walked beside me leading Eleazar, a lantern in his other hand to light our way.

It was a beautiful evening, clear and a little cool, with a brisk wind blowing off the sea. We walked together in silence for a while, through the gates and down the track that led to the cottage.

"I wish you hadn't told me you were sleeping with Lannes," he said at last.

"I didn't tell you I was sleeping with Lannes," I said. "I told you I was here with Lannes, which is true."

Michel glanced sideways at me, his expression impenetrable in the night. "You implied it."

I sighed. I did not want to fight with him. I had hoped we could be civil. "Michel, why does it matter?"

"Because it was very painful."

I stopped. He led Eleazar two paces before he did too. "Please don't start this."

He turned around. "Start what?"

To my horror I heard my voice choke. "You are the one who left me. You are the one who ended it three years ago. You have nothing to say about who I do or do not sleep with. It's not your business."

"You are the one who came to Boulogne." He had dropped the reins, and behind him Eleazar stood patiently, looking perplexed.

"You think I came to Boulogne for you?" I tried to laugh, but it sounded rough even to me. "You think I followed you here in hopes of getting you back? Michel, I did not come to Boulogne for you. I came in spite of you. You are the last person I want to see."

He stood absolutely still, saying nothing.

"If I had wanted to follow you around pathetically, don't you think I would have found you in Paris? Or followed you to Switzerland last year? It's no mystery where you are."

"I suppose not," he said. He sounded sad.

For a moment I was ready to tell him exactly why I was in Boulogne. After all, the Emperor had said he would not forbid me to, because he knew I would. But I would not. I had better sense than to blather to Michel about things that most certainly were not his secrets to keep. I am on the Emperor's mission, I thought, and with that thought my voice was easier to master. I took a step toward him. "Michel," I said more gently, "You ended it. It was your decision, and we both must live with it."

"How could I do anything else, Elza? I was getting married."

"It was your decision to get married," I said. "No one made you do that, Michel."

He threw his head back, the lantern in his hand casting shadows across the track. "What was I supposed to do, Elza? Stand and wait forever? You wouldn't marry me."

"I don't recall you asking," I said sharply.

"After your husband died, when you could have, you said you never wanted to marry again. You said it was slavery, and you would never put your head in the noose twice."

I took a step past him, stepping up to Eleazar's head, walking toward the cottage, my back to him. "I don't know how you could imagine that I would," I said, my face averted from him. "You know what that marriage was like, what it was for me. You know I was twelve when I married him, pregnant before I even bled once. How would you think I would take my freedom and turn around and give it into your hands? That being rid of one master, I would immediately seek another?"

"I never wanted to master you, Elza," he said, and his voice sounded tired.

"Then why would you want to marry me?" I heard myself choke. "We were happy. We were so good together just as we were. Why would you want to change it, except to master me?"

"A home," he said quietly. "A family. Children."

"I never said I didn't want children." He had to follow me, walking up the track, Eleazar at my heels. "I never said that."

He caught up to me with his longer stride. "And what would you have me do? Father children and not marry their mother? Raise children to be bastards on purpose? Only the lowest kind of man would treat his children that way."

I spun around, my face practically against his shoulder. "Michel, you are a Marshal of France. You're not a poor cooper. You can perfectly well support any natural child of yours. And I have no doubt that you would."

"Of course I would!" he shouted. "But that wouldn't fix it. It wouldn't make my sons not bastards. It would mean they would live their whole lives under a cloud."

"A cloud?" I shouted back. "Like who? Like Charles de Flahaut, Talleyrand's son? Everybody knows he's illegitimate, but he's a count and an officer! Tell me what cloud he lives under! Michel, when you have plenty of money these things don't matter at all!"

Michel glanced suddenly about, as though he expected Charles de Flahaut, who was after all Marshal Murat's aide de camp, to suddenly pop out of the sea grass and overhear. "It's still wrong! It's the wrong thing to do, to father children and leave them nameless."

"Fine." I turned around and stalked off. "You have your legitimate children. Happy?"

"No," he said quietly.

I stopped, tears pricking at the back of my eyes. "That is your own doing."

"I know," he said. He had not moved, the lantern in one hand. "Tell me you're happy."

I turned around, took a step back toward him and the patient Eleazar. "What do you want?" I asked him, meeting his eyes. "Do you want me back?"

He drew a breath as though he had taken a blow. "I can't," he said.

"Then why are we having this conversation?" I asked. "Michel, there is nothing good that can come of it. Why are you doing this?"

"So I can see you," he said, and his mouth twisted in something like a smile. "When you're yelling at me I can see you."

I closed my eyes. "You want to see me that much."

"Yes."

I took a step forward, and I knew without looking he would be there, that I would rest my cheek against his chest, my shoulder against his, the smell of his shaving soap and sweat, the feel of his coat against my face. He took a ragged breath and laid his head against my hair, though his arms did not go around me, one being full of the lantern and the other of

Eleazar's reins. Eleazar made a horsy noise of contentment, as if to say he preferred this to all the yelling.

"I still love you," he said unnecessarily.

I felt his breath on my brow, his cheek against my hair. "I know," I said. "And I you."

"I can't betray Aglae. I can't." He sounded like a man who was trying to convince himself. "I should have waited. I should have said that it didn't matter if we never had anything normal, if I never had a family or a home to come back to. I should have said it didn't matter and been content with what there was."

"Michel, that's not who I am," I said. "If you wanted a good woman who would stay at home, I cannot be that woman. You know that. And you weren't willing to have what we could." I opened my eyes, looked up at him. "I would have been willing to compromise," I said. "If you wanted children, I would do that. But I can't not be Charles. I can't not be who I am. And I would embarrass you. Can you see me a Marshal's wife, trotting along at court with Joséphine's train?"

"Madame Lefebvre was a laundress," Michel said stubbornly. "At least you wear shoes."

I laughed at him. "Says the cooper's son!"

"Coopers are a good deal above sutlers," Michel said, but he was grinning. "I would never be ashamed of you."

I took a deep breath, watching the sea breeze ruffle his hair. "I will come back to you," I said, "If you ask me to."

"I can't ask you," he said, and I saw his eyes glittering with tears. "I can't do that."

I swallowed hard. "Then say goodbye and let me be."

"I can't do that either."

I opened my mouth to say, Michel, you're a pain in the ass, but he kissed me and I kissed him, and it was fire on fire, flesh on flesh, our tears mingling on my face. The world tilted around me, night and wind and Michel.

He struggled up like a swimmer in heavy seas. "Let me put the lantern down," he said, "Before I set your skirts on fire."

I started laughing through my tears, and we put our arms around each other and held on for a very long time. There was no need to say anything, or perhaps words were inadequate. There was no need even for a kiss, just to stand like that, holding on, as though all the winds in the world might drag at us unpurposefully.

"I have missed you," I whispered. "I have missed you so much."

"I missed you too," he said. "I missed you every day."

I looked up at him, raising an eyebrow. "Every day? With your wife?"

He swallowed. "It's not the same."

"I told you it wouldn't be."

"It's not that there's anything wrong," he said. "There's nothing wrong. I have nothing to complain of. But she doesn't love me."

I shook my head and laid it against his chest. "Michel, do you think so well of yourself that you believed that you could simply marry any girl who happened along and have her fall in love with you? It's a bit more complicated than that."

"I thought she did. I thought she would," he said. "Why else would she marry me?"

I squeezed him tight. "That's not how aristocratic matches are made. I'm sure she liked you or she needn't have consented. Joséphine would never have pushed her into a marriage she objected to. But aristocrats don't marry for love, Michel. If one is fortunate, one finds someone compatible and pleasant, someone congenial that one can respect. Young ladies of good family aren't supposed to fall in love. At least not until they've been married for some years and take a lover." I looked up at him. "Besides, you don't love her."

He took a breath and let it out, as though letting go of something tight. "I thought I would. I thought I would learn to. I've tried to."

"And?"

He laid one calloused hand against the side of my face. "It's not the same."

Tears came brimming to my eyes again. "Tell me you love me again."

"I do," he said. "Always and always and always."

We walked back to the cottage, our arms around each others' waists, Eleazar walking along companionably behind us. I drew him into my bedroom and he blew out the lamp so that only the moonlight through the thin drapes illuminated us, silver with enchantment. He closed his eyes and bent his face to mine, a kiss long and tender and languid, as though we could simply melt into one another, shadow to shadow, moving in the quiet darkness of the room. We did not even whisper. Any sound might break the spell, undressing in silence, skin to skin still standing in the middle of the room while the sea wind stirred the curtains, body to body entwined.

The night breeze raised gooseflesh on his arms and shoulders. Warmth and cool, skin and air, his breath against my hair like a whisper as I kissed his throat, the plane of his chest, hands roving over his flesh. He might have been a statue carved out of marble, pale skin over defined muscles, a statue come to life for me like Pygmalion, the sum of my dreams.

"You are my dream," he said, his eyes closed and his lips against my hair, as if he had heard my thought.

"And you are mine," I said.

He smiled at that, his arms about my waist as I looked up. "Who dreamed who, do you suppose?"

"I was in your dream and you were in mine," I said. "For what are we but dreams given flesh?"

He shook his head and bent again to me, flesh to flesh like one of those statues that is never on public display, Mars and Venus carved from marble, lovers entwined, bodies yearning but not quite joining. Three years apart, but still we knew each other. We knew every touch, every pause. There were no mysteries, only sweet returning.

Tender, yes, but I pushed him as he needed, goading him at the last, and he clutched at me like a starving man, with a desperation I had never seen in him before. "You must," I said, riding him as he lay upon my white sheets, the moonlight making a stripe across the bed and wall, the shadow of the window frame across his shoulder like a brand. "You must."

His hands tightened, frustration and desire warring for a moment.

"I will not let you stop," I said, low and dangerous, and that was enough, enough to tip him over the edge at last, his groans loud enough to hear outside, were there anyone to hear them.

Michel reached for me then, drawing me down blindly against him, his face to my breast and his eyes shut. I could feel his heart thudding against me like the tattoo of distant drums.

"There, my darling," I said, my hands on his tight shoulders. "There, my dear. It is all right now. It is all mended."

"It isn't," he said. "It will never be right. There is no choice which is right now. I've broken my vows."

I closed my eyes. "You were mine first." The sea wind blew in the curtains, cooling my heated skin.

"I can't do it, Elza," he whispered. "Aglae, my sons…."

My eyes popped open and I raised up on my elbow. "Aglae isn't here, is she? What she doesn't know won't hurt her."

"It's still wrong," he said. "And I should not have done it. It's wrong whether or not she knows."

I shook my head, fresh pain gathering in the pit of my stomach. "And your eventual punishment in purgatory is so much more important than my happiness. The state of your soul is so much more important than I am."

"You make fidelity sound like nothing but a self-indulgence."

"Isn't it?" I asked bitterly. "You say you love me, but I don't really see you very concerned about whether or not I'm happy. You married Aglae from ambition, pure and simple. Marrying the Emperor's goddaughter did you a lot of good. All those private conversations with the Emperor, all those intimate little dinners and family gatherings. Spent a lot of time with him, have you? His Hephaistion!"

Michel flinched as though I had slapped him. "No," he said quietly. "Actually I don't see him very often." He turned his head so that it was in profile to me, harder to read, especially in the moonlight. "I was sent to Switzerland, not that I minded, as it was a job he needed done and he said he could count on me to do it. And then he gave me the corps command here, and the School of War. Which is everything I ever wanted, of course. But I don't see him very much, no."

I opened my mouth and shut it again. Impossible, but I knew him. Impossible, but I knew how he was with Charles.

He looked at me sideways, eyes keen and overly bright, furious and pained at once. "What?"

"Michel, you didn't," I whispered. I couldn't even....

"Of course not," he said levelly. "You can't imagine such a thing. It would never cross his mind, and anyone who suggested it would be insane, or at least deluded and perverted at once."

And anyone who did would find themselves with a very honorable and pleasant command far from Paris. Anyone who was his Hephaistion.

I put my hand to my mouth. Not two weeks ago I had sat in the Emperor's study, receiving orders for Boulogne, orders that he knew would land me in Michel's lap. He had even told me I might confide in Michel if I wished. I had assured him it was over between us, but the Emperor had only smiled. Oh yes, I was here to catch a spy, providentially here to solve Lannes' problem of needing a Dove, but if it killed still another bird with the same stone, was that not to the benefit of everyone? I should be happy, Michel should be satisfied, and Napoleon would have to see nothing that should prove awkward to see.

Wheels within wheels within wheels, all the workings of that complex, elegant mind....

I opened my mouth and shut it again, and for the first time sober and waking really, truly believed. "He is Alexander."

Michel nodded, a rueful smile on his face. "Yes."

I bent my forehead against his shoulder, cool and yielding like marble half made flesh. "This is all real."

"Yes."

I could count every freckle on his skin, redhead fair where the sun did not touch it. "The witches of England, the rituals, the angels, the gods...." My voice caught in my throat. "It's all real."

"This is one of the Great Stories, the Emperor's Tale," Michel said, shifting onto his back so that I lay against him, his arm beneath me. "Again and again this wandering Prometheus passes through the world with fire that burns and lights, as much punishment as reward. And we are his Companions, bound by our own wills, by our oaths and our desires, to journey in his train."

"We?"

"Lannes and Noirtier and Subervie and Reille, Corbineau and Duplessis and the others. You saw some of us tonight. You know what we are."

"The Knights of the Round Table. Charlemagne's Paladins...." My voice failed me. I looked up at him, but his blue eyes were perfectly serious, light touched and clear. "You really believe."

"I know," he said.

"Not a metaphor. Not a joke."

"No." He stroked my hair with one hand. "I know. And so do you."

It was as though the world had turned on its axis, as though vast tides had shifted, as though at last everything fell into place with a great and perfect stillness. It was as though at last I looked at it whole, not fractured pieces in a blackened mirror, a thing so perfect and impenetrable that understanding it was almost beyond me, like looking for one moment into the mind of God, or seeing the world as an angel must see it.

"If I dare to believe it I will be mad," I whispered.

"If you dare to believe it you will be whole," Michel said, and cupped my face in his hand. "The world is a numinous place, Elza, for people who dare to see it. There is magic in every tree and stone, and angels walk beside us. We are spirits given flesh, and we are older than the stories they tell about us."

I blinked as the tears spilled from my eyes.

He brushed one away with the pad of his thumb. “Say my name,” he whispered, as though it were challenge and affirmation both. “Look at me and name me.”

I looked, and in his beloved face I could see the others, shadows beneath the surface, all the things I had tried not to see. Red hair, yes, that rose from his brow, and brown eyes and a broad forehead….

“Hephaistion son of Amyntor,” I said, and felt my voice grow stronger with each syllable, as though an organ spoke below my tone with a deep note on the edge of hearing. “Patroklos of Achaia. Marcus Vipsanius Agrippa. Jonathan.”

He bent his head beneath my words.

“Bedwyr ap Griffyth. Hroudland of the Breton March. Flavius Aetius.” Too fast, too strong, like a dam washing away in a flood. “Erik Thorfinnson, Khanefernumut, Robert Dudley. Izabela of Falkenau.”

“You are our oracle,” he said. “Priest and Companion at once, born in a body with a Dove's power.”

And the Emperor's agent, I thought. Michel did not know all. He did not know what I had promised, that I had knelt knowing I had said those words before, imagined the night garden in Babylon, the King's hands burning with fever. He did not know all. He did not know that Napoleon himself had named me, five years ago in Milan.

“Why here? Why now?”

Michel shrugged. “I don't know, but I can guess that it is because the flood has come, that the world is changing as dramatically as it ever did in Alexander's day, in any other day where we have walked. We come when the flood comes.”

“Awaken from sleep in the hollow hills,” I said. “Return like bulbs in spring, sprouting underground and clawing upward toward the light.” I looked at him, touched his face with compassion. “Oh, Michel. As though you did not already have too much responsibility!”

His mouth twisted in a rueful smile. “We are what we are.”

“And you have worked this out? You and these men?”

Michel nodded. “Not all those names you said. I don't know them all. I don't know all the stories. I don't see things for other people, just bits and pieces of things I remember. And until I got here, I didn't talk about them with anyone.”

The sea wind lifted the curtains, blowing in from the Channel, a breath of cool. "Until you were at the School of War, reminding yourself every day. Until you were in this Lodge."

"Yes," Michel said. "And how not, when we are playing our own battles, reminding ourselves of what we already know?"

I blinked at him as suddenly another thing became clear. "You're doing it on purpose," I said. "You're deliberately finding Companions by giving men these campaigns to play and seeing what it stirs up. You're watching to see who reacts to what."

"And to which stories. Corbineau's one of the few who has faced firearms before. He knows what to do with a wheel-lock pistol, too."

"Of course he does," I began. Snow swirling around us, the snows of Hohenlinden in my memory when I had stood with Corbineau, but not the first time. A heavy man with a dark beard and a scarred face, Polish or Bohemian, a sash of Imperial scarlet over a buff coat....

Michel was looking at me, and for the first time I deliberately finished the thought. "Of course he does," I said. "He served with Wallenstein, in the Imperial Army."

Michel took a deep breath. "And before that?"

"I don't know," I said. "I've never tried to look on purpose, not except in the rituals." I met his eyes again, the wonder creeping over me. "Michel, it's all real."

"It's real."

"You never told me you remembered these things," I said.

"You never told me you did séances," he replied.

"It was before I met you," I said. "It frightened me, and I'd given it up before we were together. There didn't seem to be any reason to tell you." I looked at him. "You were in a lodge then, weren't you? The last months we were together? I thought it was ordinary Masonry."

"I am in an ordinary lodge," he said sheepishly, "And this one too. I didn't lie to you. I just didn't tell the whole truth. It's not the kind of thing you're supposed to tell people, Elza."

I put my head on his shoulder. "So many things I never knew," I said. "So many things for us still to learn."

He leaned his face against my hair, his lips just brushing it. "It doesn't change anything, Elza."

I looked up at him. "What do you mean, it doesn't?"

Michel swallowed, his face pale in the moonlight. "We can't do this. We can't be lovers. I want to, Elza, but we can't. I'm married."

I closed my eyes. "You are determined, then."

"I should never have done this," he said. "It was a moment of weakness. I can't help how I feel about you, but I can help what I do."

I dug my nails into his shoulder, deep enough to hurt, deep enough to draw blood. "Then hear me on this, Michel. Don't do this to me again. I can't do this. Don't come back to me again unless you mean to stay." I choked, and pressed on. "I can't live like this, waiting for you and hoping for you. I will find someone else, and I will be happy."

He flinched, but he did not move, though my nails drew blood. "You should. You should find someone else. You should be happy."

"Yes," I said, and lifted my head. "Surely there's another Companion out there. Corbineau's trying to set me up with his friend, Reille, after all!"

Michel gulped. "I would wish you and Honoré every happiness."

"Like hell you would."

He sat up, the covers around his waist. "I will try to," he said. "I will honestly try. I want you to be happy, even if...." Even if he could not be. He had made those decisions, and now he must live with them.

I took his hand, running my fingers over its familiar contours for what might be the last time, feeling the shape of every tendon. "Michel, don't go."

"I have to," he said. "Elza, we have to try to be good."

"My definition of good is not the same as yours," I said.

"No," he said sadly. "I see that it's not."

We dressed and I walked him to the door. Eleazar was placidly dozing, tied up to the post. The wind was blowing off the sea, and in the east the stars of morning were rising, Venus burning brightly ahead of the sun.

He turned and put his arms around me once more, and I held him for one long moment. "Goodbye, love," I whispered.

"Well, until Thursday," he said. "We've still got to work together."

"I know," I said. I felt a strange sense of peace about it, not angry, not frustrated anymore. This was as it was because we were ourselves, and that was what was most precious, companions rather than lovers. "But now maybe we can put it behind us, like a fever that burns away. Now maybe we can see each other without it hurting so much." I hoped so. I should have to see him over and over for who knows how long, until my mission was accomplished. And not much of an incentive to finish, I said to myself.

Involuntarily, I glanced toward the sea, where Lion patrolled in her endless offshore loop. There was a light bobbing along the cliff.

"Michel, what is that?"

He looked about. "A lantern?" The one he had carried had been put out long since.

"Who would be there with a lantern before dawn?" I asked, but before the words were even out of my mouth the sound of laughter and girls' voices came on the breeze. They came closer, four young girls in bonnets, long aprons over their cotton dresses.

"Girls who work in Boulogne but live in one of the villages down the coast," Michel said. "They go home at night to their families and come in to work in the morning. Lots of servants who work in Boulogne are from the villages. We've brought a lot of work to the area, good paying jobs in town."

They were giggling and joking, and as I watched one swung around poking another, who danced away down the path, taunting her with what sounded like a boy's name.

Now I am ridiculous, I thought. I am seeing mysterious things under every stone.

"Goodbye," Michel said.

"Good night," I said, and kissed him once more before he mounted up on Eleazar and rode away.

Patrons and Possibilities

In the morning Subervie and I went out early to walk along the cliffs.

“I didn’t see anything last night,” he said, “But that doesn’t mean there was nothing to see. The cliffs are treacherous. I didn’t try climbing down to the beach in the dark.”

It was another beautiful day, with the sun glancing golden off the waves and the gulls twisting and twirling in the warm air. I wore my thinnest muslin dress and a straw bonnet, but even so I was hot before we had gone far. Out to sea, Lion was making her way northward, sails set.

“I take it you didn’t see anyone,” I said.

Subervie shook his head. “No, but it took a while to get here. Our man could have been and gone. In fact, he probably was.” I appreciated that he did not add “if he were ever here.” I thought he believed me, believed what I had seen. It was something of a relief to be taken seriously.

We walked along the top of the cliffs together. In many places they were not high, only ten or twelve meters, but at high tide the sea came right up along the base. At low tide, as this was, there were stones and occasional strips of sandy beach at their base.

“You won’t see anything down there,” Subervie said as I looked over. “Tide’s been in and out. Any footprints or places where a boat was brought in would be smoothed out.”

“Yes, I see,” I said, leaning over. There were sandy pockets here and there, and even some struggling beach grasses tucked among the stones. It might be possible to climb down to the beach. For a nimble man. I looked at Subervie’s feet, clad in their customary cavalry boots with a heel. My little thin slippers were actually more practical for climbing. But how anyone would do it in the dark….

Subervie shaded his eyes, looking out to Lion’s wake. “I just don’t see how he’s doing it.”

I shook my head. "I don't either. But if he can figure out how to do it, so can we."

Where the track curved back toward the marshes, toward Montreuil, I stopped. A small sandy path led down two meters or so, curving behind a boulder. "What's down there?" I asked.

Subervie shrugged. "Nothing. It goes down behind that rock and stops. It's sheer cliffs below that another nine meters or so. It doesn't go anywhere. You can't get down that way."

"Nevertheless," I said, and began to climb down. Shrugging, Subervie followed me.

The boulder jutted out above, providing a patch of shade over an area large enough for Subervie and me to stand together comfortably. In the shade was a weather-beaten old blanket, threadbare and faded, wadded up against the stone. I picked it up.

"A lover's lane?" Subervie suggested. "It is private. You can't see it from the path above. If one of the men is meeting one of the village girls, this would be a good place. It's got a romantic view."

"It does, doesn't it?" I said. It offered a panoramic view of sea and sky, of Lion with her white sails stretched against the waves. Subervie was right, though, that there was no way down. It was a steep drop to the jagged rocks below.

And yet it could not be seen from above.

I clutched at Subervie's arm, and he steadied me as though he were afraid I might fall. "Careful, Madame," he said.

"Elza," I said. "Please." An idea was forming. "What if no one climbs down to the beach?" Subervie waited, sweat beading on his forehead, and after a moment I continued. "What if nobody ever goes up and down at all? What if they're doing it by signals?"

"Like flags or a semaphore?" Subervie nodded slowly. "We use the semaphore all the time, and of course their navy has flag signals." He frowned. "Lion can get in close enough to read a signal, especially through a telescope. But somebody wandering around the cliffs with a bunch of naval flags would be pretty obvious."

"Not flags," I said. "Lanterns." I watched the idea sink in. "People walk along this path with lanterns all the time. I did it last night. I imagine you did too. Nobody would ever pay any attention. It wouldn't look odd at all. And what you'd need would be a place to get off the path easily, a place where the light wouldn't be visible from above when you opened the shutters to signal."

"A place just like this." Subervie nodded. "You'd never see it from the path. The boulder is in the way. And if I were on patrol and I saw a man coming back from here with a lantern, I'd assume he'd answered a call of nature."

"Especially if he were in uniform, and were someone who would reasonably be supposed to be here," I said. "Someone who is quartered in Boulogne but attends the School of War? Someone quartered in Montreuil but who has duties in Boulogne?"

Subervie whistled, wiping the sweat from his brow. "That's a lot of men. Hundreds, probably. But it makes sense. It completely makes sense."

"We need to watch this spot," I said. "We need to see who comes here."

"Or just guard it," Subervie said. "That would stop him."

"For the moment," I said. "Until he found some other place along the coast, or some other way of communicating. Interdicting his communications would be useful if we can't do anything else, but let's try catching him first. After all, if that fails we can always then guard it."

Subervie nodded. "There is that." He took my elbow and helped me back from the edge, up the steep incline to the top of the cliff. "Let's go report to Marshal Lannes. Watching this place is going to be interesting. Not much cover."

"We're going to need more men on this," Lannes said. He stood in the stableyard, where a groom was leading out a beautiful white Andalusian for him.

Subervie nodded. "I hesitate to just detail a company to guard duty. Then everybody in the army will know by tomorrow."

Lannes stopped sharply, one hand on the reins. "Not that," he said. "We need to catch this man and make an end to it. If you detail a company to guard duty, he'll hear about it and change how he communicates with Lion. No, this has to be handled very, very discreetly. No more than a few people on it, all officers you can trust. And Madame St. Elme, of course." He nodded at me. "Good work, Madame."

"Thank you," I said.

"Assign in pairs," Lannes said. "Sunset to sunrise, every day. We'll just have to keep an eye on the place. Though for all we know it may be one of several places he uses. If he gets there and there are other people around, he may go on to another location. Still, if we watch long enough we should catch him."

"About the only place you can't see from the track is behind the boulder itself," Subervie said. "We'll have to sit there and wait for someone to come. It's the only place entirely covered from the path above that's within sight."

"Fine," Lannes said. He clapped Subervie on the shoulder. "Patience, Gervais. We'll get our man!"

Thus it was with a distinct feeling of satisfaction that I left Subervie about this business and went to find an early lunch at one of the cafes in Boulogne. I had slept perhaps two hours between dawn and morning, and thought that if I did not find some coffee immediately I would probably fall asleep in the street. No doubt Michel was in the same predicament, over at the School of War, losing another ancient battle....

I blinked, sitting in the sun, waiting for the waiter to come. I would not think about Michel. Not until I had some sleep. Not until I had at least scrubbed the scent of him off my hands, washed away every kiss.

Even now, even this moment, I wanted him.

But it was not as though he could fail to see me. The Lodge and Napoleon had guaranteed that. For the next weeks at any rate he should have to see me several times a week. And we had much to talk about.

The waiter came and brought my coffee, which I drank liberally mixed with milk. In the light of day, sitting in a café off the square before Boulogne Castle, the things we had talked about seemed incredible. And yet this time I did not retreat. Each time before I had nearly come to something, nearly said that I believed, I had backed off again in light of day. This time I did not.

Honoré-Charles Reille had said that one of the basic principles of the work of the Lodge was that everything followed natural law, whether we understood it or not. Simply because something seemed fantastic was no reason to dismiss it, especially when there were the observations of many. I might be mad. I had admitted that long ago. The things I remembered in flashes, the things that seemed true to me on some inner level, might be no more than the products of a deluded mind. But were these men mad? Sober men, responsible men, leaders of France? They were not drunks and opium eaters or madmen scamming the credulous. They were not bored women with nothing to do or whores and actresses. They were responsible, reliable people, men at the top of their profession, doctors and soldiers and in Noirtier's case apparently scholars. I could not dismiss my own memories and perceptions so easily if they were shared.

I took another long drink of coffee. Angels and elementals and ancient gods. Were these things any less likely than the teachings of the Church? Of course my father would have said the Church was nothing but folly, and Victor Moreau would have agreed with him. And yet were they more credible witnesses to the universe than Michel or Lannes, than Corbineau and Reille? Should I dismiss my own experiences because long ago my father had taught me that it could not be true?

I shook my head. In so many ways his memory was sacrosanct to me, my perfect, lost protector. If my father had lived, how different would my life have been!

But as I neared the age at which he had died, twenty-eight to his thirty-six, I began to wonder if he had indeed had all the answers. Perhaps he had been like me, an adventurer adrift in the world, making his way by his wits and protecting those he loved as best he could. Perhaps we were very alike in ways I had not imagined when I was a child, in ways I could not have understood then. He had done the best he could for me. I knew that. It had not been enough to keep me safe, to save me from life's storms, but it had been his best. For that I would always adore him. But it was possible he had been wrong about some things. It was possible he had made poor decisions, had not understood. He should have listened to my mother when she told him doom waited in Amsterdam, rather than dismissing it as a product of her derangement. She had told him the truth.

He had died the third day after we came to Amsterdam. It required no curses, no secrets, for a man to be struck with apoplexy, even a young man, when he had drunk too heavily for too long, eaten too richly and well, after a tiring journey when burdens weighed heavily upon him. He collapsed and died. There was no more to say of it.

I had stood beside his grave wearing black, listening to the unfamiliar words of the Dutch Reformed service, wondering if he would mind that there was no priest. Probably not. There was no God to him, no God who would care.

My mother did not move or speak. She stood there in her widow's weeds, still and lovely as a flower stricken by frost. She did not scream or cry or lose herself. She had known this would happen. She believed the curse had claimed her, as she had always known it would.

All the women in our family are Doves, she had said. Now that I could not ask her, I wondered where she had heard that, where she had found that word. Once again, she had been right.

I blinked, looking into my coffee cup. I could choose. I could choose what to believe, and in choosing decide who I was. Was I nothing but an adventuress, one blonde among many, a bad actress, sometime medium, former mistress of two generals who was even now losing her looks? Was I one more woman on that progress from respectability to unmarked grave?

Or was I a Companion, a rare and fabulous thing, an ancient soul on a journey unfathomably strange and wonderful?

Was I an abomination or a treasure? I had asked that of Napoleon in Milan, and he had only smiled and given me my freedom and said he would see what I did with it.

And I came back to his hand, sure as a falcon to the sun.

Companion, I thought, and raised my head. I am a Companion. That is what I choose to be, how I will live my life. It is who I am. I choose to be a treasure. I choose to believe.

I had almost finished my lunch when Corbineau cleared his throat. I spun about and he dropped into the empty chair opposite me, a critical look on his face. "Don't you look like the morning after the night before!"

"God, Jean-Baptiste!" I groaned. "Is that all you have to say?"

"More or less," he said, with a smirk. "But this morning it was not I who crept in at dawn, unshaven and disreputable! No, it was a certain substantial red-haired gentleman of my acquaintance! I trust that all is well?"

"No," I said shortly. "It isn't. Nor is it likely to be."

Corbineau folded his hands on the table. "Is he truly that big an ass?"

"He's married," I said. "And determined to be true to his wife. Tell me, Jean-Baptiste, is she such a naïf that she expects that?"

He shrugged. "I've only met her a dozen times socially, and I don't know her well, but no, I don't think she's a naïf. I'd say Aglae's fairly astute, actually. She's quiet, but I've never gotten the impression that she's stupid. And remember, she grew up in Joséphine's house during the Directory. I'd say she knows what's what."

"Then why in the world did she marry Michel?" I asked.

"Who wouldn't?"

"I wouldn't," I said.

Corbineau laughed. "Then you can hardly mind if someone else did."

"I don't mind that he married her. I mind that he won't have me as well," I said, taking a last vicious stab at my lunch.

"Ah."

"Ah what?"

"Ah that's it," Corbineau said. "He won't come out and make an offer like a gentleman."

I threw my hands up. "Jean-Baptiste, I don't even mind that! I'd be perfectly happy to be his lover without any financial support at all! I don't need it right now."

He looked at me, and his eyes were keen. "And I don't suppose you'll tell me how that came about." He leaned forward, dropping his voice. "I think it's time to level with me, Elza. I know that you didn't come to Boulogne for the Lodge. The first time I mentioned it you didn't have any idea what I was talking about. I've heard four different stories now, and all of them untrue. You're not here with Lannes, you're not here with the Marshal, and you're not here with Subervie. So now's the time to tell me why you're actually here. The truth, Elza."

I sighed. I should have anticipated this. Corbineau was too smart not to have seen holes in the story, as well as he knew me. I glanced about. It was early, and the tables around us were empty except for an enterprising seagull hunting crumbs under the chairs. If Subervie were recruiting officers to help us watch, one of them might as well be Corbineau. "Jean-Baptiste, you must not repeat this."

"I am the soul of discretion," he said.

"I am on the Emperor's business to catch a spy."

He nodded slowly. "You work for Fouché?"

"No," I said. "I work directly for the Emperor himself. I had my orders from him, face to face. I report in the field to Marshal Lannes."

He let out a long breath, and I could almost see the wheels turning in his mind, things adding up. "This has something to do with Lion, doesn't it?"

"Yes," I said, and told him the whole story.

When I was done, Corbineau nodded gravely. "I can help with that," he said. "I'll take a watch. Gervais knows me, and he knows I can keep my mouth shut. Does the Marshal know?"

"No," I said. "And I don't see any need to tell him."

"You think it's someone on his staff," Corbineau said. "Someone other than me, I mean. And you think I can help with that."

"I do," I said evenly. "Jean-Baptiste, when I was in his quarters he had the cipher key lying out on the desk. Anyone who came in while you were at the exercises could just help themselves. You know I love him, but he's completely impossible about things like that. He'd trust the wrong person and there are too many officers with axes to grind, with old grudges."

"That's why you were asking me about Honoré," he said. "About his brother-in-law who went to the guillotine. You're wrong about that one, Elza. Honoré is as solid as anyone. I'll buy that it's someone on the Marshal's staff. I won't buy that it's Honoré."

"Maybe not," I said. "I don't know him. But it's somebody, and it's somebody that seems above suspicion."

"Not him," Corbineau said stubbornly. "I'd bet my life on it."

"Would you bet everyone else's life too?" I asked. "Because that's what we're doing."

He paused for a second, then nodded. "On Honoré? Yes."

"Why are you so sure?"

Corbineau shook his head. "I just am. He's a good fellow, Elza. I know that like I know my own name."

I glanced around again. The waiter was helping people at a distant table, but was not close. "Do you remember things? Things long ago?"

He looked startled. "The Marshal told you that business, did he?"

I nodded.

"No," Corbineau said, and I thought there was something sad in his tone. "I don't. Except that I know how to do things sometimes the first time I try them. I have feelings about people. I'm a good judge of character, they say. I can pick a good one out of the crowd."

"Like you did me in Bavaria," I smiled.

"Like that. I knew I liked you when I met you. I knew we were friends." Corbineau spread his hands. "That's all. I'm not a Dove, and I don't see things in mirrors."

"And your friend Reille?'

"We haven't talked about it directly," he said. "But he's got to have been Persian, hasn't he, the way he keeps getting stuck with the horse archers? He's the only one who can figure out what to do with them." He looked at me with a little smile. "Why don't you look and see?"

"Can I just do that?"

"How should I know?" Corbineau laughed, and signaled for the waiter himself. "You're the Dove."

"I don't really know what I can do," I said slowly. All of my effort in the past had been put into not doing.

"Well, now that you're doing it for France, don't you think you'd better learn?" Corbineau asked. The waiter leaned over him. "I'd like the gratin dauphinoise and the ham, if you still have any. And a pot of mustard, please."

It was a new and strange thought. I waited until the waiter left again. "How does one learn these things?" I asked. "It's not as though one can go to school."

"Apprenticeship." Corbineau shrugged. "One is admitted to the Lodge as an Apprentice, and then you learn from others longer in the service. I've not been in but a year myself, an Admitted Apprentice. That's why my sash was white the other night."

"And the colored sashes?" I asked, thinking of the blue one Lannes had worn, and the red one of Michel's.

"They've taken a higher degree," Corbineau explained. "When you become a Journeyman, you are dedicated to the service of a particular patron, and you wear their colors. Which isn't to say that you don't work with or invoke anyone else, or that you can't stand any quarter, but you have a special relationship with your patron. You can still work with others, though, especially if you have an affinity for the work. The Marshal called Serapis the other night, and he's not a dedicant of Serapis."

"Who is his patron?" I asked, though I thought I knew.

"The Archangel Michael."

Original Sin

"I can't get through."

I sat in the midst of the circle for the third time in a week, the candle on the table burning low before me. About me the gentlemen of the Lodge waited, their white robes glimmering in the candlelight. Wordlessly, Lannes reached around me to offer me a glass of water he had waiting. I took it, my hand shaking.

"Are you all right?" he asked.

I gulped the water and nodded. Three times I had done this, three times fled from the air elemental called into being over the Channel. Each time it got easier. Each time the return to my own body was smoother. I drank the water down, letting it ground me.

"I can't get past it," I said. "This time I tried going southwest, far out to sea, but as soon as I turned north again and came in on the coast of Britain it was there. I must have been somewhere west of Portsmouth. It shows up as soon as I get a mile or so from shore."

Reille cleared his throat. "It's been tied to the boundaries somehow. I don't think we can take this thing down without knowing how it was summoned."

"I can't go through it," I said.

"I don't imagine you can," Reille said.

Subervie nodded. "The same thing happens to our ships. The winds are foul constantly. If we try to sail into this, we'll be blown straight back to Boulogne."

"If we're lucky," Lannes said. "Remember, part of the Spanish Armada was wrecked off Scotland!"

"We need to find out how it was summoned," Reille said. "Jean-Baptiste, any luck?"

"Oddly enough there aren't many rare books about British folklore lying around Boulogne," Corbineau said testily. "In fact, there aren't any.

The only thing about swans I've got is a nursery story about a princess turned into a swan in Ireland." He looked at Michel. "You need a scholar at La Sorbonne on this, not me."

"We don't have time for that," Michel said. "That could take months."

Lannes looked at Michel over my head. "Then you know what that means. Are you willing to try it?"

Michel nodded, his face grave in the flickering light of the candles. "I don't see how else to do it quickly. If Noirtier thinks it's possible."

Noirtier steepled his hands before his chin. "I think it's possible. Whether or not I can do it, and whether or not you are a good subject for this practice is unknown. But it is worth a try, if you are willing to risk it."

"I am," Michel said.

"What are you talking about?" I demanded. "What kind of risk? What are you going to do to Michel?"

Noirtier looked vaguely surprised. "An experiment, Madame, which may give us some answers. Marshal Ney has said that he has vague memories of a past life during the time of the Spanish Armada, a life in which, if he is not mistaken, he may have been the Earl of Leicester."

I met Michel's eyes. It was I who had named him thus, who had given form to the memories.

"Your pardon, but most of us have no idea who that is," Corbineau said.

"Robert Dudley, Earl of Leicester, was Queen Elizabeth's favorite for thirty years, and was Captain-General of the Queen's Armies at the time of the Spanish Armada," Noirtier said. "He was also a student of Dr. John Dee, the most noted alchemist and magician of his time. Whatever working was done against the Armada, it is indisputable that Robert Dudley would have known the innermost secrets of it. If it is true that Marshal Ney was indeed Robert Dudley in times gone by, he already knows the things we seek. It's only a matter of finding those memories in his mind."

"And how do you propose to do that?" I demanded. "It is not as though past memories lie near the surface, and finding them at all is very rare. You are talking about very complicated things too, not just someone's name or a flicker of memory."

"That is the challenge," Noirtier acknowledged. "However, a colleague of mine in Paris, Dr. Franz Mesmer, has produced some amazing results with a technique of his."

Subervie stirred. "The man who was thrown out of Vienna for bizarre experiments with animal magnetism?"

"Dr. Mesmer is a scholar whose work is not yet fully appreciated," Noirtier said stiffly.

"Is this safe?" I asked hotly.

Michel raised a hand as though he meant to touch me, then dropped it. "No, Elza. It's not safe. Noirtier has never done this before, and I have no idea what will happen. But it must be tried. If I do know the information we seek, it will save us months of work."

"You're going to let him experiment with your mind," I said flatly.

"Yes."

"Do you have a better idea, Madame?" Noirtier asked. "You can't get through their air elemental, and we do not know how it was called. If the Marshal can remember it, then we can order our counterattack."

"And if it goes wrong?"

"Elza, how wrong can it go?" Michel said, his eyes on mine. "There's nothing I'm afraid of inside my own mind." I looked in his eyes and knew that was a lie. "I need to do this."

I threw my hands up. "I have nothing to say about this," I said.

"Then move back by Subervie," Michel said. "Corbineau, can you cut a gate and go get a blanket?"

I waited while they went through the ritual of opening a gate in the circle with a sword, and stood while everyone rearranged things, a pallet of two blankets on the floor for Michel to lie on in the center instead of my scrying table. Subervie shifted into Michel's place in the circle at the northward quarter, and I into where Subervie had been, between him and Dr. Duplessis. Michel lay down on the pallet, his head to the east near me, and his feet almost in Lannes' lap at west.

"I will need quiet for the first part of this," Noirtier said. "But after a while he will not hear you. Also, it would be helpful for someone to take notes."

There was another stir while Subervie cut a gate for Corbineau to go out for paper and ink.

I looked at Michel and he looked at me. His mouth twitched. "Now who's telling who what they can do?" he said softly. "You are as bad as I am."

I shook my head. "Michel, be careful," I said. I glanced around at everyone still busy. "I don't see anyone saying you need to take your clothes off!"

"I don't think I need to be naked to find my own mind," he said.

"Quiet please!" Noirtier said, and gradually everyone settled back into their own places, with Corbineau designated as scribe. Noirtier lifted the candle in its base, now burned down to less than a hand's width.

Michel looked up at it as it cast strange shadows across his face as Noirtier moved it, his blue eyes very bright. It came to me that perhaps this scared him as much as the scrying had me.

I reached out and touched his shoulder with my hand. "It will be well," I whispered. "I'm here."

"Focus on the candle flame," Noirtier instructed. "I will begin to make passes with it, and you must follow it with your eyes. Focus on the flame and nothing else. Watch how it burns, and let it fill your mind." As he began to speak, he moved the candle slowly back and forth before Michel's gaze, left and right, back and forth. "Focus on the flame. Let it fill you. See how it burns, and watch it."

It seemed to me that the flame burned more brightly, that the shadows danced like waves across the room, brighter and brighter as it filled my gaze.

"See nothing but the candle. Watch the flame. See how it burns, and focus on it with your mind. Let the flame fill you."

Back and forward again, the movement of light and fire. Back and again, Noirtier's voice cool and calm, just at the edge of hearing. Back and again. The light flickered off Michel's face, changing and shifting.

"There is nothing but the flame and the light." His eyes flickered. "You can close your eyes. You can still see the flame on the back of your eyelids, still see the light surrounding you as you float, light and soft as a dream amid the flame."

I swayed and caught myself on my hands, glancing at the dark around me in startlement.

Subervie squeezed my hand. "All right?" he mouthed.

I nodded. It was easy, whatever this was. If this were a spell it was one that was so easy to fall into. Looking around the circle, I could see that Lannes was as entranced as I had been, Reille's eyes huge and dark, drifting closed. Corbineau, however, was doodling on the edge of his paper. That was oddly reassuring.

I looked back at Michel, the rise and fall of his chest with his breathing even and slow, as though he slept. It seemed that this went on and on, oddly repetitious, fire and flame and the same words again and again. It might have been a quarter hour that we sat thus. It might have been half the night.

There was a pattern to the passes the candle made across Michel's body, from his right wrist to his left shoulder to his right shoulder, from his right shoulder to his left wrist to the crown of his head to his right wrist. I caught my breath.

Reille's eyes were open, and he leaned closer to whisper, "It's an invoking pentagram. Don't worry. It's nothing bad."

If that was supposed to be reassuring it wasn't, but Noirtier did not hush us, so intent on Michel was he. Michel seemed oblivious. I would have thought he slept deeply, so still was he, the light dancing off his face. For a moment I thought I saw gold coins resting on his eyelids, heavy tetradrachmas with a king wearing rams' horns on his brow....

"You are standing at the top of a flight of stairs," Noirtier said, and I jumped. After so many repetitions I had almost forgotten him, let his voice become part of the flame and movement. "A flight of stairs spiraling down into the past, into your past. Are you ready to walk down them?"

Michel's lips moved laboriously, as though sunk in some illness. "Yes," he whispered, a thread of sound.

"Then begin walking down the steps. And as you walk, you will see many doors that open onto the stairs. Each door represents a life that you have lived, a past that has been yours. Do you see the doors?"

Again the whisper. "Yes."

"Go down the stairs," Noirtier suggested. "Go down and down the spirals, past the doors, until you come to the one that conceals behind it the moment where begins the problem foremost in your mind. When you reach that door, stop."

For a long moment nothing happened. I wondered what spirals Michel was walking in his mind, long counterclockwise stairs deep into the heart of himself. I could almost see the cressets along the walls, the dark stone, almost see them as though I walked with him into the dark.

"I am there," he said, and his voice sounded a little stronger, though his eyes did not move beneath their lids.

"Can you open the door?" Noirtier asked.

"Yes."

"Then pass through."

His face changed. I knew no other way to describe it. While his features were the same that I had always known, the set of his lips, the way he held his chin, the lines about his eyes all changed. Younger, yes, with a different way of holding himself, a different expression....

I had hardly begun to catalog it when Noirtier spoke. "Where are you?"

"At a wedding." His voice was different too, lighter, the words spoken a little slower.

Corbineau scratched madly on paper with his quill.

"Whose wedding? What do you see?" Noirtier prompted.

His eyes flickered beneath his lids, as though Michel were looking about at a scene only he could see. "Hanging lamps. Tables. Food on the tables, servants going around with wine. It's the wedding banquet."

Lannes and Noirtier exchanged glances and Lannes shrugged as if to say he had no idea.

"More tables. Cups. There's a musician."

Hanging lamps? I mouthed at Lannes. I didn't think that Tudor England used hanging lamps, though I was no expert on such things.

"Incense smoke everywhere. The tumblers are coming in. They're mixing more wine in the krater. No more water!" he called out, as though directing a servant.

Incense? Krater? Corbineau was writing away. Reille looked up like a hunting dog on a scent.

"No more water! Give it to me neat, man!" He stirred a bit as though reaching for something, his voice slurring a bit.

"Is he drunk?" Subervie whispered. "He sounds drunk...."

"He's not in Elizabethan England," Reille whispered back.

"Fill it all the way! That's it!"

"What do you see?" Noirtier asked. "Who is around you? What are you doing?"

For a long moment he said nothing, though his eyes continued to move.

"Where are you?" Noirtier asked. He was beginning to sound a little rattled.

"Outside," Michel said. His voice was softer now. "Outside. I'm walking along the wall and going out on the overlook. It's night and the moon is reflected in the river at the bottom of the cliff. I can see it making a path across the water. I'm climbing out on the rocks. It feels like halfway between water and stars."

A chill ran down my back. I could see it in my mind's eye, the river like a silver snake through the gorge beneath, the fires behind me sending up sparks to heaven from the wedding feast, the drums and wild notes of flutes on the breeze, ecstatic and Dionysian.

"What are you doing?"

"Sitting. Just sitting and drinking. Watching the sky." His voice trailed off.

I could see him there on the edge of the precipice, the night breeze stirring his long red hair….

Perhaps in some other world, Noirtier and Lannes were whispering furiously, Reille leaning in. "Are you the only one who knows any damned history?" Lannes hissed to Reille.

"This is not the Tudor period," Reille hissed back. "I don't know what you've got but it's not the right thing."

"I asked for the roots of the problem uppermost in his mind," Noirtier replied hotly. "Dr. Mesmer said never to specify a date or a person's name."

"Your hair smells like incense from the feast," Michel whispered, and I knew that tone, the softest tone he took with me after, when we lay replete in each others' arms. "Fourteen years, my friend. Since I was a boy. The gods know I have never wanted it to be more difficult than it had to be."

"Oh love," I whispered, wondering what he saw, what moved his face to that tender expression. I had seen it before.

"Black hair like a raven's wing, smelling of myrrh and mystery," Michel said softly. "Those eyes that see too much…. You are always temptation, a beautiful thing unknowable and within reach, seeming simple and yet labyrinthine enough to lose myself in forever…."

"Well, this isn't it," Reille hissed at Noirtier. "You've got some assignation with a black-haired lady a thousand years earlier!"

Not a lady, I thought. Not hardly. I swallowed hard.

Noirtier cleared his throat. "I want you to step away from the scene and go back out the door. Can you do that?"

It was almost painful to watch that expression fade from his face, to see his face relax into familiar lines. "Yes."

Noirtier looked at Reille, who made scissor motions with his fingers as though walking upstairs. "I want you to go up the stairs. Go up until you find the summer of 1588, the summer of the Armada. Find the door that leads there."

"All right." His voice was level and timbreless. For a long moment he was silent before he spoke again. "I have the door."

This time I was prepared for the change when he stepped through. His chin rose, the set of his shoulders changing, his brows rising as though in pleasure and astonishment.

"Where are you?" Noirtier asked.

"On the Field of Tilbury," he said, and his voice was deeper, more resonant, older.

Reille nodded sharply and encouragingly.

Noirtier looked at him. "Go on," he whispered. "He won't notice a change in questioner."

Reille leaned forward. "What do you see?"

"My men," he said, and there was a pride in his voice I had heard before. "All the Queen's men. We stand united as Englishmen this day, with no division of shire or party between us."

"And the Queen?" Reille asked.

"She is ahead of me on her horse, a steel cuirass about her and ropes of pearls in her hair. Not the Son of Venus, but Venus herself, Gloriana of the Waves!"

Again a chill ran down my spine, the magic in his words, repeated as she spoke in memory, "Therefore I am come among you as you see at this time, not for my pleasure or sport, but being resolved in the midst and heat of battle to live and die among you all...." Michel's mouth quirked, as though he spoke to a friend at hand, "Has ever a man served such a queen? Ever, since the world was made?"

Reille frowned, as though working out a mathematical equation in his head. "My Lord of Leicester, do you know how the fleet of Spain was routed by the wind not a fortnight ago, preventing their first landing?"

He moved, and I thought if his eyes had been open they would have been keen and penetrating. "Yes."

"I am not asking you to tell me," Reille said quickly. "I am asking you to fix those facts in your mind, to recall exactly what you know of how it was done, in the most minute detail. And when you wake, you will recall those facts exactly. You will know them waking precisely as you do dreaming. Is that clear?"

"Yes," he said.

"Then fix them in your mind." Reille sat back, looking at Noirtier, who spread his hands. "It's the old trick of asking the genie for more wishes," Reille whispered.

"That's usually not allowed," I said with a smile.

"We'll see if it is." Reille smiled back.

Noirtier took it up again. "If you have fixed those memories in your mind, then pass back out through the door."

I saw it leave him, like wind washing over water, and I wished for a moment we might stay longer. I had not known this man, and I thought that I wished I had.

"Ascend the stairs," Noirtier said. "As slowly or as quickly as you wish. Up, up, up. Higher and higher, until you return to yourself, until you return to the present day, to the personality that matches the body you wear, that of Michel Ney."

I watched him climb, his face settling as he did, familiar lines of tension returning. When at last he opened his eyes they were the same I had known, sleepy, as though wakened suddenly from a deep sleep. His hands moved, and his brow furrowed.

"Noirtier?"

"Do you remember what I asked you to?" Reille asked.

He hesitated, then nodded.

"Good," Reille said. "Now before you do anything else, tell Corbineau what you remember. Sit there with him and give it to him straight." He glanced around the circle, and then at Lannes. "I think we can take the circle down while he does it. We're all exhausted."

I let out a breath. My legs were cramped, and Michel sat up with difficulty, stiff as though he had been in the saddle all day.

"Let's take down," Lannes said. "Subervie? Take North if you will. Let's keep Michel off a quarter for a while yet."

With a nod Subervie stepped up, and I sat with head bowed while the Lodge took down the circle, distractingly aware of Michel on the other side of the circle talking to Corbineau in a tone too low for me to hear. I thought Reille wanted to hear too, but as he was calling the south quarter he couldn't move until the benediction was complete.

As soon as it was, and everyone moved at last, Reille scooted across to loom over Corbineau, listening intently.

"Let him be," Lannes said to Noirtier. "It's a good thing one of us knows some history." He caught my eye and grinned. "My father ran a livery stable. I didn't learn much history there!" I doubted that Subervie had learned much as a busboy, or Corbineau as a groom either, though presumably Duplessis had some education to become a doctor.

I stood up, stretching. "I will go change then," I said. "If you do not mind." It was somewhat irritating walking around in a sheet, but I thought

I was beginning to get the hang of draping it.

By the time I returned the servants were bringing in a cold collation, and Subervie and Duplessis were already helping themselves, still attired in their white silk robes with white sashes. Michel, Corbineau and Reille were in the corner, Corbineau scratching away madly.

"Eggs, Madame?" Subervie offered. "Very sustaining."

"Which we need after four hours," Max Duplessis said, a slice of ham on his fork.

"Four hours?"

"It's nearly one in the morning," Duplessis said. His glasses were perched on the end of his nose. Behind them were a very keen pair of gray eyes. "That was as long as it felt."

"I had no idea," I said. The food looked very, very good.

In the corner the group was breaking up, Michel and Reille heading off to change, still talking animatedly. Michel moved stiffly, but otherwise seemed unharmed. Of course he was stiff, I thought. He had lain in one position for more than three hours, caught in Noirtier's spell.

I went and stood at Noirtier's elbow as he helped himself to strawberries. "Monsieur, a word with you."

"Yes?" He looked surprised, as I had hitherto avoided him.

"How do you do that?"

"It is called Mesmerism, Madame. A technique invented by my colleague, Dr. Franz Mesmer. His initial application was the reduction of pain in patients who are chronically ill. As you may know, tuberculosis and certain cancers can cause a great deal of suffering before finally resulting in death, and the administration of opiates in quantities large enough to reduce pain often leaves the patient unconscious, and certainly incapable of spending their last days with their loved ones in any meaningful way. It was his discovery that the application of these mental principles often resulted in a considerable reduction in pain without reduction of the patient's mental clarity."

"Colonel Subervie said something about animal magnetism?"

Noirtier nodded. "Dr. Mesmer believes that there are electrical forces in the body, tiny charges that move along pathways we do not understand, and that the flow of these electrical forces can be influenced by the use of magnets. Thus, in theory, fluids could be prevented from pooling in one organ or another, or even the heart be restarted by sufficient magnetic or electrical force. However, his experiments were not uniformly successful, and with a charge of heresy hanging over him he left Vienna for Paris some four years ago. I have been privileged to see some of his more esoteric workings in Paris, as we are fellow members of the Lodge of Nine Sisters."

"The Grand Orient Lodge in Paris?" I was a little startled, as it was well known and thoroughly above board.

"The Masonic lodge of Voltaire and Franklin," Noirtier said proudly. "I was also pleased to stand as a sponsor for your friend Ney when he joined the Nine Sisters several years ago."

I blinked. Michel had said nothing of that, other than that he belonged to a more conventional lodge as well as this.

"In any event, I had seen a demonstration of this, but had never performed it. I am quite pleased the operation was successful."

"I want to learn it," I said.

Noirtier's eyebrows rose. "You are a woman, Madame."

"I have noticed," I said. "Is that germane?"

He spread his hands. "Of course. This sort of working is the province of men. Women are Doves, not magicians."

I had thought he would say that, but I knew where his weakness was. "Can you imagine a better way to control oracular talent?" I asked. "Do not some of the outer trappings, including the smoke and incense, remind you of the descriptions of the great oracles of the past? The oracle at Delphi, for example, sat on a tripod breathing in the scented smoke, while priests chanted about her. You have seen what I can do, untrained and spontaneously. Don't you want to see what I can do at my best?" I gave him a sweet and disingenuous smile. "Dr. Mesmer's techniques hold great promise in helping me improve upon the talents that Nature has given me. Think of the good we could do for France!"

His eyes brightened. "There is something in that," he said.

"I should like to ask Dr. Mesmer when I am next in Paris," I said. "All I ask of you is a letter of introduction. If he will not see me," I shrugged. "Then of course I will bow to his greater judgment."

"I suppose there is no harm in asking," he said.

Everyone had full plates by now, and the servants were being ushered out by Subervie. Lannes rang his fork against his glass. "May I call you back for a moment, gentlemen?"

The room quieted, and I turned, plate in hand, to watch. "Thanks to the good work of Marshal Ney, ably assisted by M. Noirtier, General Reille and the scribing talents of Major Corbineau, we have a good deal more to go on." He glanced at Reille. "General, would you like to briefly explain what we've got?"

Reille seemed even more tall and lanky as everyone turned toward him, a little awkward in a way that many women would find charming. "It's complicated, but I'll try to boil it down. If they're doing this the same way they did the Armada working, we're in trouble. It's a fairly simple working, actually, more low magic than high Hermetics, but very effective and with a lot of energy behind it. They're running that air elemental off an almost unlimited source of power, and without disrupting the physical components of the working wherever they are in England," he paused to let that sink in, "we're going to have to fight the thing."

"Physical components in England?" Duplessis asked. "What kind of physical components?"

"Elemental symbols, a conjuration circle of some kind, possibly centered on a relic. My guess would be the drum once belonging to Sir Francis Drake." Honoré Reille shook his head. "We don't have any idea where they are, nor could we get to them. And then there's some physical component that they've put on every British ship to serve as a guide for the power, and also to exclude their ships from the air elemental's attacks. We'd have to find out what it is and remove it from every ship."

"Like the colors or something? Something of symbolic nature that would be on every ship?" Subervie asked.

Reille nodded.

"If we could remove the colors from every British ship we would have already won," Corbineau observed dryly.

"Which leaves 'punch through it,'" Reille said. "And it's got an absolutely enormous amount of energy."

Lannes shook his head. "Where are they getting that kind of power? They'd need a dozen Lodges at work all the time around the clock!"

Reille looked at Michel, who nodded and stepped up. "Not if they've tied it into the power of Story itself, into the Robin Hood and King Arthur, into the sword in the stone and Drake on the deep, into the primal folk beliefs of Britain itself. Green Albion sits unconquered and unconquerable, guarded by the seas, guarded by Bran's head and Solomon's seal. It's running on the belief of tens of thousands of ordinary Britons who believe." Michel looked solemn. "Tens of thousands of people who believe that Drake will come when his drum is played, and Lionheart died for England."

"That's almost unlimited energy," Lannes said.

"Yes," Michel said. "That's the problem." A ghost of a smile played across his face. "We did set it up rather well."

Subervie blew out a long breath. I could not see how it was to be done. I had seen the power in the air elemental, and I knew I could not touch a hundredth of it.

"Fortunately," Honoré said, "I have an idea." Everyone turned and looked at him again. "You fight Story with Story."

The Symposium

The Lodge broke up within the hour, Honoré to work on his idea, and the others to go get some sleep before the School of War convened the next morning. Lannes was talking to Michel by the buffet table, and I heard him ask quietly, “Michel, do you want to stay here tonight? It’s a castle. It’s got lots of guest rooms. And you don’t look like you’re riding back to Montreuil tonight.”

Michel did look fairly terrible. He hesitated, then nodded. “If you don’t mind, Jean. I’ve got to be back here for a staff meeting at ten anyhow. I’d appreciate it.”

“It’s no trouble,” Lannes said. “We’ve got plenty of guest rooms. I’ll send my man to turn down a bed for you.”

“Thanks,” Michel said. He looked utterly exhausted.

I caught up with Michel in the hall. “Are you all right?” I did not trust Noirtier not to have made some sort of mistake.

“Just tired.” We stood in the hallway for a moment, looking at one another. There was a strange expression on his face, as though something disturbed him still. What had he seen? What had he remembered?

“What was it like?” I asked. “Being someone different.”

“Interesting. Strange. And not strange at all.” He was still looking at me that way, as though he sought something elusive in my face.

“In the service of Queen Elizabeth.”

“Oh. Yes.” His brow furrowed. We were standing too close in the empty hallway, the sounds of everyone else leaving muted behind us. “You were worried about me.”

“Of course I worry about you,” I said. “I never said I didn’t. Don’t you think I will worry about you when you’re off to invade England?”

“I suppose,” he said.

I put my head to the side. “And doesn’t the Earl of Leicester have decidedly mixed feelings about that? Invading England is bad?”

Michel smiled ruefully. "I begin to think that in my time I have invaded nearly everywhere and defended nearly everything. I have been left for the kites by Romans, and returned to kill as one. I have to place my allegiance in something bigger than national borders or people who speak the same language."

"In what, then?" He smelled like wine and sweat, as though he had brought a hint of incense from the wedding feast. Though of course it was our incense, in the circle.

"In God," he said. "And in this temple we are building, all of humanity together. I have to believe there is purpose to it, that God needs a man who works in the slaughterhouse."

I put my hand on his arm. "Michel...."

He flinched as though my touch burned. I lifted my hand carefully away, feeling that flinch stab me through the heart. I should have known it would affect him, and I was breaking the rules already.

He seized my hand and put it back, his mouth set. "I'm sorry. I don't mean...."

"No," I said, my hand still clasped between his. "I'm sorry. I should not...."

"I never listen to you."

"You never shut up long enough," I said, but I smiled. I could not quite see what had brought this on.

"I don't," he said. "It's a flaw."

"All this from the Earl of Leicester?" I asked.

Michel snorted, looking over my shoulder at the distant wall. "And there's a man who made a pretty mess, spending his life between defending himself for the murder of a woman he didn't kill and the accusation of fornication with the woman he didn't marry."

"That's gone over my head, Michel," I said. "I haven't read a lot of modern history either."

Michel shrugged. "Never mind. It was two centuries ago."

"I don't understand," I said.

He squeezed my hand between his. "I know. But it doesn't matter. Good night, Elza." He let go and went off down the hall to the guest room Lannes had offered him.

Corbineau came up behind me. "All over between you?" he asked with an arched brow.

"Jean-Baptiste...." I put my head in my hands.

Corbineau gathered me against his chest in a warm embrace. "Here now, dearest. Men are shit, aren't they?"

I laughed and put my head against his breast. "Some of them. Not you."

"I'm glad to hear that," he said. "Come on. I'll walk you back to your cottage, not that I think you need protecting. God help the footpad who ran into you!"

"I'm not particularly armed at the moment," I said.

Corbineau held me at arms' length and looked at me seriously. "You might want to reconsider that. The closer you get to finding our spy, the more desperate…."

I nodded. "You have a point. I'd best start carrying a pistol. It's a little more discreet than walking about in a dress wearing a saber."

"Speaking of which, do you want to join me at the fencing salle tomorrow afternoon? You could probably use some practice, and because there's a senior staff meeting tomorrow we don't have an exercise to play."

"That sounds wonderful," I said.

The next day I met Corbineau at M. Clanet's salle, dressed as Charles and ready for practice. It seemed that much of Boulogne kept late hours, or perhaps it was too beautiful a day to spend indoors, but in early afternoon there were only a few men there. One was clearly there for a private lesson with the maestro, while others were practicing in pairs. Corbineau had paid a membership fee, so we took off our coats and went to work.

It felt very good. I was not as smooth as he was, but we were of a height and build, so neither of us had much advantage. His style was dirtier than mine, the style of a man who had learned first in the field and then refined it with lessons, whereas I had begun as a child under my father's tutelage learning the formal style of the duel when I was six years old.

We had been at it nearly an hour, working up a good sweat, when Reille and Subervie came in, so we stopped and watched them for a bit. I watched Corbineau lose money on a wager match.

"It doesn't matter," Corbineau said. "Not when my friend Charles here could roll Gervais up."

Reille's eyebrows rose. Most of the members of the salle might be convinced I was some friend of Corbineau's named Charles, but the Lodge members knew I was a woman.

"I can't say I'd take that bet," Subervie said, coloring. "Wouldn't be sporting."

At that there were derisive hoots from the men who didn't know who I was.

"So little confidence?" Corbineau asked lightly.

"I wouldn't want to hurt the …er…young man…." Subervie stuttered, looking daggers at Corbineau.

I decided to rescue him, as I liked him very much. "I am not so young, nor in fear of your sword, Colonel. I would be delighted to make a match with you," I said, with a courteous bow.

"I'm going to kill you, Jean-Baptiste," Subervie hissed. "I can't fight a…."

"Gentleman so young?" Reille put in, a smile playing about his lips. "Then I will relieve you of the burden." He gave me a sharp nod. "I'm handicapped here, so I will give you this—hold me off five minutes from a body touch. Limb touches don't count."

At that the gathering crowd ooohed and started placing bets, as Reille was well known as a fencer. And, standing well above six feet, he had both the reach and weight of me.

"Done," I said with a negligent shrug, the excitement already chorusing through my veins. "It will be my pleasure, General."

"Fifty francs on my friend Charles!" Corbineau shouted. The bookmaker started giving him six to one odds.

I took my coat back off and made a few more passes with the practice foil. Corbineau leaned over and whispered in my ear, "Damnation. I thought you could take Gervais."

"Thank you for the vote of confidence," I said, but I was anything but sanguine about fencing Reille, myself. I'd seen him cross blades with Michel, and I had never been anywhere near Michel's league.

Subervie leaned in on the other side. "Madame, you don't have to do this. Some harebrained scheme of Corbineau's…." He gave Corbineau a stern look. "It's most unsuitable."

"My dear Subervie," I said. "I am most unsuitable, as you are no doubt learning." I pushed my hair back behind my ears and stepped out in to the center to salute.

Reille had taken off his coat as well, and fenced in dark blue waistcoat and breeches. He gave me a courteous nod. "Ready?"

"Ready," I said, and when the timer gave the signal we began.

Our blades barely kissed in the middle, sliding together and then apart.

He waited in guard, his eyes on my face.

Pretty dark eyes, I thought, and fierce at last. This was something that moved him to passion.

Yet he was cool. A quick exchange of points, but he did not even change expression, collected and still. He is a thinking one, I thought. He doesn't go hot in the field either, I imagine. He goes cold. Ice is worse than heat, sometimes.

And he was fast. I almost missed the disengage, the quick thrust that should have hit my left shoulder. Instead it hit the back of my hand, stinging and leaving a welt along my thumb.

"Hand touches don't count," Corbineau reminded everyone loudly. "Come on, Charles."

Gamely I put my best into it. He was not used to a left-handed opponent, and that gave me something to play with. A quick riposte, a step back giving ground to lead him, and I almost had it. A quick disengage, and I pinked the elbow of his sword arm.

"Body touches only!" Corbineau said, but I heard the exhalation run around the room. It was something to have hit Reille at all.

His lips compressed, and the blades touched again, scraping and flying like fire. He was fast, fast as a much smaller man, though he stood over six feet, tall and thin and all lanky muscle. Still he hung back, not pressing me though he could. He had the reach. I had to get in close and he didn't need to, so he could afford to play me at the point, waiting for me to make a mistake.

I could try to hold him off. The victory condition was that he had to hit me. Most of these men were aggressive fencers, and his stand back and wait style would be very effective against them, men who would rush to close and tire themselves out in attack while he simply defended until they were exhausted. But this victory condition made it my game. He had to touch me. I just had to not be touched.

At that I began to fly from his blade, backing quickly around the room, circling out of reach, not even trying to connect but only to defend.

I saw Reille's eyes narrow. He knew what I was doing, and that he would need to change strategies accordingly. Riposte, riposte, beat and beat and beat. Now he was chasing me, circling with his longer stride. Only the tips of our blades connected, parry and parry and parry.

I saw the movement in his eyes first, before in his limbs, and he flew into a beat attack that could only end in a thrust. My blade came up, dropped below his beat and caught his disengage awkwardly. He beat....

"Time!" Subervie shouted. "Five minutes is up!"

...beat again, and slipped under my guard for a beautiful touch on my right shoulder, solid as anyone could want.

Corbineau cheered. "It was after the time! It doesn't count! Pay up, my friends! I told you my friend Charles was good!"

Reille saluted solemnly, and I returned it, my shoulder aching all to hell. It was a tipped foil, but it hurt all the same. He shoved his sodden hair out of his face and came over to me. "Are you all right, Madame?" he asked quietly. "I didn't mean to hit quite that hard."

"I'm fine," I said. "And I'm amazed I held you off long enough. You're good."

"You're fast," he said. "And the left handedness throws me a little. I don't have too many sinister friends."

"Of both sorts?" I smiled. "Are your friends right-handed, or simply upstanding fellows?"

"Both," he said. He had a disarming smile, pulling the right side of his mouth more than the left, which gave him a charmingly lopsided look. "We're good boys really."

"Are you? I hope you're not too good. Virtue can be terribly boring."

"I try not to be dull." Reille said, and I thought he blushed a little. "But I have the reputation of being a bookworm."

"Because you finish your homework?" I asked.

"And everyone else's. But that's what it's about, isn't it? Learning to be a team. It's good to be competitive, but when we get in the field we need to be able to put that down." He shrugged. "We'll be there soon enough, I suppose."

"I expect you will," I said. I felt eyes upon me, and glanced about to see Michel in the doorway watching, his hat in his hand. Before I could say anything, he spun around and left.

And what if he did? We were done with each other. There was no reason in the world I couldn't talk with a handsome young man my own age who happened to be an excellent swordsman and a bachelor besides. If it sent Michel scurrying out of the room, it was really his problem.

Reille was waiting for me to answer something.

"I'm sorry," I said, "I didn't hear you. What?"

"I asked if you'd like to join me and Subervie and Corbineau for dinner. After we all have a chance to clean up, of course. The senior staff meeting will go late because Marshal Berthier is here, and unless someone sends for us, we're free."

He meant the Lodge of course, but I doubted Lannes would come straight out of a meeting and want to go into ritual, even if the meeting ended by six o'clock. He'd probably want some dinner of his own, and possibly a quiet room!

"That would be wonderful," I said.

Like any army town, Boulogne had sprouted a fine crop of taverns and restaurants. They had their favorite, and I joined them at a tavern in a narrow street off the citadel, where actual tablecloths marked it one of the better ones. I had gone back to the cottage and cleaned up, but I put on Charles' good clothes, a dove grey coat, well cut, with a taupe waistcoat and snowy linen. Fashionable, but I needed to keep up with the company.

"The boys," as Reille called them, were all well turned out too. It is the pride of our men to look fine, and all of them did in their undress uniforms, a superfluous amount of gold braid present. Subervie had a short blue pelisse trimmed with fur, which must be hot as hell in the summertime. Corbineau's collar was embroidered with enough gold lace to hurt his neck, and Reille had epaulets the size of well-grown pigeons on each shoulder. All of them wore white trousers tight enough that one would have thought sitting uncomfortable. On the other hand, it did suit them.

"What a handsome group," I murmured as I sat down at the table.

Subervie stood, as though uncertain what to do about my feminine status, but the others plopped directly into their chairs and then stared at him, at which he took his seat abruptly.

Corbineau give me a brilliant smile as if to say, here we are as your chaperones, now go after Honoré!

I shook my head at him ever so slightly. If I were bent on seduction, I would have worn women's clothes and not had Corbineau along. Sometimes, I thought, I did actually want to talk to someone without getting them straight into bed. Michel's subordinate under Michel's very nose would be poetic justice, for he would be determined to not be Moreau. He would bend over backwards not to blame Reille and to show no lack of preferment because of it. If I were looking for a way to hurt him, that would be it.

But I wasn't. Being entirely candid with myself, I didn't want to revenge myself upon Michel. I wanted him back.

I flashed Subervie a brilliant smile. “So how did you gentlemen all come to know one another?”

Subervie fussed with his napkin. “Honoré and I have known each other for a long time,” he said. “We were both in the Army of Italy on the First Italian Campaign. I was Lannes’ aide, and he was Massena’s. We were both lieutenants then.” He gave Reille a quick glance. “It’s been a long strange road, hasn’t it?”

“It has indeed.” Reille settled into his chair with a bit more grace.

“I know Jean-Baptiste’s older brother, Claude,” Subervie continued, “So when I was posted here with the Marshal last year I ran into Jean-Baptiste. Now I’m Lannes’ ADC and he’s Ney’s, so we deal with each other a lot. And then Honoré came to join the party at the School of War, and like I said we go way back.”

“And the other…gentlemen in your company?” I asked. I was curious as to how the Lodge had recruited.

“Max is Ney’s pick,” Subervie said. “He’s one of VI Corps surgeons and none of us knew him before. Most of the others are Marshal Lannes’ Masonic brothers, or else they were with us in Italy.”

“A lot of us are from the Army of Italy,” Reille said, helping himself liberally to the pâté and fresh bread the waiter had set before us. “Though I missed most of the Second Italian Campaign because I was wounded at Genoa just before the surrender. I’d brought a message from the Emperor to Massena,” he said.

“You are too modest,” Corbineau said, eager to impress me with his friend. “He makes it sound as though he were the postman! No, he swam ashore through a British blockade! He got a fishing boat to take him out and then slipped over the side in the dark and swam through the blockade by stealth into the besieged city. It was quite the feat!”

“Really? It sounds like something out of the most thrilling novel,” I said.

Honoré had the modesty to look embarrassed. “I was very fortunate,” he said. “And also very fortunate not to be killed in Genoa. We were fairly hungry before the end. And then I got shot. But it all came right. We held long enough, and the Emperor defeated the Austrians.”

“And now we’ve trouble with the Austrians again,” Subervie said. “Another round of threats, another round of alliances.” He shook his head.

“They won’t rest until the Bourbons are back on the throne of France,” Corbineau snorted. “Until all of us are sent back to our places in the kitchen. We do not belong at the table, the likes of us! If we'd known our place and not gotten uppity, we'd still have the Austrian Queen ruling over us, with a pack of bishops and dukes to keep us there."

Subervie nodded. "My father thought I might turn out well to be a gentleman's valet instead of a busboy. I don't suppose he ever thought I'd be the gentleman." He glanced down at his immaculate fur collar with an ironic smile. "He's happy enough now."

"I was a groom," Corbineau said as the waiter arrived with a tureen of carrot soup. "All of sixteen when I talked my older brother into letting me come with him when he went back to the army. Never had a pistol in my hand before. Didn't know anything more about swords than that the pointy end went in the other fellow. They said, child, what can you do? I said, sirs, I can ride."

Reille paused with his spoon halfway to his mouth, grinning. "I bet they got a surprise when they saw you!"

"They did," Corbineau said. "Little skinny kid, looking about thirteen. But I could stick on any horse ever foaled. I could get down on his neck and ride through anything! So they made me a message rider. I could go through the worst of it and never injure the horse, and always bring the message in. So in good time they made me a chasseur, the lightest of the light scouts. And from there it's been one good thing after another."

I looked at Reille. "And you? What's your story?'

"I was in school," he said a bit sheepishly. "It seemed awfully dull to have a revolution going on and to be stuck declining Latin nouns instead. So I sent my father a long letter to be delivered after I was gone, and ran away to join the army. I had a horse, so they said I was cavalry."

"This was the Year II," Subervie said. "When that was about the only qualification!"

"It was the only one I had," Honoré acknowledged. "I'd had a few fencing lessons, how to duel like a gentleman, not much use in a real fight. But it kept me alive until I learned better. And you?"

"I traded my husband for the Army of the Rhine," I said. "And a good trade it was."

"So you see we've everything to lose," Subervie said. "All of us, and thousands more like us. Max is Protestant, and you know what the history of that looks like, massacres of Huguenots whenever Church and King decide. He wants freedom of religion. And most of the rest of us don't want to go back in the kitchen just because our blood's not blue."

Honoré looked down in his soup plate. “You watch them and you say, why do they get everything for nothing, when there is no way I can earn it? I wasn’t born poor, like some other fellows. But it rankles just as much to watch boys your age with less talent and brains go on past you because you’re a filthy bourgeois and they have a pedigree. If there is to be an aristocracy at all, let it be an aristocracy of merit. Let each man earn his laurels based on what he can do.”

“In whatever field,” Subervie added. “How can we study astronomy when the Church still says that the sun goes around the earth? If we can’t get our damned universities to teach real science, then we may as well give up and hand the world to the British!”

“Well, now we can,” Corbineau said. “Let us make Paris a second Alexandria, where the best of all arts and sciences are met.”

“I’ll toast that,” I said.

We did, raising our glasses together.

“Another toast!” Corbineau said. “To love!”

I rolled my eyes. “Really, Jean-Baptiste?”

“What is love?” Honoré said, waving his glass with the air. “A symposium on the subject.”

“Love is overrated,” I said.

“Love is as inevitable as digestion,” Jean-Baptiste said. “Don’t you agree, Gervais?”

“I think that’s a perfectly disgusting metaphor,” Gervais Subervie said. “And are we talking about love, or conquests?”

“Love,” Honoré said. “The nature thereof. The quids and quos. It’s an ancient and suitable topic for discourse.”

“Not until the dessert course,” I said, smiling. “In a proper symposium.”

“Not so,” Honoré said, his eyes twinkling. “It comes in with the wine, and as we’ve already got the wine we can go ahead.”

“If Elza agrees,” Jean-Baptiste said. “Love. Is it real?”

Subervie snorted. “That’s like asking if air is real. You’ll have to do better than that.”

“All right,” I said. “Is adultery justified by love?”

“Or fornication,” Jean-Baptiste put in. “I think we’ve all been guilty of that one.” He glanced at Honoré. “Some of us more than most.”

Honoré ducked his head. “Women like me,” he muttered.

Subervie cleared his throat. “To my mind, fornication is worse than adultery, because it’s more likely to leave a young woman in trouble with a fatherless child. If she's pregnant she may have nowhere to go and no one who will take her in and care for her. That's worse. If she's married, there may be talk that the baby's not her husband's but no one can prove it. She's still got her name and her livelihood. I think it's a lot worse to risk a young woman's life that way than it is a married woman's. It's more irresponsible."

"I think you have a good point," I said. "And many couples come to quite an amiable arrangement after a few years, where each pursue their own interests. Certainly my husband wanted to."

"And you were not happy with that?" Jean-Baptiste asked, refilling my glass.

"I wanted him to love me," I said.

"I've saved a lot of trouble by marrying a woman I loved in the first place," Subervie said. "We grew up together, but you might say I was well beneath her since her father was a factor at the Chateau de Parenchere. When I was made an officer she married me." He helped himself to the chicken with lemon and thyme offered, a shy smile on his face. "We've been very happy. Our son, Jean, is four and we've a new baby. Aimeé is five months old."

"He's the settled and happy one," Honoré said. "The one who is truly lucky in love."

"Is your wife in town?" I asked.

"We've rented a cottage on the Paris road a few kilometers out," he said. "Everything is ungodly expensive in Boulogne, and with two little ones and her sister come to help we can't manage in town in just a room or two, and we can't afford a house in town. I don't make that much!"

Jean-Baptiste looked at him. "And how about adultery? Do you cheat on your wife?"

Gervais didn't look offended. "No. Because it would hurt her. And I'm a terrible liar. She'd find out. I've never wanted to enough to be worth the pain it would cause."

"And if the wife doesn't care?" I asked.

He shrugged. "Better than fornication. Like I said. I think it depends on the harm done, or the lack of it."

"Like sodomy," Honoré said, studiously not looking at Jean-Baptiste. "As long as it's not in the chain of command, it's like adultery with a woman who has an understanding. No harm, no foul. We all have our vices and it's really no one's business."

"I would agree with that," I said. "And a very sensible conclusion for a symposium. Plato would be proud."

"Would he?" Gervais asked.

"Plato held that true love could only exist between equals, and since a man and a woman can never be equal, the purest love can only be between men, between brothers in arms," I said.

"That's a different kind of love," Gervais said, also carefully not looking at Jean-Baptiste. "It's not sexual."

"Is it not?" I asked. "I have found that it can be."

"But you are a woman."

"And therefore can never be a man's equal?" I said, raising an eyebrow.

"I don't think it makes a damned bit of difference," Jean-Baptiste said, downing the rest of his glass in one gulp, not looking at any of us.

Honoré shrugged, glancing from one to another. "I think it's all shades. We know what brothers in arms are like, and we all know that things happen when feelings run strong and so does drink. It's all shades of love, different colors and intensities, but all the same thing, like refracted light. And when you walk with death as we do, those shades are very precious." He lifted his glass. "Let us give Love his due, rather than Death."

"I'll drink to that," I said, and touched my glass to his.

"Love and friendship," Honoré said, looking at Jean-Baptiste, who at last lifted his eyes and glass at once, a sideways smile on his face.

"Love and friendship," he said.

Wargames

It was a few days later that Lannes sent for me. I sat down with him and Subervie in the stuffy office, which was far too hot for the wool coats they were wearing. Presumably the window was closed for the sake of confidentiality, and as soon as we were done Lannes could get some relief.

"Watching the spot on the cliffs isn't working," he said bluntly. "Nobody has seen anyone."

"Or rather," Subervie said, "We've all seen everyone. There must have been five hundred people past there with lanterns in the last week, everyone from Marshal Ney to fifteen-year-old serving girls going home from work. There has to be a better way." He looked at me significantly. "And we've just had word that the Emperor is coming to Boulogne week after next."

I let out a long breath. The Emperor's presence in the camps of the Army of Coasts of Ocean might be the final prelude to invasion. If it were, then it was imperative that we find our man quickly. "A new strategy?" I asked.

"Yes," Lannes said. "There are twenty men who have access to the most sensitive material, whose deliberate treason would be most costly." He raised a finger. "I say deliberate for this reason—I do not mean that someone else has access to their papers—I mean that they, themselves, are the spy."

I nodded. Not Michel, in other words. Not a man who might unwittingly give something away.

"I propose to tell these twenty men the date of the invasion," Lannes said. "Each one of the twenty will be told in strictest confidence a different date in the next two months, each told that it is the real embarkation date. And then we will wait, and see which date comes back to us from our spies in Whitehall. Since each date will only be given to one man, the date that comes back will tell us which man was the source."

"That's very clever!" I said. "And then we can at least concentrate on one person, or on his contacts. If we knew which man it was coming from this would be much easier."

"That's the idea," Lannes said. "So let us see what it brings us. Meanwhile, I assume you will be available for Lodge day after tomorrow?"

"I am at your service," I said.

The following week passed slowly. My nights were spent scouting for the Lodge, gathering such information as I might while Honoré worked on his idea for a way to successfully attack the air elemental. My days were spent pleasantly enough, fencing and dining with Jean-Baptiste and his friends, most often dressed as Charles, or riding down to the beach or across the fields in the bright summer air.

I did not see Michel except at Lodge, and we were very polite to one another, though we did not speak deeply or privately. Whatever it was that had so disturbed him remained a mystery to me.

The week ended, and the next began. The Emperor was scheduled to arrive within days. I began to pester Subervie.

"We have heard nothing," he said. "Nothing whatsoever. Our men in Whitehall report that there is no change in the British preparedness. One man who is keeping tabs on the incoming correspondence from Lion reports that he has not seen any date discussed, just a general state of high alert."

"What is he doing?" I asked, pacing toward the seaward window of the office. "What is the spy thinking? Why isn't he sending Captain Arnold the date?"

"It's possible we don't have the right man at all." I turned to see Subervie tapping the edge of the desk impatiently. "If all the men we told were honest men, then none of them are our spy. Nothing would come back to us."

I sighed. "If they are all honest men…."

"Then we have no idea who's doing it. We're right where we were in the beginning."

"At least we will have cleared the twenty officers," I said. "If they were told the embarkation date and proved not to be the spy, that is something. It is more men we can trust." I did find myself pleased that Honoré had been on the list of twenty, given a date of August 4. Perhaps he was as trustworthy as Jean-Baptiste thought.

"There is that," Subervie said. "That's pretty much what we're concluding."

"So what's next? We're back to watching the overlook?" I asked.

"I think so," Subervie said. "Unless you've other ideas? You're the espionage agent, after all."

"Yes, of course," I said. I had no idea how to do this. It had been a stroke of luck, finding the spot, but I didn't know what happened next. And if we were back to the broad list again, anyone who might walk along the cliffs, I still had no idea how to narrow it down. "I take it we can at least recruit out of the twenty cleared men to help us keep watch."

Subervie nodded. "That should be fine. I might tell Honoré myself. I've been wanting to, and he's clever. Maybe he can think of something."

"That sounds like a fine idea," I said. "Perhaps we should get dinner together and fill him in."

Honoré leaned back in his chair in the almost deserted restaurant. It was late on a Wednesday, nearly eleven, and in Boulogne people ate earlier than in Paris. The restaurant was nearly empty. "The Emperor arrives day after tomorrow," he said.

Gervais Subervie nodded.

"If I were the spy, I'd wait and see what the Emperor was doing here before I reported to Lion again," Honoré said. He looked at Subervie. "Are we getting the embarkation order?"

Subervie regarded him levelly. "You know I can't tell you that."

"I know."

"Everything will be clear when the Emperor arrives," Subervie said. "You can trust me on that, Honoré."

The waiter leaned in to refill my cup, and I stirred my after dinner coffee. "Whether the embarkation date is next week or next month, we're running out of time. It has to be one of the men assigned to the School of War, or to headquarters. We've got to narrow the list down somehow."

"No, it doesn't," Honoré said.

"Doesn't what?" I was perplexed.

"You were born upper class, weren't you?" he asked.

"In the sense of having parents with pretensions to gentility, if that's what you mean." I felt a bit odd, classing my parents as upper class when I suspected my father was little more than an adventurer.

"But you were raised in nice houses, weren't you?" Honoré pursued. "Didn't wash your own clothes or dishes? Didn't do your own cooking?"

"No," I said.

Honoré looked at Subervie meaningfully over the rim of his coffee cup. "How many people are in this conversation?"

"Three." Gervais stopped, and I saw his face change. "Four."

Honoré nodded. "That's right."

"What?" I said, confused.

The former busboy nodded gravely. "The waiter."

"It doesn't have to be a man assigned to the School of War or to Headquarters," Honore said. "There are a hundred servants in and out. You don't even see them. And you don't see the way they come and go." He gave me a cockeyed smile. "I saw that when we tried to break into your old lodging. You had two ways to do it—through the front door or through the window. But there's a back door too, and the back door is usually open. Probably we could have just walked around the back and come in through the kitchen, but it never even occurred to you. Well-bred people aren't supposed to see servants. They're just there." He glanced at Subervie. "The busboy is supposed to be invisible."

"If he's not it's because he's dropped the china," Subervie said. "That's the only time people notice him. And yes, he's supposed to be invisible. Guests aren't supposed to pay him any attention. It's rude."

"It's a sign of poor breeding," Honoré said. "Don't you think so, when men are ogling the waitress or watching the parlormaid?"

I let out a deep breath. "Oh, my God."

"We're not looking for a soldier. We're looking for a servant," Honoré said. "Someone who goes in and out all the time, someone who's supposed to be there. Someone we never see. How secret is a Lodge meeting after all? Do you think the buffet appears out of thin air?"

Subervie snorted. "I've no excuse for missing that. I've thought about it, actually. The setting up and serving while we're still robed and half the time still talking about what we're doing. The footmen can see this is no staff meeting. They have to see it."

"Yes," Honoré said. "A servant to a senior officer, either at Headquarters or the School of War."

I shook my head, baffled by my own idiocy. "Michel had the cipher out on his desk. Someone must make his bed, empty his chamber pot. There must be servants in and out. You're right. I never see them. And I'd never thought about it."

"We don't even know who half of them are," Subervie said. "If they're not military personnel, they're locals hired by the permanent staff.

Boulogne Castle, for example, has a permanent chatelaine who's here all the time, Madame Dumont. She's completely in charge of hiring and firing household staff. I only deal with the military personnel who are directly assigned to Headquarters or to the staff of V Corps."

"Are they all local?" I asked. "Or as busy as it is, as much extra work as there is, would it be reasonable to hire someone from outside who came with references?"

"It probably would be," Honoré said.

Subervie sighed. "And over in Montreuil who's doing the hiring?"

"We hired a lot of people locally," Honoré said. "And there are a bunch of enlisted men's wives who take in the laundry. Sophie Henri is the one who does mine and who cleans my room. I have no idea who does anyone else's. It's not my job. I'm cavalry training right now, so my attention's on the stables."

"We're going to have to close the meetings and close Headquarters," I said. "If we can't know who we've already got, the only thing to do is assign military personnel to all the support tasks in Headquarters. It's a precaution for the Emperor's visit or something like that."

"Soldiers gossip," Subervie said. "I'm not sure it's more secure."

"It's more secure than the spy we know we have," Honoré pointed out. "Yes, some private from the Vosges can be plied with drink and pumped for information, but that's not as bad as what we've got. Besides, it will take time for our man to do that. We can stall him for a week or more with this."

"I'm not sure that helps," Subervie said thoughtfully.

I saw Honore's eyes flicker, and I knew he had heard the same thing I had: that it wasn't a matter of stalling for a few days until the Emperor arrived and we embarked. If it were, delaying him would be all we needed. No, there would be no embarkation next week, and Subervie didn't seem to realize he'd said it.

"Close the Headquarters except to military personnel," I said. "And we'll have to step up surveillance on the coast." I looked at Subervie. "I don't suppose Marshal Lannes can tell me when the embarkation is."

Subervie met my eyes candidly. "He said your efforts would be the same regardless, and therefore it was not necessary."

"True enough," I said. My work would be the same whether we planned for early, mid or late August. And the fewer people who knew the fewer who could let something slip.

"I'll take a turn watching," Honoré said. "The more the better. We're going to have to catch someone actually signaling."

"When the Emperor is here," I said. "That's the thing. That's when the British will be desperate to get news, when they're expecting embarkation. All the servants know the Emperor is coming. What if we give them something to report?"

"A boat drill," Subervie said. "I can set up a boat drill for V Corps in the middle of the night when the Emperor's here. A demonstration for him that we can embark in an hour and a half, men, horses and guns. You can see it from the town, so there will be plenty of people who know. And then we watch the overlook."

"I'll do it myself," I said.

"I'll come with you," Honoré said. "I'm with the School of War, so I'm not involved in V Corps' boat drill, unlike Subervie who'll have to be there."

"Let's give them something to look at," I said with satisfaction, "And see what we can catch."

"A plan," Honoré said, pushing himself back from the table. "Now I need to go read Diodorus tonight."

Gervais swore. "Oh the damned exercise tomorrow! What are we doing, anyway?"

"Ptolemy versus Perdiccas. The Battle of Memphis. Don't you ever read your homework?" Honoré asked. "It's only ten pages of Diodorus in translation."

"Is this the bloody war elephants? And who's supposed to win, anyway?"

"Yes," Honoré said, grinning. "The bloody elephants. And Ptolemy wins."

"Very handily," I said. I had always been rather fond of Ptolemy.

"I don't see why we have to study war elephants," Subervie grumbled. "Unless there's a new Prussian Elephant Corps I don't know about, or we decide to invade India."

"You never know," I said. "The Maratha princes have envoys in Paris right now about an alliance against the British. They want arms and support for a mass rising centered on Delhi and Hyderabad. A treaty with Napoleon would give them a lot. You might be off to India sooner than you think."

Honoré gave me a sideways look. "And where would the Emperor's agent be in that?"

"I'd be off to Delhi in a heartbeat if Napoleon asked it of me," I said. "I imagine it would be fascinating." I took a sip of my long-cold coffee. "The exercise tomorrow—out of curiosity, what are you playing?"

"I've got Ptolemy's cavalry," Honoré said. He looked at me keenly. "Want to come watch?"

"Could I?"

"I don't see why not. We've had a bunch of guests in there before, and there's nothing particularly secret about the outcome of a battle two thousand years ago. Come along if you like, Madame."

Michel would be there, probably. But then, was that a reason not to do something that I really wanted to?

"I'll come," I promised.

I suppose I had expected that the exercises were conducted in an office, or perhaps in some sort of cabinet room, but the actual facility looked more like a mess hall. It was a big flat building constructed of wood, with broad windows on all four sides that let in a wealth of summer sunlight as well as a pleasant cross breeze. In the middle of the room was a massive table fully twenty feet square, made up of several smaller tables intended to fit together. Around it, as around a giant billiards table, were a bunch of billiard cues. There were smaller tables around the walls, one of them bearing a coffee service for the fifteen or so men who milled about, some of them already without their coats in the warmth of the morning. They scrambled to put them back on when they saw me, as I was dressed nicely in women's clothes today, a white lawn dress with a turquoise shawl.

Honoré came over to greet me eagerly. "Let me show you the set up," he said, leading me to the table. "Jomini and his assistant were here at six getting ready. You know Jomini, don't you? The Swiss volunteer that Marshal Ney has commissioned because of his work on the theoretical nature of warfare?"

"I've not met him yet," I said. He was one of the men I'd had my suspicions of, though he had been given the date of July 30 and it had not come back from Whitehall.

"He'll be here in a bit," Honoré said. "He runs the simulations and keeps us from killing one another." He ran one long hand along the edge of the table. "So here's the set up."

"It's gorgeous," I said, and it was.

The table was covered in what appeared to be a very elaborate chart, depicting in beautiful colored detail the banks of the Nile. At the far left was laid out the city of Memphis, her white walls coming down almost to the river, while on the right bank of the Nile were trees and fields colored green to indicate growing crops. In the middle of the Nile a little upstream from Memphis was an island.

I frowned. “Why are the fields green?”

“I think the battle was fought in June. Why?” Honoré asked. “Shouldn’t they be?”

“I don’t know,” I said, but it bothered me. It did not seem right that the battle was fought with crops in the field. The fields should lie fallow.

“The chart is based on Diodorus,” he said, “And on Denon’s sketches of Egypt when he was there. He did a few charts himself for us to use as reference.”

“Do you mark up that lovely thing?” I asked. The playing surface looked almost like a work of art itself.

“No, we use toys.” Honoré grinned. “I’ll show you.” He fetched a box from the side table and opened it. It looked like a set of little wooden toy soldiers, each with his armor painted golden and a tiny red plume on his helmet, each clutching a tiny sarissa. “Each one counts as twenty men. We can arrange them and move them about, because the chart is made to scale. That way we can visualize the entire battle and we never mark up the chart. You can see the current positions of all units.” He handed me another box.

“Those are lovely,” I said, picking out one of the perfect miniature elephants, its caparisons painted gold and scarlet, an archer on its back with bow drawn.

“Each elephant counts as two,” Honoré said. “They take up more room. Here are my favorites.”

He opened a third box. Against the black batiste lining were a dozen horse archers, each one painted in exquisite detail, dark beards and dark eyes. One horse tossed her head, while another archer was arrested in the motion of reaching over his shoulder for a fresh arrow. “Persian horse archers. I’ve used these a bunch of times now.” He gave them a friendly pat. “They always come through for me.”

“Do you have any today?” I asked.

“I’ll have five of them,” Honoré said. “To be Ptolemy’s fifty horse archers with the cavalry.”

“Don’t you think fifty is too many?” I blurted.

Honoré winked. “I do, but I’m not complaining about having a few extra! After all, Diodorus doesn't say exactly how many Ptolemy had left at this point, and Jomini has decided it's five facings, not three." He dropped his voice. "So don't tell him he's wrong!"

"I wouldn't dream of it," I assured him. I had no idea why Honoré and I should both think there ought to be thirty. It was somewhat disturbing.

I looked up and straight into Michel's eyes. He did not look away, but just nodded at me as though I were a friendly acquaintance. Which was, in its own way, worse.

"Ptolemy's men, over here!" Subervie had come in and was calling out. "Everybody who's one of Ptolemy's men, come here!" He waved a hand with a cup of coffee in it. "Conference time, my brothers!"

"Excuse me," Honoré said, "I need to go." He handed me the box of archers.

"Of course." He and four or five others joined Subervie in the corner, heads together, no doubt plotting mayhem. I wished I could join them.

I didn't have to look around to know that Michel had come to stand beside me. "You're not one of Ptolemy's men?"

"No," he said. "I'm afraid not. I'm Perdiccas today."

"And who's Ptolemy?"

"Subervie." Michel cleared his throat. "Lannes is tied up with the Emperor arriving tomorrow."

I turned and met his eyes, so very blue and so grave. "Perdiccas dies," I said.

"Only because he loses," Michel said. "Murdered by his own men for losing. If he'd won, he'd have prevailed."

"I'm not sure Seleucus would have suffered him long," I said. "Or Roxane." It was hardly fair that our minds worked the same, that we could slide through the centuries like this, in perfect accord.

"Perdiccas and Roxane got on well enough," Michel said easily. "But he wasn't much of a general. He was adequate, but that was an age of giants."

"So is this," I said.

He nodded, then gave me a sideways smile. "But I'm still better than Perdiccas ever was!" He raised his voice and his arm. "Perdiccas' men! Over here! Come over here if you're with Perdiccas!"

I stepped back and let him confer, thinking it would not be fair to hear what he said. After all, I was quite certain I wanted Ptolemy to win.

A few minutes later, the room was called to order by a weedy-looking young officer with glasses and a sheaf of papers over his arm. "Everybody?

Attention?" From this I assumed he must be Jomini, the young Swiss that Michel had decided was a tactical genius. The room quieted, the two camps about their respective leaders, while he explained the technical parts of the exercise in great detail. Each turn would be five minutes of battle time, and there would be ecological changes as the battle progressed, mirroring the changes in currents of the Nile on the real day. Each team would receive such warning of those changes as a man at the scene might find observable, but no more. The exercise would begin at battle noon, to compensate for the time that Perdiccas had spent moving his men to the island in the morning. Each team could place their initial pieces in order of battle, Perdiccas' men on the island, and Ptolemy's on the left bank in any location.

I watched each side set up. Michel's set up was rather crowded and predictable. It was more a matter of fitting all his units onto the small island than anything else. Subervie chose a rather conservative order of battle, taking the infantry himself in the center with a man I did not know, with more infantry on his left and Honoré with the cavalry and horse archers on the right. There were three young subcommanders, one of whom asked Jomini if the commanders' deaths were possible.

"If the unit to which a commander is attached suffers more than 50% casualties, you may assume that the commander is incapacitated," Jomini said quickly. "Commanders, you should designate a subordinate in that event. You will have to step back along the wall for the remainder of the action if that occurs. And you must be quiet. You can't give orders when you're dead."

"Where are you attached?" Subervie asked Honoré, leaning over his shoulder. I stood behind Honoré, my foot tapping.

"Here," he said, tapping a Companion Cavalry piece on a white horse. "That's me."

"Ready?" Jomini asked. "Marshal Ney, you have the first move."

Michel nodded quietly from across the table. "Renaud?"

One of the young subordinates took up a pool cue and with it reached across the map, gently scooting the first units forward from the island into the Nile, a wedge of five elephants. Behind them, the other elephant units waited, with infantry to the side, moving up to prepare to cross.

"That's not right," I whispered. "It's supposed to be Silver Shields infantry." A chill ran down my back, coldness down my arms. I could imagine it too clearly, the stillness on the riverbank in the heat of the day, the bright sun glancing off their helmets as they waded forward into the water, sarissas leveled. I could see the water flashing reflections of the sun like fire, while far above a falcon turned on the wind.

Honoré leaned in, no doubt assuming I'd read Diodorus the night before too. "He doesn't have to play it the way it actually happened. That's the point. Gervais has set up with Ptolemy's actual order of battle, but it seems like the Marshal has other ideas. We'll just have to take it as it comes."

"No move," Subervie said steadily. "We're holding position."

Michel moved the elephants forward to midstream, the other elephants following. Behind, the Silver Shields locked into position in the rear of all twenty of Perdiccas' elephants. "Silver Shields, prepare to form the tortoise," he said in the same tone he would have taken in the field, as though it were all real. As though black arrows would rain down upon them when they began to come ashore.

Honoré nodded to his young subordinate. "Horse archers, down behind our infantry. Get in range to fire on the elephants."

So few. My hands clenched together around my reticule, as though this were a real battle, as though I were seeing as the gods might. We have so few horse archers, even with the extra two facings Honoré conned Jomini out of. There are too many elephants.

And then I saw what Michel was doing. He was using the elephants like cavalry. What was lumbering through the water toward us was a flying wedge, a sword with a two-ton point, ready to drive into the phalanxes waiting, snapping sarissas and sending men flying. When the elephants hit shallow water they would increase speed, charging down like a lightning bolt.

I put my hand to my mouth. Surely Subervie could see it! Surely he would! But what was the counter to it, with no elephants of our own?

"No move," Subervie said. "Steady."

Honoré walked over and leaned on his shoulder and they whispered together.

"Forward," Michel said. The elephants moved forward another space. Behind the wedge the Silver Shields stepped into the water in battle order.

Pull the cavalry out of line, I thought. Pull them back. They're going to have to countercharge the side of the wedge after it breaks through. And it will break through. The elephants will go through our line like fire.

"Can we do that in one move?" Subervie said in a low voice.

"I don't know," Honore replied, "But we'd better try, don't you think?"

Subervie nodded sharply.

"Your move?" Jomini asked. He was standing on a chair where he could see the board from above.

"Reille, pull the cavalry back. Out of line and toward the center. Infantry, divide in two and prepare to change facing," Subervie said.

"Objection," Michel said mildly. "They have leveled sarissas. They can't divide and change facing in one move. If they do it, there's a chance they'll foul each other."

"Crack troops," Honoré said. "These men are veterans of Alexander the Great's army. They can walk and scratch their ass at the same time."

A ripple of laughter ran around the room. Meanwhile, one of the sub-commanders was pulling Ptolemy's Companion Cavalry back, just on the line I would have chosen. They would be in position on the right flank of the wedge when it came through. But I seriously doubted the infantry could divide in time.

"On a five or six," Jomini said, and tossed something to Gervais Subervie.

He caught it with a flick of the wrist and sent it spinning across the table, a black and white die. It came to rest with five pips showing.

Honoré whooped. "Now we're back in business," he said to Michel.

"Divide in two and change facing to the middle," Gervais said. "Couch sarissas and stand to receive!"

Stand to receive! Echoes woke in my head, spiraling away like distant horns. The riverbank and bright sun…stand to receive….

"Your move, Marshal?" Jomini asked.

"Turn the wedge 45 degrees right," Michel said coolly. "We're going into their left rather than center. And there should be contact on this turn."

"Oh shit," I whispered, forgetting I should be quiet, forgetting I was a lady at all. I could see how it would be, the phalanx in the middle of changing facing, the elephants changing their line of approach toward our left, where our cavalry could do no good with the main body of our infantry in between, the elephants charging straight toward the units to which Subervie was attached, driving straight for Ptolemy's white plume…. There was no way we could get over in time.

The lines moved together, the first elephants occupying the same space as the infantry. Only now the infantry were facing in the wrong direction.

"40% bonus for the flank, 20% bonus for elephants on infantry, 20%

bonus for the charge," Jomini said. "That's 80-20 in Perdiccas' favor. Colonel Subervie, you can consider those front units 80% incapacitated."

"Shit shit shit," I whispered, clasping my hands to still them.

"Horse archers to the fore," Honoré said, white lipped. "We're barely in range."

"You're still in the penalty zone," Jomini said. "30% dropoff for extreme range."

"We'll take the shot anyway," Honoré said.

There was an exchange of fire, some damage. The cavalry was working their way around, but could not engage on this turn.

"Change the facing back," Subervie said.

"Not while engaged on the flank," Michel said tranquilly.

Jomini nodded. "I uphold Marshal Ney."

Subervie snorted. "This is going to be shorter than Cunaxa," he said under his breath.

"Forward elephants," Michel said. "Press the charge straight into the rank behind. Silver Shields, form the tortoise against horse archer's fire." The Silver Shields were nearly on dry land.

"Now would be a really good time for some crocodiles," I muttered.

"We have 60% damage on your attached unit," Jomini said to Subervie. "You must consider yourself incapacitated, sir."

"Damn!" Subervie swore and stepped back to the wall, Ptolemy down under the feet of the elephants.

"The command is yours, General Reille," Jomini said. "He had designated the Hipparch of Companion Cavalry in this instance."

I gulped. "The river…." I whispered.

Jomini had heard me. "Does not rise for four more turns, Madame."

"By which point I'll be out of the water," Michel said smugly.

I clenched my fists.

A sub-lieutenant hurried in, dashing up to Michel, who bent so that he could whisper in his ear.

I saw his face change as they exchanged a few words and then Michel turned. "My apologies, gentlemen. I'm afraid we must call this exercise to a close. I have just been informed that the Emperor is five kilometers from Boulogne, and is arriving a day early. Subervie, Marshal Lannes would like you back in Boulogne directly. Everyone with VI Corps, please prepare to turn out for review this afternoon instead of tomorrow. Reille, I want a Guard Cavalry honor guard in Boulogne in an hour!"

Everyone started running madly about, with the controlled chaos of a military unit about to be unexpectedly reviewed by a head of state. I didn't even see Subervie leave, so fast was it.

I was standing by Honoré's coat as he came over to get it, still talking to Michel. "Well done, considering," Michel said to Honoré. "You were in a bind."

"If you'd been the Regent for Alexander's son, Ptolemy wouldn't have won," Honoré said.

Michel looked at him, a rueful expression on his face. "If I'd been the Regent, Ptolemy would have never had to take up arms."

"A different ending," Honoré said. He paused a moment as if thinking, then shrugged. "I'd better go find that honor guard."

Echoes

I dreamed, and in my dream I fought on horseback on the riverbank, a sword in my right hand, the reins wrapped around my withered left hand. I fought on the riverbank under the scorching sun of midsummer, steel breastplate on fire from the heat, and about my horse's legs I felt the river rise.

"Get back! Everybody out of the water!" I shouted. The current swirled sharply, mud and blood and all else whirling on the waters, dark as creation, dark as the beginning of the world. Swollen by rains in distant lands, I felt the Nile rise. Elephants trumpeted and wounded men screamed, while far above on the winds of day a desert falcon turned on the wing, watching over the slaughter below.

Son of Egypt, you have your miracle, something whispered within me. Son of Egypt, you are whole.

I woke, and there were tears on my face. They did not flow for sadness, but for the beauty of it, for the completeness of that moment, for things I did not remember, waking. I sat up in my bed in the cottage. It was two hours yet till dawn, the cool morning of another beautiful summer day.

Had I been there? Had that battle they had played yesterday been mine? It seemed the most incredible arrogance to think so.

And why not, some part of me wondered. Because I now wore a woman's body? If I were a man, I should be a soldier. There was no reason to think I would be worse at it than Corbineau or Subervie. Arrogance or not, I was no less than they. Were I a man I would be here still, a student of the School of War, perhaps a member of the same Lodge.

Only I would not be the Dove. I sat a moment in the dark before dawn. I would not be the Emperor's agent, charged to find a spy. If I had that life, I would not have this. If I had those talents, I would pay for them with others.

No one gets everything, I thought, at least not at once. Given world enough and time, perhaps I could play all parts. But not at once. If I were a man, I would be a soldier and magician. But then I would not be Dove or the Emperor's agent. And those things were valuable too. In fact, there were many apprentices in the Lodge, but I was the only Dove. Lannes would surely rather have me with my unique mix of talents than another Corbineau. After all, he already had one of those.

Seized with restless energy, I got up and dressed by starlight, a thin white lawn dress that I would not hate in the heat of the day, and walked outside in the cool hour before dawn. It did occur to me to bring a pistol, which I tucked neatly inside an oversized crocheted reticule. Perhaps I would go up to the cliffs and see how the watchers fared. At least I could see if Lion were there, going back and forth in her endless patrol, waiting for a lantern signal.

I knew that I couldn't sleep again.

The moon was setting in the west, and the sea grasses blew softly in the dawn breeze. Below the cliffs, the breaking waves showed white against dark water. The sea was empty. Lion was not in sight, too far out to sea to be seen, or off about some business of her own. It was very clear. A distant pinprick of light on the horizon might have been a ship, or it might have been England.

I was not surprised to see Michel. The way he stood, the set of his shoulders, was unmistakable silhouetted against the sea. His hat was under his arm, and he had no lantern. I came and stood beside him and he did not even flinch, as though he had expected me. We stood for a moment in moonlight above the precipice below, the sea sighing and receding below us as the tide began to go out. We stood, and for a moment I was very aware of us, of who we were just that moment, of the whisper of my white dress against my legs, the sea breeze flirting with my uncurled hair where it escaped from the bonnet, of the way he looked in profile, his face less than handsome and more dear than treasures.

"Why didn't you tell me you were the Emperor's agent?" he asked quietly, his eyes on the sea.

"Who told you that?" I asked, lifting my face to the night breeze.

"The Emperor." He glanced sideways at me. "You could have told me that. I thought you trusted me that far."

"Michel, it's not mine to tell," I said. "I have a job. I have work to do. Yes, I wanted to tell you. But I couldn't."

"You could have."

I tilted my chin up, looking him full in the face. "Really? When is the invasion? What is the embarkation date? If you've just come from a meeting with the Emperor, surely you know."

Michel swallowed, and in the moonlight his eyes were shadowed. "I can't tell you that."

"You could if you wanted," I countered.

"Elza, fewer than thirty men know the plan, and half of them only found out tonight. I can't tell you."

"Then do not ask me to confide in you things that I should not," I said. I put my hand on his arm, as he was standing so very close. "I am a Companion too, with my own oaths and my own work. The time is past when I would have been here only for you."

Michel's eyes roved over my face, as though looking for something, and I was acutely conscious that I had not even combed my hair before I came out. I was not far short of thirty, and I had not touched the rouge pot. "So different," he said, "And so much the same. Dark hair, dark eyes, but your expressions are the same." He reached up and touched my cheek with one finger. "You're fair, not dark, but even the shape of your face is the same."

"As who's?" I asked, trying not to let my voice choke at the expression on his face.

"I don't know your name." He shook his head sadly. "It doesn't work that way for me."

I lifted my eyes to his and made the guess that had been in my mind since the moment he began speaking of that memory during the ritual. "Not a dark lady."

"No." He half turned, toward the sea, away from me.

"Michel, what does it matter?" I asked. "We are more than these costumes we wear, now or in centuries to come. My soul knows yours, and love is without end. What does it matter if then I was a Companion cavalryman who worshipped you?"

His face was in profile. I could not see his expression clearly. "What ever happened to you?" he asked quietly. "I've wondered. What happened to you, in the bloodbath after my death?"

I blinked, knowing that my eyes filled with tears. Of course he would wonder that. Of course he never knew what happened to me. I had never reached for it quite like this, but it was simple as breathing, tonight in the moonlight on the cliff, the day's game behind me. "I lived," I said simply. "I lived forty years after you. I fought beside Ptolemy in that battle you staged today. I had the job Honoré played today, Hipparch of Ptolemy's cavalry. I was not flattened by an elephant, and we won the battle, the gods of Egypt fighting beside us. I lived, and I had a lover I cherished. I married a priceless woman, and I came to love her and our children that came after. I fought at Rhodes and in Syria, and carried Ptolemy's banner on many fields before I was old." My mouth ran on as fast as my vision, my voice choking. "I had a house by the sea with a garden, and my grandchildren played in the shade of the peach trees. The gods blessed me every day of my life."

A single tear ran down his face. "You did all right, then," he said.

"Yes. I did all right." I put my hand on his arm. "I helped found a city that became the greatest in the world, and kept alive the memory of the time that was, of all that I had known and those I had cherished. I could ask for nothing more than to hold that standard proudly again in my own time. Love is without end, Michel. And nothing is gone while I remember it."

"And you remember forever, and in your words conjure new worlds, or raise places long lost like Atlantis rising from the sea," he said. "You are a witch."

"I expect I've been burned as one," I said levelly, "But I'd rather not think about that right now."

"So have I," he said.

I put my head on his shoulder, my cheek against his gold oak leaves. "I thought that was as a heretic."

"Heretic, sorcerer, worshipper of Baphomet..." There was almost a smile in his voice as he turned, leaning against me as I leaned against him. "I've lost track of all the charges."

"As I recall the Templars were also accused of sodomy," I said, and felt him stiffen. "Beloved, whatever you may remember, here and now I am very conveniently a woman. We got along well enough before, in spite of Charles."

"Not in spite of." His arms tightened around me and we stood thus, two shadows made one in the long moonlight. "I don't love you in spite of the things about you that are a bit strange. I love you because of them. When I saw you at Apfing wading into the fight with Corbineau, possessed by that same divine battle madness, I knew I would never be over you. I don't love you in spite of being a Companion. I love you because you're a Companion." He leaned back, trying to see my face shaded beneath the brim of the bonnet. "And I don't know how to stop."

I closed my eyes and rested by cheek against his chest, breathing in the warmth of him, his familiar scent. "Is it always going to be like this, coming and going? Never stopping needing you? Never stopping wishing we had time?"

"I am beginning to think so," he said, his face against the top of my bonnet. "Something occurred to me the other night, after Noirtier's operation, when I remembered...you. I'm not even sure how to say it."

I waited, letting him find the words.

"I am always sure I know what is best for us. And it doesn't usually work. So I'm asking what you want, here and now, with the mess we have. It may not be something I can agree to, but I'm asking you want you want."

I took a step back, not quite stepping out of his arms, but able to see his face rendered beautiful by moonlight. When I spoke, it was to put my heart in his hands. "I want you back," I said. "As my lover. I will not be your mistress, living in your house on your money. I don't need that. I have work of my own for the Emperor. And I would not be your wife, not if she suddenly died tomorrow." He flinched. "I want to be your lover, your companion in danger, your female eromenos. As much as we can have, as long as we can have it, Companions together under the eagle, building a new world."

He took a deep breath, and I saw the lines in his face tighten. "And what about my promises to Aglae?"

"That is between you and your conscience, Michel," I said. "Do you think your angel will abandon you?"

Michel smiled ruefully. "My angel says I'm a colossal fuck-up. How can even I make such a mess of something so simple? If I were going to do that, I should not have married, and should have been true to you."

"You always think you should be true to one alone," I said, "When it is against your nature. Is it kind, do you think, to expect one person to be everything, to be wife and Companion, lover and soldier and intellectual equal and mother and friend and confidant and brother at once? How can any one person fulfill all of the things you are, and not leave you still starving for what they are not? I have not asked you to have no one but me, to need nothing I cannot give you. I see that you need things I cannot give. And I will try so very, very hard not to be jealous when you seek those things, when you go home to your family and your peace. Cannot you give up resenting Aglae for not being me and me for not being Aglae? Is that fair to either of us?"

He blinked. "You make monogamy seem like nothing but selfishness."

"How can any one person be everything another will ever need? People break each other, begging and demanding things that can never be, or go through their lives starving for what they might have had. Is it not better to say, this is the place we match, and these are places where each of us matches another better?" I asked. "Whether that is lover or friend, brother in arms or child, to put all that on a husband or a wife is nothing but a modern convention, and not one that works very well. Two hundred years ago no one expected marriages to be made for love, nor resented other emotional connections' depths."

"Adultery wasn't fine two hundred years ago either," Michel said wryly.

"No, but two hundred years ago you should not have expected your wife to love you," I said. "Or expected that she would make you happy. Have you ever asked her what she wants?"

Michel blinked again. "No. I mean, isn't it obvious? I mean, how could you have a conversation about something like that with your wife? It would seem like I was accusing her or something."

I shook my head. "Even a good woman has opinions. You might find them quite surprising."

"We don't talk very much," he said. "Not about personal things. If we did, there are too many things she'd be appalled by. I mean, I have to be on good behavior, you know. She...."

"Would hate you if she knew what you really thought?" I finished.

He nodded miserably.

I took a deep breath. "You don't really know that, do you, Michel? Do you actually know what she thinks about anything?"

"She's a good woman, a good mother. She can't understand...." There was so much unsaid, but I knew what it was, the blood lust, the dark places, all of the parts of his soul that did not bear the light of day. "I don't want to hurt her. I don't want her to hate me."

I considered my words carefully. "I'm not suggesting you drop everything on her at once. But you could sound her out and see what she thinks about things. Don't you talk at all?"

"About the children," he said. "We talk about the children. But whenever I try to spend time with them everyone gets very upset about it. I have about ten minutes before nurses are taking them away so they won't bother me. The minute one of them is hungry or dirty they're whisked out of the room. I don't mind. I would be happy to clean them up."

"Michel, Marshals of France don't change diapers!" I said. "Gentlemen of breeding ignore their children, except properly turned out for ten minutes before dinner."

"But that's not what I wanted," he said. "That's not it at all."

I put my arms around him again and held him tight. "I know, dearest. But it's what you signed up for. If you want something different, you're going to have to make it different. You are the master of the house. Stop trying to be good enough for your wife and servants! Stop worrying about whether you have less breeding and manners than your butler! Do as you like. It's not as though your servants can throw you out of the nursery."

"It's a moot point," Michel said. "I won't see them again before...."

"Before the embarkation?"

He nodded but did not meet my eyes.

I tightened my hands on his arms. "Michel, if you ask me to, I will come with you to England. If you agree to my terms, I will come on this campaign with you."

His eyes searched my face. "I have to think about it."

"Think about it," I said. "You asked what I wanted, and you've heard my proposal. Think about it and decide." I took a step back. "But time is not infinite. You know the date you have until, and I don't. That's how long you have."

Michel nodded gravely. "I understand," he said.

Subervie came to see me in the morning, which surprised me, as surely with the Emperor in Boulogne he had a great deal to do, and I said so.

"I do," he said, flourishing a piece of folded paper, "but the Emperor asked me to bring this to you personally. He said to tell you he could not send for you here, as it would be tantamount to advertising that you are in his service, but I should bring you this and wait for your reply."

"Thank you," I said, and tore it open with trembling fingers. It was short and to the point.

Madame,

Nearly two months have passed since our last interview. While I am given to understand that you have provided invaluable service to Marshal Lannes, so far you have not yet secured the identity of the man in question. Time is running out, Madame. You must complete this quickly, or the price in French lives will be very high indeed.

N.

I folded it up very tightly, my cheeks flaming. Subervie was too well trained to ask me what was in it, but I saw him glance sideways.

"He says to hurry up and find the spy," I said. "That time is running out."

Subervie snorted. "We know that, don't we? Well, you'll have my best shot tonight. The boat drill is scheduled for an hour after midnight. If you and Honoré will be in position, we'll see what we get."

"We'll be there," I said grimly. "And hopefully this will wrap it up. If it doesn't?"

"The Emperor leaves next Thursday," Subervie said. He looked at me significantly. "Summer is wearing away."

He would not give me a date, but his meaning was obvious. We were getting into August. Fall would come soon, and the Channel would be rolled by storms, cool weather and rains coming in. Yes, the south of England had mild winters, but the north? Wales? We should not want to begin a campaign in the fall, knowing it might take many months to fight. That was against all established military wisdom. We must begin by the end of August. I did not need to know the exact date. We only had two and a half weeks left.

The Eagle

Reille and I sat side by side in the dark, my shoulder almost against his, our pistols across our laps. Below the boulder we sheltered behind, the sea cliffs dropped away steeply, twenty-five feet to the waves below, breaking white on the rocks. It was very quiet. Orion had risen clear and cool in the sky with his belt of fire.

"It's well after midnight," Reille said quietly. "The boat drill must have begun by now."

I nodded even though he might not be able to see me in the clear starlight. "We wait."

The spy would surely hear of the boat drill. Half Boulogne would hear the commotion. He would take the time to confirm that the landing craft were indeed being boarded and that the troops were embarking before he hurried to report. With any luck, Lion would not be lying directly off the coast and this would take some little time: to hurry out from Boulogne with a lantern and wait for the path of Lion's patrol to bring her within sight of his observation point.

Where we waited. Hopefully the spy would get a surprise tonight and I would complete my mission.

Time passed. We could see nothing from here, nothing except empty sea. The port was too far and the shape of the headland hid it from us. Sirius rose, the dog star bright in the sky before dawn.

"The heliacal rising of Sothis," Reille said quietly, his dark eyes on the sky. "That used to mean something, didn't it?"

"Yes," I said. "How do you know that?"

"I read a lot." Reille looked at me sideways. "I've never done the type of operation we did with the Marshal the other night, the Mesmerism."

"But would you?" I asked.

"Of course I would," Reille said with a smile, as though it should be patently obvious. "Wouldn't you like to know if you could?"

"I don't know," I said. "I have spent a good deal of my life trying not to know."

He shrugged as if he found that inexplicable. "I'd like to know everything." He leaned back against the boulder, the pistol shifting in his lap. "Besides, isn't it fun?" I looked at him dumbfounded, and Reille smiled. "We have good friends and good work, a part in the greatest events of our age. We ought to enjoy it. There will be enough time for regrets later."

I looked at him, and it was as though I saw him for the first time, tall and lean, dark-haired and dark-eyed, long-limbed and contained, with a sideways smile that was a twist of kindness, not irony. A happy man, I thought, and one whose happiness is a banked fire for those around him. No wonder the world loved Reille. He loved the world.

And with that thought came an unlooked for rush of desire. His shoulder was very warm against mine, dark blue wool coat blending with the shadows. His thigh was not quite pressed against mine, attired in Charles' black breeches and riding boots. His hands were long and lean on his pistol, beautiful hands with the quick skill of a fencer. He smelled of vetiver and lemon toilet water, and the slightest hint of his own body beneath it.

I shivered. And what was this, entirely inappropriate and unexpected?

He looked at me and shrugged just a little. "It takes some people that way," he said. "Danger as an aphrodisiac."

I felt the blood rising in my face, but there was no censure in his expression. Perhaps he felt it too. Perhaps daring was also arousing for him.

"It's one of those things," he said. "But I don't think we'd better do anything about it since we're on watch."

"No, probably not," I agreed. "That would be inattentive." I swallowed hard. The shape of his lips, the tiny nick at the corner where he had cut himself shaving....

Smiling, he shifted his seat, putting a few inches further between us, his pistol carefully resting over his lap. "So where are you from?"

"Amsterdam, I suppose," I said. "But it was never home. I never had a home until I came to Paris."

"There is nowhere like it, is there?" he said. "I could pass my days in Paris in perfect contentment."

"Are you not more likely to pass them in the field?" I asked.

Reille shrugged. "As long as I can always come home."

He would have said more, but I raised my hand and he fell instantly silent. I thought I had heard a sound above.

A long moment of silence. Perhaps I had imagined it. No, there it was again, repeated. It was the soft sound of sand shifting beneath feet, someone beginning to make their way down the steep path.

Reille was on his knees now, gathered up like a cat to spring. Not a stone beneath us stirred as I got slowly to my feet.

No further sound on the path. Had he stopped? Was this nothing at all except some ordinary passerby? I did not hear anything. The wind off the sea whipped away the sound of breath. I was smaller and lighter than Reille, closer to the edge of the boulder. Carefully, I crept forward until I could look around.

At the top of the path was a man silhouetted dark against the stars. Only a few rays of light shone through the shuttered lantern he carried, and I could see nothing more of him than the shape of his hat against the sky, a bicorn without plume or cockade.

"Stand where you are!" I shouted, coming from behind the rock to level my pistol at him in the starlight. "Put the lantern down and get your hands up."

"Oh for the love of God!" Corbineau said. "Elza, put that thing down before you hurt me."

Behind me Reille swore.

Corbineau opened the lantern shutters so I could see his face, and just incidentally so he could see the path ahead as he descended. "I came to tell you that Lion is standing off Boulogne. They've come in close enough with the tide that they can see the men disembarking after the drill. There's no need for the spy to show himself to signal to Lion. Those peerless sailors can see for themselves."

"Bad luck," Reille said, coming around the rock.

"Bad indeed," Corbineau said. "A high tide, and Lion up at the north end of the patrol circuit by chance. We'll get nothing tonight. I suppose I could have let you sit out here until dawn, but I thought I'd rescue you." He gave me a tiny wink as though to say that he thought Reille probably needed rescuing from me.

"Many thanks," Reille said, uncocking his pistol. "Then we'd best call it a night."

"Yes," I said.

The Emperor would not be pleased that we had accomplished nothing. And I would be the one who would face his displeasure.

When I returned to Boulogne in the gray light before dawn I was unsurprised to find Subervie waiting for me, a grim look on his face. "Did the boat drill go badly?" I asked.

"The boat drill was fine," he said quietly. "The Emperor wants to see you."

I squared my shoulders. "I was afraid he might," I said. Chances were that he would turn me out of his service. After all, what use was an agent who never accomplished anything? Is it not customary to fire someone whose work produces nothing?

Subervie led me into the fortress by the back way, up servants' stairs that were entirely deserted despite the hour of the morning. Surely the servants should be busy at this hour, lighting fires and bringing breakfasts and preparing for the day? Or perhaps, I thought, Lannes had indeed closed headquarters for the length of the Emperor's stay.

It was not quite six by the clock on the console table in the hall when Subervie led me to the door of the second floor drawing room that the Emperor was using as an office. Unsurprisingly, he was already at his desk, steam curling up in thick spirals from a cup of black coffee on a leather roundel placed on the fine walnut. He wore a plain chasseur's uniform, and he looked up from the papers before him as we entered.

"Madame St. Elme, sire," Subervie said, his eyes front and center rather than on the Emperor.

"You may stay, Subervie," he said. "We will only be a moment."

I swallowed. "Sire."

He looked up from his desk, his tone mild. "You have not yet caught the spy, Madame."

"No, sire."

"No excuses? No explanations?" He did not raise his voice or stand. He did not need to.

"No, sire."

"Do I need to reiterate the importance of this mission?"

"No, sire." Beside me Subervie was a model of military stiffness, and I resolved myself that I would do no less. I would not beg and plead and whine.

"Lannes says that you have made yourself helpful to him." I wondered in which capacity Lannes had meant it.... Surely the Emperor did not know of the Lodge? "You must do better."

"I will, sire," I said.

"There will come a time not far off when the die is cast," he said. "If this matter is not laid to rest before that day, it will cost many lives. Secrecy is essential to our plan, and if this spy is still at large…." He shrugged.

"And many of those lives may be those dear to me," I said. "Sire, if I fail it shall not be through want of effort!"

"I believe that, Madame," he said gravely. "But let us see your success as well as your industry." He stood up, reaching for another sheaf of papers on the side table. "Subervie, show Madame St. Elme out."

"Thank you, sire," I said, and went with great relief. He had not relieved me, not yet. I had not yet failed, though I thought I could read in his words just how little time remained before the embarkation, before all was lost or won.

The Emperor left for Paris that afternoon, putting the lie to the rumor that the embarkation was imminent. Surely if it were he would have remained in Boulogne, the better to have operational control of the invasion himself! There was nothing in Paris so pressing as this war.

And so, I thought, we have some small amount of time, some few days before we are wakened by the flying hooves of his big Berlin on the cobblestones of Boulogne, his arrival our only warning that the time has come. A few days, or perhaps a few weeks. No more than four weeks, surely. This must come by mid September or not at all.

That night, at dinner with Corbineau, I said as much.

Jean-Baptiste took a quick sip of his wine. "You know I don't know the date either."

"That's why I'm talking to you," I said. "Subervie will think I'm trying to wheedle it out of him, which I'm not. I'm trying to figure out how to best calculate our opportunity to catch the spy." I rested my forearms on the edge of the table. "There is the weather to consider. Fall gales in the Channel."

"That's not the only thing of course," Jean-Baptiste said. "There are naval maneuvers we know nothing about. Our ships must lure the British fleet away, or at least engage them and draw their attention so that we have a clear passage. We need seven hours to get across. That's all. But we must have seven hours without the Channel Fleet. Or," he looked at me pointedly, "without other interruptions."

The air elemental, of course. Otherwise our fleet would suffer the same fate as the Spanish Armada, and Jean-Baptiste, Michel and the rest would be cast into the sea, landing craft swamped by eldritch waves.

"I do not see how we are to do it," I said, shaking my head. "The power of that creature...."

"Honoré says he has a way," Jean-Baptiste said, glancing up over my shoulder in the nearly empty tavern. "Why don't you ask him? Honoré, will you join us? This capon bears remarking upon."

Reille had come in behind me, and now loomed over me in an uncertain sort of way, as though wondering if he were really welcome. "If you don't mind," he said. "Madame?"

"Call me Elza," I said warmly. "And do join us. We were just speaking of you."

He looked startled and a little pleased. "Oh."

"I was saying what a great buffoon you are," Jean-Baptiste said with a grin.

"He was not," I said. I dropped my voice. "We were discussing how to get rid of the creature."

"That." Honoré sank into the chair to my left. "That is the question."

"To which you are expected to provide an answer, if I understand correctly," I said. "What is it you mean for us to do?"

He reached for the wine bottle and filled an empty glass with the air of a man settling in for a long explanation. "The only way to fight Story is with Story. That creature is drawing its power from the belief of Britons, from the core mythology of the British Isles themselves, that Albion is protected by the encircling seas, inviolable and uninvadable. Thousands of people know the stories—Drake's Drum and the Armada, Robin Hood and King Arthur, Bran's head...."

I must have looked blank, having never heard of Bran's head.

"It's a very old tale," he said, "but the specifics aren't important. The thing that's important is that thousands of people believe that the seas and skies will rise against an invader. They believe it in their core, in the very heart of their being. That is a powerful, unshakable thing. We can't hope to touch that."

"So what do we do?" I asked.

"We must attach our efforts to a story of successful invasion," he said. "To a counter story of equal power."

Jean-Baptiste looked keen. "Hastings?"

"Not enough," Honoré said, shaking his head. "There isn't enough power in that story. Really, when it comes to it, who adores William of

Normandy? Who dreams of him as the model of a king, or for that matter the model of a man? He is no great hero of France. And even more importantly, none of us, so far as we know, have the correct correspondences to tap into that story."

"Correspondences?" I asked. I thought I knew what he meant, and it sent a shiver up my spine.

His dark eyes were level. "None of us were there. As far as we know, none of us were present at Hastings. On either side."

"That is what I thought you meant," I said. My throat was unaccountably dry, and I took a quick gulp of my wine.

"What then?" Jean-Baptiste asked.

Honoré smiled, and lifted the front of his coat, displaying the facing to us. "What do you see?"

Dark blue wool, of course. White lining, black braid about the button holes.... I drew in a deep breath, reached out and touched one of the brass buttons. "Imperial eagles," I said. Each button on his uniform coat was the new style, spread-winged eagles rather than the old ones of the Army of the Republic. They glittered in the candlelight, almost as though their feathers shifted a little. Eagles on our standards, each regiment with its own, given to them by the Emperor's own hand, like the legions of old. All that was missing was the legend SPQR beneath them.... "Julius Caesar invaded Britain," I said, and I was proud that my voice did not shake. "Caesar did it. Before the civil war, before he came to Alexandria."

"And Lannes was with him," Honoré said in a low voice.

I had not thought about it, but now, bending my head over plate and glass, the slightly wavering surface of my goblet reflecting the candlelight, I could see him clearly, a young man with a sharp, handsome face wearing leather beneath his red cloak, his hair grown out long like the Celts he commanded rather than cut short as a Roman's. I could see him in the dining room of some old palace, striding in among the couches with a piece of news, vital and hurried, making his way about the antique krater on its stand....

"Pollio," I whispered, the name coming to me unbidden.

Honoré started, dark eyes rising to meet mine.

"You served him," I said, the certainty of it making me bold. "You were one of his men."

And there was something there I did not wish to see, some old sorrow that blurred my eyes, that my gaze shrank from.

“That could well be,” Honoré said gravely. “Asinius Pollio commanded Caesar’s cavalry for many years.”

“Celtic auxiliaries,” I said. No, there was something there I did not wish to see, something too painful, a time I did not wish to return to, even in thought....

Jean-Baptiste touched my hand. “What’s wrong?”

A white palace in slanting light, late summer sun....

“There is something I do not want to see,” I said, a note of rising panic in my voice. “I do not want this!”

Honoré took my other hand warm in his, met my eyes with compelling authority in his voice, like that which he had used in the operation with Michel. “You do not have to see anything you do not wish to,” he said. “You are the master of your soul. The choice is yours to see or not.”

I felt the terror subside a bit, answering to the command in his face. Oh yes, I thought irrelevantly, there is some part of me that desires to be commanded yet. Would I find that imperative in him?

“You do not have to see,” he said. “Not unless you choose to.”

I nodded, my grip on his fingers tightening. “Do you remember?” I asked. “Do you know what it is that I don’t want to see?”

He shook his head slowly, his eyes never leaving mine. “No,” he said. “I don’t know.” I heard his unspoken thought as though he had said it aloud—but I can guess. Honoré was the one who had read history, who knew what books told us befell these people. I did not know who I was to have known Lannes and Honoré in that life, but he had drawn his own conclusions based upon study, not dreams.

“Well, it’s nothing to me,” Jean-Baptiste said. “No affinity for Caesar whatsoever. Unless you mean Borgia.” He squeezed my other hand. “I’ve an utter terror of the Italian Renaissance, just for your information.”

“I will keep that in mind,” I said, releasing both their hands. Whatever it was, the strangeness had subsided now. I must learn to control this lest it control me. It was too strong, too powerful to leave alone, too dangerous to leave that doorway half open. Perhaps Noirtier’s Dr. Mesmer could help. Perhaps those techniques could give me mastery of the things that resided in my own head, these far memories which proved both so important and so distressing.

“That’s what technique is for,” Honoré said. “Technique teaches control. That’s why the esoteric has always been a hidden path of study. It’s not easy. It’s a demanding calling requiring much of one. Misused or half-understood, it can be very dangerous." He looked at Jean-Baptiste. "I wish Noirtier would agree to let Madame St. Elme join as an Entered Apprentice."

I looked from one to the other as Jean-Baptiste shrugged. "I do too, but only Lannes among the Journeymen agrees, and he can't overrule his own Master."

"An Entered Apprentice?"

"If you're going to work with us, it makes sense," Jean-Baptiste said. "Better to have official standing."

"Better to have actual teaching and discipline," Honoré said.

"But I am a woman," I said.

He seemed unconcerned. "There have been circles that admitted women before," Honoré said. "Just not...."

"...the Pléiade," Jean-Baptiste finished. "God love the Pléiade! We must do nothing differently than the Pléiade did! As though this were the seventeenth century!" He reached for his wine glass. "I say we make it up for ourselves."

"Have any of us the theory for that?" Honoré asked. "And us both still Apprentices ourselves?"

"We shan't be forever, shall we, child?" Jean-Baptiste smiled. "And one must break some eggs to make omelets. We are too cautious, and these are not times for caution. We'd have got nothing out of the Marshal if we hadn't tried Mesmer's techniques, and you know that's not Pléiade."

"Not hardly," Honoré said. "But I'm not conceited enough to think that two years' study makes me a Master. We have a long way to go, Jean-Baptiste."

He shrugged negligently. "Well. But when you are Master indeed, I'll be just there to back you up. And if you want girls in the Lodge, so be it."

"I am several years your senior," I said sternly. "I hardly think I am a girl."

Jean-Baptiste winked at me. "You are an oldster like Honoré, then. Would you believe that he has just passed his thirtieth birthday? A fire-breathing Leo. And you?"

"I will be twenty-nine in the fall," I said. My own true age, my own birthdate. "I am a Libra."

"Balance in all things," Honoré said. "Or perhaps just being caught between."

"Something like that," I said. I took up my glass again. "So. Caesar.

What is your plan for using this Story to invade Britain?"

"Albion's Tale is strong," he replied. "But so is the Emperor's Story. There is a wind through the world that cannot be stopped, a force that sweeps all before it, legions and ships, orthodoxies and customs alike. We claim that Story, that force. We claim our mantles, and all of the strength and passion that entails to sweep away any obstacle in our paths. We ride the wave."

"We are Companions," I said, and I blinked hard. "We have the right because we are us." I looked at him. "If we do that, it cannot be undone."

Jean-Baptiste whistled softly. "I take back my accusation that you are over-cautious. To call that power into ourselves, to claim the sword...."

"I'll do it," I said. I lifted my chin. "Absolutely."

"Good," he said, and there was in his even gaze a daring to match mine.

You are my brother, I thought, *my kin, my soul's friend. Oh yes. We understand one another.*

"Why ever not?" I asked. "It might be fun."

Invasion

"Dis," who dwells below, lord of the dark places and their hoarded treasures, of mines and hidden things, of the grain in the ground and the caves of concealing night...." Michel's voice was strong and even, and I felt a shiver run through me even though the light of the candles played against the lids of my closed eyes, kneeling in abeyance between Honoré and Lannes. His was the last quarter of the circle to be called.

I had not shivered when Lannes spoke, addressing himself to Venus of the Seas, lady of all the oceans of the world, mother of the Caesars, nor when Honoré had, addressing himself to canny Minerva, or Max Duplessis to swift Mercury. But Dis... one does not even address Dis by his proper name where he sits below, eternal consort of the Lady of the Dead, merciless in his judgment.

I had lost the thread of the ritual, and it surprised me when Michel turned back to the center and knelt in his place, his red hair burnished bronze in the dim light. "Very well," he said, looking at Lannes.

Lannes took a deep breath, as though steeling himself for some passage of arms. The incense smoke from the censer curled around him in its path to some chink in the windows, a breath of frankincense. "Let us begin," he said. He lifted up the wrapped bundle in front of him, a piece of white silk around something roughly the size of his hand, and then opened it in the candlelight. Flame glinted off gold.

It was an Imperial eagle, the bottom of it fitted as for a staff, and I knew in that moment what it was—one of the eagles from V Corps regimental colors, the ones handed out by the Emperor only a few months past that his troops would march under.

Subervie shifted, and Honoré caught his eye. "Correspondence," he said quietly. "Our eagles and Caesar's."

"Reille, if you'll assist me with this?" Lannes asked, but it was an order, not a request. I knew why. In that time we reached for, that distant lifetime we were attempting to grasp for its power, Honoré had served under him as now he served Michel. I could almost see that man's face in the candlelight, wavering just out of reach.

"Sir," Honoré said, reaching for the eagle and laying it out reverently on our central altar. The long sets of lines were his, long sections that had to be memorized and delivered like an actor. I wondered if he'd written them as well. I doubted Subervie was up to composing in Alexandrines. It wasn't so different from provincial theater, after all.

While he began, my eyes ran over the table draped in white. The eagle, and of course my mirror. A thick white candle in a silver stand. The censer. A worn cloth-covered copy of De Bello Gallico filled with schoolboy scribbles. I wondered whose it was. The handwriting was unfamiliar. I opened it to the title page. Duplessis. Max shrugged at me across the circle, the corner of his mouth twisting.

Honoré had stopped, and now Lannes took up the narrative, minus poetic Alexandrines. His voice was businesslike, as though he were giving a report. "On the 23rd of August 55 BC we embarked in the third watch of the night, from this place in which we stand, then known as Portus Itius. We sailed through calm seas until at dawn we came to Dobris, where the chalk cliffs guard the seaward watches of Britain. But there were men drawn up upon the cliffs with spears and bows, and so we waited for a favorable tide and until the ninth hour of the day, making our way a short distance up the coast to an open beach which now they name Deal. Thereupon we disembarked into deep water, wading ashore while the catapults of our navy engaged the chariots upon the beach to clear the way for us. Caesar set his foot upon the land, and thus Albion was drawn into his story, an outlying land no more, but part of the World That Is Known." He looked at me and nodded to the mirror. "The seas are Caesar's to cross if he wishes. And by this power we have the right."

I nodded in return, and with careful hands took up the eagle, heavy and solid in my hands. I held it to my breast, feeling its cool weight through the draped linen of my robe. Material correspondence: our eagles and Caesar's, our forces and his. Caesar had camped here long before Boulogne existed.

But not before we had. Not before we were Companions.

Lannes sat beside me, his shoulder not quite touching mine. "Asinius Pollio," I whispered, and closed my eyes. I could see him so clearly, the lines of his face, his hair grown long like the Celts who served under him rather than cropped Roman short, could see him bending over Caesar's couch in some elegant dining room, a dispatch in his hand. Asinius Pollio, who had ruined himself rather than take arms against Antony.

Imagination, some logical part of me whispered. You are imagining those you know in an old story, making up things to pretend to importance.

Old doubts. I would not give them sustenance, not tonight. I pushed against it, forcing the picture in my mind clearer. It was easier than I had expected. There was Caesar, his mobile face changing as he read the dispatch, one knee forward beneath his scarlet tunic. Behind him stood a massive bodyguard, his arms crossed, blond beard trimmed to a point beneath his chin. I felt a wave of warmth, of friendship and love. I knew him, dear man whose name I could not quite touch! And yet he was here. He felt the same as Subervie in some indefinable way.

Two, I thought. Pollio and the German bodyguard. There should be three. There should be four.

Honoré. Pollio's man. Long brown hair caught back in a tail, the faded leathers of the Celtic auxiliaries, with beautiful long hands....

Michel. A boy on the last couch barely out of adolescence, light brown hair waving close to his scalp, and his eyes on me as though I were something out of a dream....

After all, something whispered within me, nineteen hundred years was such a little time....

And with that I cast myself aloft, flung my winged soul into the sky.

The sea rushed by beneath me, the moon making a path across the water toward Dover. Fast and sure I drove toward it, a white gull made of moonlight and mist, gray water beneath my wings. Power crackled above me and around me, a lone scout, the first line of the advance.

And yet I was not alone. All their strength channeled through me, all their determination. I could feel each of them as though I held separate reins in my hands, a chariot pulled by eleven fine horses, each of them a fillet of silver, a cord slender and shining as steel. Max Duplessis was bright as fire, will and purpose wrought by faith. Michel was solid as the earth beneath my feet, glossy black stone found far underground. Honoré's mind played over mine like light on water, skipping and illuminating. Subervie's stubborn strength, Jean-Baptiste's flashing power, Lannes elusive as mercury, thoughts sliding away from mine, keeping his secrets.

It rose out of the sea a mile off shore, a vast cloud tipped with lightning, winds buffeting at me. Every instinct screamed. I must veer off. I must shear away before it ripped me to pieces. I was only a gull and it was a hurricane. It would catch me up in its power, leave only ragged feathers and a storm-tossed body discarded on the beach.

Not a gull, something whispered inside me. Far away I held it to my chest, felt its power seep into me. Not a gull but a golden eagle, hard as bronze.

Lightning flared around me and did not scar, its power feeding my own. Shadows followed me, dark triremes against the water, ghost ships risen in my wake as my wings beat ceaselessly, driven by the primal power of Story, straight into the heart of the storm.

Demon-worshipper, it screamed at me, *driven by the powers of Hell, you cannot prevail!*

I do not believe in demons, I replied. *I am older by far than your stories of the devil, and I do not believe them.*

White cliffs beneath me glimmering in the moonlight.

You cannot hold the seas against the Sea Lady's son! I was a golden eagle like an arrow in flight, straight through the clouds rendered insubstantial by its passage....

...a garden bathed in moonlight, an old woman raising blue eyes to the sky, a swan's wing in her hand, Albion's power invoked and strengthened. I plunged like an arrow to her breast, stooping on the wind.

What are you? she thought for one moment as her eyes dimmed.

I do not know, I said, and witch to witch I slew her there, power burning through her and leaving her cold upon the ground.

The skies were clear above the Channel.

I shocked back into my body shaking, every muscle seizing as though electricity ran through me. I looked up into Subervie's face. "The way is clear," I said through chattering teeth, and I knew no more.

I woke lying on a bed, a cool cloth across my eyes. I caught at it and gentle hands lifted it away. Max Duplessis bent over me. "Madame?" he said. "Are you returned to yourself?"

Of course it was he. He was one of the VI Corps doctors. Of course it was he rather than Michel.

"I killed her," I whispered. "Their Magister."

Max's gray eyes were kind. "It is war, Madame. People die."

I closed my eyes, seeing her again in my mind's eye, older than I and so much stronger, or so I had thought. But not stronger than Story. Not stronger than the wave I summoned, all the weight of belief and history. I nodded slowly. What had to be had to be. She had put her life in the balance for her country as I did for mine.

"What happened?" I asked.

"They have closed the circle again while I wait with you," Max said. "Jean-Baptiste has gone scouting to see if the elemental is truly gone."

"He's terrible at it." I tried to sit up. "Jean-Baptiste won't be able to tell...."

"Lie down," Max said. He pushed me back down gently. "You've done enough."

"But Jean-Baptiste...."

"Will have to do his best," Max said. "I forbid you to get up. Your pulse was seriously slow."

"Slow?" It seemed to me that I had been exerting myself considerably.

"Yes." He shook his head. "Lie still and rest. There is nothing further you need to do tonight. And if you have defeated that elemental...." His voice trailed off. "I cannot imagine."

"We defeated it," I said. "All of us. This leviathan that is the Emperor's Story...." I did not even have words for what I meant, for the thing that we had wakened. Or perhaps it had always been there, simply waiting for us to claim its power.

Max smoothed my hair back from my forehead, his hands as gentle as a father's, checked the pulse at my throat. "That is stronger now," he said. "Good. Madame, I do not pretend to understand everything we are doing. But I do know that it must be done. You have done your part for tonight. I will fetch you some warm milk to strengthen you, as you should regain your energy, and then you will sleep here where I can keep an eye on you until I'm certain you are fully recovered." He got up with a reassuring smile. "I'll be back in just a few minutes." Quietly, he pulled the door shut behind him.

I lay in the warm candlelight in the bed piled with blankets. It felt chilly for all that it was the twenty-eighth of August. This room must be Lannes' own, or that of one of the senior officers. Max had not undressed me, for I was still in my linen from the ritual. They must have carried me in while I was in a dead faint.

Some part of me that was not lulled and drowsy, so bone tired, wondered why Max had gone to get milk himself. Oh yes. The servants. They'd locked down headquarters during the rituals and meetings. If the doctor wanted warm milk, he'd have to go warm it himself.

So nice of him, I thought, and closed my eyes. I would just doze until he came back. It was safe here beneath wards and stones, quiet and warm and safe. I could just hear the faintest murmur of voices down the hall, the circle still about their business. Besides that all else was still. I turned my head, sinking deep into the pillow. Perhaps I dozed, and perhaps not. I woke to the sound of Max's steps in the hall. The milk, I thought.

And yet the door didn't open. The footsteps passed the door and went on toward the stairs.

I opened my eyes. That was wrong. He should be coming from the stairs, coming up from the kitchen. Even if he decided I was asleep and he would not disturb me for me to drink the milk, he would open the door to check on me.

I heard nothing. The building was absolutely silent, save the soft flickering sound of the candles and the distant voices. And that was wrong as well. Why would the doctor be standing silently in the hall?

I sat up gingerly, waiting a moment for the wave of vertigo that washed over me to subside. Something was very wrong. I tiptoed to the door, my bare feet cold on the floor and turned the handle, praying that it was well oiled. It worked silently and I peered out.

The hallway was lit by a pair of sconces at the far end, at the head of the stairs. Beyond them were the double doors that led into the room we had used for the ritual. And next to them….

A man was quietly closing the door of the first room to the right, the dim light of the sconces gleaming off his white wig, off the dull sheen of his livery. A footman, an ordinary domestic, a man who would not merit a second glance. Except that the servants had been sent out. Quickly he turned and hurried down the stairs, his shoes almost silent on the treads. I did not see his face.

I hurried down the hall, my heart pounding in my chest, and opened the door he had just closed. A private office, papers and maps neatly arranged in folders, a stack of orders at the ready. The top one was in the Emperor's hand.

I knew.

Cursing myself for a fool, I ran the few steps to the double doors and flung them open. "He is here!" I shouted as they all turned, posed in tableau in the midst of their work. "The spy. He was on the stairs and he just went down. He had been in the office next door and there are papers there. He is dressed as a footman!"

Chaos ensued. Subervie started for the door, coming up short as though he'd hit an invisible barrier, his hand going to his forehead as he collided with the energy of the cast circle.

"You great fool!" Honoré exclaimed, sweeping his sword around. "Let me cut a gate!"

"No need now," Michel said, dropping to a crouch as though to deposit something heavy on the floor, and I felt him absorbing it, the shock of the loosed energy, forcing it into the ground, into the stones of Boulogne.

Subervie reeled and Jean-Baptiste ran past him, dashing for the stairs in a sprint. "I'll get him!" he yelled.

Lannes swore, looking down at his white linen robe. He couldn't very well chase after someone dressed like that, not when he was a Marshal of France.

I made a beeline for the dressing room. Thankfully I'd arrived with Charles' clothes tonight instead of bonnet and gown, and so it was the work of a moment to change. I had just begun to pull the trousers on when the door opened and Subervie barged in, and then barged back out. "Beg pardon."

"Come in and dress!" I yelled. "This is more important than my god-damned modesty!" I stuffed my shirttails into my trousers and threw on my waistcoat as Subervie barged back in with Lannes.

"Excuse me," Lannes began.

"I'm leaving," I said, tearing out with my coat in my hand.

Honoré had been wearing shirtsleeves under his robe, and now he stood at least half dressed in front of Michel, who was still robed. "Go after Corbineau," Michel was saying. "Quietly. Subervie will get patrols out, but of necessity they'll be somewhat behind." He looked at me, taking in my dress in a moment. "Did you see his face?"

"No, but I would know him," I said. "His stature, his clothing, his way of moving. I'm going with Reille."

For a moment I thought he would argue with me, but he didn't. "Here," he said, and thrust a pistol into my hand, his own I presumed. "It's loaded."

"Thank you," I said. A single shot.

Honoré had his saber belted on but no coat. "We have to go," he said urgently.

"Yes," I said, and we turned about as one and bolted for the stairs. Whatever weakness I had felt earlier was gone now, lost in the pounding need of the chase. Down the stairs and across the stable yard….

"Not the horses," Honoré said, grabbing my arm. "They won't have them. A footman can't be seen on horseback, remember? And Jean-Baptiste didn't have time if he was on his heels."

I hoped a footman didn't carry a gun either. Jean-Baptiste was unarmed, and while he'd hold his own hand to hand it wouldn't do much good against a gun.

We pelted up to the guardpost, the confused soldiers coming to attention when they recognized Honoré. "Did Major Corbineau come this way?" he demanded.

"Yes, sir," one said.

The other cut in. "He ran off toward the town. He said that a footman had stolen his purse. We said that the man just left and…."

"That way?" Honoré demanded, and at the man's nod pelted after with me in his wake.

Halfway down the hill to the fountain square I caught up to him and grabbed his sleeve. "Wait!"

He halted. "What?"

"Stop a moment," I said, my breath coming hard. "We're not going to catch him this way. If he knows the town he may have already gone to earth and we've run straight past him. We have to think."

Honoré nodded, his dark forelock dripping with sweat. "Yes." He lifted his head as though he could scent the wind like a hunting dog. "What did he see?"

I had only looked for a moment, just an instant, long enough to see the Emperor's signature. "I'm not certain," I said. "But I think it was the embarkation order. It was an order of march for V Corps." I took a deep breath. "And the date. Five days from now."

Honoré's eyes met mine. "He has to communicate that to Lion. Immediately."

"The seas are open now," I said. "If they are warned this could all be for nothing." I looked about. The square was not yet deserted. A few people were still walking to and fro, a tavern was still open, lights spilling out into the street. It could not yet be midnight. "Where is Lion?"

"She came about off Boulogne at four," Honoré said. "She ought to be at the far southern end of her circuit, or thereabouts."

"Then our man can't wait," I said. "He can't hole up in town. He has to go south along the cliffs and transmit tonight. By the time Lion gets back here it will be near dawn in high summer, five hours and a bit."

Honoré nodded again. "If he has any sense he lost Corbineau in town. Then he'll go along the cliffs to find a place to signal. You're right that he can't wait. Not with this."

There was a clatter on the stones behind us, Subervie charging up at a run, saber in hand. "Did you find him?"

"No, nor Jean-Baptiste either," I said.

"But we think we know where he'll have to be," Honoré said.

"The guard's turned out, but…."

"This is for stealth," Honoré said. "Gervais?"

"I'm with you," Subervie said grimly. "It's time to put an end to this."

Beyond the edges of the town the night was quiet. The road to Montreuil curved away from the sea, while the other track meandered its way along the cliff tops. We took that one wordlessly. There was nothing for our spy in Montreuil tonight.

We had no light, and the moon had set early behind a few scudding clouds in the west, but the stars were enough to light our way somewhat. Here, far from the smoke and haze of a city, they were astonishingly bright.

"You were right," I said as we walked along, Subervie just ahead of us, surprisingly quiet for a big man. "He was dressed as a footman. A servant."

Honoré gave me a quick smile. "Thank you. People don't say that often enough."

"Say what?"

"That I'm right." He grinned.

I smiled back at him. "You're right. I will absolutely give credit where it's due." The night air was cool with the breeze off the sea, lifting my hair from the back of my neck, clearing my head. "You have to wonder, though," I said contemplatively. "What leads a man to do that. To become a secret agent."

"What indeed?" He looked at me sideways.

"It's a very long story," I said. "Involving love and war and a great many unpleasant events."

"Surprising," he said.

"Why?"

Honoré shrugged. "You seem so happy."

I had not thought of it quite that way before. "I suppose I am," I said. "Despite all tumults and alarms."

"A very deep keel," he said. "Like a ship. When the keel is deep below the waterline it's stable despite the waves and storms. Perhaps your soul has a deep keel."

There was a movement ahead, and we all froze momentarily, then crept forward together. It looked like the movement of white cloth. Yes, that's what it was. It was a man's back in shirtsleeves going forward cautiously over the stones. We were very near to the overlook we had marked before, and it looked as though the man approached it cautiously, moving down the edge of the cliff at an angle toward it, as though he wanted to look over the edge before he got there.

Honoré glanced meaningfully at my pistol and I shook my head. It was too far, and the light was too uncertain. I had only one shot, and at this distance I could not count on accuracy. If I wasted it we would alert him to our presence.

He disappeared for a moment, ducking down behind a stone.

I looked at Honoré and he moved his hands apart, then circled them around. We must separate and try to get him between us. That would be the surest thing. Nodding so that he knew I understood, I started working my way to the left, southward, Subervie fanning out in the other direction to come upon him from the right. I would get ahead of him and Honoré would be behind.

Suddenly a light flashed out like a star brought to Earth, not where the man I had seen was but a little further on, a shaded lantern being opened. Once, twice.

Out to sea to the south there was an answering blink, a point of light upon the sea replying, Lion at the extreme end of sight working her way northward against the wind.

Now or never, I thought. If he signaled what he'd seen we were lost. I sighted along the gun barrel but I had no target. I could see nothing. The man holding the lantern might be to its left or right depending on how he stood, but either way he was wearing dark clothes against dark ground and sea.

There was a rush suddenly, the sound of feet running hard over stones, and in an entirely different place the white shirt sleeves bobbed up in answer. I understood in a moment. The white shirt had been Corbineau, trying to keep low since he was more visible than his quarry, and the running feet....

"Get him!" Subervie shouted, running at the light, which winked out suddenly. He must have caught our man in a flying tackle, for there were scuffles and grunts. Off to my right Honoré abandoned all pretense of creeping, dashing toward the fight. Pistol in hand I took off too, though I could see nothing more than a dark form thrashing about on the ground, presumably Subervie and the spy entangled.

One of them got up and broke away and the other followed, catching his quarry right at the edge of the cliff. A blow, a grunt—I still could not see. One staggered on the edge, and I saw the other strike, a gut punch that would have winded a man on a flat floor. It was too much, and he staggered back, misstepping at the very brink, then going over in a flailing of arms.

The survivor ran, and in that moment I knew which was which. If the spy had gone over, Subervie would have looked after him. It had been Gervais Subervie who had gone over, that fearless family man with his two small children. It was the spy who escaped.

Curses, and Jean-Baptiste was at the edge, "God damn you, you great stupid brave idiot...."

The spy was running full out along the cliff, southward away from us, his lantern deserted on the ground behind, as the light would give him away.

I could not hope to bring him down hand to hand, not smaller and lighter as I was, if he'd done for Subervie. But I still had one shot. And so I stopped and took it, lining up carefully in the pale starlight as he clambered over the stones, moments long as hours, blood cold as ice.

It took him full in the middle of the back. He screamed, a terrible bellow of pain, and pitched over the edge.

I ran up and looked over, leaning out on the stones like a parapet. His body lay unmoving on the rocks at the base of the cliff, his head at an unnatural angle, blood pooling around him like a dark tide. I swallowed bile but did not look away. Only a coward looks away from what they have done.

"Elza, help!" shouted Jean-Baptiste.

I turned and ran back toward where Subervie had gone over and hurried to the brink.

"Elza!" Jean-Baptiste was stretched full length on a ledge about five feet beneath the edge, his legs spread for greater purchase on the rocks, his shoulders at the edge and his arms over the drop. He had Subervie by one arm, and as I watched Subervie tried to fling the other up to catch at the stone, his fingers scrabbling for a hold. The sea sang around the rocks below. "I've got him but I can't haul him up like this," Jean-Baptiste panted. "If I move his weight will drag me over too."

"A moment," I said, scrambling down to the ledge as quickly as possible. Of course he couldn't lift a man heavier than he while lying flat on his stomach! It was only the most exceeding stubbornness that allowed him to hold on at all.

"Give Elza your other hand," Jean-Baptiste directed. "Let her take some of your weight and I can get in a better position to pull."

I got my hands around his wrist and braced myself as well as I could, but even so the strain on my shoulders nearly pulled me forward. "Hurry," I said.

Jean-Baptiste got into a better position and pulled, getting Subervie's left shoulder even with the ledge so that he could get purchase, and then hauling on him beneath the arm. After that it only took a few moments before we all lay there on the ledge together, panting and staring up at the stars.

"Many thanks," Subervie said, still trying to catch his breath. "I thought I was done for a moment there. I caught the ledge as I fell but I couldn't get up nor hold on forever. Jean-Baptiste…."

"Any time," Corbineau said, resting his head back against the stone. "It's my pleasure to rescue you, child." He looked almost giddy with the relief of it.

"I suppose the spy got away," Subervie said regretfully.

"No," I said. "I shot him to death."

A momentary silence greeted that revelation.

"Well," Subervie said. "Good. The Emperor ought to like that."

"I like that," Jean-Baptiste said.

We all just lay there for a moment.

"What do you suppose has become of Honoré?" Jean-Baptiste asked.

"I haven't the faintest," I said, and got to my feet.

Light beamed out from above, the flashes of a lantern blinking in code, the shutter opening and closing. Out to sea, Lion answered.

I scrabbled up from the ledge.

Honoré stood at the top along the cliff, the lantern in his left hand while he worked the shutter with his right, holding papers open before him.

"What in the devil are you doing?" I demanded as Subervie and Corbineau popped up behind me.

Honoré's look of concentration didn't change. "If the three of you are through lying around down there, there's work to do."

"What?" Subervie demanded, whether for the charge of lying around or utter bafflement.

"The spy dropped his code book with the lantern," Honoré said. "Lion is sitting offshore waiting for a message. We might never have an opportunity like this again." He glanced back at the papers, then opened and shut the lantern swiftly three times in a row.

"What are you telling them?" Subervie demanded.

Honoré repeated the last group of signals and looked at Subervie. "This three times and then this." He pointed to a line of code which I wasn't near enough to read in the dark.

Subervie was. "Embarkation in progress. Invasion imminent? What in the hell do you think you're doing?"

"Shaking things up a bit," Honoré said. "The boy who cried wolf. Full out alert, Boney's coming in a rowboat and all that. Tonight's the night." He looked at the book again, then gave a different signal. "Capture expected. Farewell."

A chill ran down my spine as Honoré sent gallant last words from a man already dead. They would believe he had given his life to save them, when instead he had failed and died.

"For verisimilitude," Honoré said with a sideways look at me, but I did not believe him. Not entirely.

"The Marshals will have fits," Subervie said. "For that matter, the Emperor will have a fit! How could you take that on?"

"We had one chance to do it," Honoré said, setting the lantern down. "Lion had already given the countersignal. It's not as though we could wait for orders from Boulogne!"

"Gentlemen," I said. "Let's get back to headquarters. Marshal Lannes will want to know what's happened and send a detail to recover the body. And…." Words failed me.

"I'll take full responsibility for this," Honoré said stiffly. "It was my initiative and mine alone."

"Back to town," Jean-Baptiste said, putting a hand on each of their shoulders. "And pray we'll meet a patrol on the way."

We started along the cliffs together. I looked back. Lion was spreading all canvas, and over the water I could hear the shouts on her deck as she prepared to come about, Captain Arnold standing out from the French coast with all possible haste and a fair wind for Dover at his back, carrying the message of invasion. On her deck a light winked and then ceased. Godspeed.

Lannes boggled. So did I, when I saw the clock. All of that and it was only half past twelve! It seemed that several nights must have been and gone. Michel sat down heavily in a chair and didn't look at me while Lannes paced. Honoré, of course, had to answer some rather penetrating questions from the both of them.

"This may be to the good," Michel said, looking at Lannes. "Misdirection."

"It could be." Lannes nodded gravely. "I'll get this coded and sent by semaphore at first light. We'll see what the Emperor says."

Honoré straightened his shoulders, eyes front.

"You can go," Michel said, and I thought he was pleased with Reille rather than the opposite. "Corbineau, Subervie…get some clean clothes and something to eat. There's the buffet laid and no one's touched it."

"Yes sir," Jean-Baptiste said with a smart salute. He looked a bit the worse for wear, but entirely self-satisfied, as though it had been a good adventure all around. And he thought I was the crazy one!

"Stay, Madame," Lannes said as they went to the door, and I waited while the door closed behind them. He sat down on the edge of his desk, white trousers immaculate even at this time of night. "A very good job," he said. "The spy disposed of, and Lion making for Dover leaving Boulogne entirely unattended and unobserved."

"Are you thinking…" Michel began, looking up at Lannes from the chair.

"Will there be a better time?"

"Not likely." The devil's smile played about Michel's lips.

"Then," Lannes said.

"Then." They looked like boys daring each other on.

"You are not going to launch the invasion in the teeth of the alarm!" I burst out. "Surely that will be more dangerous!"

"You will see what we will do," Lannes said. He went behind the desk and fetched a small packet of papers. "But you had best report to the Emperor immediately. My own carriage is waiting to take you to Paris without delay. You'll change horses at each posting station and travel through the night. The semaphore message will pass you in the morning, but I'm sure the Emperor will want your report in person. I've sent a man for the clothes you left here for after the ritual and to put up some cold supper for you to take with you. But you'd best be off." He handed me the packet. "It has been a pleasure working with you, Madame St. Elme. I would be delighted to see you in my command at any time."

He made to bend over my hand, but I took it and shook it like a man. "The pleasure has been entirely mine, Marshal. I hope that our paths cross again."

"I hope so too, Madame," he said. "You are a worthy addition to our Lodge."

"I appreciate your trust," I said.

He glanced at Michel rather transparently. "If you'd like to show the lady down, I have things I must attend to."

"It's no bother at all," Michel replied, and closed the door behind me as we stepped out into the hall and went down the stairs. It was no longer silent. I could hear the swift tattoo of a drum beating to arms, the sounds of men assembling in the courtyard, horses being led out.

I stopped at the bottom of the last flight. Amid the orderly chaos of the courtyard, Lannes' black traveling coach was waiting. "Michel…."

He took both my hands in his. "I know we've only a moment," he said. "And I don't know when I'll see you again. But yes."

"Yes what?"

"Yes, I'll take your proposition," he said, his eyes roving over my face. "We've already ruined so much, but if there's any chance…. We'll do this your way. I don't know if it will be enough, but you say that's what you want…."

"Shut up and kiss me," I said, and drew him down.

It was a very long kiss, thorough and deep and replete with everything we hadn't said when there was time, but now there was none. Our hearts raced in time to the drum's roll and the night was speeding fast. Time was tearing ahead of us.

"I'll see you as soon as I can," I murmured, my forehead against his stubbled chin, drinking in the scent and feel of him, the faint hint of incense clinging to him.

"I love you," he said unnecessarily.

"And I you." I rested my cheek against his shoulder for a long moment. "Be safe."

"I always try to be," he said, and stepped back, that quirk at the corner of his mouth again. "I don't enjoy getting shot. It just happens."

"As soon as I can," I said, and stepped out into the courtyard with Michel at my back.

He opened the carriage door for me and handed me up though I wore dirty and stained man's clothes, leaned in a moment. "Always," he said.

"Yes."

And then he closed the door and spoke to the driver, looking back as the wheels began to turn. He lifted a hand as we turned at the guardpost and held it while I waved back, trying not to cry. About him the regiment was forming up at arms. Ahead was the road to Paris.

I ate the cold supper Lannes had caused to be packed and changed into clean clothes. I couldn't wash, and I was certain we'd stop no longer at posting stations than absolutely necessary to change the horses and tend to vital functions, but at least in a sprigged muslin dress and bonnet I looked somewhat more respectable, perhaps Lannes' mistress rather than his stableboy!

I had not thought I could sleep. The rigors of the night crowded in, one thing upon another, but the motion of the carriage was soothing, horses trotting smoothly over well maintained highways. I had not thought I would, but before long I leaned my head against the cushioned frame of the door and closed my eyes.

Up and down, rising and falling, the gentle give of the carriage springs....

Rising and falling, leaping through choppy Channel rollers, colors spread against the night sky, Dover Castle now in sight. There was a man on the foremast, shuttered lantern in his hand, signaling the moment the pinnacles appeared over the horizon. Embarkation in progress. Invasion imminent. Invasion imminent. Captain Arnold paced his quarterdeck, his eyes on the light above, while his lieutenant squeezed every bit of speed from Lion. Invasion imminent.

An answering light, and I swooped low like a gull in flight, hearing our drums echoed in the answering tattoo at Dover, the garrison called to quarters in the predawn stillness.

Embarkation in progress. Invasion imminent.

Church bells rang out across Kent, alarm pealing clear and loud over fields and towns. Invasion imminent. The sky was paling as home guardsmen assembled in lanes with antique fowling pieces, ready to repel.

The sun rose over London, church bells carrying the word swift as semaphores, the bells of London crying out alarm, repeating and repeating from high streets to low. Invasion imminent.

Drake's drum sounded its relentless beat beneath it all, while high and clear the bells of St. Martin's answered. A white gull turned among the pigeons, wings tireless and strong, London spread beneath her wings....

The carriage stopped, bumping into a posting station, and I jerked awake. It was just after sunrise, and a riot of birds sang in the trees. The bees were in the lavender. I climbed stiffly down from the carriage and used the necessary while they changed the horses. I stood and washed my face at the pump, letting the morning sun kiss the water from my cheeks. The ostlers brought out the new team. On a ridge beyond a field the massive arms of a semaphore turned, telegraphing the news toward Paris, Lannes' report passing me and charging on through the morning.

I felt light, thin as a cloud and twice as attenuated. I got back in the carriage and slept before we were moving again.

I woke as we clattered into the village of Pontoise. Afternoon shadows were lengthening. A sergeant at the posting station passed me a basket of cold chicken and bread, and I ate as we lurched on again, a new team eating up the miles. Dispatch riders passed us still, chasseurs galloping wildly on errands. All France was on the move.

Were even now the beacons burning on England's southern coast, our landing craft seen from shore? Were even now they coming under fire from naval guns?

Michel.... My heart yearned for wings again, but now I was awake and fed and it was only me. I could see nothing, could not launch into that unseen wind. The sound of the wheels was his name. Michel. What was happening even now?

We rolled into through the Barrière de Clichy into Paris at evening, with all the lamps new lit and the streets full of people. Cafés spilled their crowds into the street on a warm August night. In the west the moon was setting ripe and bright. An escort of hussars fell in beside the carriage, clearing traffic as though I were Lannes himself.

The Tuileries blazed with light. Every window was lit, open to the river breezes, white curtains moving, silhouetting figures behind them.

"Madame St. Elme," the driver said at the guardpost, and the soldiers let us through immediately. When we stopped beneath the portico I could hardly get down, so much had I stiffened from sitting so long. A sprigged muslin dress and bonnet was hardly appropriate for the Tuileries. I should have been in satin and diamonds.

"This way," a footman said, and I followed him.

This time the anteroom was full of military men, mostly chasseurs waiting about to carry orders. The marble bust of Alexander smirked at me, and it occurred to me that it was real, the Guimet Alexander wrought two thousand years ago. “A very good likeness,” I said aloud.

“I am glad that you approve, Madame.”

The chasseurs had all come to attention and the Emperor stood in the doorway to the inner office wearing a plain undress uniform. I made my courtesy as swiftly and with as much grace as possible.

“Come in,” he said, and gestured for me to precede him.

“Sire,” I said.

He shut the door and grinned at me, a boyish look of sheer delight that utterly transformed him. “I knew you could do it,” he said triumphantly, as if he’d won a schoolboy bet. “Oh, well done, Madame!”

“Thank you, sire,” I said.

“Lannes says that you have given perfect satisfaction in every way, above and beyond any expectations of you. You have saved many French lives, and you have my gratitude.”

I bowed my head under the weight of his approbation. “It is enough for me if some of them are the lives of my friends,” I said. “I beg you, let me return to Boulogne and cross the Channel with our reinforcements! Surely there will be more ships attempting the crossing even if the British Navy….” I stopped short at his incredulous expression.

“Has no one told you yet? I thought Ney would leak like a sieve!”

“Told me what?”

“There is no invasion of England, Madame.” He crossed behind his desk and sat down. “There has not been since the spring.”

“What?” My mouth hung open. “All those ships, all those men….”

“All of those ships and men are engaged in a campaign against Austria,” he said. “It is time to bring our wars with Austria to a close. Their empire will never accept the Revolution, not so long as the specter of Marie Antoinette hangs over all and they believe that the Bourbons may yet be restored to the French throne. Austria, not England, is our nemesis. Fox can be reasoned with, and men like him, but Austria? They cannot afford for us to exist, as every day that we do their subject peoples grow more and more restive on the idea of revolution.”

“Austria?” I felt rather stupid, still a step behind. “But the British navy, the landing craft, the Lodge….”

“It was imperative that the Austrians and British both believe that our goal was England. But that has not been the case since March. Long before you went to Boulogne, Lannes knew what the real plan was. He wrote it with Berthier and two others. The most senior officers and some essential aides were informed when I was there last month, because they should have to arrange the execution of the plan—two massive army corps spinning on a coin and attacking east instead of west, a complete and total surprise! This is the secret for which men and women have died, Madame."

"So what I saw on Lannes' desk...."

"...were V Corps' orders to pivot and march east four days from now. That is the secret that the spy would have reported, a secret that would have brought the whole plan down in ruins." The Emperor leaned forward on his elbows. "If not for you and that peerless band of gentlemen."

"Reille was doing his best, sire," I said. I thought I owed it to Honoré to try to get him out of hot water.

"A young man with initiative," he said. "Thanks to him the British and Austrians both believe that our troop movements are the precursors to an invasion at any moment, successfully screening our real purpose. There is a decoration in it for him, and an appointment to my staff. I think he'd make a fine Aide de Camp for me!"

"Sire," I said rather breathlessly.

The Emperor opened a morocco folder on his desk. "And now there is the matter of your payment." He handed me a sheaf of papers. "This states that you are one Ida St. Elme, born in the village of Vallombreuse in the Department of Haute Savoie, daughter of a Protestant minister and his wife. A copy has also been filed with the Mayor's office there, in case there is ever any question. You are a citizen of France named Ida St. Elme. There is no Elzelina Ringeling who is wanted in Holland."

Haute Savoie. My eyes ran over the paper as though I could hardly believe what I read. Safe. Safe for the rest of my life. They filled with tears.

"You shall never be deported. A fresh start," he said. He wiggled a finger at the rest of the papers. "There is also a bank draft for you of some size. I do not want you to find me parsimonious."

"I am sure I shall not, sire," I said rather breathlessly. I lifted the first page and looked at it. Generous, but not excessive—precisely what I was worth to the sou. "And the other papers?" There were several others beneath.

"Orders for posting houses allowing you to requisition fodder and supplies, passes and that sort of thing." He looked up at me and there was a mischievous expression on his face. “If you hurry, I imagine you can catch VI Corps at Strasbourg!”

I could not help it. I burst out laughing, as it was that or tears.

“I have no doubt I will see you soon,” he said. “I am certain you will be needed.”

“You may count on it,” I said.

Author's Note

The Emperor's Agent is based on a true story. Elzelina Versfelt, aka Ida St. Elme, was an adventuress, courtesan, soldier, and ultimately author of her memoirs of the Napoleonic Wars. She was also, quite possibly, a spy. Her loyalty to the Emperor was unimpeachable, and she followed him not only to Moscow and back, but to Elba and through the Hundred Days. Her relationship with Michel Ney is real, as are Lannes and the other "boys of Boulogne." Later in life she wrote her memoirs—and several other books—that have served as the basis for this story, for *The General's Mistress*, and for my forthcoming books about her. Elza's story will continue in *The Marshal's Lover*, out in 2014 from Crossroad Press.

About the Author

JO GRAHAM worked in politics for fifteen years before leaving to write full time. She is the author of the Locus Award nominated *Black Ships* and the Spectrum Award nominated *Stealing Fire*, as well as several other novels, including the Stargate Atlantis Legacy series and *The General's Mistress*. She lives in North Carolina with her partner and their daughter. She can be found online at jo_graham.livejournal.com.

CROSSROAD
PRESS

CPSIA information can be obtained at www.ICGtesting.com
Printed in the USA
BVOW11s2040050914

365715BV00005B/40/P

9 781937 530488